Night Shift
Dragons

DFZ Book 3

Rachel Aaron

Series Information

Minimum Wage Magic

Part-Time Gods

Night Shift Dragons

More Books in the DFZ

Nice Dragons Finish Last

One Good Dragon Deserves Another

No Good Dragon Goes Unpunished

A Dragon of a Different Color

Last Dragon Standing

Copyright and Publishing Info

*In memory of my dad, Rob Aaron,
who was not a dragon,
or cruel, or neglectful,
or any of the horrible things I always make parents in my books.
He was wonderful, and he will forever be
very, very missed.*

Prologue

The white dragon crashed into the shallows of the Detroit River like a meteor. The dark water exploded when she hit, flinging rocks and sticky mud high into the air as her huge body plowed up the waterway's Canadian bank before finally coming to a rest against the rotting hull of a long-forgotten tour boat. The stinking mud she'd sent flying landed on top of her a few seconds later, hitting her broken scales in a staccato patter of soft, wet slaps.

Ow.

Chest heaving, the dragoness known as White Snake, youngest daughter of the previous Great Yong of Korea and dragon of nowhere in particular, cracked open her glittering eyes. Across the churning water, the skyline of the DFZ was still undulating angrily, its elevated roads twisting like vines around the place where her hateful brother and his human pet had vanished. No, not vanished. The city had *eaten* them. Snatched the bleeding dragon right out of the sky. Right out of her claws.

White Snake had no idea what Yong had paid to get the god of the city on his side or how he'd done it, but it was most definitely done. With one well-hurled truck, the DFZ had smashed the victory White Snake had given everything to obtain. It had taken centuries of patient waiting to find a flaw in her brother's control, years of watching and biding her time before the Great Yong had made a mistake great enough to give her a chance. She'd planned the events of these last few weeks down to the second, mortgaged her resources and connections down to the hilt to bring it all together. And now, in the space of an instant, it was over. Smashed, wasted, *ruined.* Her greatest plan, her chance of a lifetime, gone forever. And if she didn't do something about this bleeding soon, she would be too.

Groaning, White Snake closed her eyes and tried to push herself up, "tried" being the operative word. Great Fire, that city hit *hard.* Even with the river to cushion her fall, it felt as if every bone in her body had been shattered. The only positive she could see in her current situation was that at least she'd landed on the Canadian side of the river, outside the city limits where the DFZ couldn't reach to finish the job.

That was lucky, she supposed, but the city wasn't the only—or even the most dangerous—thing she had to worry about right now. As a small dragon with no clan to back her up, White Snake had always taken care never to make enemies, but there were no politics in the world good enough to save a downed dragon. A predator that could no longer defend itself was everyone's prey, and the DFZ had slapped her out of the sky in front of the entire world. It was only a matter of time before another dragon showed up to take her fire as its own. If she wanted to live, she had to move.

Growling deep in her throat, White Snake dug her broken claws into the mud. *Move,* she ordered herself. *Move, weakling, or you're dead. They will eat your flesh, scales, and bones. They will steal your fire until you're left without even a ghost.* **Move.**

But she did not move. No matter how she struggled or how fiercely she clawed the sucking mud, her mangled body did not budge. When she collapsed panting back into the bloody water, the truth of her situation hit her like a second truck to the face. She was going to die here. Die alone in the dark, in mud that smelled of dead fish, on an alien shore, without ever seeing her beloved homeland again.

Roaring at the loss, White Snake surged upward. Pushing with all her fear-driven strength, she managed to pry herself a few feet up the bank. She was about to try again when she heard the unmistakable sound of a truck rolling to a stop on the road above her, followed by the pounding of booted human feet.

No.

White Snake began to thrash wildly. This was it. They'd come for her. She didn't know who "they" were yet, but only another dragon could have moved so quickly. She had to get out of here before their mortals cornered her. Had to run before their teeth found her exposed throat and—

Her panicked thoughts froze as the wind shifted, bringing the smell of gunmetal and plastic and human, but not dragon. But while she didn't scent another of her own kind, she *did* smell blood. That wasn't unusual when dealing with humans, but the amount she scented now was absurd. The stench rolling down the bank was enough to fill the river. Human blood, animal blood, magical blood, more blood than she'd seen spilled in all her life put together. The sheer scope of it overwhelmed her pain-addled brain, leaving her dizzy and confused for several moments. A critical several moments, it turned out.

"Hello, lovely."

White Snake bared her teeth. She'd only heard one truck stop, but there must have been several, because when she looked up, the riverbank was crowded with humans in black armor pointing weapons at her face. But the mortals weren't what concerned her. Her attention was locked on the man standing behind them. The surprisingly normal-looking, middle-aged man in an expensive suit who was the source of all that blood.

"You are the one they call White Snake, yes?"

White Snake took a breath in reply, sparks popping around her mouth as she prepared to drown these fools in fire. She didn't know what the man was, but no one who smelled of that much blood was good news. But as the first licks of flame climbed in her throat, the bloody man lifted his hand.

"I wouldn't do that if I were you," he said, reaching out to tap his fingers against the barrel of the huge gun the armored soldier next to him was pointing at White Snake's snout. "These aren't ordinary weapons. They're anti-dragon guns. A bit of a specialty firearm, but in a city this infested with dragons, it seemed a smart purchase. Not that I ever expected a treasure like you to fall out of the sky, but that's the joy of being prepared." He grinned. "Victory always favors you."

White Snake growled deep in her throat, but she swallowed her fire. Now that he'd drawn her attention to it, she could indeed see that the guns pointed at her were much bigger than usual, their huge barrels stamped with an A surrounded by cresting waves. The Lady of the Great Lakes hadn't been seen above water since the Spirit of the DFZ defeated her twenty years ago, but every dragon with a brain still recognized the symbol of Algonquin's dragon hunters. It could still have been a bluff, but White Snake was in no position to call it. If a lifetime in exile had taught her anything, it was never to gamble what you couldn't afford to lose.

With that, the last of her flames snuffed out, and the man's smile widened. "That's better," he said in a deep, pleased voice. "Now we can negotiate."

"It's not much of a negotiation if one of us is talking at gunpoint," White Snake said, eyeing the armored humans, who had yet to lower their weapons. "But you don't look like one who values fairness."

"Quite the contrary," the blood-smelling man said. "There's nothing I love better than a fair fight. That's actually what I wanted to talk to you about. I'd like to offer you a job."

White Snake couldn't have heard that right. "Do I look like I need a job?"

"You look like you need a lot of things," the man replied, his dark eyes gleaming in the reflected light of the city across the water. "Fortunately for you, I can offer most of them. I can protect you from the rest of your kind. From your brother's wrath. Protect you even from the spirit of the city herself. I can shelter you in your weakness until you are strong enough to stand on your own once more, and all I ask in return is a few evenings of your time."

White Snake sank deeper into the mud, her glowing eyes flicking across the river. The DFZ's undulating skyline was settling down at last, but she could already see dragons gathering on the roof of the Peacemaker's consulate. Dragons who would be coming for her if she didn't do something fast.

"I'm listening."

✳✳✳

"Sir?"

The man who smelled of blood turned away from the team of hired muscle hefting his newest star off the riverbank to glare at the mage kneeling on the road behind him.

"What is it, Kauffman?"

Andrej Kauffman winced at the coldness of his voice, but what else did the boy expect? He'd lost, and there was nothing more despicable than losers. If he hadn't made himself so critical to the operation, he'd be dog food.

"I have the footage you requested," the mage said, holding out his phone. "The dragon taken by the DFZ was indeed Yong of Korea, but my media team also managed to ID the girl riding on his back. As I suspected, it's his adopted human daughter: Opal Yong-ae."

"Opal, eh?" The man grabbed Kauffman's phone to get a closer look at the grainy, zoomed-in picture on its screen. "Isn't that the name of the Cleaner girl sniffing around my Mad Dog? The one he broke your face over?"

Kauffman's newly reconstructed jaw ticked. "Yes, sir."

The bloody man's mouth split into a grin. "Tonight just gets better and better. If Yong and his brat have truly been eaten by the city, they'll be in there for a while. The DFZ doesn't surrender her prizes lightly. Meanwhile, Kos will be left on his own." He tossed the phone back to Kauffman, who barely caught it. "Looks as if you've been given a chance to redeem yourself, Andrej. Let's give Kos a few days to get nice and desperate, then we'll send him a message offering to help with his…problem."

The mage blanched. "With respect, sir, Nik swore he would never—"

v

"I don't care what he swore. This is the same Cleaner girl he gave up the cockatrice payoff for, right? The Asian one who blasted you with your own magic?"

When Kauffman nodded, the bloody man spread his hands. "There you go. Kos *never* turns down money. I don't know what angle she's working, but she's hooked him hard, and you know what a stubborn dog he is. He'll beat himself bloody against the city hunting for his lost jewel. Then, after the DFZ breaks him, we'll swoop in to put the pieces back together into something better, just like always."

From the look on his face, Kauffman didn't believe that, but the mage had always been small-minded. Brilliant, which was why he was still here, but tragically lacking in vision. He saw Kos as a simple thug, a killer for money. He'd never understood that under his "leave me alone" exterior, Nikola Kos was a savant. A glorious, snarling animal just waiting for its stage, and that was back when he'd been fighting merely for cash. Now that he had something real to go to war over, he'd be incomparable.

Cackling with delight, the bloody man looked over his shoulder at the dragoness who'd just now healed up enough to transform into a shape capable of fitting inside the armored van they'd brought. After years of waiting, it looked as if his stars were finally lining up. He'd known it would happen eventually—luck always hit if you waited long enough—but he'd never dreamed things would come together this explosively. This was the chance of a century. All he had to do now was strike, and who better to strike with than his favorite runaway weapon, dragged home at last?

"Just make sure you're ready to receive Kos when he arrives," he ordered his mage. "My best dog escaped once. We mustn't let it happen again."

"I will tie him tight," Kauffman promised, but his face was still weak. "But what if he *doesn't* come? Not that I doubt your vision, but Nikola Kos isn't the man he once was."

The bloody man scoffed. "Every man wants to win, and a dragon's daughter is a hell of a prize to lose." He shook his head. "No, Andrej. Kos will come. He'll come and he'll fight and he'll win. He'll do whatever I tell him to. That's why he's the dog and I'm the master. Though with the ways things are aligning"—he jerked his head back at the defeated dragon—"I might just become master of everything."

Maybe Kauffman wasn't as small-minded as he'd feared, because the mage smiled greedily at that. "Yes sir," he said, lowering his head once more before slipping away to rejoin the rest of the hirelings. When he was gone, the bloody man turned back to the DFZ, the glittering prize across the water that would soon—*at last*—be within his reach.

Chapter 1

"**I** thought we'd try something bigger today."

I froze, the spoonful of wheat berries I'd been about to eat stopping halfway to my lips. I was in Dr. Kowalski's house in the woods, sitting on a stool in the tiny kitchen and holding my bowl above a battered wooden table too cluttered with ancient magazines, gardening tools, and piles of produce to actually eat on. Across from me, the sadly deceased but still world-renowned expert on Shamanic magic—and my new teacher—stood in the doorway to her backyard, holding an orange squash the size of a beach ball between her dirt-covered hands.

"It's a pumpkin," Dr. Kowalski announced at my horrified stare.

"I can see that," I replied, swallowing against the sudden dryness in my throat. "It's just, I have kind of a...*thing* about pumpkins, and that one's really big."

"Beauty, isn't she?" Dr. Kowalski said proudly, setting the giant gourd on the crowded table with a *thump*. "But don't worry. You'll be fine! You haven't cooked a potato since week one, and you're going to want the big guns for today. We're moving that trellis by the southern edge, and I'm counting on you to do all the digging and lifting."

I groaned internally. I'd been training with Dr. Kowalski for the last eight weeks. At least, I thought it had been eight weeks. The days had all kind of blurred together since I'd sold myself to the DFZ in exchange for saving my dad. Every morning, I got out of bed before dawn and dragged myself over to Dr. Kowalski's for Shamanic magic lessons. After all her talk about riding the lightning and shaping magic in real time, you'd think that would be exciting, but so far "training" seemed to be a euphemism for "farmhand." I'd load up on as much magic as would fit inside the day's chosen vegetable, and then I'd use all that fantastic power to dig holes or haul water or whatever else Dr. Kowalski needed until it was time for lunch or I collapsed from exhaustion, whichever came first.

All this magical-manual labor was *supposedly* teaching me to handle larger and larger amounts of power without burning myself out. Privately, though, I was beginning to think it was just an excuse to make me do all the grunt work she didn't want to do herself. Like moving a giant plywood trellis from one side of the garden to the other.

"Why are you still sitting there?" Dr. Kowalski scolded, clapping her hands at me. "Hustle up! We're burning daylight!"

I set down my half-eaten bowl of stewed wheat berries—organic and grown right here in the garden, which would have made them delicious if Dr. Kowalski had believed in sugar, salt, or dairy products—and stood up, wrapping my arms around the massive pumpkin she'd set in front of me like I was giving it a hug. When I had a good grip on the slippery squash, which had to weigh thirty pounds at least, I lifted it off the table with a grunt and followed Dr. Kowalski through the back door into the sunny autumn garden that had become my temporary home away from home.

"Okay," Dr. Kowalski said when we reached the aforementioned trellis. "We'll start by pulling up the posts. I'll hold it steady. You do the digging. Remember: feather the line. Grab as much magic as you can handle and not a drop more. Keep control. Keep it even."

I nodded, setting my pumpkin down on the flagstone path. When I was sure it wasn't going to roll away, I put my hands down on top of it and started pulling in magic very, very slowly. Probably too slowly, but as I'd said earlier, I had a *thing* about pumpkins and magic. Even the smell was enough to make my stomach clench, but as Dr. Kowalski had said, I'd been doing really well. I hadn't cooked a vegetable, or myself, in weeks. I could handle a pumpkin. This one wasn't even a kabocha variety. I could do it. I could—

Magic flooded through me, making me jump. Even after two months, the wild power that lived out here in the DFZ's private urban wilderness preserve still caught me by surprise every time. Reaching for it felt like shoving my hand under a raging waterfall, but at least these days I didn't get washed away. I went with the flow instead, catching the rushing magic and redirecting it in a controlled, even stream straight into the pumpkin at my feet.

Technically, I didn't actually *need* to put the magic inside it. Like the potato Dr. Kowalski had given me when we'd first met, the pumpkin was only a guide, a visual aid to help me grab *some* magic instead of *all*. But I'd gotten used to putting my magic into things before I used it, and I had a score to settle with this pumpkin. I filled it as gently as a summer shower, letting the magic drip through my fingers until I had exactly the amount I needed to grab the six-foot-tall wooden post my teacher was holding steady and yank it out of the ground.

"Good!" Dr. Kowalski said excitedly as the sharpened two-by-four popped out of the soil. "Little slow, but excellent form. Now do it fifteen more times."

I groaned externally this time. Using magic for physical stuff like this was *exhausting*. I might have been garbage at Thaumaturgy, but at least there the spellwork did all the heavy lifting. The freewheeling flexibility of Shamanism meant you had to do everything yourself, which got *really* tiring when you were using magic for things magic wasn't actually good at, like pulling up stakes. I'd only done one so far, and I was already soaked in sweat. But hey, at least I hadn't exploded the pumpkin.

That victory got me through the rest of the trellis. I only used the pumpkin a few more times. Once it was clear that I was grabbing the correct amount of magic, Dr. Kowalski had me shift to holding the power inside me instead, drawing it in with one hand while I cast out with the other. The balancing act was time-consuming and fiddly and made the work ten times harder, but I understood why she was making me do it. Vessels like the pumpkin were good for teaching me how to control my off-the-charts magical draw—my number one problem and the reason I used to backlash myself every time I attempted serious magic—but it was ultimately a crutch. Real Shamanism was active.

Unlike Thaumaturgy's spellwork equations and endless circles, Shamanism had no setup. There was nothing to draw, nothing to write out in advance. It was all about understanding and working with the power that was in the world around you in the moment. For me right now, that was the magic of the forest: a feral, stubborn power that smelled of loam and damp and slid through my fingers like wet pine needles. As with all wild things, it required a firm hand. If I let up for even a second, the magic would wiggle away from me like an angry badger. I had to be calm, steady, and in control. Not generally things I was good at, but that was what practice was for.

By the time I yanked the last wooden stake out of the ground and flopped exhausted into the dirt, I felt like I'd run three marathons back to back. I'd been concentrating too hard to notice the passage of time, but the sun, which had been barely over the treetops when I'd started, was now riding high in the clear blue autumn sky. I was staring up at it and gasping in air when Dr. Kowalski's shadow fell over me.

"Excellent work," she said, reaching down to help me up. "Take a five-minute break, and then it's time to move all this wood over to the other side of the garden and put it back up."

I nodded and grabbed her offered hand, panting too hard to speak. The thought of having to put all those stupid pieces of wood back into the ground I'd just yanked them out of was making me twitchy, but I didn't dare complain. I was the one who'd signed up for this, and as painful as it was, the thrill of actually being *good* at magic for once in my life outweighed the suck. Before Dr. Kowalski, I couldn't remember the last time a teacher had watched me cast without wincing. I also couldn't remember the last time using magic had felt natural. I wasn't sure if it had *ever* happened, to be honest. But while yanking up posts with nothing but raw magic was exhausting, it was a good, physical sort of tired. It didn't hurt or feel scary and out of control like my casting used to, and the effect that change had on me was hard to put into words. I'd happily pull up posts for the rest of my life if it meant I never had to go back to fearing something that was such an intrinsic part of myself.

"Sounds as if you've had a breakthrough," Sibyl said glumly in my earpiece. "Hooraaaaaay."

I frowned at the flatness in my AI's normally overly cheerful voice. "Are you okay?"

"No, I'm not okay!" Sibyl cried. "I've been cut off from the internet since you came here! Don't get me wrong, I'm super happy you're finally dealing with your casting issues, but I haven't had a security update in eight weeks and it's *making me crazy.*" Her voice grew pleading. "Can you ask her to let me back onto the wireless for one minute? I swear I won't broadcast any location data. I just want to ping my update server, that's all."

There was only one "her" in the garden with me, but I knew Sibyl wasn't talking about Dr. Kowalski. She was talking about my real boss, the god for whom I was currently a provisional priestess: the Spirit of the DFZ.

"Sorry," I told my AI as I brushed the dirt off my butt. "But you already know that's a no-can-do. We're on a strict no-internet policy."

"But—"

"I'm the one who asked her to cut us off," I reminded Sibyl harshly. "Do you know how many people are looking for me?"

"No," she snapped. "And neither do you since we've had no contact with the outside world for *two months!*"

"Yeah, that's what 'hiding' means," I reminded her, walking over to the water pump and shoving my face under it until my mouth no longer felt like the Sahara. "Dad still hasn't woken up. Until he does, we're easy prey for any dragon who wants to finish him off."

"But they *can't* finish him," Sibyl argued. "So long as you're under the DFZ's protection, no dragon can mess with you."

"That won't stop them from trying," I said, shaking the water off my head. "With my dad out of the picture, there's no one protecting

Korea. Power vacuums like that don't come up often, and the Korean peninsula is one of the richest territories in the world. White Snake's probably already up and trying to claim it as we speak, along with every other greedy snake on the planet."

"So let them fight each other," my AI grumbled. "Your dad had so much private security he practically ran his own army. What's the point of paying for all that muscle if you're not going to use it when the time comes?"

"Because no dragon worth the name is going to assault Korea directly," I said, exasperated. "Dragons are ruthless tyrants who don't give a damn about human life, but they're not stupid. They *could* go to war against the combined might of my dad's forces and the Korean military, *or* they could just search the DFZ until they find us and kill him here. Despite the Peacemaker's efforts, duels are still a legit way to claim territory. No dragon anywhere is going to dispute the claim of someone who shows up with Yong's head, and since the other option is fighting an entire country, which do *you* think they're going to pick?"

My AI made a pleading sound, and I shook my head. "Sorry, Sib. The whole world is looking for my dad right now, and since I was on his back the last time he was seen, that applies to me as well. I know you need updates, but opening ourselves to the public is just too risky. Until Yong is awake and able to get himself home safely, the internet stays off."

"I'm going to die," Sibyl moaned. "That's what happens to AIs that don't update, you know. They just *die*."

"That's just your programming making you want to update," I told her. "No AI has ever actually been deleted because her security certificates were out-of-date."

"You don't know that! You can't, because there's no internet for you to look that information up! We're living in *darkness*!"

There was more to her rant, but I'd heard it all before, so I just hit mute and concentrated on drinking my water. Honestly, I was as tired of living in a black hole as Sibyl was. I hadn't even been able to let Nik know that I was alive yet, or my mom for that matter. She was probably losing her mind, but Nik and my mom were both obvious targets for any dragon looking to finish off my dad. The less they knew about our situation, the safer they'd be, and it wasn't as if this would last forever. Dad had to wake up sometime. When he did, he'd re-establish his position, push back the interlopers, and this would all be over.

"How do you know?" Sibyl grumbled. "Yong hasn't moved in two months. He could be in that coma *forever.*"

"*Hey!*" I yelled. "What part of 'mute' didn't you understand?"

"Why should I listen to your input commands?" my AI wailed. "Nothing matters anymore! There's no internet, and for all we know, there will never be again! It's the end of everything!"

I rolled my eyes. "Would you tone down the drama? Seriously, who's the mental health AI around here?"

"Sorry," Sibyl said. "But you don't know what it's like! I'm built to be connected to the cloud *all the time.* Being offline means the only real 'me' that exists is the one on your phone. If something happens to my file, there is no backup!" Her voice grew small. "If I die here, I die for real."

"If I die *anywhere,* I die for real," I reminded her. "Welcome to my life."

"Machines weren't meant for mortality!"

I sighed and pulled her bud out of my ear, cutting off our mental connection. It wasn't that I didn't feel for Sibyl; I absolutely did. We were foxhole buddies at this point. She was like a sister to me, but there was nothing I could do for her without risking my dad's life, and seeing as I'd just sold myself to a god to save him, I wasn't willing to throw away that sacrifice quite yet. It'd be a hell of an update when we finally reconnected, but Sibyl could survive a little longer without the internet. Meanwhile, I was going to focus on keeping my chin up. When your immortal father refused to wake up and your mental health AI was having a nervous breakdown, soldiering on was all you could do.

"Opal!"

I jumped. Dr. Kowalski was waving at me from the new trellis site across the garden, but the voice that had called my name wasn't hers. It was younger and infinitely more powerful. The doctor's wrinkled face looked decades younger as well, which could only mean one thing.

The DFZ was here for her daily check-in.

I caught my wince just in time. I was still only a priestess on a trial basis, but it was never good to insult a god, and as creepy as it was to have my teacher get randomly possessed by the living spirit of the city, this was actually the DFZ's way of being polite. My first week here, she'd just popped into my head whenever she'd wanted to talk, which I *hated*. I'd accepted that my life wasn't going to be my own until my dad was up and my debt to the city was repaid, but was it too much to ask for privacy in my own brain?

Thankfully, the DFZ had been able to feel my displeasure along with everything else, so she'd started speaking through Dr. Kowalski instead. I didn't know if that was better since I was pretty sure the god was still inside me at all times, but at least this gave me the illusion of autonomy, and Dr. Kowalski didn't seem to mind at all. As she loved to remind me, she was already dead. Technically, her body was only a manifestation of the DFZ's will, which I guess made being turned into a telephone whenever the city wanted to chat seem pretty trivial by comparison.

"Hey!" the DFZ said, bounding over to me with a boisterousness that looked absolutely ridiculous in Dr. Kowalski's stocky old-lady body. "Dr. K tells me you're making fantastic progress on your magic. Great job! I knew you could do it!"

"Thanks," I said, flattered despite myself. I was perfectly aware that I was being buttered up, but dammit, it was so *nice* not to be seen as a failure anymore. "How are you doing? You only stopped in once yesterday." She normally popped in on me three or four times. I didn't know if that was because I was really that important or if her divine ability to be in multiple places at once enabled her micromanaging, but it was a remarkable day when I only saw the DFZ once.

"It's been hectic," the spirit said with a shrug. "Who knew smacking a dragon out of the sky would cause so many problems?"

I had. I could have told her *exactly* how big a hornets' nest she was kicking by taking Yong and me in. If she'd known, though, she might not have done it, so now as then, I kept my big mouth shut.

"It's only temporary, though," the DFZ went on. "Technically, I'm violating my agreement with the Peacemaker to leave all dragon affairs in the city to him, but since he's only here by my goodwill in the first place, he's not complaining. And compared to my predecessor Algonquin, who had every dragon shot on sight, I'm practically a champion of the species, so really, what's he gonna say?"

She looked pleased by that logic, but I couldn't stop my nervous shaking. "Is the Peacemaker mad?"

"Yeah, but he's being a good sport about it as always," she said. "But I don't know how much longer he'll be able to hold things up. The pressure on him is getting intense. Apparently the various draconic powers started divvying Korea among themselves the moment I sucked you two in. They've been pressuring the Dragon of Detroit to declare Yong dead for weeks so they can officially fight over his land. So far, the Peacemaker's been living up to his name, but things are getting heated at the Dragon Consulate." Her orange-glowing eyes looked hopefully at me from Dr. Kowalski's transformed face. "Yong hasn't woken up yet, by any chance?"

"You'd be the first to know if he had," I promised, which was silly. In addition to being in my brain at all times, the DFZ was the one keeping my apartment hidden from the rest of the world. There was nothing I did or thought that she wasn't privy to. Hell, for all I knew, she watched me pee.

"I don't watch you pee!"

I gave her a look, and she held up her hands. "Sorry, sorry," she said, not sounding sorry in the slightest. "I know you hate it when I do that, but in my defense, your mind is *really* loud. That huge magical draw of yours acts as a megaphone. It's what makes you such great priestess material. And speaking of!"—she waved her hand between us, and a wooden desk covered in papers popped out of the garden's turned-up dirt like a mushroom—"it's time for our monthly accounting."

Fighting the urge to wince, I sat down hard on the cushioned office chair that had popped out of the ground behind me. Unsurprisingly for the soul of a city of commerce, the DFZ was a *big* fan of accounting. She kept meticulous records of everything: how much rent she was owed, who was behind, who was ahead, maintenance costs, subcontractor fees, etc. And as the current leaseholder on over four hundred units, a depressing number of the lines in the old-fashioned ledger book she pulled out of the desk's bottom drawer were for me.

It was my own damn fault. Thanks to my brilliant decision to raid units for salables to pawn for gold so I could beat my dad, my name was attached to apartments, lofts, houses, garages, and storage lockers all over the city. If I'd actually done my job as a Cleaner, all of those units would be sorted, scrubbed, and back on the rental market, but I *hadn't* been doing my job. I'd been ransacking, taking the valuables and leaving the rest a filthy mess.

Worse, due to my busy schedule as the DFZ's newest priest-prospect, I hadn't had a spare moment to go back and fix any of my mistakes. All of the units Nik and I had bought were still in the exact same state of chaos we'd left them in, which meant they couldn't be re-leased to new tenants. But just because the spaces weren't being lived in didn't mean the rent didn't still come due every month, and since my name was the one on the lease, it came to me. Six hundred thousand dollars and change, every damn month.

"So here's the total of what you owe for all your units, plus maintenance fees and utility bills," the DFZ said, pointing at the terrifyingly huge number rounded to the nearest tenth of a cent at the bottom of her ledger page. "How will you be paying?"

I couldn't. She *knew* I couldn't pay, but she also knew that I couldn't default. If I failed to honor even one of those leases, I'd be in violation of my Cleaning contract, which meant I'd lose my Master Key. Without my key, I couldn't be a Cleaner anymore. Staggering debt or no, I wasn't ready to give my old life up. Dammit, I'd *just* gotten rid of my dad's bad luck curse! If I could only get out of this situation, I could go back to Nik and we could actually make the bank I'd promised him so many times. I refused to let that hope go just yet, but until my dad woke up, there was nothing I could do.

"I see," the god said when I didn't reply, her face lighting up in a salesman's dazzling smile. "Looks like you'll be working for me for another month, then!"

I nodded, fighting the urge to cry. It wasn't that I was unhappy here. I enjoyed the work I did for the city, and I *loved* having Dr. Kowalski as a teacher. I'd made more progress on my magic in the last eight weeks than in all the rest of my life combined. I also had no right to complain. Working off what I owed for all those apartments had been *my* idea, the only thing I could think of to save my dad without actually signing my soul over to the DFZ's priesthood. It had seemed like a great plan at the time, but now that the emergency was over, I was trapped again. All that work to get clear, and here I was right back in debt, only this time I was on the hook for a lot more money to a *much* greater power.

It was depressing in the extreme. No matter how hard I worked, I only ever seemed to end up digging myself deeper. At this rate, I'd be a billion dollars in debt to multiple gods by the end of the year.

Hyperbole aside, I actually did have a plan to get out of this mess. Like everything else in my life, though, it depended on my dad waking up, which reminded me, "Can I ask you a question?"

"Sure," the DFZ said, making a note on my rolled-over debt and shutting her ledger. "A god is always there for her loyal followers. What can I do for you?"

"Actually, it's about my dad."

To her credit, the city spirit made a solid effort at looking concerned. "Is he getting worse?"

"No, but he's not getting any better, either," I told her. "He still looks exactly the same as when you rescued us. He doesn't move, he doesn't eat, he just…lies there. It's freaking me out."

Honestly, it was doing a lot more than that. Despite living in the shadow of one my entire life, I knew jack squat about how dragons actually functioned. I knew they generated their own magic in the form of dragon fire, but when I'd poked at my father's chest where his flames normally lived, I hadn't felt a thing. If he hadn't been breathing, I would have sworn he was dead. He certainly looked like a corpse, all still and pale and haggard. But dragons were famously hard to kill, so I'd left him alone on the assumption he'd get better, except he hadn't. He hadn't healed, hadn't changed, hadn't moved at all, and after two months, I was starting to lose hope that he would.

"You could ask the Peacemaker," the DFZ suggested as she did every time I brought this up. "He'd help you."

"I'm sure he would," I said. "But as I told you last time, I can't go to him. My dad isn't part of the Peacemaker's Accord. I know everyone says the Dragon of Detroit is different, but he's still a dragon. I've never met one of those who could resist exploiting weakness, and a kitten could kill my dad right now. Even if the Peacemaker *did* agree to help us without demanding some kind of horrible debt in return, word of my father's condition is bound to get out. The only reason we've stayed safe this long is because I've been super careful to stay off the internet and never go anywhere that's not under your direct control, like this garden. I know the moment there's even a whisper of a rumor that the Great Yong is one pillow-to-the-face away from dead, we'll be up to our eyeballs in murderous dragons. From what you said earlier, they're already circling, which means going to the Peacemaker would put my dad at *more* risk, not less."

"What about his own people?" the DFZ asked. "You're always complaining about Yong's overly worshipful mortals. Can't you just hand him off to one of them?"

I shook my head. "No, and for the same reason. I'd *love* to foist Dad off on his servants, believe me, but while my mom would slit her own throat before she put her dragon in danger, the rest are just employees. Stupidly loyal ones, but there's no keeping a secret this big down. The more people who know about my dad, the bigger the chance that the truth will escape, and the Great Yong's household doesn't move in groups of less than a hundred. The only reason it hasn't slipped out already is because we're the only ones who know, and neither of us is talking. I thought that would be enough to buy him the time he needed to heal, but he's *not* healing, and I don't know what to do."

That last bit came out in a pathetic warble. I *know* I'd just said, "Keep my chin up," but there were limits, and mine were crashing hard into reality. It was easy to be brave when it was just me going through my daily routine, but saying these things out loud made them feel bigger and scarier. Unbeatable. Gods were supposed to help you deal with that, but mine just sighed.

"I don't know what else to tell you," the DFZ said, leaning Dr. Kowalski's dirty, wrinkled elbows on the desk she'd summoned from the garden bed. "I want to help, but you've shot down all my good ideas multiple times, and you don't want to hear my bad ones."

"You have more?" I asked eagerly, but the god waved her hand.

"I just said you don't want to hear them."

"Try me," I urged. "I've made bad ideas work before, and I'm pretty desperate."

The DFZ arched one of Dr. Kowalski's bushy gray eyebrows at me. "I thought you didn't even like your dad."

"I don't, that's why I'm desperate. You think I *like* being trapped in my apartment with the monster I've fought my whole adult life to escape?" I shook my head. "Just because I'm not willing to throw him to his enemies doesn't mean I want to be his nurse. The sooner he's off death's door, the sooner I can ship him back to Korea and out of my life."

And make him pay all the bills I'd racked up saving his scaly bacon. My debts at the moment were all arguably Yong's fault, and I intended to make him pay back every damn penny. It was the least he could do after putting me through all this, because I *definitely* wasn't sheltering him out of the goodness of my heart. I'd thought that was obvious, but it must not have been clear to the DFZ, because the moment I said I wanted him gone, her face lit up like downtown on New Year's Eve.

"Well, why didn't you say so? If you just want him gone—"

"Gone from my apartment," I clarified sharply. "Not gone from this mortal coil."

"Of course, of course," the god said flippantly. "But all this time I thought you were fretting over his well-being! If you just want him out of your life and you're not picky about the how, *you* need to talk to the Spirit of Dragons!"

The blood drained from my face. I didn't know much about the Spirit of Dragons, but what I'd heard wasn't good. "Why would she help me?"

"She wouldn't," the DFZ said. "But she *would* help your dad. She has to, because he's part of her domain. Just as I am bound to everyone who lives in my city, she's bound to him. As an all-knowing spirit, she's *also* already aware of his condition, so you wouldn't even have to worry about his secret getting out! It's *perfect.*"

It did sound pretty great, which made me nervous. "If she's so perfect, why did you classify talking to her as a 'bad idea'?"

"Because she's a dragon *and* a god," the DFZ said despairingly. "That combination creates a near-dysfunctional level of ego, unfortunately.

But if anyone can help your dad, it's her. She knows everything there is to know about dragons and their fire. We just have to get her attention."

I still didn't like it, but it wasn't as if I had other options on the table. "How do we do that?"

"Same way you get any dragon's attention," my god said with a smirk. "Bribery. Copious amounts of it. Fortunately, I know what she likes best. Gimme a sec."

The city spirit vanished, leaving Dr. Kowalski standing confused at the desk. "Huh," my teacher said, looking down at the scattered leather-bound ledgers. "Is she done, or—"

Before she could finish the question, the god came back, taking over the old lady's body again in an instant, only this time she was holding a plastic box full of something that rattled musically.

"Here," the DFZ said, setting the crate down on the desk with a *thunk*. "This should be everything you'll need."

I rose nervously from my chair to take a look. Given that this was bribery for a dragon god, I was expecting piles of gold or severed heads, but the inside of the crate wasn't glittery or grisly. It was filled with liquor bottles. There was rum, gin, tequila, whiskey, and a whole pack of those red plastic cups. Most surprising of all, though, was that none of it was expensive. Every dragon I knew wouldn't touch something that wasn't world-class, but there wasn't a single handle of booze in the box better than mid-shelf. Some of it looked distinctly lower, and I bit my lip nervously.

"Are you *sure* this is what she wants?"

"Trust me, this will do the trick," the DFZ said, handing me the crate, which was even heavier than I'd expected, and I'd braced for a lot. "Just take this to where your dad is, put out the cups, and start pouring libations. She'll come. The Spirit of Dragons can't stand to see good liquor go to waste."

My rich-girl snob days were far behind me, but I still wouldn't have called anything in the crate she'd handed me "good liquor."

"Hangover-in-a-box," maybe, or "frat-house punch." But gods were famous for their mysterious ways, so I hefted the booze under my arm and promised to do as she asked.

"Fantastic," the DFZ said, scraping all of her ledgers into the drawer again before sinking the whole desk back under the ground without a trace. "Just make sure you do it on your own time. You've got a lot of work to do, and you're losing enough hours to training as it is."

"My training was your idea," I reminded her.

"And it was a wonderful one," she agreed. "You're making marvelous progress! But that doesn't mean your other priestly duties don't still need to get done." She sighed. "When you're a *real* priestess, I'll be able to take over your body and remove your need for sleep. Until then, we'll just have to limp by on aggressive scheduling."

She smiled eagerly at me. I did my best to return it, but my face was already slipping. I knew she didn't mean to be creepy, and again, I *liked* my life with the DFZ for the most part. The training was great, and my work was interesting. If that was all there was to it, I'd probably have agreed to join her priesthood already, but then she went and said stuff like this that made me want to run for the hills.

I knew she didn't mean to be a tyrant, but the DFZ wasn't exactly a city known for her relaxed pace or healthy work-life balance. People died of overwork here on the regular. *I'd* almost died of it during the crazy three weeks Nik and I were raiding. My service was *supposed* to be strictly voluntary, just a temporary gig, but I'd clearly been here too long. Now she was talking about taking away my sleep like it was a done deal, and I just couldn't. I *had* to get my dad up, get this debt paid off, and get away from this situation before I slipped and accidentally ended up in the DFZ's service for the rest of eternity.

"Thank you for the help," I said, bowing reverently to hide the nervous sweat rolling down my face. "I promise I won't fall behind on my duties while attending to my father."

"You never do," she said in a voice that was equal parts praise and warning. "Just make sure to stay on your guard when you do the summoning. This may come as a shock, but the Spirit of Dragons has a bad habit of taking what isn't hers. I know she's stolen priests from other spirits. Not saying it'll happen to you, but I wanted to give you a heads-up."

"Don't worry," I assured her. "The last thing I want to be is owned by a dragon ever again."

"That's my girl," the DFZ said proudly. "Dr. Kowalski is getting nervous, so I'll go ahead and give you back to her. Good luck on the rest of your training today, and keep me posted on what happens with your dad. I'll already know, of course, but I still like to hear your version."

"Thanks," I said flatly, but the god was already gone, fading back into Dr. Kowalski, who gave herself a shake.

"She's chatty today," my teacher said, blinking rapidly as if she were getting used to being back in her own head. "Not that I mind being a vessel for the divine, but I don't understand why she feels the need to check in on you so often. She can see your progress through my mind anytime she wants."

"You mean she doesn't do this to all her priests?" I asked, carrying my crate of liquor over to the kitchen door so I wouldn't forget it when I left.

"No way," Dr. Kowalski said. "She's normally pretty hands-off, but I guess she doesn't need to keep tabs on those of us who've already committed like she does for you."

I could have done with far less tabbing, but arguing with gods didn't normally end well for mortals, so I let it go and moved on. "Ready to get back to the trellis?"

"Absolutely," she said, rolling up her sleeves. "But let's do it by hand this time. We don't want to overwork your magic, and a strong body is also part of being a good Shaman!"

I shrank back with a shudder. I know I'd just been complaining that pulling up stakes with magic was hard, but that was a *lot* of holes to dig by hand.

"Don't make that face," Dr. Kowalski scolded. "Weren't you a Cleaner? You should be used to hard labor, so grab a shovel and let's do this. Gardens don't tend themselves, you know."

With a mournful look at the sun riding dangerously close its zenith, I retied my sweat-damp hair into a higher ponytail and got back to work, reminding myself over and over that this was my chosen torture and a lot better than the alternative, which was dead.

***

By the time we got the trellis set up in its new location two hours later, I was done both physically and mentally. Dr. Kowalski fed me lunch as always, setting out the usual spread of boiled beans, grains, and fresh vegetables from the garden. There was steamed pumpkin this time as well, which I didn't have the heart to tell her I couldn't stand. Even though the orange North American pumpkins tasted nothing like kabocha, the smell still made me ill. I couldn't even eat pumpkin pie, which was a tragic loss if American holiday specials were anywhere close to reality.

Technically, Dr. Kowalski didn't need to eat since she wasn't actually alive, but that didn't stop her from wolfing down her half of the meal, encouraging me to eat more between giant bites. I did so to be polite, though to be honest, I was getting pretty sick of the leafy greens and quinoa parade. But free food was free food, so I forced down as much as I could stomach, washing my plate in the sink and placing it on the drying rack before grabbing my crate of booze and heading for the back door that led to the garden.

At least, that was where the door *normally* went. But being a priestess of the DFZ wasn't all downsides. There were definitely a few perks to the job, and one of those was getting to travel as the DFZ did. All

18

I had to do was turn the doorknob while picturing where I wanted to go. When the back door from Dr. Kowalski's cozy kitchen opened this time, it was no longer into her sunny garden, but a small one-bedroom apartment that had been recently refurbished.

"Take care!" the doctor called, waving at me from the cluttered table. Shifting the heavy crate to one arm, I waved back and stepped through into my apartment, shutting the door behind me. The moment the latch clicked, the sounds of Dr. Kowalski's house in the woods—the wind in the trees, the drone of insects, the casual rustles of another person going about their day—vanished, leaving me in the deep, unnatural silence of a place lost in time and space.

I let go of the door with a wince. It didn't matter how many times I did this, I was never going to get used to coming back here. Technically, it was still my apartment. All the tacky furniture my mom had bought was long gone, but I'd managed to scavenge enough replacements to make the place livable again, including a couch, a vintage wicker peacock chair, and a super-cool coffee table made from recycled hammered-tin ceiling tiles. They were all solid vintage pieces that matched my admittedly eclectic aesthetic. My stuff, in other words, which should have made this *my* home. But no matter how many quirky pillows I piled on my sofa or how many curtains I hung over the terrifying chaos that existed outside my windows, I couldn't make the place feel like anything other than what it was: a detached set of rooms floating like bubbles in the void. If I focused hard enough, I could actually feel the floor moving under my feet, which was why I didn't do that anymore. If it wasn't for my dad, I wouldn't come here at all.

And speaking of.

I set the crate of liquor down and walked to my bedroom. Unlike the living room, I hadn't replaced the furniture in here yet. I'd cleaned up the blood as best I could, but otherwise the small room still looked exactly as it had when the DFZ had brought us here after the fight with White Snake, right down to my dad's body on the floor. He was still naked under the blankets, his body lying on what had once been my mattress on the floor. I knew I should have gotten him clothes and a real bed, but other than cleaning the blood off his skin, I hadn't done a thing. It wasn't that I didn't care—the last two months were proof of that—it was just that touching my dad felt wrong on a level I couldn't describe. He wasn't deathly cold or anything obvious like that, but his face was the color of ash and his skin just felt…empty. Like tapping on a hollow shell.

It was insanely creepy. He hadn't moved since we'd arrived. There'd been no fluids in or out, no bed sores or soiled linens or any of the biological unpleasantness I'd braced myself to deal with as caregiver to someone in a coma. I supposed I should have been happy we'd both been spared the indignity, but I would have far preferred emptying a bedpan to this unnatural stillness. He barely even breathed anymore.

"Hey, Dad," I whispered, crouching down beside him. "How are you doing?"

He showed no sign he'd heard me. He never did, but I still spoke to him every time I came in because talking made the situation feel less scary. I was pretty sure I'd said more words to my dad in the past eight weeks than I had in all the years since I'd turned thirteen. I just wish I knew if he'd heard them. I'd even welcome a growl at this point, anything to let me know he wasn't actually gone.

"I think I've finally got a lead on something that might help you," I said, carefully avoiding looking at how sunken his cheeks had become. "I'm just going to shower first and then I'll be back. Don't move."

I used that same joke every time I talked to him. It made me feel more in control, a necessity since seeing him like this always threatened to send me right back into the despairing panic I'd felt the night this happened. Neither of us had time for that, though, so I forced myself to chin up and slipped into the bathroom to wash off. It felt like stalling, but if I really did manage to summon the Spirit of Dragons, I at least wanted to greet her without dirt on my nose.

Since the DFZ had already warned me about punctuality and I only had forty minutes left in my lunch break, I cleaned up as fast as possible, resisting the urge to soak my aching body under the detached apartment's miraculously never-ending hot water. When I'd gotten all the mud I could see off my skin, I grabbed a fresh set of clean work clothes from the small set of plastic drawers I'd moved into the bathroom since there was no way in hell I was changing in front of my dad. Unconscious or not, there were some lines that should not be crossed.

Thankfully, the DFZ handled my laundry in the same mysterious way she handled my plumbing. Stacks of fresh clothes appeared every morning, while my dirties from the hamper were whisked away. I didn't even know if I'd worn the same clothes twice since they all looked the same, a never-ending parade of mom jeans, thick white T-shirts, and work boots. It was boring as hell and definitely not my usual style, but it was traditional for priests to dress humbly, and it wasn't as if I had anyone to impress. Also, I'd been poor for too long to turn up my nose at free clothes *and* no laundry. I put on my dull outfit without complaint, pausing just long enough to twist my wet hair into a bun before I stepped back out.

"Okay," I told my unconscious father as I hauled the crate of liquor into the bedroom. "Let's do this."

As the DFZ had suggested, I put out the red plastic cups first. She hadn't specified how they were to be arranged, so I just placed them around my dad in a circle, doing my best to keep the spacing as neat and even as possible. When the whole fifty-pack was down, I grabbed a bottle at random and started pouring, filling each cup to the brim in what I hoped would be interpreted as reverent silence.

By the time I was done, I understood why the DFZ had given me mid-shelf booze. Filling all those cups had taken thirteen bottles in total. By the time I finished, the smell of booze was so strong in the room that I was having trouble breathing. I couldn't exactly open a window thanks to the whole floating-in-a-mind-destroying-nothingness situation, though, so I just tried to move quickly, stacking the empty bottles neatly along the wall in the hopes that the Spirit of Dragons enjoyed order as much as other dragons did. My father certainly loved for things to be extravagantly neat. He probably would have loved this as well if not for the insulting cheapness of the booze. Again, I *really* hoped the DFZ knew what she was doing. The setup I'd just made looked more appropriate to summoning the Spirit of College Binge Drinking than dragons. I just prayed she wasn't insulted. If I got eaten over bad booze in plastic cups, I was going to be *really* pissed off.

Done was done though. The libations had certainly been poured. I would have offered prayers as well if I'd thought the Spirit of Dragons cared about the opinion of humans. The chance of accidentally insulting her was too high, though, so I just settled in to wait.

After ten minutes of nothing, I decided to try the prayer thing. Dragons always loved it when you got on your knees, right? So I got down on mine, bowing over my dad with my hands pressed together. *Please*, I thought, trying my best to broadcast the words through my supposed megaphone soul. *Please, great spirit. Please, please, please.*

As prayers went, it wasn't the most poetic, but I was counting on sincerity to make up for what I lacked in eloquence. I wasn't even sure what language the Spirit of Dragons spoke. I was contemplating trying again in Korean and Cantonese just to be sure I was covering my bases when I realized the room had gotten uncomfortably warm.

My eyes popped open in alarm only to instantly slam shut again as sweat poured down my face into them. I wasn't sure when it had happened, but my bedroom was suddenly hot as a furnace. It also felt unusually crowded, and when I finally got my shirt up to wipe the stinging sweat out of my eyes, I saw why.

There was a dragon made of fire sitting practically on top of my dad, a red plastic cup pinched delicately between her burning claws. All the other cups I'd put out were already empty and scattered across the floor, their shiny plastic sides blistered and warped from the heat. She drained the final cup as I watched, tossing the cheap liquor back with a gulp of greedy satisfaction. When it, too, was empty, she tossed the melting cup away and sat back on her haunches to flash me a grin full of sharp, flaming teeth.

"Hello, mortal," the god said in a sweet, deadly voice. "You libated?"

Chapter 2

I bowed so fast my forehead smacked into the floor. "Great dragon!" I gasped, not even realizing I'd said the words in Korean until they were out. I started to sweat harder. Panicking in front of a dragon was the *worst* thing you could do. Best-case scenario, the fiery god would find my fear amusing and try to scare me more. Worst case, she'd see it as a prey reaction and eat me.

In my defense, I hadn't actually expected this to work. I mean, what kind of dragon—or spirit, for that matter—came down for offerings of strip-mall liquor-mart swill served in red plastic cups? I would have considered it beneath *my* dignity to reply to such an invitation, and I wasn't even immortal. Or dignified. But while none of this made sense to me, the Spirit of Dragons was most definitely here, and from the way the tip of her fiery tail was twitching, she was starting to get annoyed.

"Would you get up?" the god snapped. "Not that I don't appreciate a good grovel, but it's impossible to hear what you're saying when you're talking to the floor like that."

"Sorry, Great Dragon," I whispered, pushing myself up so that I was sitting on my knees.

"Quite all right," the fiery dragon said benevolently. "You're only mortal, so I don't hold it against you. Now let's have a look."

She lowered her flaming head, which was so tall I wasn't entirely sure how it fit inside my bedroom. There was definitely some space bending going on, because now that I was looking straight at her, there was absolutely no way she could be contained by such a small room. We *were* inside a magical apartment floating in a void, though, so a dragon god cramming her fiery body into somewhere it shouldn't technically fit was hardly the weirdest thing going on.

"My, my," the dragon spirit purred. "You're quite the package, aren't you?" She breathed in deep through her nostrils. "Polite, off-the-charts magical potential, good facial symmetry, and you're a *Shaman*! That's a nice change. Haven't seen one of those in years." She sniffed again and frowned. "Already attached to the Spirit of the DFZ, though. *Such* a pity. That dirty upstart of a city will never appreciate you properly. But you don't smell like you're fully dedicated yet." The giant flaming head moved a little closer. "It's not too late to trade up, you know. The DFZ is powerless outside her borders, and I'm always in the market for a new priestess."

Her eye ridges wiggled suggestively above her beautiful flame-colored eyes, and I jerked back in alarm. "Uh...no. No thank you, I mean! I am most flattered and humbled by your attention, but I am happy in my current situation."

"*Really?*" The dragon god looked skeptical. Then she looked suspicious. "Well, if you're not auditioning for a divinity upgrade, why *did* you call me?"

I shifted nervously. Was this some kind of trick question? My eyes darted to the still body of my father between the god's flaming feet. I wouldn't have thought she could miss him, but looking back over the last few minutes—which was easy since the mortal terror had etched every second into my brain—I realized the Spirit of Dragons had never actually looked *down*.

"With utmost respect, Great Dragon," I said, speaking as slowly as I could to try and feel out if she was really confused or if this was a test I was failing. "I called on behalf of my father, the Great Yong of Korea."

"Yong?" The spirit huffed. "That old stick-in-the-mud? Isn't he—*Oh!*" She gave a little jump, looking down at last. "Well, what do you know? He *is* here! I didn't even notice him."

I boggled at her in disbelief. This *was* the Spirit of Dragons, right? I mean, she *looked* like a dragon made of fire, but she wasn't acting like any dragon I'd ever met, and it didn't seem possible that she wouldn't know what was going on. Spirits were created by their domains. Just as the DFZ was the living embodiment of the city, the Spirit of Dragons drew her power from all the scheming snakes of the world. She should be the most dragony dragon that ever dragoned, and she should *definitely* know where all of her supplicants were at all times. The DFZ felt it when someone knocked over a trash can. How was it possible this spirit didn't already know why I'd called her here? Had I screwed up and summoned some sort of party god by mistake?

While I was silently freaking out, the fiery dragon lowered her head to my father's chest and breathed in deep. When she breathed out again, a cloud of smoke left her mouth in curling tendrils that hooked into my father's body like claws. It was insanely creepy to watch, but at least it calmed my fears about the spirit's identity. I'd been nearly burned alive by dragon fire enough times to know the stuff when I saw it, and that smoke was *definitely* draconic. It also didn't look good, because when she breathed the smoke back in, the god shook her huge head.

"I understand now why I didn't notice him," she said, turning back to me. "His internal flame is so low it barely registers. He shouldn't be alive, and yet somehow he is." She tilted her head at me with new curiosity. "What did you say your name was?"

I hadn't, but like hell was I telling her that. "I'm Opal Yong-ae."

"Ah!" she said, her huge eyes burning brighter. "That explains it! You're the Dragon's Opal. I've heard about you."

I winced instinctively. Nothing good usually followed a dragon recognizing me. Really, though, I felt as if she should already know all of this. Not to be cocky, but my dad's mortal collecting habit was pretty famous, and it wasn't as if there were *that* many dragons running around. Not to keep comparing, but the DFZ knew the full history of every brick and manhole cover in her city. How could this god not know such an obvious detail about one of her oldest and most established dragons?

"Don't look at me like that," the spirit said. "Just because I don't bother learning all the petty details of my subjects' lives doesn't mean I'm slacking. Why should I learn about them? I'm *their* god. They should be trying to impress *me.*"

"I meant no offense," I assured her, uncertain if she'd read the thought out of my mind or guessed what I was thinking the old-fashioned way. "It's just…You're *very* different from other spirits I've met."

The god snorted. "I suppose you mean the DFZ. Of course we're different! She's a city, which means she's a horrific busybody who constantly feels the need to control everything. Dragons, by contrast, are independent creatures, and they're self-important enough without me puffing them up more by knowing their names when they call." She turned up her nose with a snort. "If a dragon isn't audacious enough to demand my attention, they don't deserve it."

I nodded, lowering my eyes. Well, at least that solved my doubts about who she was. This was most definitely the God of Dragons. I just hoped I hadn't insulted her to the point where she no longer wanted to help.

"I see you are both wise and powerful," I flattered, trying to get this conversation back on the "helping my dad" track rather than the "punish the uppity mortal" one. "I hope you can help me understand as well. You said my father is alive when he technically shouldn't be. How is that possible?"

The dragon shrugged. "Not sure, but it's probably because of you."

"*Me?*" My eyes flew wide. "But I'm not a dragon!"

"I know," she said testily. "That's what makes it so odd." She lowered her head to sniff at my dad's chest again. "I don't understand it myself, to be honest. There's no way a fire that small should be able to support his body, or even keep itself alight, but it *is*." She sniffed another time. "Fascinating."

That wasn't the word I'd use. "But how is it happening?" I demanded, forgetting myself in my rush to understand. "And what does it have to do with me?" Because if I was the reason my dad was alive, I needed to know how that worked and how I could do it harder.

The dragon god sighed at my questions and sat back on her flaming haunches. "How much do you know about dragon fire?"

"Nothing really," I said, which wasn't precisely true. My dad never told me anything about his magic, but I'd figured out a great deal on my own through observation and publicly available information. But while I was reasonably confident I could hold my own in the conversation, I'd never met a dragon who didn't love showing off their knowledge, and I had a lot of ground to make up from my earlier blunders. "Please, great dragon," I said sweetly. "Would you explain it to me?"

As I'd hoped, the Spirit of Dragons preened at the request. "Oh, you're *good*," she said, flicking a long claw to summon a torch-sized tongue of glittering orange-and-gold fire from her body. "Dragons don't have souls like humans. Instead, we have this." She extended her claws, holding out the glittering flame until it was all I could see. "Dragon fire is the font of our magic and the source of our life. It sparks before we hatch and grows with us as we age. That's why ancient dragons are so much more powerful than young ones: the bigger the fire, the better the dragon."

I nodded, remembering how much larger my father had been than his little sister.

"Fire is what makes a dragon a dragon," the god went on, her voice grave. "This is critical to understand. Unlike humans, our bodies can recover from almost any injury, but if our fire goes out, we die. It *is* our life. That said, it is also still just fire. It can be smothered or doused just like a normal flame. It can also be stolen, which is precisely what White Snake was attempting to do to your father. She wanted to leapfrog her own abilities by eating Yong's flame and adding his power to her own. That's by far the easiest way to get a leg up if you're small. But White Snake *couldn't* eat Yong's fire, because by the time she cornered him, his flame was already gone."

My stomach sank. Despite claiming not to recognize me, the Spirit of Dragons seemed to know a lot about my family affairs. "So White Snake's attack wasn't what did this to him?" I asked, nodding at my dad's comatose body.

"I'm sure she didn't help," the spirit said. "Getting slashed up and losing most of your blood is taxing for anyone. But ultimately speaking, this situation was all Yong's doing. He had no business casting such an open-ended curse or holding it for as long as he did. Remember what I said about fire being our power *and* our magic? When Yong cursed you to have bad luck, he was doing the magical equivalent of burning the candle at both ends, giving you an open tab on the magic he also needed to stay alive, which is how he ended up in this predicament." She scowled down at my father. "*Really*, a dragon his age should know better. But while he is very low, he hasn't burned out yet. That's the nice part of having fire for your magic. Unlike humans who are tied to their biology, we dragons can reignite. Even if our physical bodies are destroyed, so long as a single spark of our fire persists, we can always come back. Trust me, I know from personal experience."

There was a world of history in that last sentence, but I was too excited to follow it. "So my dad *can* recover?"

"So long as his fire hasn't completely gone out, yes," the dragon god said, but she wasn't smiling. "Unfortunately, this is where your situation gets…odd. Remember how I didn't notice him when I came in? That wasn't just me being dismissive. I literally could not feel his fire. If I wasn't standing here watching him breathe, I'd say his last spark had already burned out. But his body is still functioning, so there must be *something* in there. Unfortunately, I'm not actually sure what that is."

My body slumped. The god of dragons had been my last hope. If she didn't know how to fix this, we were lost. The defeat I felt at that thought was enough to send me to the ground. I'd almost folded all the way over when the dragon's fiery tail smacked me in the face.

"Stop that," she commanded, snaking her head down to glare at me. "Now's not the time to be a sad sack. As a famous human once said, 'mostly dead is still partially alive,' and alive for us means fire. Yong's flame *must* be in there somewhere or he'd be totally dead. Since he's not, all we should have to do to bring him back is build that fire back up."

"How?" I breathed.

The dragon tapped her burning claws on my bedroom floor, singeing the wood. "That's a tricky question. Usually a dragon's flames come back on their own, though they can also be fed through other sources. Usually by killing and eating another dragon, but there are less gruesome means of getting fire, one of which is family. The more dragons you have in your clan, the more power flows up the chain back to you."

"Wait," I said, confused. "You're saying dragons share power with other dragons they're related to?"

"Not *share*," she scoffed. "Dragons never *share*. Clan fire is a strictly top-down affair. If you're at the bottom of a clan, your fire gets sucked up the pyramid whether you like it or not, which is why most dragons prefer to be at the top." She flashed me a toothy smile. "Haven't you ever wondered why dragons have such big families despite our bad habit of murdering each other?"

I started to shake my head then stopped and changed to a nod. My father had no clan, so I hadn't given the contradiction much thought. Now that she mentioned it, though, it did seem odd. Her words also reminded me of something my father had said a long, long time ago. So long that I couldn't remember the exact conversation anymore, but I think it was in response to a very young me asking how I could be his daughter if I wasn't a dragon. He'd replied that he was happy I wasn't a dragon because all dragons were murderers. If I'd been his real daughter, he would have had to live in fear that I'd grow up to kill him and take his power just as he'd done to his own father. But I wasn't a dragon. I was human, and that meant he was free to treasure me.

Those words made me cringe now, but at the time I'd thought it was his way of saying he loved me. That I was his child in spirit, if not in blood. I'm sure my father would have called that idea sentimental garbage, but in the context of what the Spirit of Dragons had just said, it made me wonder. "Could *I* be feeding his fire?"

The spirit sighed. "Thirty minutes ago, I'd have called that nonsense," she admitted. "But I am the most attuned being on any dimensional plane when it comes to dragon fire, and I can't feel so much as an ember smoldering in the Dragon of Korea. He should be ash, and yet he lives, which means something that's not his fire *must* be keeping him going. It's the only explanation, and you're literally the only thing around, so it has to be you."

"But I'm human," I said, stating the obvious.

"I'm aware," the spirit said flatly. "But clan is more about mindset than blood. Case in point, the infamous Marlin Drake is the head of a clan of clanless dragons. The whole thing's a violent hodgepodge of misfits who've been kicked out of their own families for various reasons. None of them are related, yet Drake still manages to draw power from his position at the top, so it's clearly possible."

"But they're all still dragons," I argued. "I'm not."

"Again, I'm aware," she said. "But I think that's actually working to your advantage here. Small and weak though you may be, humanity's superpower is the ability to grab magic from one place and move it somewhere else. Everyone knows Yong considers you his daughter, because that's what he called you when he took his case to the Peacemaker, and a dragon as stodgy and proud as he is wouldn't use that word unless he meant it. Likewise, you've only called him by his actual name once since I arrived. *Normal* human servants address their dragon by title, but you call Yong 'father' and 'Dad' without even thinking about it. It's natural for you, just as calling you daughter is natural for him. It's obvious you both think of each other as family on a deep, reflexive level. Now combine that with the draconic ability to draw magic from clan ties *and* the reflexive human instinct to shove magic at anything they consider important, and what have you got?"

I held my breath, barely daring to hope. "You think I'm pushing magic into my dad."

"I don't think," the god said haughtily. "I *know*. It's the only way any of this makes sense. Humans are *constantly* sending magic into things they value. That's how spirits like myself and the DFZ are made. When enough people all start believing in the same thing, their subconsciouses fill that idea with magic until it reaches critical mass and *poof!* A god is born. This same phenomenon also works on a small scale. Because you are human, all the love and worry you feel for your father translates directly into power. Power he is capable of receiving because *he* considers you clan. Neither of these factors would be enough on their own, but put them together, along with what is clearly an off-the-charts ability to move magic on your part, and you've got just enough oomph to keep an otherwise dead dragon alive! Technically. He's basically on life support, but you get the idea."

I thought I did. "Let me make sure I've got this straight," I said, pressing my hands to my temples as if I could physically squish all the whirling ideas together in my head. "My worrying about my dad caused me to send him magic subconsciously, and he was able to pick that magic up because he considers me his actual daughter." When she nodded, I broke into a grin. "So does that mean I can revive him by channeling more magic in?"

My excitement grew with every word. It had never occurred to me to try just shoving power into my dad. Living things usually didn't work that way. If you could heal someone just by filling them up with magic, hospitals would be out of business. Ditto for funeral homes. As always, though, dragons were different. If I'd been keeping Dad alive all these weeks with just my subconscious, imagine what I could do if I actually paid attention! Dad was huge, but I had a god on my side. The DFZ wanted him gone as much as I did. If she volunteered her magic, I could funnel it into him and have Dad back on his feet in a week. He'd be saved, and I'd be *free*! But even as these wild thoughts were rushing through my mind, the Spirit of Dragons was shaking her head.

"I can see the conclusions you're jumping to," she warned. "But it's not going to be that simple. The fact that this is working at all is a miracle all by itself, but you can't just shove magic into a dragon."

"Why not? There's tons of records of mages pulling magic *out* of dragons. Why can't I put it in?"

"You're a Shaman, and you're asking me this?" the spirit said, exasperated. "Parts aren't parts! You can't put magic back into a dragon for the same reason you can't put chicken nuggets back into a chicken. Dragon fire is *alive*. If you want it to grow, you have to feed it."

"Okay," I said. "How do I do that?"

She tapped her claw thoughtfully on her chin. "Stealing fire from someone else is the quickest solution. Is there anyone you don't like that you could feed to him?"

It was a sign of how desperate I'd gotten that I actually gave that question serious consideration. "No one I could catch," I answered at last. "I'd happily feed him White Snake, but we only got away from her the first time with the help of the DFZ. I don't think I could take her alone."

"I don't know," the spirit said thoughtfully. "White Snake's got her own problems right now, which makes her a softer target than you might think. That said, I don't know how we'd feed her fire to your father if he's unconscious, and I probably shouldn't be selling out my dragons. Not that I care about their good opinion, but I am technically the caretaker of all fire, and I try to maintain a minimum level of neutrality. If I didn't, a lot more snakes would be dead, believe me."

I sighed. Of *course* the one dragon in the world who could have made this easy for me was also the only one who actually sort of cared about fairness. Maybe my bad luck curse wasn't broken after—

I froze, eyes going wide. "What about the curse?"

"What about it?" the god asked.

"You said the reason my dad is in this state is because of the curse he put on me," I said. "He tied his fire to my luck, and then I burned it up by forcing his magic to sabotage entire currency markets. I thought the curse broke on its own the night he was attacked, but looking back, I don't think he ever actually removed it. I think it just stopped working because he ran out of fire to fuel it."

"Makes sense," the spirit said, looking more interested. "Go on."

"We've already established that I can't just shove magic into his body like I would to fill a circle," I continued. "But if I was able to use up all his magic, that proves there's an open connection between myself and his fire. A live wire, so to speak. Is there any reason I couldn't hack that wire to go the other way and send power back in?"

The Spirit of Dragons frowned thoughtfully. "Maybe," she said after almost a minute. "There is definitely a connection of some sort, but how would you use it? You burned up Yong's magic the first time by forcing his curse to do crazier and crazier things until his fire could no longer keep up. I don't see how that works in reverse."

"But the *link* is still there," I said eagerly. "White Snake said he was a fool for tying his fire to me, and obviously he was, but if the curse isn't actually broken, if it's still there binding us together, that means I've got a main line straight into my dad's fire. Shoving magic into his body obviously won't work for all the reasons you just mentioned, but if I use that connection to send magic straight into his fire, could I reignite him?"

"You mean like jumping a car?"

I'd been thinking dragon-fire defibrillator, but that worked too. When I nodded, the Spirit of Dragons opened her mouth only to close it again just as fast. She sat in silence for several minutes, tapping her tail on the floor so hard the empty cups bounced.

"I don't know," she said at last. "And that is *extremely* vexing. I can't think of a concrete reason why it *wouldn't* work, but there are so many conflating factors going on here that I can't say for sure that it *would*."

"Is there any harm in trying?"

The dragon god lapsed back into another long thought session, smoke curling from her nostrils. "Probably not. If it doesn't work, you run the risk of smothering whatever tiny spark he has left. If you don't do anything, though, he'll eventually grow so weak that he'll no longer be able to keep up his end of the connection. You're basically doomed either way, so I don't see a reason *not* to give it a go."

That was hardly a ringing endorsement, but even long shots looked good when you had nothing else. "Let's do it, then," I said, rising to my feet. "I'm ready. I just need a minute to go get Dr. Kowalski."

The dragon spirit blinked at me. "Doctor who?"

"My teacher," I explained, going for the simplest answer since I didn't know which of the DFZ's secrets were common knowledge among the spirit community and which weren't. "And a much better Shaman than I am. She'll know the best way to handle this."

"What?" the dragon god cried angrily. "No, no, *no!* You can't bring in another person! This is dragon business. The only reason you're allowed is because Yong considers you clan, and you're already in the middle of this mess. You have to be present, but we're going to be digging into the innermost workings of dragon fire with this. Outside consultants are strictly *not* allowed."

"But I can't do it on my own! We're basically talking about performing magical surgery, and I only became not-terrible at casting two months ago!"

"It *has* to be you," the fiery spirit argued. "You're the one with the connection to your father, and it was *your* idea. All you have to do is follow your own instructions and you should be fine. I'll even get you started."

She took a deep breath and leaned over, blowing gently above my father's chest until one of the sparks from her breath caught on the tip of his nose. If I hadn't known dragons were fireproof in every form, that would have freaked me out, but the ember didn't even blister his skin. It just sat there glowing with a smoky, burning power I could feel from two feet away, a tiny fleck of dragon fire from the world's purest source.

"Don't tell anyone I did that," the dragon god warned, swiveling her head around to glare at me menacingly. "If word ever gets out that I gave away fire, every dragon in the world will be on my tail trying to pitch me dark bargains in exchange for power. I'll never have a moment's peace again, so lips shut!"

"I'll tell no one," I promised, truly moved by her generosity. "Thank you."

The god rolled her eyes. "Don't look at me like that. I'm not doing this to be *nice*. I'm just extremely curious if your plan will work. Now get a move on. That ember won't burn forever, and I'm not giving you another."

I nodded and dropped back to my knees, reaching out to cup my hands around the precious spark she'd given us. It was a *spark* too. The glowing dot of magic on my father's nose was barely larger than a grain of rice, but that wasn't the point. As the Spirit of Dragons had said earlier—and Dr. Kowalski constantly reminded me—magic wasn't "parts is parts." This was the sort of spell that Thaumaturges with their homogenizing circles couldn't do. Even with the curse connecting us, if I wanted to feed magic back into my father, it was going to have to be in a form his body could accept. It had to be dragon fire. As a human, I couldn't make that myself, but I *could* mimic the power I saw flickering in the glowing dot the Spirit of Dragons had given me.

At least, that was my theory. For all that I mashed around handfuls of it every day, Shamanism was normally about changing the spell to fit the magic, not the magic to fit the spell. I wasn't sure I *could* shape the oily, slippery city magic of the DFZ into something that mimicked dragon fire, but the ember she'd breathed out was already fading, so I chucked my insecurities and went for it.

Picturing the pumpkin I'd used earlier today in my mind, I reached out to grab a handful of the rich, chaotic power of the DFZ that constantly churned through my apartment. The city's wet, chaotic magic seemed as far from the pure, hot dragon fire as you could get, but—as Dr. Kowalski also loved to remind me—Shamanism was all about being creative. With no circles or spellwork to smooth everything out, we had to work with what we had. Fortunately for me, the DFZ and dragons had a lot in common.

They were both ruthless and intolerant of weakness. They both loved money and power. They were both unfair. Just like fire, the city moved constantly, and both could eat you in a second if you let your guard down. The similarities were everywhere if you stopped being literal and left yourself open to interpretation, and I was a magical art history major. Finding abstract concepts in literal representations was my *jam,* and the more ways I found for these two to overlap, the more the magic came together in my hands, growing and heating and turning over on itself until the spark was no longer a spark, but a roaring ball of dragon fire precisely the size—and, oddly, the shape—of a pumpkin.

"Nicely done," the Spirit of Dragons said, swiveling her head to observe the ball of fire that was floating above my father from all angles. "Not quite sure I understand the shape, but that feels more like dragon fire than anything I've ever seen a mortal make. You've got a real knack for this." She looked at me greedily. "Are you *sure* you don't want to switch divine patrons? I don't know what the DFZ is offering, but I'm positive I can do better."

I shook my head, too focused on controlling the pumpkin of fire raging in front of me to answer in words. This was the hard part. I'd practiced holding magic with Dr. Kowalski, but now I had to actually send that power into my father—*without* smothering his own flames—and that was something I'd never done. I supposed I could have compared it to putting magic into a circle, but I was terrible at that, so I banished the thought and focused on the curse instead.

I'd felt it before, that oily shadow of draconic magic crawling over my soul, but even knowing what I was looking for, finding it was hard. My father's magic was so subtle, I hadn't even noticed I was cursed until another dragon had pointed it out. That made finding it now, when it wasn't powered, pretty much impossible. For once, though, my obsession with my dad's meddling in my life actually worked in my favor. I might not have been able to actually feel his curse anymore, but I remembered exactly where it was, so that was where I sent the flame, channeling the ball of fire into my own chest, through my magic, and up the connection I *knew* still hung like a shadow between us.

Once I got it going, the transfer was actually easier than I'd expected. I'd thought sending fire to my father would be a fight for every inch, just like everything else between us. In hindsight, I should have known better. My dad was my dad, but he was also a dragon. The moment I offered him a flicker of power, he started sucking it down with classic draconic greed. Seconds after I began, the pumpkin-sized ball of fake dragon fire I'd created had been drained dry.

And he *still* wasn't moving.

"Did it work?" I asked breathlessly, crouching over my father's unconscious body, which still looked exactly the same.

The Spirit of Dragons leaned over him as well, breathing in deeply. "He doesn't smell different."

"Does that mean anything?" This had been my last shot. If fire didn't work, I didn't know what I was going to—

Yong's body spasmed on the floor, making me jump. I scrambled away the second I recovered, ducking behind the Spirit of Dragons in case he woke up roaring and ready to fight. But he didn't wake up. Instead, his mouth opened to let out a billowing cloud of smoke. There was so much, it filled my bedroom. I was starting to choke when the gray-black clouds suddenly condensed, pulling together like joining beads of water to form a familiar, humanoid shape.

Eyes still watering, I poked my head out from behind the dragon spirit's flaming haunch.

"Dad?"

The shape looked up when I said his name, and my eyes went wide. It *was* my dad. My father, the Great Yong, Dragon of Korea, was standing in front of me, except he wasn't. His body was still on the floor. What I was staring at was a figure made of smoke. A transparent shadow in the shape of my father.

"Oh my god," I whispered, pressing my trembling hands to my mouth. "He's a *ghost.*"

"Huh," the Spirit of Dragons said, reaching out to pass a fiery claw through Yong's transparent head. "Didn't expect that to happen."

The smoke shadow looked up at the spirit's voice, and his face—also smoke, but every bit as detailed and expressive as the real thing—pulled into a furious scowl. "*You!*" he snarled, stabbing a transparent hand at the dragon of fire.

I jumped again. Before this point I hadn't been entirely convinced, but that was my father's voice for sure. It really was him standing there! Just, you know, made of smoke.

"Is that how you speak to your god?" the Spirit of Dragons asked in a dangerous voice.

"You're not *my* god," my father spat, his smoke eyes moving to me. "Opal, get away from that charlatan."

"She's not a charlatan, Dad," I said nervously, staying right where I was. "And she's helped you a lot, so maybe you should show a bit of gratitude."

"Why should I be grateful for *this?*" Yong demanded, holding up his see-through arms. "What happened to me? And why is my body on the floor?"

"The first is too obnoxious to answer, but the second's a good question," the Spirit of Dragons replied, squinting down at my father's comatose body. "It seems you've gotten disconnected somehow." She shifted her glare back to the Smoke-Yong. "How hard have you been trying to wake up?"

"With all my might," he replied. "My sister tried to kill me, my territory is unprotected, and my daughter is still living in this trash heap of a city. What did you think I would do? Lie there and take it?"

"Spoken like a true dragon," the spirit said, turning back to me. "He dislocated himself."

"Is that fixable?" I asked nervously.

"Hard to say," she replied, poking my father's body with the tip of her burning tail. "His physical form seems unharmed, or at least no worse than it was before, except he's no longer in it. Normally dragons are trapped in their bodies because that's where their fire burns, but you just gave him a new source, so…" She trailed off with a shrug. "My best guess is that he was *so* eager to move, he jumped up to grab the fire you were offering and got stuck."

That didn't sound good. "So I trapped him outside his body?"

"He trapped himself," the Spirit of Dragons corrected. "You didn't do anything wrong. He's just a greedy dragon." She flashed Yong a burning grin. "See? You *are* mine."

"I am no one's!" my father said, but the Spirit of Dragons wasn't listening.

"I think we can still count this as a success," she told me. "You know what dragon magic feels like now, and the curse connection obviously works. Great thinking on that, by the way. Really out of the box. And I'm dead serious about the job offer. Just let me know, and it's yours."

"I'm good, thank you. But what do we do now?" I pointed at my smoke dad. "He can't stay like that."

"He won't," the god assured me. "Just keep feeding him magic and he should get strong enough to reenter his physical body eventually. Or he'll disconnect permanently and die. It's up to him. You've already done all you can. Until he puts himself back together, though, he's going to be entirely dependent on you for fire, so consider yourself haunted, I guess."

My eyes went wide. "You mean he has to stay close to me? As in follow me around?"

"Pretty much," the spirit said. "You were keeping him alive before, but now you are *literally* his life's fire. And considering how much of that a dragon his age needs, he's going to be stuck on you like a baby koala for the foreseeable future."

This could not be happening. "How am I supposed to live my life with the *ghost of my dad* following me around?!"

The Spirit of Dragons shrugged. "Dunno. If it helps, I'm pretty sure only spirits and other dragons will be able to see him like this. I'd call that a plus, but pretty much every dragon in the world wants to kill Yong of Korea at the moment, so maybe not so much."

Definitely not. "Can he be killed in this form?"

"I don't know," the god said. "Let me try."

Before I could stop her, she lashed a burning claw through my father, completely dissipating his smoke. I was about to scream when he suddenly re-formed, his transparent body coming back together even faster than the first time. Faster and angrier.

"*How dare you!*" he roared.

"He's fine," the dragon god said, turning back to me. "Just make sure *you* don't die. Until he gets himself back together, you're his lifeline. Also, I'm pretty sure you don't want to die for your own sake. Most mortals don't."

I absolutely did *not* want to die. Especially not for my ungrateful bastard of a father. Unfortunately, it looked as if my hopes of getting him healed and out of my life had just gone up in literal smoke. At least when he was a vegetable I could leave him in the apartment. Now he was stuck to me like a giant target.

"I'm doomed," I groaned, putting my face in my hands.

"Don't be like that," the spirit said, patting me on the head like a dog. "You've done an excellent job at staying hidden so far. Even *I* thought you were dead! Just keep it up a bit longer, keep the magic pumping, and Old Grumpy Smoke should be back on his scaly feet in no time."

That made me feel a little better. "Will *you* keep it secret?"

"Absolutely. You think I want word of my kind and generous nature getting out?" She gagged. "I won't tell a soul, and I'll kill you both if you breathe a word about what happened here to anyone."

She looked one-hundred percent serious, but the death threat actually made me feel better about all of this. Dragons were only trustworthy when they were threatening to kill you. "Thank you for your help, great spirit," I said, bowing low.

"Your gratitude is accepted," the god informed me, reaching over to grab the last liquor bottle I hadn't emptied for the summoning. "And if you change your mind about the priestess thing, you know how to ring my bell." She wiggled the plastic bottle of Canadian whiskey at me with a wink. "Farewell, Yong's Opal. You're an interesting little mortal. Don't die too soon!"

"I'll try not to," I said, but she was already gone, her too-huge fiery body vanishing in a poof of acrid-smelling smoke, leaving me alone with the faded ghost of my dad.

"She's an embarrassment to all our kind," Yong growled, waving his hand at the smoke she'd left behind, which did nothing since he was made of the same stuff. "How we dragons ended up with a drunken, selfish, egotistical snake like her as our god, I'll never understand."

"I don't know," I said sourly. "I think you just made a pretty good argument for her divinity."

He turned up his nose. "Believe me, there's nothing 'divine' about that one. I knew her before she became a spirit, and I'd be hard-pressed to name anyone less qualified for the position."

I had no idea what he was ranting about, and I didn't care. Now that it was over, I was starting to realize just how much zapping my dad back to life had taken out of me. Add in my morning of intense physical labor, and I was ready to sleep for a week. As ever, though, my father couldn't let me have a moment's peace.

"What's our next step?" he asked, looming over me.

"I don't know," I replied, flopping onto the ground. "You're the one who made himself a ghost."

"I'm *not* a ghost," he said stubbornly. "This form is merely a temporary inconvenience. Just put more fire into me, I'll get back into my body again, and we can deal with things properly."

"Yeah, well, I can't do that. As much as I'd love to get you out of my hair, I'm too tired to make fire again today."

"Nonsense," he said, his smoke jaw clenched. "You can't leave me like this, Opal."

If it were anyone else, I'd have said he sounded panicked. My dad *never* panicked, though, so I wrote it off as exhaustion-induced hysteria. "If you're that eager to get moving, you should call Mom," I suggested. "She's the one who'd do anything for you. I'm sure she'd be happy to—"

"I can't let your mother see me like this," my father said, his smoke face horrified. "I'm her dragon! She serves me because I am strong. If I appear before her in this...this *state*, she'll never look at me the same way again."

I rolled my eyes. "Dad, she worships you. Like crazy cult levels of worship. You could probably appear before her as a cabbage and she'd still bow down to kiss your leaves."

"Don't insult your mother," he said, glaring down at me. "How long must you rest before you can feed me fire again?"

I had no idea. I didn't even want to think about magic right now, and his entitled attitude was really pissing me off. "You know, a 'thank you' wouldn't be amiss. I've saved your life like ten times over in the last two months, and—"

"Two months?" my father interrupted, his eyes going wide. "You mean I've been lying incapacitated on your floor for *two months*?"

"To the day. The DFZ just gave me my end-of-the-month report this morning."

That statement seemed to make him even more confused. "DFZ? What are you talking about?"

Hoo boy. "Remember back when White Snake had you trapped and the city helped us escape by smacking White Snake into the river?" I asked, sitting up. "Well she didn't do that out of the goodness of her heart. I agreed to be her priestess in exchange for help."

And debt relief, but I was going for maximum guilt here, so I left that part out. It was working too. My father looked shaken, his smoke hands trembling so hard they couldn't hold themselves together.

"You sold yourself to a spirit?" he whispered at last. "To save *me*? But I thought—"

"Don't read too much into it," I warned, crossing my arms over my chest. "Just because I wasn't willing to let White Snake murder you doesn't mean everything's hunky-dory. I'm still not going home. Ever. And now you can't make me." I grinned wide. "Guess turning you into smoke has benefits after all."

This was usually the point in the conversation where my father would say something nasty about me being an ungrateful, spoiled child with no respect for her elders, but he didn't. He didn't say a word. He just sat there staring into the distance like a trauma victim.

It was pretty unnerving, and not just because he was made of smoke. I was so used to my father acting superior, like he knew everything. Seeing him like this, like he was lost, it felt wrong. So much so that I almost wished he *hadn't* woken up. At least when he'd been lying on my floor he'd just looked like he was asleep. As scary as that had been, it was better than seeing him like this. My dad seriously looked like he was about to cry, and I didn't know how to handle that.

"Whoa," I said nervously, putting up my hands. "Dad, I—"

A loud buzzing sound came to my rescue. Down in my jeans pocket, my phone was going off like a noise grenade, informing me that my lunch-turned-spirit-summoning break was over.

"I've got to go to work," I said slowly, pushing myself up. "Why don't you stay here and rest until—"

"You can't leave," he said, his voice dead calm even though his smoke was shaking wildly. "This is an *emergency*."

"I don't get a choice," I told him. "I work for a god. They don't tolerate tardiness."

"Then take me with you," he said, stepping closer. "We're tied together, remember?"

As if I could forget. "What about your body?" I asked, trying another angle.

"What about it?" he shot back, pressing a transparent hand against his transparent chest. "Everything that is me is here in the smoke. *I* am here." He looked over his shoulder at his pseudo-corpse. "My body's been lying on your floor for eight weeks. It can handle one more afternoon. But I'm not leaving you, Opal. You're my fire now."

That *was* what the giant dragon god had said, wasn't it?

"Fine," I grumbled, stomping away to go grab my work bag from the living room. "You can come, but don't get in my way. The DFZ's already warned me about slacking off to care for you, and she's not someone you want on your tail."

My god could be surprisingly kind, but when it came to work, she was every bit as ruthless as any other DFZ employer. Family emergencies were no excuse. If I didn't show up and do my job, I'd end up on the street before I could blink.

"I won't be a burden," he promised, looking affronted that I'd even thought such a thing. Then his face grew curious. "What manner of work does a city god require?"

"One very suited to my skills, actually," I said, walking straight through him to grab the doorknob to my bedroom. I closed the flimsy door and my eyes at the same time, picturing the destination in my mind. When I had it good and clear, I opened the door again and marched through. The curse stretched as I went, the line of magic growing taut, and the smoke shadow of my father was jerked off his feet, yanked like a dog on a leash after me into the dark.

Chapter 3

When I opened the door from my apartment, the scene waiting for me on the other side was the same one I always saw: an empty city, floating in the dark.

Like Old Detroit, it was arranged into blocks, but these roads had never been driven on. The asphalt here was still new and black with fresh yellow paint that had never touched a tire. So far as I could tell, the roads were only there to divide the buildings into a grid for organization, which was good because there were a *lot* of them. Structures of every size and from every time period spread out in all directions, forming a ghost town of boarded-up shops and shuttered houses, failed banks and abandoned tenements, crumbling department stores and forgotten Masonic temples. Some of the dark structures were collapsing, others looked brand-new, but every single one of them was empty. Aside from the single orange streetlight shining above the intersection where my door appeared, there was no light anywhere. No sound or movement. Even the rats didn't make it down here.

"What is this place?" the shade of my father whispered, looking nervously at the empty blackness above our heads.

"I'm not really sure," I replied, setting my work bag down on the table that was usually next to my door, though sometimes it wasn't. Despite the dead quiet, this place could be surprisingly energetic. The grid layout was always the same, but the buildings themselves changed all the time. It wasn't unusual to open my door and see an entirely new skyline waiting for me, but what else could you expect from the private stash of a city that couldn't stay still?

Fortunately for my sanity, today was a table day. A nice polished mahogany one that must have been someone's showpiece dining table before it had been forgotten. I was unpacking my things carefully so as not to scratch the finish when my father walked his smoke body *through* the table to force me to look at him.

"How do you not know where we are?"

I rolled my eyes and slapped the pair of reinforced work gloves I'd just pulled out through his chest. "First rule of working for the DFZ: you must accept that space is flexible. Nothing in this city stays put. Even the Dragon Consulate moves around."

"Yes, but I can still always reach it." My father pointed up at the flat-black nothing that served as the sky here. "This is a ghost town floating in the void!"

"That's not the void," I said authoritatively. "*My* apartment is floating in the void, and if you looked out my windows, you'd know it's way scarier than this." I waved at the blankness. "What you're seeing is just background, a courtesy curtain installed by the DFZ to hide the fact that this place doesn't exist in a way non-divine brains can understand."

My father scowled. "That's surprisingly thoughtful of her."

"Try practical," I said with a snort, unpacking my magnifier set. "If that blackness wasn't there, I'd be too busy having an existential crisis to do my job, and when it comes to the DFZ, *nothing* is more important than the job."

And speaking of jobs, I was late for mine. Digging into my bag, I pulled out my hard hat/headlamp combo and slapped it down on top of my hair. I pulled my phone out of my pocket next and powered it down since this place always sent Sibyl into a next-level freak-out. Even with her GPS disabled, my AI simply couldn't handle being somewhere that didn't technically exist. I'd tried talking her through it, but we'd ultimately agreed that turning her off was the kindest thing for both of us.

"So what work do you do in this place?" my father asked as I lovingly stowed my phone.

"My official title is 'Appraiser,'" I told him, reaching up to turn on my LED headlamp. "But I don't like it because I never actually appraise anything. I'm really more of a curator. My job is to go through all of the random stuff the DFZ has collected over the years and tell her what's worth keeping and what isn't."

Yong still looked lost. "Why would she need you for that?"

"Because she can't do it herself," I said, exasperated. "The DFZ is a place, not a person. She's fantastic at understanding city things—roads, traffic flow, zoning, and so forth—but that still leaves a ton of really important stuff that she has no idea about. For example…"

I waved my hand at the blocks of silent buildings around us, some of which were covered in decades of dust. "Notice how there's no scrap metal here, or old cars? That's because the DFZ already knows what to do with those. Ditto for recyclables, old lumber, broken cement, et cetera. Anything that has a fixed resale value she's already on top of, but there's plenty of material in a city that *doesn't* fit that criteria. Antiques, art, historical pieces: anything whose worth is measured in human interest rather than price-per-ounce. She *knows* it's valuable because she sees people valuing it, but the hows and whys of that value are completely beyond her ability to comprehend."

That was the part of priesthood that had taken me the longest to understand. Because she was capable of talking and acting normally, it was easy to think of the DFZ as just a really powerful person, but she wasn't. She was a spirit, the magical embodiment of a concept. She'd been shaped by human perception—what *we* thought the DFZ was—but she wasn't actually one of us. Since she was a city with all the human social interactions that implied, she was better at pretending than most spirits, but that's all it was: pretending. At the end of the day, the DFZ was as much a slave to her concept as the Spirit of the Forgotten Dead. She couldn't leave her city, couldn't understand things that didn't have to do with it, and didn't particularly care. The only reason she hadn't recycled everything down here into raw materials for new buildings already was because it went against the DFZ's thrifty nature to destroy anything that might have value whether she understood that value or not.

I understood it, though. That understanding was why the DFZ wanted me as her priestess so badly. It wasn't just my magical potential or the fact that I wasn't a sociopath, which was apparently uncommon enough to be notable. I was valuable because, unlike her, I actually understood why people had treasured this stuff and these places. I could see that the amazing Art Deco facade on the front of that collapsing bank was beautiful and rare and worth way more than the granite blocks that made it up. I knew which pieces of colored glass were Tiffany and which were beer bottles. She'd saved this stuff for years because she knew it was worth more than the sum of its part, but she'd never been able to tell more than that until me. I solved a problem the DFZ couldn't solve on her own, and so, true to her nature as a city of capitalism, she'd hired me on the spot, given me a quota, and put me to work.

And I *loved* it. Working here was all the best, treasure-huntery parts of being a Cleaner with none of the actual cleaning, bidding, or risk of opening a door and getting a shotgun in your face. In addition to the blocks of buildings—all of which were too run-down to be usable but still possessed enough potential architectural, cultural, or historical significance that the DFZ hadn't felt comfortable junking them for parts—there was an aircraft-hangar-sized warehouse one block over that was jammed to the rafters with all the random stuff people lost, hid, or threw away.

Some of it was legit trash, some were consumer goods that, though interesting, weren't actually rare or valuable, but a surprising amount was actual treasure. In just the last two months, I'd discovered hundreds of museum-quality pieces, including several that appeared to have been looted from the old Detroit Institute of Art. I'd found paintings, I'd found historical artifacts, I'd even found an entire wall from Diego Rivera's lost *Mural to Industry*! It was hands down the best treasure hunting of my life. If it hadn't been for the fact that I was owned by a god and making no actual money, just putting off a debt I couldn't pay, I could have done this forever.

Unfortunately, my father didn't seem to understand at all when I explained this to him. He'd never understood my fascination with Cleaning either, though, so I wasn't sure why I'd bothered. For the millionth time, I wished Nik was with me. He would have understood the wonder of this place. Also, it would have been really nice to have someone made of metal to hide under when the rickety old buildings I poked through every day started dropping pieces. Mostly, though, I missed his company. Working alone was, well, *lonely*, and for someone who'd ghosted on all her friends and made a new life in a city famous for lonely people, I handled that surprisingly badly.

"All right," I said, reaching through my dad to mark my arrival on the time sheet taped to the post of the single working streetlamp. "Enough talking. Time to get to work."

"You can't just 'get to work,'" my father argued. "You said the DFZ wouldn't tolerate you being tardy, but you've already checked in. You should be fine, so let's make a plan."

"You're free to plan all you want," I said, setting off down the dark street in what I considered my "lucky" direction. "But I'm not getting a god on my case for you. I have quotas to meet."

Yong made an insulted sound and hurried after me. "Isn't your job to find culturally valuable objects? How can she put quotas on *art?*"

I also thought the quotas were stupid, but, "She doesn't understand, remember?" I said defensively. "And the quotas aren't about flogging value out of me. She just likes to know I'm not slacking around down here." The DFZ *hated* slacking.

"Sounds like you work in a salt mine," my dad huffed. "But very well. What's the minimum you have to produce before we can get back to more important matters?"

"You mean *you?*" I said, rolling my eyes. "You *do* remember that we're inside a god, right? One that saved us both? You might want to think twice before you talk out loud about how much more important your interests are than hers."

"Gods can take care of themselves," Yong said dismissively. "And my needs are obviously more pressing than sorting through a bunch of rotting buildings that have been here for years."

Some of the stuff down here *was* pretty old, but that wasn't the point. "I don't work for you," I snapped, stopping to glare at him. "The only reason I let you come down here is because we're stuck together, but contrary to what you *clearly* believe, you are not entitled to my time. Now shut up and let me do my job, or I'm going to tie you to the lamppost to wait for me like a dog."

My dad's response to that was a long, put-upon sigh that made me want to strangle him, but he didn't yell, which was a surprising and welcome change. It was no secret that my dad brought out the worst in me, but that was usually because he could never let a conversation pass without asserting his dominance. But the dynamic was different now. My dad was no longer huge or powerful compared to me. He was weak and dependent, which meant I no longer had to care.

That was an amazingly freeing realization. I'd never had the luxury of just *not caring* what my dad thought or did before. I was still struggling to wrap my brain around the concept when my dad cleared his throat.

"If your god will punish you for not working, then that's what you have to do," he said in a voice that was clearly straining to remain calm. "But the task will go faster if we do it together, so what does the DFZ require?"

I still didn't like the unspoken implication that I would help him once I was done here, but that was a fair observation. Having my dad work with me would be a lot less trouble than arguing with him for the next eight hours, and there was no one more knowledgeable when it came to antiques. I'd learned some stuff at school, but most of what I used on a daily basis came from my father. If nothing else, having him around to double-check my finds would save me a lot of research time on the ancient library computer the DFZ had installed in the warehouse for reference purposes.

"I have to check three blocks worth of structures and mark them as either renovate or tear down," I said, pointing at the dark buildings we were walking past. "Every room has to be checked, because you never know what's hiding behind a boring front. One time I found an entire Prohibition speakeasy hidden inside a basement! It had an Art Deco ballroom with a full orchestra stand and a fifty-foot bar lit with real Schonbek crystal light fixtures! The rest of the building was a teardown, but I had the DFZ move the entire basement as-was into the warehouse. We're just waiting on the University of Chicago to send us some experts on the time period so we can restore the club to its former glory."

It was going to be magnificent too. The wood paneling was cracked, and the gilding on the bar had long since worn off, but I could tell that with a little TLC, that place was going to be a window into a lost world. Finding it had felt like walking into a pharaoh's tomb. Just thinking about it was getting me excited all over again when my dad asked, "Why?"

I blinked at him in confusion. "Why what?"

"Why are you renovating an old speakeasy?" my father asked. "I can understand restoring valuable antiques, and beautifully renovated historic buildings always fetch high rent, but what does the DFZ care about recreating a historically accurate Prohibition Era drinking club? What's she going to do with it, charge admission?"

I looked down at my feet, because I didn't know. The DFZ had hired me to sort through all of this because she couldn't do it herself, but so far as I could tell, she had no actual plans for anything I'd found. Whenever I brought the subject up—suggested building a museum or loaning the things I'd found to somewhere that already had a similar collection—the DFZ was completely uninterested. She didn't even seem to care about selling it. All that mattered to her was that nothing valuable was thrown away, which was good, but still left me feeling lackluster about what we were doing here. I mean, what was the point of saving all this stuff if you didn't show it off?

Unfortunately, it wasn't my choice to make. That was the downside of this job: everything I found here belonged to the DFZ, not me. Until my debts were clear—or until I decided I really did want to worship a city for the rest of my life—I was just the hired help. Now that my dad was up, though, I hoped it wouldn't be too long before I was free again. And speaking of…

"So," I said as we climbed the steps to our first target, a listing structure that had probably been an incredibly charming Gothic cottage once but now looked more like a haunted house. "How much more magic do you think you'll need before you're back on your feet?"

My father thought about that for a moment, his smoke form almost impossible to see in the dark as we stepped through the building's sagging doorway. "Hard to say," he replied at last. "I don't feel as though I have any fire at all right now."

"The Spirit of Dragons warned us it was small," I said, swinging my light around the house's fire-damaged interior. "But you've clearly got something burning in there or we wouldn't be having this conversation. I'm not trying to fire-shame you. I just want to know how big a tank I'm trying to fill up."

My father's smoke face pulled into a scowl. "You mean, 'how much longer until I'm no longer dependent and you can ship me back to Korea?'"

When I didn't dispute that, his scowl deepened. "It doesn't matter how long it takes. I'm not leaving you here, Opal."

"That's not your call," I said, shining my light in his face. "We're *done*, Dad. I paid my debt. I saved your life! You don't get to control me anymore."

"I wouldn't have had to control you if you'd been reasonable," he argued, which was exactly the wrong thing to say.

"*Reasonable?*" I cried. "You're one to talk about *reasonable!*" I stabbed my finger into his smoke body. "You're not like this because of anything White Snake did. This happened because you used up all your fire trying to control me. All I wanted was to live my life dragon-free, but you couldn't let me have *one day* where I wasn't under your claws! In what world does that make *you* the reasonable one?"

"I admit things got out of hand at the end," my father said in a strained voice. "But my actions were well-intentioned. I am the Dragon of Korea, and you are my child. That position makes you an obvious target for everyone who wishes me harm. What was I supposed to do? Let you run free?"

"*Yes!* Because I'm a *person*, not a weakness."

"It wasn't as if I ruined anything important," he argued. "You were living in squalor, working as a subcontracted manual laborer."

"I was living *my* life! And if it wasn't up to your standards, that's because of *you*. I was doing fine until *you* buried me in bad luck!"

I was screaming by the time I finished, my body clenched so tight with rage that every muscle hurt, which was not how I wanted to spend my afternoon. Dammit, how did my dad always manage to get under my skin? Even when he was nothing but a smoke ghost, just hearing him talk made me feel like I was sixteen again, and I *hated* it. I hated everything about this.

"You know what? Forget about helping. I'll do this faster myself. Just shut up and stay out of my way. The sooner I meet my quota, the sooner I can go home, go to bed, and get the sleep I need to give you enough fire to *get out of my life.*"

My father tried to say something, but I'd already stomped away, keeping a mental hand on the curse that connected us to make sure he couldn't get too close. We fell into a long, angry silence after that. I stalked through the crumbling house, too mad to see more than the most obvious details. I knew that put me in danger of missing things, but I was having trouble caring. My dad's questions had reminded me that the DFZ wasn't actually doing anything with the stuff I found, so what was the loss? All I wanted was to get my work done to the minimum acceptable standard and get this forced daddy-daughter time over with.

Fortunately for me, the house I'd chosen to start with turned out to be a pretty easy call. There was some nice brickwork on the front facade, but it wasn't anything I hadn't seen before. That didn't mean it wasn't amazing. *All* old Detroit houses from this period were amazing. Back in the glory days of the auto factories when they'd actually paid line workers good money, immigrants had flocked here from all over the world. Eager to put down new roots, they'd built their homes like castles, creating beautiful structures of stone and brick made to last for generations. I would have saved every last one of them if I could, but even the DFZ didn't have unlimited room, and this particular house-castle had a collapsing roof *and* a cracked foundation. Sighing at the loss, I pulled out my tiny can of spray paint and drew an X on the front door, marking the building for demolition.

The moment I was done, the whole building started to shake. I barely had time to scramble off the porch before the listing house sank into the ground, sucked down by the city to be digested into materials for new buildings. Sad to see it go but happy to have an item off my list, I moved down the street to my next target, a cement office building from the nineteen seventies with some *very* unusual design elements.

And so it went. Save, pitch, save, pitch, all the way down the line. But while my bad mood stuck around for the first block, by the second, the work had sucked me in. I couldn't help it. Even knowing it wasn't going anywhere except into the DFZ's warehouses, I was a sucker for a treasure hunt. I'd just started digging into a rotting industrialist mansion from the Gilded Age that I had high hopes for when my father spoke up behind me.

"Found something."

I jumped into the air. He'd been so quiet and hard to see in his smoke form, I'd actually forgotten he was there. Being reminded now brought my anger rushing back hot and sharp, but I was sick of feeling that way, so I pushed it aside, focusing instead on the small lump he was staring at by his feet, its rounded surface glittering dully in the glare of my headlamp.

"What's that?"

"A silver sugar dish," he said, scooting around to point at the tipped bowl's heavily tarnished bottom. "Looks like a Lamerie."

"No way." Paul de Lamerie was one of the greatest English silversmiths who'd ever lived. His work was still prized all over the world. My expectations for this place might have been high, but there was no *way* my dad had just found a priceless silver treasure lying on the ground.

"Let me see that."

"I'm not wrong," Yong said confidently as I snatched the little footed bowl off the dusty floor. "His mark on the bottom can be forged, but there's no counterfeiting Lamerie's exquisite attention to detail. Just look at the tiny swirls of oak leaves on the handles. Who else in the medium could create movement like that?"

I didn't know. I wasn't an expert on silver, but my dad was. When it came to treasure, Yong was an expert on everything, and as deeply as I resented his company, *I* hadn't spotted that bowl.

"Nice catch," I admitted grudgingly, placing the maybe-priceless piece of silver into my bag. Then, after a long, resistant pause, I added, "See anything else?"

I shouldn't have asked. I should have known better than to give him so much as a toe into my life again. But like I said, I'd gotten pretty lonely these last two months, especially when it came to work. The DFZ didn't understand or appreciate any of the stuff I brought her, and Dr. Kowalski never wanted to talk about anything that wasn't gardening or magic. But while we argued over literally everything else, my dad and I had always been able to talk treasure. Even in my current grumpiness, I wasn't going to pass up my first chance in weeks at a real conversation on the topic that interested me most. I'd also be a fool to give up the opportunity to go treasure hunting with a dragon. Forget quotas and jobs and the fact that no one was ever going to see this stuff. My dad could sniff out valuables better than anyone alive. If there was something truly amazing hidden down here, he would find it. Surely that was worth a little suffering, especially since I was stuck with him anyway.

That greedy mindset made tolerating my father much more bearable, particularly since I was right. Between his encyclopedic knowledge of everything valuable, his supernatural ability to see in the dark, and the fact that being made of smoke meant he could pass right through obstacles that would normally be too dangerous for me to cross, Yong was a treasure-finding machine. All he had to do was look at a building to know if it had valuables and where they would be. Plus, he pointed out tons of stuff I hadn't even known to look for, things like vintage toasters and an ugly tangle of colored glass tubes that I'd thought was a bong but was actually an *epergne*. I knew what an *epergne* was, of course, but the giant Victorian centerpieces had always been so kitschy and ridiculous, I'd never bothered to study up on them.

My dad didn't have that blindness. This stuff wasn't history to him. He'd lived through the periods when the things we saw as antiques had been popular, and he remembered all of it—what was good, what was bad, what was worth buying, and what wasn't. His reptilian brain was a catalog of art and fashion trends going back thousands of years, and while his taste had always been a bit stuffy for my liking, there was no denying his eye. He could recognize a Monet even if another lesser artist had painted over it, and for someone currently employed as a treasure finder, that was *gold*.

I was so busy freaking out over the never-ending parade of amazing stuff he was turning up, I actually forgot that I was mad at him. For a few blissful hours, it was like we'd gone back a dozen years to the time when we'd done stuff like this for fun. It felt incredible, as if a dragon-sized weight had been lifted off my chest. So, naturally, my father had to go and send it crashing back down.

"Why do you serve her so faithfully?"

"Huh?" I asked, looking up from my pile. We'd finished our house quota thirty minutes ago and moved on to the shipping containers, the huge open bins where the DFZ threw all the little things that fell down storm drains or were tossed out of cars or otherwise didn't filter down to her inside buildings. This was exciting in and of itself—I normally never made it to the containers!—but my good mood soured when I looked up to see my father's scowling face.

"The DFZ," he clarified, his voice grudging and heavy, as if the words had been building up inside him for a while. "She works you like a dog, keeping you tied up with quotas and time sheets, and yet you haven't said a word against her. Why? Are you afraid of making her angry?"

"If that was the case, I couldn't admit it out loud to you, could I?" I quipped. "But seriously, no. She can be pretty terrifying, but I'm not doing this out of fear. I work for the DFZ because I owe her, because she keeps me safe, and because it's not so bad. I get free food and a roof over my head, and treasure hunting is pretty awesome even with the quotas."

Given how we'd spent the last few hours, I'd thought that would be obvious, but my father looked angrier than ever. "You owed me as well, and you didn't behave like this. You fought tooth and nail against every opportunity I gave you no matter how generous. Why is it different with the DFZ?"

"Because she's not you," I snapped, all good feelings forgotten.

"She's worse," he argued, his lip curling into a snarl. "I gave you comfort and luxury! She's barely provided you with a furnished apartment."

"Actually, *I* furnished my own apartment using stuff *I* found down here," I said sharply, crossing my arms over my chest. "I *like* picking out my own furniture, but you don't care about that. You've *never* cared about what I like. The DFZ might be a taskmaster, but at least she listens when I talk. At least she respects me. If I told her I didn't want to be a priestess anymore, she'd try to change my mind and hold me to my debt, but she wouldn't keep me against my will. You did. That's the difference."

My father started to grind his teeth only to stop when he remembered that he had none. Just smoke and anger, so much that his edges were starting to go fuzzy. "If debt's the problem, I'll pay it. I won't have my daughter enslaved to a cheap god who makes her dig through condemned houses for trinkets!"

"Damn straight you'll pay my debt!" I yelled, shooting to my feet. "You're the reason I'm in this mess to begin with!"

"You don't want to get into the blame game with me," Yong warned, holding up a smoky fist. "Let's not forget whose fault *this* is."

"Yeah, *yours!*" I cried, balling my own fists. "You want to talk about enslavement? How about a dragon who uses monthly payments to control his adult daughter from across the ocean because she had the audacity to want her own life *away from him.*"

"It was for your own good," he said without a trace of remorse. "Mortal life is short, and you were wasting yours. I had to make you come home somehow."

"*I'm never coming home!*" I screamed at him. "Don't you get it yet? I'd rather work for the DFZ forever! I'd rather be *homeless* than go back to Korea with you!"

My father's eyes went wide. If he'd been in his normal body, this was the point where flames would have started pouring out of his mouth. Coincidentally, this was also the point when I typically started backing down, but to hell with that. He couldn't do shit to me like this, and I was so *sick* of being afraid of him. So sick of letting him rule my life even when he wasn't there.

"Just leave me alone!" I yelled before I remembered that he couldn't. We were stuck together, which only made me angrier. Even when he was practically dead, I couldn't escape my dad.

In the end, I compromised by turning my back on him. Wherever he went, I faced the other direction. It was petty and childish, but I just couldn't stand to look at him right now, which sucked because we'd actually been getting along for once. I'd *actually* been enjoying his company for the first time in I couldn't even remember how long, and then he'd opened his mouth and ruined everything, just like always.

For such a stupid reason too. I'd been too mad to notice at the time, but when I went back through the argument in my mind, I realized he'd been *jealous* of the DFZ. Dad wasn't concerned that I might be trapped in unwilling service to a god. He just couldn't stand that I was being a good little mortal for her but not for *him.*

Thinking about it that way made me want to throw in the towel on both of them, but that would have been unfair. This wasn't the DFZ's fault. She'd done her best for me, given me everything I'd asked for that was within her power. The reason I had quotas and strict work times was because that was the sort of god she was, not because she wanted to control me. Unlike my dad, she'd *never* wanted that. She was the city of free will. She hadn't even let me join her until I'd proven I was doing so of my own volition. She tallied my debts as a point of order, not a lever to crush me into submission. That was my dad's game.

And he wondered why I couldn't stand him.

I didn't find so much as a collectible sports cup for the rest of my shift. I dug through the containers because that was my job, but I was too angry to actually see anything I was looking at. Angry at my dad, angry at life, angry at the world, angry at myself, just *angry.*

God, I wished Nik was here. He always knew how to put things into perspective, and while we were at it, I could also really use a hug. But there were no hugs here, so I settled for slumping against the wall of the shipping container and poking at random objects until my shift was over. It was a blatant and complete waste of time, but the DFZ had no grounds to complain considering all the treasures I'd sent to her warehouse today. Also, all that moping gave me a chance to recover my magic, which was great since the sooner I recharged my dad, the sooner I could kick him out for real.

I absolutely intended to do it too. I didn't care how many of his enemies were stalking the streets. He was a big dragon with billions of dollars and a household full of people who worshiped the scales on his feet. He could take care of himself. I was the only one who could take care of me, and at the moment that meant getting as far away from my father as possible.

"Hey," I called, finally looking over my shoulder. "Time to go."

The words echoed through the dark without reply, and I scowled. Seeing a figure made of smoke was always hard in the dark, but even using my light, I didn't see my dad sulking around the containers or anywhere else. I could feel the thread that connected us, so I knew he couldn't have gone far—or died, still a possibility—but I had no idea where he'd run off to. I was about to just yank him over using the curse when I spotted a plume of smoke rising from the ancient stone chapel across the street.

Sighing deep in my chest, I walked out into the road to get a better view. Sure enough, I spotted my father lying on the slanted roof just below the steeple, staring at the emptiness above our heads as if he'd lost something precious up there in the dark. It was an absolutely pathetic sight, and I didn't have the patience to deal with it.

"Get down here," I ordered.

Naturally, he didn't move. Furious, I grabbed our connection to give him a good tug when his voice floated down to me through the dark.

"Do you hate me that much?"

I stared up at him in disbelief. "You're really going to do this now?"

"Just answer the question," he said. Then, quietly, he added, "Please."

It was the "please" that did it. I'd never actually heard my father use that word non-sarcastically. The shock alone was enough to make me let go of his leash. When I came back to myself, he'd slid down the slate roof to land on the ground, staring at me from across the empty street with the same lost expression he'd used on the sky.

"Don't," I said.

"Don't what?"

I didn't feel like explaining myself, so I answered his first question instead.

"I don't hate you," I said. "If I did, I wouldn't have sold myself to save you, and we wouldn't be here. At this point, I don't think I'm capable of hating you, but I hate everything that you do. I hate how you talk to me and how you act."

My father looked supremely displeased. "That makes no sense. How is hating everything about me different from hating *me*?"

"It just is," I said with a shrug. "I can't explain it. I guess it's because you're my dad. No matter how badly you treat me or how little you deserve it, part of me will always love you. I know it's pathetic, but there it is."

He stared at me in confusion. "How have I treated you badly?"

My jaw fell open. "You *can't* be serious."

"I am very serious," he said angrily. "Everything I've ever done has been for your sake. Even the curse was an attempt to guide you. I never wanted you to suffer, but I couldn't ignore that you were making terrible choices. I tried to help you, to give you advice, but you refused to listen, so I cursed your luck in an attempt to make things go *so* badly for you, you'd come home of your own accord. I can see how that might appear heavy-handed to you, but it was done with good intentions. I've only ever wanted what's best for you, Opal."

He sounded utterly sincere, which was the only reason I didn't blow up. Once I realized I wasn't getting mad, I fought to stay that way because I blew up every time we had this conversation, and it never helped. My father wasn't stupid, but he was so backwards when it came to me, it felt like we were speaking different languages. I'd always thought that was because he was a cruel dragon who couldn't understand human relationships, only ownership, but there was nothing cruel in his voice now. He sounded really hurt, as if he were just as confused by my reaction as I was by his. I didn't know if that was good or bad, but it was a different path from the usual screaming rut we typically fell into, and after months of debts and curses and fighting and both of us nearly dying over this, I was just desperate enough to give it a shot.

"All right," I said, taking a deep breath. "I'll bite. You say you only want what's best for me. What exactly do you think that is?"

"You coming back home to Korea," he answered instantly. "I can provide everything you could want there, and you would be safe from my enemies. It is what's best for both of us."

"But what if what I want isn't something you can give?"

My father frowned, clearly not comprehending the question, and I sighed. "You say you want what's best for me," I said again, trying a different angle. "But 'best' is subjective. You wouldn't want to live what the Peacemaker considers your 'best' life, right?"

"That is completely unrelated. Stop sidetracking the issue."

"I'm not," I said, fighting to keep my voice calm and level so he wouldn't stop listening like he usually did. "This is exactly the problem. You say if I come home, you'll provide me with everything I want, but you *can't*, because the life *I* want is here." I waved my hand at the darkness above our heads. "I *like* living in the DFZ. I *like* Cleaning. Every day was a new surprise, a new treasure hunt, and I was good at it! Before your curse took me down, I was a rock star. You can't give me that again if I go home."

"I can give you something better," Yong said stubbornly. "It is to your credit that you were able to make a life in this dog-pit of a city, but don't confuse successful survival with actual happiness. I can give you so much more."

"More of what?" I asked, looking him straight in his smoky eyes.

"Everything," he replied. "Clothes, jewelry, food, security, comfort. Everything humans desire."

It was a sign I'd spent way too much time around dragons that I almost laughed at that. "Not all humans want the same stuff, Dad."

"Perhaps, but I've yet to see anyone turn down a life of leisure and luxury," he said peevishly. "Why won't you just let me take care of you?"

"Because I don't like your brand of care," I replied, straining *really* hard now to stay calm. To make him hear me. "I'm not so spoiled that I can complain about your generosity. You were always an excellent provider. You and Mom gave me everything I asked for, and I'm grateful for that, but there's more to life than things. You want me to act like all your other humans, to do and say and be exactly what you want all the time, but I'm not like them. They left their old lives voluntarily to come and serve you. I didn't get that choice."

"I don't see how there's a choice to be made," Yong said. "There is no better life than what I provide."

"I'm sure you don't think so. But has it ever occurred to you that what you want for me and what I want for me are two different things?"

"That is because you are young," he said dismissively. "When you're older, you'll understand I was right."

It took a heroic effort not to roll my eyes. "*Dad,* I'm twenty-six. I have two college degrees. I've survived four years in the DFZ on my own. I'm not some fourteen-year-old runaway going through a phase."

"Then why do you act like one?" he snapped. "If you're so grown-up and self-sufficient, why are you still so reckless?"

"Probably because *someone* keeps putting me in horrible situations!" I yelled, then I stopped and forced myself to take a breath. No, Opal. Anger bad. I was a calm and rational adult, dammit. I could do this.

"I know I don't always make perfect decisions," I continued a moment later in the most mature voice I could manage. "But who does? As you love to remind me, I'm human. Humans make mistakes."

"And it is my job as your father to stop you," Yong replied sternly. "Doubly so because I am a dragon. I am older and wiser and more experienced than you could ever be. What is all that knowledge for if I don't use it to help you?"

"Helping doesn't mean living my life for me," I argued. *Calmly.* "If I turn to you for all my decisions, that's not living. It's just following instructions, and what kind of life is that?"

"A long, happy, safe one," he replied without a trace of irony.

I took a steadying breath as I struggled to think of how I was going to deal with this one. "Would *you* want that?" I asked at last. "If there was a bigger, older, more experienced dragon ruling your life, would *you* like it?"

My father's jaw tightened. "I would listen to and value his advice."

"Now who's side-tracking the issue?" I taunted. "I didn't ask if you would listen. I asked if you would enjoy being in my shoes, and I don't think you would. You wanted to rule on your own so bad, you killed your father."

"My father was a tyrant and mad. He also has nothing to do with this. I see perfectly well what you are trying to do, but it won't work. You are not a dragon, Opal. You're a little girl, and you have no idea what you want. I know what is best for you, and if you'd stop being stubborn for one second, you'd see that."

I closed my eyes with a frustrated sigh. And here we were again. I'd thought I was making real headway this time, but no matter what I said, no matter what I did, we always ended up back in the exact same place.

"Do you think so little of me?"

My father jerked back. "Of course not," he said. "I treasure you. But you are—"

"Do you think I am weak?" I demanded, rising up on the balls of my feet to bring myself closer to his towering height. "I figured out how to defeat your curse. I saved you from White Snake. I faced *two* gods to bring you back to life, and I am currently the *only* thing keeping you that way. I was good enough to do all of that without your help, and you still claim I don't know what I want or how to get it? You think I need *you* to tell me what to do? Do you really think I'm that stupid and helpless?"

"That's not what I meant."

"But it is," I argued. Angrily, admittedly, but not in the usual way I was when we fought. I wasn't mad at my father. I was righteous for my own sake. I was *insulted.* I'd survived so much these last few months, more than even I thought I could, and I'd still come out on top. I'd climbed over every damn mountain he threw at me, and he had the *gall* to say I wasn't good enough to think for myself?

"You can't have it both ways," I told him. "Either I'm the mage who convinced a living city to save you from your enemies, or I'm a foolish little girl who can't be trusted to live on her own. One or the other, Dad, because I can't be both. You don't get to lean on my strength one second and scold me like a misbehaving dog the next. You say you want me to come home because I'm too reckless to live outside your watch, but I built a life of my own in this city that was *so* successful, you had to curse my luck to stop it! In fact, *all* of my problems since I left home have been of *your* creation, so I don't think the problem is me. I think it's you."

My own words left me shocked. I'd always blamed my dad for everything, but I hadn't put the whole picture into perspective until this moment. Now that I had it laid out in front of me, though, I felt like an idiot for not realizing the truth sooner.

"I'm not too foolish to live without you," I said, staring at the smoky ghost of my father with new eyes. "You're the one who can't live without *me*."

The look of anger on his face then was the one I used to fear above all others. He'd never struck or hurt me, but it was impossible to be around a dragon that mad without being terrified. Looking at him now, though, I couldn't be afraid. He was just smoke. Without my magic holding him together, he could have been taken out by a stiff breeze. It was pathetic, really, and from the way his furious expression began to collapse, my dad knew it.

All at once, he sat down hard on the street. Just dropped straight down to the pavement as if someone had cut his legs out from under him. All his draconic dignity and presence went with them, leaving him nothing but what he was: a sad, old shadow, crumpled in the dark.

"Dad?" I said nervously, worried I'd gone too far. "Did I—"

"What did you say that wasn't true?" Yong asked, looking down at his transparent hands as if he didn't know whom they belonged to. "But you can't understand what it's like. When you're as old as I am, time goes by so quickly. A moment ago, you were this adorable, bumbling, helpless creature who needed me for everything. Then I blinked, and suddenly you were a stranger who wanted nothing to do with me. I tried my best to bring you back. How could I not? You were my Opal. But the harder I reached for you, the more you slipped from my grasp, and I..."

He trailed off with a sigh, slumping even farther. "I never sought to control you for my own sake, but this world is dangerous. Every time I turned my back, you ran headfirst into trouble, and I didn't know how to make you *stop*." He looked at me pleadingly. "Do you know what it's like to watch your greatest treasure throw herself into danger over and over and *over* again while refusing to accept your help?"

"No," I said, sitting down beside him. "But do *you* know what it's like to build a life from scratch—a life you love, something you're proud of—only to lose it to your own father, the one who should be helping you the most, because he's afraid?"

Yong gave me a scathing look. "Don't try to make it sound so noble. You were a garbage picker."

"That's wrong and you know it," I said sharply. Then I sighed. "But it doesn't matter. There's no shame in being a garbage picker. There's no shame in doing anything you enjoy that doesn't hurt others and earns you a living. Being a Cleaner isn't so different from what we did today, and you saw me in there. I love this stuff! I loved my old life too. I was successful, I was happy, I was even safe. Until you started making a fuss, no dragons ever bothered me. My life here already had everything you just said you wanted to give me, and you were the one who ruined it. Do you see why I'm so mad?"

"No," Yong said, pressing his hands over his face, which didn't work nearly as well as he wanted since his hands were transparent. "How could you possibly be happy here? How could you prefer *this*"—he waved at the empty buildings—"to living in a palace in Korea? It makes no sense."

"It doesn't have to make sense to you," I said. "My happiness isn't something that requires your understanding or permission. But I still hope you'd be happy for me. Isn't that what parents are supposed to do?"

"You were wasting your mortality," he snapped.

"How so?" I asked, refusing to rise to his bait. Now that I'd realized I had the upper hand, it wasn't even a struggle to stay calm anymore. I was no longer afraid, no longer panicked. I could do this.

"How was a happy, stable life doing work I enjoyed 'wasting my mortality'? You knew exactly how successful I was as a Cleaner because that was why you cursed me in the first place. You keep trying to make this about saving me, but I was doing fine. *You* were the one who couldn't handle me being gone, which is ironic because if you'd just let me live my own life, you wouldn't have needed to control me. I would have happily taken your calls and come home at holidays like a *normal* adult child. You talk about me when I was young like I'm a completely different person, but I never stopped being your daughter. You were the one who pushed me away by refusing to accept anything in my life that wasn't *you*."

To my father's credit, he thought about that for a long, long time. "If I stopped…pushing you," he said at last, "would you come home?"

"I can't be a Cleaner in Korea," I told him honestly. "But if you stop trying to run my life *and* I feel like I can trust you not to trap me there, I'll promise to visit."

He lifted his nose like an offended cat. "I wouldn't *trap* you."

"You locked me in a shooting closet in Canada two months ago," I reminded him.

The offended look vanished. "I was in a highly stressed state. It was a poor choice."

I rolled my eyes. "I think the words you're looking for are 'I'm sorry.'"

"I will never be sorry for trying to help you," he said stubbornly. Then his face fell. "But I can admit that, in hindsight, I did not make the right decision. I was afraid for you. Afraid for both of us. My fire was nearly gone at that point, and I didn't know what to do. I thought I was going to lose you, and I allowed fear to cloud my judgment."

"Everyone screws up," I said with a shrug. "But it came from a good place. So long as you admit that you were wrong—and *never* do it again—I'm not mad about it anymore. I mean, I have every right to be, but I'm tired of being angry at you all the time. It's exhausting, and I've got enough on my plate as it is." I smiled at him. "How about we make a deal? If you promise to trust me not to swallow my own tongue and stop trying to control everything I do, I promise to try being less reckless. It should be easy if you're not putting me in corners all the time."

"I don't know about that," my father said skeptically, but I could see the wheels turning behind his smoky eyes. "Would you come back to Korea? Just for a little while?"

"If you buy my airfare, sure," I said. Then I bit my lip. "It'll have to wait until after I stop working for the DFZ, though. I don't think her priests can leave the city."

"That's not a problem," he said. "I can get you the money you need to buy your freedom as soon as I'm back in my body."

My eyes narrowed. "I don't know. Do I have to pay you back?"

"No," Yong said, his shoulders slumping. "I am done trying to control you with money. It's never worked, and only fools keep banging their heads against stone walls. Besides, you were willing to nearly kill both of us for a few hundred thousand. I don't want to know what you'd do to settle a god's debt."

Couldn't argue with that logic, but it was still...nice. I'd always intended to make him pay, but it was nice to hear my dad offer to do it of his own volition, no strings or wires or chains attached. I'd figured I'd have to withhold his physical body until he swore on his fire to pay my debts. Honestly, though, the money had always been my thing. Yong had never made me pay for anything before I'd broached the idea of paying him back for my schooling as part of my escape plan. This offer was much more like the generous father I remembered as a child. I was smiling about that when, suddenly and without warning, my father leaned in and wrapped his arms around my shoulders.

I jumped in surprise. I couldn't even feel it since he was made of smoke, but not counting all the incidents where he'd yanked me around or shaken me, this was the first time my father had touched me kindly in years. I couldn't actually remember the last time he'd given me a hug. Probably not since I was eight or nine. I didn't know if this counted, but I took it anyway, leaning into his smoke as best I could without actually going through him since that probably felt weird.

The resulting position was super awkward for both of us, but I didn't care. I was too relieved to not be black-out mad at my father for once to mind anything. I was sure I'd be pissed at him again soon enough, but there was no denying that something fundamental had changed between us. Hug notwithstanding, I couldn't remember the last time my father and I had had a conversation without screaming, and we'd had two today! I was no expert on family therapy, but that felt like a breakthrough. Again, I wasn't sure how long it would last, but I felt like I had my feet under me on this for the first time in, well, *ever*. I just hoped he remembered some of this humility when he stopped being smoke and got his power back. And speaking of…

"Come on," I said, standing up and holding out my hand. "I'm feeling like I've got one more pumpkin's worth of fire in me. Why don't we go see if we can't get you back into your body?"

"Yes, let's," my father said in a relieved voice, placing his hand in mine even though he was made of smoke and couldn't actually take it. "I'm already tired of being like this. What kind of father is dependent upon his own daughter?"

I shrugged. "Everyone needs help sometimes."

From the look on his face, it was clear that my dad had had enough words of affirmation for one night. But proving that he was, in fact, a wise old dragon, he kept his opinion to himself, following me as silently as the ghost he resembled back through the door and into my apartment.

Chapter 4

"**O**kay," I said, kneeling down beside my dad's body in the middle of my bedroom, which felt a lot bigger now that there wasn't a dragon made of fire taking up all of it. "Ready?"

"I was ready six hours ago," Yong replied, sitting down inside his own chest, which was both freaky and probably the exact right place for him to be. "Give me as much as you can. I can handle it."

I'd given him as much as I could last time, but I was flattered he'd thought I'd held back. Since he was good to go, I went ahead and closed my eyes, reaching out to grab the city magic that floated all around us.

It was harder to get things started without the Spirit of Dragons to give me a light. My dad had a bit of his own fire now, though, and after some fumbling, I got the flames to spark again. My soul still ached from the last time I'd done this, more than it had since Dr. Kowalski had taught me how to stop backlashing myself, which was pretty scary. But I was a much better mage these days, or at least a more disciplined one, and I held it together, feeding careful handfuls of magic into the flame I'd created until I had another pumpkin-sized ball of dragon fire floating in front of me.

Now that I wasn't in a panic or being watched by a dragon god, I realized I probably *could* go bigger. The burning magic definitely felt easier to handle than I remembered it being this morning. Tempting as it was to keep going, though, I stayed mindful of the strain on my soul and kept things reasonable, sending my pumpkin-sized ball of dragon fire up our connection just like I had before.

The flames went out instantly, leaving me blinking spots out of my eyes. For a horrible second, I thought I'd screwed up, then I realized the flames hadn't vanished. My father had sucked them in, devouring the fake dragon fire like the greedy monster he was. His smoke form had vanished at the same time, leaving me alone in the bedroom with Yong's still body.

Sweat dripped down my forehead as the seconds ticked by. Maybe I *had* screwed up. The Spirit of Dragons had warned me that I could snuff him out if I pushed too hard. I'd thought I'd done it just like before, but it was difficult to read the size of flames accurately, *and* there'd been that weird pressure to keep going. Maybe I'd gone harder than I'd realized. Maybe I'd killed him! Oh God, it would be just my luck if I killed my dad right after we finally made headway on our relationship. This was a crisis! I had to—

My father's body jerked on the ground, knocking me out of my panicked thoughts.

"Dad!" I cried, grabbing his shoulders. "Are you okay? Can you hear me?"

He answered with a coughing fit, curling into a ball on his side. This was a fabulous change after two months of nothing, but it sounded like he was hacking up a lung. I wasn't sure if the problem was magical or physical, but I figured water couldn't hurt. Thankfully, there were still plenty of red plastic cups lying around from the summoning ritual for the Spirit of Dragons. I grabbed the least melted one and ran to the bathroom, taking care to rinse the remaining alcohol dregs out thoroughly before filling it with clean water and rushing it back to my dad.

He drank the cup dry in one gulp then downed two more in rapid succession. By the fourth, he'd managed to stop coughing long enough to sit up, wiping his eyes wearily as he looked at me.

"Well?" I asked nervously, touching his shoulder with shaking fingers. "Are you, you know…normal?"

He didn't look normal. For all that he was awake and moving, his face was still the color of ash, and he was so thin that you could see his skeleton clearly under his skin.

"It's better than being smoke," Yong answered in a weak voice. "But I still feel like I'm dying."

"Crap," I muttered, reaching out to poke his magic. I could feel his fire now, which was good, but it was so faint. "Maybe I need to put more in?"

He absolutely needed more power. Unfortunately, I didn't think I could give it to him. Even though I'd been careful to keep things manageable, that last batch of fire had left my already sore soul feeling like a wet dishrag. I didn't think I could have moved a pea's worth of magic, never mind a pumpkin. I was scrambling to think of a way we could get him another dose of fire without burning myself out when his stomach made a gurgling sound, and I realized I was being an idiot.

"Dad," I said, biting back laughter. "I think you're just hungry."

His stomach growled again in answer, and I started to laugh.

"It's not funny," Yong said angrily. "I haven't eaten in two months. Do you even have food here?"

I had no idea. Dr. Kowalski always fed me when I was at her place, and I didn't dare go out in public, which meant no trips to the grocery store. Add in the fact that I'd been basically living with Nik for the three weeks before the DFZ had grabbed me and I couldn't actually remember the last time I'd bought food to prepare myself at home. Sure enough, when I went to the kitchen to check my fridge, the only things inside were a jar of pickles with nothing but the brine left and an expired bottle of ketchup.

I had a bit more luck in the cupboards. All the fancy health food my mother had stocked for me was long gone, either resold or eaten, but I did find a dusty bag of generic cereal that had fallen into the gap between the fridge and the wall. The printing on the bag was so faded that I couldn't figure out what well-known brand it was supposed to be knocking off, but the nice part about super-processed carbs was that they never really expire. When I presented my prize to my father, though, he looked less than impressed.

"Opal," he said in a scornful voice. "That is not food."

"Sure it's food," I said, ripping the bag open to release a cloud of sweet-smelling cereal dust. "And before you say it's past its date, I already checked and there *is* no expiration date! That means it's perfectly safe."

My father's scowl deepened, and I glared back stubbornly. "Do you want to starve or not?"

With a sigh that shook the floor, the Great Yong took the bag and tilted it up to pour the dusty cereal down his throat. Seeing where this was going, I went ahead and got him another glass of water. He downed that one just as fast as the first four, using the gulps of liquid to keep his throat lubricated as he choked down the sugar-covered cardboard.

"I've lived through countless famines," he told me when he finished. "And that was, without question, the worst substance I have ever eaten."

"You're welcome," I replied, but I knew we weren't out of the woods yet. Though technically food, the cereal I'd fed him was completely devoid of actual nutrition. He needed something real to eat, and he needed a *lot* of it. If it hadn't been so late, I would have taken him to Dr. Kowalski's. She had enough squash and potatoes lying around her place to feed an army. But while my mentor didn't actually need sleep as a manifestation of the DFZ's magic, she still behaved like the old lady she resembled, which meant she didn't like being bothered after nine.

I also didn't think vegetables were going to cut it. Dragons could eat just about anything, but they were primarily hunters. If my father's body was going to heal, he needed meat, or at least a meat-like substance. A whole live cow would have been ideal, but while I was sure you could buy one of those in the DFZ, I didn't know where, and there was still the issue of secrecy. I'd gotten my father back into his body, but he was obviously still very weak. I hadn't worried about taking him to work since the DFZ would never allow a dragon—or any outsider—into one of her personal stashes, but the streets were another matter. Thanks to the Peacemaker, this city was always crawling with dragons. If we went outside, there was a good chance we'd be spotted, which was why I hadn't gone anywhere that wasn't directly within the DFZ's control in two months. But I couldn't feed him here.

"Nothing for it," I said, scrubbing a hand through my hair with a resigned sigh. "We'll have to go out. Can you stand?"

"I'm perfectly capable of moving," my father informed me.

"Then why haven't you?" I asked, because aside from sitting up, he hadn't budged from the mattress on the floor.

Yong arched an elegant eyebrow at the question and waved a hand down at his chest. His pale, bony, *naked* chest rising from the blanket that covered the also-naked rest of him.

"Oh," I said, looking away with a wince. "Right. You need clothes."

"Clothing is not strictly necessary," he said in a dignified voice. "But it would be useful if you don't wish to draw attention."

I'd seen a lot worse than public nudity on the DFZ streets, but my dad was a dragon. Even at death's door, his human shape was tall, imposing, and beautiful in a way actual mortals simply couldn't achieve. He was going to attract a *lot* of attention no matter what he wore, which meant we didn't just need clothes. We needed a disguise.

"You're too big for my stuff," I muttered, scowling in thought. "Don't move. I've got an idea."

He hadn't moved since he'd sat up, and he continued to stay put as I scuttled back to my front door. Grabbing the handle, I pictured the place I wanted to go. I was so nervous that it took me several tries to get it right. This was my first time trying to travel to somewhere that wasn't inside one of the DFZ's private spaces. Everything in the city belonged to her, though, and I got it in the end, opening my door into the hallway of my old apartment complex.

In hindsight, it wasn't the best choice for a reemergence after months of lying low. If anyone was watching for me, my old home was the obvious stakeout. I was still getting the hang of my powers, though, and my old door was the one I knew best. It was also right next to what I needed.

Closing the door behind me to disconnect the magic so that no one could sneak in and whack my dad while my back was turned, I hurried as quietly as I could down the hall to the breezeway at the top of the stairs where the vending machines were. Since I'd transferred all my money to Nik when I'd thought I was doomed two months ago, I didn't have any cash of my own, but the DFZ—ever practical city that she was—had given me an old-style cash card to use for expenses. I didn't know how much was on it, but I didn't have anything else, so I pulled the card out of my wallet and tapped it against the vending machine's chip reader.

When the scuffed digital display showed my account was approved, I made my selection, glancing over my shoulder every few seconds as I typed in the codes listed below the pictures on the machine's glowing front. The moment my goods landed in the dispenser tray, I grabbed them and bolted, sprinting back to my old door, which was no longer *my* door at all.

The DFZ must have moved another apartment in to fill the void, because the door that had been mine was festooned with Halloween decorations. I'd totally forgotten the holiday was approaching, but whoever lived here now was clearly very serious about it. I could barely find the doorknob under all the plastic ghosts and cheap AR projector displays of 3D laughing pumpkins and hissing black cats.

Technically, I supposed I could have used any door. The whole point of the priest-of-the-DFZ power-set was to let me move through the city as she did, stepping from anywhere to anywhere in an instant. According to Dr. Kowalski, once I got good enough, even the door wouldn't be necessary. But that was a long way away, and in my head, this was still *my* apartment. Even with the over-the-top decorations, the door still felt right and familiar, two critical factors when you were using new powers that could kill you. I clung to that familiarity, digging past all the plastic dancing candy corns and lime-green streamers until my fingers found the doorknob, which wasn't even locked.

That threw me hard for a moment. Seriously, who leaves their door unlocked in the DFZ? But I got it together and pushed through, opening the way not into the no-doubt Halloween-ified home of the overly trusting tenant who'd replaced me, but my own living room where my dad was waiting for me with a blanket wrapped around his shoulders like an ancient king.

"Did you find something suitable?"

I tossed him the vacuum-sealed packets I'd bought. "It's not Savile Row, but it should do the job."

My father scowled and ripped into the flimsy plastic bags, pulling out a black long-sleeved T-shirt with a wobbly hem, dark-washed distressed pants that were *supposed* to be jeans but contained no actual denim, and a pair of black plastic flip-flops.

"What is this?" he asked, holding up the shirt, which was so thin I could see his face through it.

"The best I could get," I said with a shrug. "I didn't exactly have the time or cash to run to a department store."

"How can they legally call these clothes? These pants already have *holes* in them!"

"They're fashionable holes."

The look on his face told me exactly what he thought of that, and I rolled my eyes. "Just put them on, Dad."

He did so with great reluctance, pulling the shirt over his head gently so as not to rip the tissue-thin fabric. Turning my back to give him some privacy, I dug my phone out of the pocket of my own sturdy work jeans to find us some food.

"Are we getting back on the internet?" Sibyl asked excitedly when I reinserted my earbud.

"No."

"Oh come *on!*"

"We can't take the risk."

"But—"

"I know it's rough," I said sternly. "But until my dad is strong enough not to keel over the moment another dragon looks his way, we stay in 'run silent, run deep' mode. End of discussion."

"*Fine*," my AI groaned. "But how am I supposed to search for a restaurant if you won't let me go online?"

She clearly thought she had me with that one, but I just grinned. "We'll use what's already in your memory cache. That thing's always taking up like 99.9% of your available space. Let's put it to work for once."

"But I already dumped most of my cache for precisely that reason! I needed the space for backups since you won't let me connect to the cloud, and all that info was out-of-date anyway. Everything is! It's been so long since I checked in with a location server, my maps would be woefully inadequate even for a city that *doesn't* move every day. In the DFZ, they're totally useless!"

"I don't need actual directions," I reminded her. "Only the pictures. Just bring up whatever you've got left from my 'Want to Eat' list, and I'll take care of the rest."

With much wailing and gnashing of digital teeth, Sibyl dug down deep to find the long list of restaurants I'd marked to check out when I got the chance. As my AI had warned me, most of the listings were just broken links, but a few had survived in the cache with their pictures intact, and after a bit of scrolling, I found exactly what I needed.

"Perfect," I said, zooming in on the street-view picture to get the details. When I felt like I had a good mental image of where I was going, I called over my shoulder to my dad, "Are you decent?"

"That's open to debate," came my father's grumpy reply. "I'm no longer naked, but do the people here really go out in public like this?"

I actually thought he looked quite fashionable. When I turned around, my dad was dressed in the outfit I'd bought him, except unlike everyone else who had to make do with emergency clothes from a vending machine, he made them look *good*.

His current gauntness actually went perfectly with the all-black ensemble. His bony shoulders made the thin fabric of his T-shirt look delicate rather than cheap, and his jeans were as skinny as they got. Combine that with his waist-length, perfectly straight black hair, and he looked like a K-pop star going through a goth phase. He also looked *much* younger, which was weird. My dad normally dressed like a bank manager in custom-tailored suits that ran the color gamut from dark gray to navy. I was the one who'd picked his outfit, but actually seeing him in streetwear was so bizarre, I did a legit double take.

"Wow," I said, looking him up and down. "I don't believe it. You're almost hip!"

"People *have* hips," Yong informed me. "If you're going to speak English, do so properly."

"Annnnnd it's gone," I said, shaking my head as I started toward the front door. "Come on. Let's get you fed before you blow away."

He followed me slowly, which was disconcerting. He might look like a young twenty-something, but he moved like an old, arthritic man.

"Are you going to make it?"

"I'll be fine," my dad said stubbornly, joining me at the door at last.

"You don't have to go far."

"I *said* I'll be *fine*," my father growled, his eyes—which were still terrifyingly dull, nothing like their usual bright mix of blue, green, and gold—narrowing with insulted pride. "Just take us to wherever we're going."

I turned back to the door with a sigh, checking the saved photo on my phone one last time. When I felt absolutely certain I knew where I was going, I grabbed the knob and twisted, stepping through my apartment door…

And into the middle of a busy sidewalk.

The transition was so abrupt, I stumbled. I'd only had a picture of the restaurant's front, so I wasn't entirely sure where the door would open, but this didn't look right at all. This place was supposed to be in a working-class area near the river. Even if it had moved—always a safe assumption in this city—the DFZ was usually careful not to relocate businesses too far from their customers. I'd assumed we'd come out in the same neighborhood at least, but the sidewalk my door had opened onto was packed with obvious tourists despite the late hour. It wasn't until I looked up to find a coral reef of flashing pink neon shining beneath the noisy darkness of a huge elevated highway that I realized the truth.

"Aw, crap."

"Where are we?" my father demanded, scowling at the flashing lights.

My cheeks began to heat. "Loveland," I answered with a sigh. "We're in Loveland."

My father arched a disapproving eyebrow, but there was nothing I could say. The tourist strip that ran along the DFZ's western border with Michigan was every bit as seedy as it looked. Nestled in the shadow of the world's largest elevated highway that connected Troy and the other Michigan suburbs to the capitalistic lawlessness of the DFZ, Loveland was a perfect overlap of the worst both sides had to offer. The shadiest businesses in the Underground *loved* to set up on the borders, preying on the businessmen, thrill-seeking teens, and other clueless normies who flocked in from all over the Midwest to get a taste of the Detroit Free Zone's infamous debauchery.

Not that I had a problem with that. I didn't care how people got their kicks. *I* was pissed because this whole place was designed to rip off tourists who didn't know better. Everything we found here was bound to be ten times more expensive than what you'd see anywhere else in the city at least. I might not use brothels, VR snuff parlors, or narcotic vending machines personally, but the ridiculous prices infuriated me on principle. The only good thing I could say about Loveland was that at least all the blinking neon and undulating, impossibly proportioned dancers shimmying through the street's shared AR kept the gawking tourists too distracted to notice my dad and I popping out of an unsupported door in the middle of the sidewalk.

"Huh," Sibyl said as the door sank back into the gum-covered pavement behind us. "Guess the restaurant got moved since that picture was taken."

"You think?" I muttered, rubbing my spinning head.

My priestess powers were supposed to let me travel anywhere in the city. Before this, though, I'd only ever moved between places I knew. I'd thought a photo would be good enough, but I didn't see the restaurant from the picture I'd memorized anywhere in the flashing lights. Had I screwed up and taken us to the wrong place entirely?

I was wondering if I should just go back to my apartment and start over when Sibyl placed a discreet arrow on the edge of my vision, the only part of my Augmented Reality field that I could see when I was using just my phone rather than my full goggles. When I turned to follow her indicator, my breath left me in a relieved rush. We'd come out facing the main drag of Loveland—what had once been known as 8 Mile Road—but just to the left was an alley that led back into the much quieter, much *cheaper*, side streets. The sort of tourists who flocked to Loveland didn't like going off the brightly lit main trench, so the alley wasn't even crowded, and at the very back of it, glowing like a treasure, was our destination.

"Good find," I said, breaking into a grin. "Guess I'm not so bad at this priestess stuff after all!"

"What are you talking about?" my father demanded, moving his body away from the crowds of humans jostling past us. "This place is horrible. I thought we were supposed to be staying out of sight?"

"Relax," I told him. "I hate it as much as you do, but Loveland is actually a great place for us. There's not a dragon in the world who'd be caught dead in a seedy tourist trap like this, and look!" I pointed down the alley. "There's our restaurant."

My father turned his head to follow my hand, and what little color he had left drained from his face. At the end of the alley we'd emerged beside, nestled between a nail salon and a convenience store advertising coupon books for popular Loveland attractions, was a bustling restaurant with a huge, brightly painted, sombrero-and-chopsticks-festooned neon sign that read *Los Hermanos Li's Famous Dim Sum Nachos. All You Can Eat!*

"You must be joking," my father said.

"What's there to joke about?" I asked, starting down the alley. "Fusion food is a DFZ classic, and the internet says it's good."

"I don't care what the internet says," Yong snapped, hobbling after me. "'Dim Sum Nachos' aren't food. They're an insult to two cultures."

"It's cheap and it's all you can eat," I countered. "Two critical components seeing how you're a starving dragon and I'm still broke."

He looked appalled. "Does the DFZ not pay you?"

"Being a priest is a calling, not a profession," I said humbly. "Also, I'm doing this to work off a debt, so a salary would be kind of counter-productive. The city does give me free room and board, though, so it's not as if I'm starving."

"I noticed." He looked down at me critically. "You've put on weight. Your mother won't be pleased."

"My mother can mind her own business," I said, shoving the restaurant's jingly door with both hands. "But I've been living on a whole-food vegan diet for two months. I don't care what they're fused with, I'm going to eat some damn nachos!"

The inside of the restaurant was every bit as tacky as I'd hoped when I'd first marked it to try months ago. It was also *packed*. The crowd looked like it was mostly locals, though. There were no backpacks or shopping bags from overpriced stores—the sure signs of a tourist—just shopkeepers and sex workers on break.

After two months in hiding, being around so many people made me nervous. As I'd just said to my dad, though, there was basically zero chance of meeting a dragon in a place like this. I was more worried about running into someone Nik and I had pissed off.

Loveland was directly below the hidden shopping-district-for-criminals he'd taken me to when we'd been looking for someone to hack Dr. Lyle's hand. Other than his cyber-surgeon Rena, I didn't think there was anyone up there who knew me by name, but we'd made quite the exit. So far as I knew, Nik hadn't gone back since. If he'd been here with us, I was sure he'd have been even more paranoid than usual. That said, if Nik had been with us, we wouldn't have come at all. He distrusted restaurants in general, but this place had *all* of his red flags: crowded tables, suspiciously low prices, and no obvious rear exit.

I didn't think I could have gotten Nik through the door of a place like this. Of course, a few hours ago, I would have said the same thing about my dad. He must have been a lot hungrier than he was letting on, though, because he didn't even growl when I flagged down the waitress.

Los Hermanos Li was a lot bigger on the inside than it had looked from the street. The main dining room was huge and packed, but in a long overdue stroke of luck, the staff spoke Cantonese. Not that we couldn't have managed in English, but you always got better service when you spoke the language. A few minutes later, I'd secured us a table right next to the kitchen door, the ultimate power position for dim sum. Every delicacy-laden cart that came out had to roll past us to get to the rest of the room, which meant we always got first pick of the freshest dishes, and just as the internet had promised, the pickings looked damn good.

Soon, our table was covered in plates of char siu served on a bed of fried wonton "chips," fried noodles tossed in queso fundido, a bowl of white cheese dip with giant pickled-jalapeno bao on the side for dipping, and various other ridiculousness. They even had a bottomless margarita made with Chinese white liquor, which I *totally* ordered. I wasn't sure that was a good idea after my first taste, but hey, booze was booze, and if I'd ever needed a drink, it was tonight.

"Are you sure this is safe?" my father asked, poking at the pile of bright-green tomatillo-and-porkbelly potstickers I'd grabbed for us. "It smells of food coloring."

I shrugged and reached over with my chopsticks to steal one of the dumplings off his plate, dunking it gratuitously in salsa before sticking it in my mouth. "Tastes fine to me," I reported. "But they have sushi on the other cart if you'd prefer."

"That's even worse," Yong said with a shudder. "As they say back home, 'if you can't see the ocean, don't eat the fish.'"

I didn't know if that old adage held true in the age of refrigeration, but sushi from a cheap Mexican-Chinese fusion restaurant on the edge of an Underground tourist trap probably wasn't the greatest idea. Honestly, though, I didn't care what he ate. I was too busy stuffing my own face. After two months of healthy living, I'd forgotten how *good* cheap processed carbs could taste. There was something about all those unpronounceable chemicals that was just so delicious. And probably toxic. I was pretty sure a margarita made with actual lime juice wouldn't be that shade of neon green, but hey! Sometimes poisoning yourself was fun, and holy crap was I ready for some fun, even if the only person I had to party with was my grumpy old codger of a dad.

Speaking of my dad, he must have *really* been starving. After barely two minutes of turning up his nose, he broke down and started to eat. Once he got going, he was a machine, tearing through plates of food as fast as the carts could bring them. By the time he finally stopped, I'd already lapsed into and come out of my carb coma. I wasn't even drunk I'd eaten so much, but I had zero regrets.

"See?" I told my dad as the busboys attempted to clear the wreckage. "Not so bad."

"It was terrible, and you know it," he said, glaring at me. "We raised you to have better taste than this."

"Expensive tastes are a liability," I replied sagely. "The wise Undergrounder cultivates an appreciation for all edible substances. I've eaten things out of food trucks you wouldn't believe."

"I don't want to hear what you've eaten out of trucks," my father said, his face horrified. "You *do* remember you're mortal, right? Vulnerable to dying from poison?"

I laughed then stopped, eyes going wide. "Wait, was that a *joke?*"

"It was a legitimate concern," he said without a trace of humor.

I should have known better, but grousing over what your child ate was perfectly normal parental behavior, so I couldn't be too miffed. Given how it had started, tonight had turned out surprisingly decent. I'd finally gotten to try a restaurant that had been on my list for over a year, and while he'd made it clear he considered eating here slumming of the lowest degree, it had still been pretty damn entertaining to watch my dad eat ten normal people's worth of food. Most amazing of all, though, nothing bad had happened. We'd been here for almost an hour, and dragons hadn't burst in to grab us. There'd been no disasters, no crises or magical apocalypses. We hadn't even argued! We'd just had dinner like two normal people.

That was a miracle in and of itself and probably a sign that we should go. While I'd clearly been right about the lack of dragons in Loveland, it was never a good idea to push your luck, especially luck as bad as mine. We'd paid the All You Can Eat fee before we sat down, so technically we were free to go at any time, but I still wanted to tip the staff to make up for the mountain of dishes my dad had generated. I was standing in line at the register kiosk by the front door to do just that since I couldn't use my phone's wallet feature without letting Sibyl back onto the internet. But just as I finished tapping the DFZ's cash card against the screen to okay the extra payment, I heard the bells on the door jingle behind me.

I can't say why I looked. The front door had been jingling every five seconds since we'd arrived. But there was something about this jingle that made me glance over my shoulder, which was how I came face-to-chest with a very armored, very upset Nik.

"Found you," he said, grabbing me by the shoulders.

"Nik!" I cried, jerking in surprise. "What are you doing here? I—"

That was as far as I got before he picked me up—literally lifted me off the floor—and kissed me.

Chapter 5

If we'd been in a movie, this was where the music would have swelled, and the colors would have turned all warm and soft as I melted against him. But my life had never been a movie—at least not that kind of movie—and the first thing I actually did was panic.

I couldn't help it! I'd spent the last eight weeks living with a comatose dragon and a deceased doctor of Shamanism whose physical body was merely a manifestation of a city spirit's will. Actual human contact wasn't something I was used to. I went stiff as a frozen fish, causing Nik to lean back in alarm, which wasn't my intention at all. I was just surprised. Once I got over myself though, the kiss was *really* nice.

I'd thought about Nik a lot over the last two months. Mostly I'd worried he'd be mad at me, or worse, forgotten me entirely and moved on with his life. That was what my other friends had done when I'd vanished to become a Cleaner, but Nik hadn't forgotten. I'd been out in public for less than an hour in a part of town I normally never went to, and he'd still managed to find me. Found me and *kissed* me like I was someone special. Someone he couldn't wait to touch. Which was good, because I couldn't wait to touch him either.

After that, I got into the swing of things pretty quick. I threw my arms around Nik's neck and pulled myself into him, freeing his arms to snake around my waist. He breathed a breath of relief against my lips, and then he was burying his head in the crook of my neck, kissing everything he could reach. I did the same, sliding my fingers up to feel the familiar cool softness of his short-cropped dark hair then down to feel the strength of his steel-reinforced shoulders. Every time I breathed, my lungs filled with the scent of him, that Nik smell of warm leather and his favorite lemony cleaning solution I hadn't realized I could recognize anywhere until just now. It was all like that: his hands, his body, the scrape of his stubble against my ear. It felt crazy that I could miss an intimacy I'd only known once so intensely, but I did. *God*, I'd missed him, but this was a really good start. Maybe he wasn't pissed at me after all!

As if he could hear my thoughts, Nik broke our embrace, setting me back on the floor with a look of such fury, it made me tremble. *Definitely* pissed.

"We need to talk."

I winced hard. Nothing good ever followed "we need to talk," but I couldn't say I didn't deserve it given how I'd left him. Fortunately for me, I had a really good explanation. I just needed time to get it out.

"I'd love to talk," I said, turning to my dad, who was stalking over from our table as fast as his body—freshly gorged, but still weak—could go. "Give us a moment," I told him in Korean.

Naturally, my father did nothing of the sort. He marched right over, glaring murder at Nik, who returned the look plus some.

"What is *he* doing here?" Nik snapped.

I winced again. Hoo boy, here we went. "It's a long story."

"'Long story?'" Nik's glare shot back to me. "Opal, he's your *abuser*. He's the one we were fighting to get you away from! Why are you eating dinner with him?"

"I can explain," I said, careful to keep my voice calm. Even without taking my eyes off of Nik, I could feel the busy restaurant going still around us. I'd stare, too, given the scene we were creating, but this was bad for more than just my ego. We were *supposed* to be keeping a low profile. Dragons might not frequent Loveland, but that didn't mean they didn't have spies here. Going out to eat was one thing, but we'd be in serious trouble very shortly if Nik kept shouting my name. He was normally super sensitive about that sort of thing, but he must have been angrier than I'd realized, because he didn't look like he was backing down anytime soon. I was about to suggest we move to the street so we could at least do this without a seated audience when my father stepped into the gap Nik had just opened between us, using his superior height to sneer down his nose into Nik's face.

"She doesn't need to explain anything to you," Yong said in a voice so dismissive and disdainful even I was surprised. "My daughter is not a criminal's concern, so go. You're causing a disturbance."

"*Dad!*" I hissed, trying to shove him out of the way. Even in his current condition, though, my father was a dragon. No matter how hard I pushed, I couldn't budge him, which was rapidly becoming a serious problem since Nik was leaning in to match him.

"You do *not* want to start this with me," he warned, glaring at my father without a trace of fear. To be fair, my dad wasn't projecting his usual level of alpha-predator menace. Even if he had been, I didn't think Nik would have noticed. I'd never seen him look this scary, and his new outfit definitely wasn't helping.

His usual dark jeans, plain T-shirt, and armored black-leather jacket were gone, replaced by a head-to-toe suit of matte-black combat armor, the serious sort you normally saw on riot police. He was loaded for bear, too, with two pistols strapped under his arms and what appeared to be a giant single-barrel, pump-action shotgun slung across his back. Add in the black combat boots with knives tucked into both tops and dude looked like he was ready to enforce a fascist agenda. It wasn't a load-out that spelled anything good, and judging from the barely healed bruises I'd just noticed peeking up over the edge of his high collar, Nik had been as much a victim of it as anyone.

"What happened to you?" I cried, reaching past my dad to touch Nik's wounded neck. At least, that was my plan. Nik caught my fingers before I'd made it an inch, squeezing my hand in his gloved, metal one.

"You first," he said, his angry gray eyes boring into mine. "You slept with me and vanished!"

"You slept with this man?" my father demanded.

"That's none of your business," I told him angrily, then I whipped back toward Nik. "Not in front of my dad!"

"Screw your dad!" Nik yelled, making me jerk back in surprise. Nik *never* yelled.

"Do you know what I've been through?" he went on, his voice as thin and jagged as barbed wire. "You trapped me with magic and *ran away*! I tried to find you, but by the time I got free, you'd vanished. I was still searching when the whole city went nuts, and I looked up into the sky just in time to watch you get eaten by a *building* while riding a *dragon*."

Before this moment, I hadn't actually thought about how our escape must have looked from the street. Hearing Nik describe it, it sounded pretty terrifying. "I was—"

"I was afraid you were *dead*!" Nik roared at me, the fear in his voice finally breaking through the rage. "Where the hell have you been? Why didn't you call me?"

"I couldn't!" I yelled back, losing my patience. "I wanted to. I wanted to do a lot of things! But I couldn't."

"Why not?"

I snapped my mouth shut. That was a question I *definitely* couldn't answer in a crowded restaurant. Before I could think of the right thing to say that would calm him down enough to get us somewhere I *could* tell him, though, my dad opened his mouth and made things worse.

"You are demanding knowledge to which you have no right," Yong said haughtily. "You should be grateful my daughter speaks to gutter trash like you at all."

Listening to those words was like watching a car crash in slow motion. I legit could not believe he'd just said that. Nik's reply, though, was totally predictable.

"You want to talk about rights?" he said, eyes narrowing in a glare that made my blood go cold. "You have no right to be anywhere near Opal, you abusive piece of shit."

My father stepped back in shock. "I have *never* abused—"

"You hurt her all the time! Do you know how hard she fought to get away from your controlling bullshit? She nearly killed herself trying to get out of the curse *you* put on her! Everything she's been through is because of *you*."

"I gave up everything for her!" my father roared, making me jump. He didn't normally lose his temper like that for anyone but me. But apparently Nik could push his buttons, too, because despite barely having enough fire to stay upright, smoke was curling from Yong's mouth as he bared his teeth at Nik.

"I don't care what you think you gave," Nik spat, ignoring the warning. "I know what I *saw*, which was a dragon throwing a hissy fit because a grown woman didn't want to be his pretend daughter anymore."

Yong's smoke thickened. "She's not my 'pretend' anything! She is mine, *period.* I am her father, and I treasure her more than an animal like you could comprehend!"

"Okay, that's enough," I said, pushing between them. "Show's over. Let's take it down a—"

"The only reason you're not dead right now is because Opal was too kind to leave you to the end you deserved," Nik said over me. "I don't know why. Her life would be infinitely better if you weren't in it."

"You know nothing about our lives!" Yong yelled. "I am her family! You're nothing but a scavenger who preyed on her while she was weak. You don't deserve for her to know your name, you worthless—"

He never got to finish. One moment my dad's body was taut as a coil, the next it went slack, his eyes rolling back in his head. He crumpled to the floor a second later, leaving the smoke version of my father standing over his unconscious body like a wayward ghost.

"Crap."

"What the—" Nik jumped back, his gray eyes flying wide in panic. "What the *hell* just happened?"

I was wondering the same thing. It looked as if my dad had dislocated himself again, probably because he'd gotten way more worked up than his weakened body could handle. Even his smoke ghost was having trouble keeping itself together, his edges swirling like clouds in a high wind.

"Craaaaaap," I said again, prodding the ambient magic floating through the restaurant. It was the same city magic that was in my apartment, but the saturation out here in the real world wasn't nearly as thick as I was used to. Even if I could have scraped enough power together, there was no way I'd have been able to manage the complicated conversion to dragon fire under these circumstances. I was too tired and too distracted. Particularly by Nik, who'd grabbed hold of my arm.

"Opal, what is going on?"

"Oh, are you ready to listen to me now?" I asked. Probably more sharply than I should have, but I was so pissed at him. Pissed at both of them for making such a mess out of what should have been a simple conversation. If their fight hadn't already been the talk of Loveland, it *definitely* was now. The story would be all over the Underground in half an hour, and then the predators would come running. I had to get us out of here before that happened, but my dad's limp body was too heavy for me to move on my own, and Nik *still* hadn't let go of my arm.

"If you want to help, give me a hand," I told him, nodding at my father's legs. "We need to get him out of here."

To his credit, Nik didn't argue this time. He just grabbed my dad's body and heaved it over his shoulder like a sack of flour.

"Nice. Thank you."

"*Not* nice," my father snarled, his furious voice barely louder than a whisper in my ear. "I don't want that filthy gutter human touching me!"

"You're in no position to complain," I whispered back as I led Nik out the door, wincing when the restaurant exploded into excited chatter behind us.

"This is just great," I grumbled, striding up the alley. "You couldn't keep your mouth shut, could you? You just *had* to go and pour gasoline on the fire."

"This isn't my fault," Nik said.

"I wasn't talking to you. I was talking to *him.*" I pointed at my unconscious father since Nik clearly couldn't see the smoke one standing beside me. "But while I'm at it, you're not off the hook. Why the hell did you do that in a restaurant? Did it not occur to you that there could be a *reason* I hadn't called, and maybe I'd rather not discuss it in front of an audience of strangers?"

"What do they matter?" Nik grumbled, though his face was turning red. "This is between you and me."

"Exactly. You and me. Not you, me, my dad, and two hundred other people who are probably posting this on social media as we speak!"

Holy crap, I hoped no one filmed that. My dad was toast if they had.

"No worries," Sibyl said proudly in my ear. "I got you."

My whole body sagged in relief. "Thank you," I replied breathlessly. Then I frowned. "Wait, how?"

My AI's voice grew sheepish. "I, um, might have been a little desperate for internet, so I kind of accidentally on purpose took over the restaurant's WiFi."

"You can do that?" I asked, shocked. I'd never installed any hacking suites on her.

"I wasn't hacking!" Sibyl protested. "Their security certificate was years out-of-date. I almost couldn't *not* take it over! But before you yell at me, I kept my location data deactivated the whole time *and* I turned off camera permissions for the building the moment you and Nik started engaging in your public display of affection. I couldn't stop people from posting text, but no one should have been able to record video or take pictures so long as they were signed into the free network, which *everyone* there was. Gotta love cheap places!"

"Oh, Sibyl," I gushed. "I *love* you! Great job!"

If my AI had had a face, it would have been grinning. "So this means you're not mad about the internet thing?"

I was, but it didn't matter. Thanks to Nik and my dad's gratuitous display, our cover was mega-blown. What was a little internet connectivity after those fireworks? Especially since it made my AI so happy. She was already getting back to work, humming to herself as she processed all the updates I'd forced her to postpone. Shaking my head in defeat, I left her to her bliss and turned my attention back to my own mess.

We'd just reached the front of the alley where my dad and I had originally come in. Now that Yong was no longer goading him, Nik seemed to be calming down, but his face was still a dark scowl when I motioned him to stop at the corner.

"Where are we going?" he asked, eyeing the wall of tourists, which had only grown thicker while we'd been at dinner.

"I'll explain everything in a moment," I promised, scanning the shops for a usable door. "But we're not safe here. I just need—*ah-ha!*"

I grabbed his hand and bolted across the crowded sidewalk, nearly getting us run over by an auto-cab as we crossed the busy street to the other side. It was much darker and quieter over here. 8 Mile Road was the DFZ's official border, but the fence didn't actually begin until the other side of the sidewalk. At least, there was *supposed* to be a fence. The United States government put up a new one every spring, but the DFZ kept tearing them down because border fences went against everything she stood for. This late in the year, the chain-link barrier was so full of gaps that it could barely hold itself up, but it still had the one important feature I needed. It had a door.

Well, a gate, really. But I was feeling lucky after coming out in the middle of a sidewalk earlier, and unlike the rest of Loveland, there was no one over here to gawk at me. Other than the cars racing by behind us, this side of the road was dark and dead, which was exactly what I needed.

"Okay," I told Nik as I linked my fingers through the fence gate, which was already so loose it nearly fell over when I touched it. "This is going to look really weird, but I need you to roll with me, okay?"

Nik nodded and secured a firmer hold on my dad, which made me smile. This was why we made such a good team. I could trust Nik to handle anything I threw at him, and this one was going to be a doozy. I hadn't even reached for the magic yet, but I could already feel the city twisting under my feet, ready to bring me home.

"Here we go," I said, getting a tight hold on the chain-link gate as I pictured my apartment. "On three. One. Two—"

I yanked the gate open. As it creaked on its hinges, the darkness on the other side—which had been a dirty alley behind a gas station—swirled and vanished, replaced by the cheery chaos of my pieced-together living room.

I stepped through the moment the image settled, waving for Nik to follow me. He did, albeit more slowly, easing his armored body through the door I'd just opened in space like he was stepping into the mouth of a giant beast, which, technically, I supposed he was. The door I'd opened led into the DFZ, but not as most people knew her. We'd been walking around DFZ the city. This was DFZ the *god*, and she swallowed us up with a silent gulp, closing over the street behind us the moment our feet hit the floor of my apartment.

I slammed my door against the void of chaos a second later, but not before Nik saw enough to make him stagger. "What was that?" he asked in a shaky voice, his eyes darting around my apartment as if he'd never seen it before. "What is any of this? What did you *do*?"

"You don't have to explain yourself to him," my father said, crossing his smoke arms over his smoke chest. "He probably isn't educated enough to understand."

I rolled my eyes and proceeded to ignore him, turning my attention to Nik instead. "You can put Dad down in here," I said, opening the door to my bedroom. "He should be fine after he rests."

Nik did as he was told, setting my father's body down on top of the blanket that covered my mattress on the floor. I'm sure his sharp eyes didn't miss the bloodstains or the crate of empty liquor bottles or the wooden boards I'd nailed over the window to hide the maddening void outside, but he'd clearly gotten over his uncharacteristic outbursts, because he didn't say a word. Only when we were back out in the living room and the bedroom door was closed did he turn to me, his face pale and bewildered.

"Opal, what is going on?"

I sighed and sank down to my overstuffed couch, patting the faux-velvet mauve cushion beside me. This was going to take a lot of explaining, but if there was anyone who deserved my effort, it was Nik. I'd treated him the worst through all of this, but no matter what I did or how badly I messed up, he'd never abandoned me. Even when I'd screamed at him and vanished into the city on a dragon, he'd steadfastly searched for me. He'd never given up, and that mattered. It mattered a lot, and I was determined to pay him back. So when he sat down beside me, I told him everything.

That was not hyperbole, either. I meant I told him *everything*, the complete narration of my life from the moment I stormed out of his apartment to just now. I told him about my dad and White Snake. I told him about the DFZ and how I'd become a priest to save my father. I told him about my work and Dr. Kowalski and learning to be a Shaman. I told him about the Spirit of Dragons and my dad's condition and why we had to stay secret. I dumped all the information on Nik that he could ever want to know, stopping only to answer his questions. My father had a surprising number of questions as well, which made sense seeing how he'd been unconscious for most of it, but I only told Yong enough to get him to stop interrupting. This was Nik's time, and I focused exclusively on him.

By the time the whole story was out, it was after midnight. I felt like I'd been talking forever. Nik certainly looked exhausted, but neither of us said anything about sleep. We just sat there together on my couch, letting the dip in the middle lean us into each other until, at last, Nik sat back with a sigh.

"Well," he said, dragging a gloved hand through his ruffled hair. "At least I understand why you didn't call me."

"I'm *really* sorry about that," I said for the millionth time. "I wanted to, and I would have if I could, but I couldn't risk anyone finding out where we were hiding, and not just for my dad's sake. I didn't want some stupid dragon torturing you for information, and the only way to avoid that was to make sure you knew nothing."

"Knowing nothing doesn't stop you from getting tortured," Nik said in a voice that gave me the horrible feeling he spoke from experience. "I just wish you'd said *something*. I didn't need details, but if you'd told me you were lying low, I would have made different choices."

He sounded super frustrated, and I winced. "Sorry," I said again.

"Done is done," he said, waving his hand as if he were pushing the whole situation away. Then his eyes went back to mine. "So you're a priestess now?" When I nodded, he added, "Does that mean you're like Peter?"

I shook my head. "Peter serves the Empty Wind. I'm with the DFZ. Totally different spirits."

"I get that part," Nik said. "I meant are you under the same rules?"

He stared at me like that was super important, but I still didn't understand. "What rules are you talking about?"

A faint red blush spread over his face. "Do you have to be…you know…celibate?"

"Oh," I said, my own face heating to roughly the surface of the sun. It was a stupid reaction. We weren't teenagers. I was a grown woman who'd happily pounced on Nik the moment I got a chance. But there was something about the shy way he asked that melted my brain into a gooey puddle. To him, me being celibate was clearly the most horrible thing in the world. Knowing he felt that way made me stupidly happy, especially since it wasn't the case. I'd already asked Dr. Kowalski this exact question before I'd taken the DFZ's offer, and she'd said the city god didn't care about that stuff. I was about to tell Nik the good news when I remembered the second part of that conversation. The DFZ might not care about sex, but she did demand to be put first.

That was going to be a problem. Nik and I hadn't officially discussed what we were to each other yet, but he definitely ranked at the top of my priorities, and I didn't know how my god would feel about that. She was in my head all the time, so I supposed she'd let me know if I went too far, but I didn't want to deal with that. I didn't want someone else telling me who I could love.

I wouldn't do that.

The sudden voice in my head made me jump, which was stupid. I'd just said she was in there. Why the hell was I surprised when she appeared on cue?

I was trying to give you your privacy, the city spirit grumped. *But I'm hurt that you think I'd stop you from doing anything you wanted. Haven't I made it abundantly clear that I'm a god of free will? I'd* never *stop you from loving anyone or anything you wanted. You just can't love them more than me and still be a priest.*

Well, that was going to be a problem.

Let's not be hasty, the DFZ said. *Your life is crazy right now, I get it. What kind of god would I be if I judged you for that? Let's just play this by ear and see what happens.*

My eyes widened. That was shockingly generous of her.

I am quite *benevolent and wise,* she agreed. *But it's not entirely altruism. I've invested way too much in our ecclesiastical relationship to give up at the first bump, and this isn't entirely about you. I don't care what happens to Yong of Korea, but Nikola Kos has been part of me for most of his—and all my—life. If nothing else, I'm interested to see how his drama plays out, and your head is a perfect front-row seat.*

Glad I could be of service.

You are an excellent servant, the DFZ said, pinching my mental cheeks. *That's why I put up with you.*

Rolling my eyes, I turned back to Nik, who was looking at me like I'd lost my marbles.

"Are you okay?"

"There's a city in my head," I explained, tapping my temple. "Makes me a little weird."

Anyone else would have *definitely* thought I was crazy after that, but Nik just smiled. "You're always weird. I'm used to it."

I laughed at that. Then I stopped, because he was right. Not about me being weird, though that was also true, but about how he accepted it. Nik had seen me through several of my lowest points and never blinked. He'd never held them against me, never judged me, always helped me. Even when I'd cost him millions or made him work three straight weeks of eighteen-hour days, he'd put up with me. The man had been a *saint*, and I'd been too caught up in my own drama to appreciate it.

"I'm sorry."

"It's all right," Nik said. "You don't have to keep apologizing. I understand why you didn't call."

"Not that," I said quickly. "I mean, I *am* sorry about that, but…" I trailed off in frustration, angry that I couldn't get this right when it was the most important thing I'd ever said. "I'm sorry for how I left you. You handed me everything, and I threw it back in your face. I was so twisted up in my daddy issues, I wasn't capable of seeing your offer to support me as anything but an attempt at control. But I know now that I was wrong. You're not my father, and you weren't trying to own me. You were trying to help me, just like you always do, and I'm so, *so* sorry for how I reacted."

Yong's smoky specter looked hideously insulted by that, but I didn't care how he felt. I'd obsessed over my dad for way too long. This was about me and Nik, so I kept my eyes on him as he processed my apology.

"You did freak out pretty hard," he said at last, rubbing the back of his neck. "But I wasn't acting my best, either. I knew how much you hated other people having power over you, but I was so excited I'd found a way to keep you in my life that I didn't think about it. Bonehead move in hindsight, but…"

He trailed off with a shrug. I was too overcome to say anything, either. Even when I was dragging him through hell, all Nik wanted—all he'd *ever* wanted—was to keep me close to him. I'd spent so long obsessing over how I was the Dragon's Opal, I'd almost missed the one person who'd never seen me like that. Who wanted me *despite* my dragon, not because of him. And I…I…

"Thank you," I whispered, reaching out to squeeze Nik's hand with my trembling ones.

It wasn't enough. No words could ever be enough for the gratitude that was washing over me like a waterfall. I didn't even want to keep talking for fear I'd gush all over him. As always, though, Nik took it in stride.

"I'll always be there for you," he said, as if that wasn't the biggest deal of my life. "As I told you before, I like you. You being gone just reminded me of how much." He lowered his eyes to our tangled hands. "I missed you. When you're not with me, it's like I'm living in monotone. Nothing is colorful or funny or interesting. It's just work and fear and watching my back. I used to think everything was fine so long as I was surviving, but then I met you, and the world got so much bigger. That's why I *had* to get you back. Pushing through life just didn't seem worth it if you weren't with me." He winced. "That sounds pathetic, doesn't it?"

"Not at all," I assured him, squeezing our hands tight. "I understand completely. And I missed you too." I leaned in to rest my forehead against his. "Let's never do that again."

For a second I worried I'd gone too far, but the look of relief on Nik's face erased my fears. "Never," he agreed, wrapping his free arm around my shoulders to pull me closer. "Life sucks without you."

I could see my dad's look of disgust over Nik's shoulder, but I didn't care. So far as I was concerned, that was the most eloquent declaration of affection I'd ever received. I was still basking in the glow when Nik suddenly moved away.

"What's wrong?"

He looked back down at our joined hands. "Now that you know how I feel, I have a confession," he told our tangled fingers. "In my desperation to find you, I might have done something…stupid."

I froze in alarm. Oh shit. I'd been so busy talking about myself, I hadn't even asked about him. Nik was clearly involved in something bad. Last I knew, he didn't even own a suit of black combat armor. That meant something in the last two months had made him buy it, and given how expensive that stuff was—not to mention all the bruises I could see even better now that were poking up above his high collar—it must have been something *serious.*

"What is it and how can I help?"

"Kind of late for that, I'm afraid," Nik said, his voice embarrassed. "When you disappeared two months ago, I panicked. I'd always known the DFZ was alive, but I'd never understood what that really meant until I watched a skyscraper eat you in front of me. After that, I didn't know what to do. You'd been taken by something I couldn't fight or bribe or negotiate with. I didn't even know where to look for you. The DFZ's temples wouldn't help me, and I couldn't find the Wandering Cathedral no matter how hard I searched. I even hired someone to hack your phone's location data, but he couldn't find it."

I felt a brief twinge of satisfaction that my anti-internet strategy had actually worked. Too bad I'd made my AI's life hell hiding from the wrong person.

"It was like you'd disappeared into thin air," Nik went on. "I refused to believe you were dead, you're too stubborn for that. But after a month of searching, I realized there was no way I was going to find you on my own. I needed help, so I went to the only person I knew who was strong enough to stand up to the DFZ."

Oh shit. "Who?"

Nik heaved a defeated sigh. "The Gameskeeper."

He said that as if I should be terrified, but it actually took me several seconds to remember that the Gameskeeper was the guy who'd hired Dr. Lyle to make cockatrices for his arena. Kauffman's boss. The man Nik had sworn he'd never work for again.

"Oh shit," I said, aloud this time.

"Pretty much," Nik agreed stoically, his eyes dropping to his fake right arm. "I always said I'd never go back, but I didn't know anyone else who could help. The Gameskeeper knows everything that happens in the

Underground. If anyone could find you, I knew it was him, and I was right." He flashed me a weak smile. "How else do you think I knew you were in that restaurant?"

I'd thought it was odd he'd shown up so fast, but that wasn't important right now. "How much did his help cost you?" Because it had to be a lot. I didn't know much about the Gameskeeper, but guys that powerful never worked for cheap. Whatever it was, I'd help Nik pay it back, but he was already shaking his head.

"The Gameskeeper doesn't work for money. He has enough of that. His price was something he couldn't get any other way." He tapped his armored chest. "Me."

The way he said that made my stomach heave. Not that I could say anything about selling yourself to save someone else, but I had a strong feeling the Gameskeeper wasn't as dedicated to fairness and personal choice as the DFZ. "What did he want from you?"

"What he always wants from me," Nik said bitterly. "A fighter."

My heart fell as my eyes went back to Nik's new armor and guns. "He made you go back to contract killing, didn't he?"

"I wish it had been that easy," he said. "Contract killing was awful, but at least I got to pick my battles. The Gameskeeper wasn't going to let me off so lightly this time. In exchange for helping find you, he wanted me for his arena."

In any other context, I'd have said that sounded *way* better. I'd seen the top of the Gameskeeper's arena from the bridge in Rentfree. It had looked like just another tourist trap with all the tacky flashing signs and busloads of gawkers. From the doom in Nik's voice, though, I knew it couldn't be that simple.

"How bad is it?"

Nik shrugged. "Not *so* bad. I used to fight there sometimes when I needed cash. It's not fun, but it's not the end of the world."

He was lying. Not only did he refuse to meet my eyes, he was rubbing his false right arm like he was trying to pull it off. He definitely wasn't as nonchalant about this as he was trying to put on, but how could he be? I'd heard what Kauffman had said about the Gameskeeper's arena when he'd tried to buy our cockatrices. He'd claimed they were good for fighting *because* they suffered. That all that fear and love and desperation made good drama for the crowd. Now as then, the idea made me sick. I hadn't been willing to tolerate that cruelty for a bunch of magical chicken lizards. Like hell was I tolerating it for Nik.

"You have to let me help," I told him. "This is all my fault. If I'd just called you like a reasonable person and told you what was going on, you never would have gone to him."

"It's okay," Nik said. "You thought you were doing the right thing. I was the stupid one who panicked."

"You're not stupid and it's *not* okay. It will be, though, because we're getting you out of this. I'll just call the Gameskeeper and tell him you found me so your deal is no longer valid. I'm a priestess of the DFZ. That has to count for something."

From the scowl I could feel pressing into the back of my brain, my god was *not* cool with me pulling rank like that. I was still ready to try it, but Nik was shaking his head.

"It's not that simple," he said, reaching up to pull down his collar. At first I thought he was just showing me his bruises, which were a lot worse than I'd originally realized. Poor guy looked like he'd been choked multiple times, but Nik didn't stop at the throat. He kept pulling the armored shirt down until he reached the base of his neck just above his collarbone where his skin was marred with thick black marks from a new, hideously ugly tattoo.

No, I realized. Not a tattoo. The thing on his neck was a *curse*. I'd never seen one dug into the skin like that, but now that I knew it was there, I could feel the malicious magic a foot away.

"What did they do to you?"

"Nothing I didn't agree to," Nik said, his voice resigned as he slid his collar back up. "I went to the Gameskeeper for help, not results.

Whether I found you or not was never part of the deal. All the Gameskeeper promised was that he'd look for you and let me know when you showed up. In return for that information, I promised to be his champion for five fights in the arena. I thought it was better to stick to simple rules, less chance for him to screw me. Unfortunately, simple cuts both ways. The Gameskeeper's job is done, but I've still got two fights left. If I don't show up, the curse chops off my head."

"Then we'll get it removed," I said frantically. "The Rentfree arena fights are to the death, right? You can't fight in a death arena!"

"It's not that bad," Nik said, still refusing to meet my eyes. "I've already done three bouts, and I'm still alive. I can handle two more. What's important is that I found you."

"You shouldn't have had to look for me!" I was really panicking now, because it was so obvious that he was lying. Nik was trying to hide it from me, but I could see the tension in every line of his body. He was terrified, and it was all my fault.

"I'm getting that thing off you," I promised. "I don't know anything about removing curses, but I found a bunch of cursebreakers when I was trying to get rid of mine. Yours isn't dragon magic, so I bet we'll have a lot more luck finding—"

"No," Nik said sharply.

"Why not? If that curse is the only thing holding you to this stupidity, why can't we trash it?"

"Because that will be worse," he said, looking at me at last. "The Gameskeeper is the only person everyone in the Underground is afraid of. He's not someone you want to piss off. We made a deal. If I break it, he'll be after both of us forever. But if I stay the course and fulfill my end, I'll be free in two more fights. It won't even take that long. My fourth bout is tomorrow, which is now tonight, I guess, but the point is I'm almost done. I just have to hold out a bit longer and then this will all be over and we can go back to how things were before."

I wanted to believe him. Going back to Cleaning with Nik sounded like heaven after everything we'd been through, but I knew it couldn't be that simple. The Gameskeeper wasn't a dragon so far as I was aware, but I'd never met a powerful person who let a weapon walk away just because the fight was done. Remembering some of Kauffman's snide remarks, I suspected the Gameskeeper had been trying to get Nik back under his thumb for a long time. Deal or no deal, there was no *way* he was going to let him go free again whatever happened in that arena.

From the look on his face, I was pretty sure Nik knew that too. He was clearly clinging to hope with all he had, though. After causing him so much hurt, I didn't have it in me to crush that, especially since I had no solution to offer in exchange.

"Can I come watch you fight, at least?" I asked, trying to smile.

Nik shook his head. "I don't want you to see me like that."

"There's nothing I could see that would lower my opinion of you," I promised. "If I hadn't been so thoughtless, you wouldn't be in this mess. The least I can do is come and cheer for you."

Nik still didn't look convinced, but I was determined to get my way. This whole thing was such a pointless disaster, but if he was going to suffer for my sake, then dammit, I was going to be there with him.

"All right," he muttered a few seconds later, pulling out his phone. "I'll tell them to hold a seat for you."

I blinked in surprise. "Really? Just like that?"

"I know better than to stand in your way when you get like this," he said in a resigned voice. "And it's not as if I can keep you out. It's a public fight. If I said no, you'd just look up the time and go anyway. At least this way I can make sure the Gameskeeper doesn't make any money off your ticket." He punched a few buttons then turned his ludicrously archaic phone around to show me the confirmation on the postage-stamp-sized screen. "There. Second tier seats. Just give your name at Will Call, and they'll hook you up. Fight starts at seven."

I winced when he said the time. I'd been so determined not to let Nik face this alone, I'd forgotten I had other obligations. His fight was right in the middle of my work block for the DFZ. If it were any other job, I'd blow it off no problem, but as evidenced by her quota and check-in systems, my god took work attendance *very* seriously. I'd never even tried to request time off, but I'd never had a reason to before this. She was already in my head, so I supposed I could ask, but I didn't think she would—

It's fine.

"Really?" I cried, causing Nik to arch an eyebrow at me.

I'm not a jailer, the DFZ grumbled. *You can make the work up later. This is important to you, and I'm all about people chasing their dreams. Go with my blessing, just promise you'll take me with you.*

That was an easy promise. With the city constantly in my head, I didn't see how I could leave her behind even if I'd wanted to. She was still waiting, though, so I nodded. "I'll take you."

Good, the god said. *Now go assure your boyfriend that you're not insane. He's getting that look again.*

Nik did look pretty freaked out. "Sorry," I said, flashing him my most confident smile. "Everything's cool. Just had to check in with the boss, but she says I can go."

"The boss," he repeated nervously, staring at my forehead as if he was trying to peer inside it. "You mean the DFZ is in your head right now?"

"A lot of people are in my head," I said with a helpless shrug. "My brain's kind of a highway these days, but you get used to it. What's important is that I'll be there tomorrow night. Do you want me to bring anything?"

"I just want it to be over," Nik said tiredly, glancing down at the clock on his phone. "I should probably go. It's late, and I've got a med check early tomorrow morning."

"Okay," I said, standing up.

Nik didn't follow suit. For all his talk of leaving, he seemed incredibly reluctant to move. I didn't want him to go, either. Not after I'd just gotten him back.

"Do you...Do you want to stay?" I asked nervously. "My dad's body is taking up the bedroom, so all I have to offer is a couch, but I'd be happy if you wanted to sleep over. You know, with me."

My cheeks were burning by the time I finished. *Real* smooth, Opal. Way to flex your pro-seduction skills, and the fact that my dad was still in the room listening was the inappropriate icing on the awkward cake. I was about to tell Nik to forget it when he lurched forward.

"God yes," he whispered, clutching me hard against him. "I'd rather be on a couch with you than anywhere else in the world."

"Absolutely not," my father said as I burst into the biggest grin.

"You don't get a say," I told him in Korean as Nik drew me back down to the couch. "This is my home. Go to your room."

My father growled, but I wasn't listening to him anymore. All of my attention, my entire world, was focused on Nik as he pulled me into the lumpy cushions, the two of us tangling into the happy, breathy heap that I'd lived without for far, far too long.

Chapter 6

Despite our best intentions, we ended up just going to bed after all. To be clear: this was *not* my fault. I was ready to go, but Nik fell asleep the second he was flat. Literally passed out mid-kiss. If I hadn't been so worried about him, it would have been hilarious. I didn't know what the Gameskeeper had been making him do between fights, but poor guy was absolutely dead. He was also far more injured than I'd initially realized.

After he fell asleep, I tried to remove his gear to make him more comfortable. I got his guns and boots off just fine, but when I tried to unzip his armored jacket, I realized someone had taped it to the bandages underneath. I didn't know if that was to help with compression or to stop the jacket from moving so it wouldn't accidentally reopen any wounds, but I wasn't about to mess with whatever system was clearly in place.

It was probably for the best. I was exhausted too. Not as much as Nik, but I had no trouble at all falling asleep next to him despite our awkward position. Since he was bigger and had passed out first, he got the majority of the couch. I had to squeeze myself into the tiny gap left between his body and the edge, but I was too tired and too happy to mind. After so many weeks of worrying, it felt like my life was finally coming back together. Not fixed, not yet, but I felt like I was on my way at last.

That hopeful thought sent me to sleep like a baby. I woke up five hours later to the sound of my morning alarm. Nik jerked awake next to me at the same time, looking around in a panic before his eyes found me.

"Hey," he said, relaxing at once.

"Hey yourself," I replied, leaning in to kiss him before swooping down to grab my phone off the floor so I could shut off the incessant beeping. "I gotta go to training."

"Do you have to?"

"Not immediately," I said, snuggling back down beside him. "I mean, if I don't show up in ten minutes, we'll probably have a god in here scolding me, but I didn't get undressed last night, so I've already got a head start."

"Mmmm," Nik said, burying his nose in my hair.

"You can stay if you want," I offered. "There's no food or anything, but the plumbing works and it's as safe as you can get in the city."

Nik thought about that a moment, then he shook his head. "I've got a checkup this morning. They want to make sure I'm okay to fight tonight."

"*Are* you okay?" I asked nervously, tapping my fingers where they rested on his still-jacketed chest.

"I'm fine."

I gave him a look, and Nik sighed. "The damage from my last fight hasn't healed as fast as I'd like, but I'll be good enough by tonight. One of the nice things about working for the Gameskeeper is that he isn't cheap. The reason they're calling me in so early is so I can take a dunk in the rejuvenation tank."

I whistled. Rejuvenation tanks were *expensive*. The nutrient-rich baths were typically reserved for critical cases like super-premature infants or billionaires over the age of sixty. Definitely not the sort of thing you expected to find in an Underground arena, but the more I thought about it, the more sense it made. I didn't follow blood sports, but you'd have to be deaf, blind, and criminally unobservant to miss the Gameskeeper's advertising. Those big weekend fights had to make him millions. That sort of money made keeping your talent in top shape a critical investment, and while I hated to think of Nik as someone's commodity, I was happy to hear he'd at least be getting the best treatment.

We lay still for a while after that. Not even talking, just listening to each other breathe. I could have snoozed on Nik forever, but five minutes later, my alarm went off again, this time with the super-critical ringtone, and I forced myself off him with a groan.

"That's the final warning."

Nik sighed and sat up as well, reaching down to grab his boots and weapons where I'd stacked them by the end of the couch. When he was shod and rearmed, he rose to his feet. "See you tonight?"

"I'll be there the moment the doors open," I promised, getting up on my tiptoes to kiss him one last time. "Good luck."

He caught me and kissed me back, crushing my body to his for a too-brief second before he let me go and walked to my door. He was about to turn the handle when I finally snapped out of my romantic daze.

"*Wait!*"

Nik stopped, looking over his shoulder in confusion.

"You don't want to do that," I said, hurrying to pry his hand off my front door. "We're kind of floating in a mind-twisting void that shouldn't exist. It's not fun to walk into."

He scowled. "How do I get out, then?"

"Let me," I said, grabbing the knob. Then I stopped. "Uh, where do you want to go?"

"Back to that weird restaurant you were at last night," Nik said. "I left my car in Loveland."

I gaped at him. Nik had left his *car* in Loveland to stay with me. I know that doesn't sound like much, but tourist areas in the DFZ were hot spots for petty crime. Leaving anything unattended in a place like that was practically asking for it to be stolen or vandalized, and Nik had left his beloved black car parked there overnight. For me.

"I put it in a deck," he said when the silence had stretched too long. "I wasn't going to—"

"Shh," I said, pressing my finger to his lips. "Don't ruin it."

He nodded, looking confused. Still sighing at his selfless romantic act, I turned back to my door and focused my mind on the picture I'd used to get us to Loveland last night. I was struggling to remember the details when I realized I could do even better. I'd never tried this particular variation on the spell before, but I'd used a fence gate to get back here last night, so I didn't think it would be *too* much of a stretch.

With that, I pushed the old image out of my head and focused on a new one. One I knew *much* better. When I had it perfectly clear in my mind, I turned the doorknob and pushed, grinning wide when my apartment door opened, not onto a busy tourist sidewalk, but directly into the cab of Nik's sports car.

"Ta-da!"

"Wow," he said, sounding legitimately impressed. Then he scowled. "Wait, how does that even work? Your door is taller than my car. It doesn't seem physically possible."

"It's not," I assured him. "But it is quite *magically* possible, and that's what counts."

Nik puzzled over that for a good twenty seconds, then he shrugged and stepped into his car.

"You know," I said as he sat down in the driver's seat. "In hindsight, I could have opened a door straight to your apartment. Then we could have spent last night in a bed rather than on a couch."

"I wouldn't change a thing about last night," he said, giving me a rare grin. "But that's a good plan for next time."

Hearing he wanted to do this again sent my heart fluttering. It felt silly since Nik had always made it clear he wanted me to stick around, but I wasn't used to being part of someone else's life like this. If you counted the two months I'd been forced to hide—which I *totally* did—Nik was by far my longest relationship. It was a new experience, in other words. Can you blame me for being excited?

"No," Sibyl said in my ear. "But you will be *very* late if you don't get a move on."

Grumbling about killjoy responsible AIs, I waved a final goodbye to Nik and shut my door. When I turned around to make sure I had everything I needed for my morning training, I spotted my dad standing in the bedroom doorway. My *actual* dad, not the smoky ghost from last night.

"Hey, you're back in your body!" I said, walking over to grab my bag off the kitchen counter. "How'd you do that?"

"I just stepped back in," he said curtly. "It is *my* body."

I'd thought it would be more complicated than that, but, "If it works, it works," I said, slinging my bag across my chest with a joy nothing could bring down. Not that my dad wasn't trying.

"Where is your criminal?"

"His name is Nik, he's not a criminal, and he had to go to an appointment," I said, refusing to let him rain on my parade. "Speaking of, I've gotta get to Shaman training. I'll bring you back some vegetables or something."

"You're not going anywhere without me," Yong said sternly. "The fire you gave me last night is already fading. I barely managed to climb back into my body this morning."

"Well, maybe you should climb back out of it," I suggested. "Being corporeal seems to drain you faster than being smoke."

"Perhaps," he admitted. "But I'd rather drain more quickly as myself than live a half existence as an ashen ghost."

I supposed that was fair. I *had* promised to keep him supplied with fire until his own came back, and while I didn't appreciate him disparaging Nik, my dad had gone to his room last night when I'd told him to without a fight. That counted as a petition for sainthood given who we were talking about, but as I was reaching for the floating magic to give him the boost that would hopefully keep him together until I got home from my lessons, I realized I was going about this all wrong.

"I've got a better idea," I said, reaching out to grab my dad's hand instead. "Come on, we're taking you to the doctor."

"Which doctor?" he asked in a voice that almost sounded nervous as I dragged him toward the door.

"She *is* kind of a witch doctor," I agreed, laughing. "But she's the best there is."

That joke only made him look more wary, but I'd already seized the doorknob, twisting the magic to open a portal to the one destination I never had to think about.

I don't think I could have made Dr. Kowalski happier if I'd brought her back to life. The moment I dragged my dad into her kitchen, she was on him like a bloodhound. While I helped myself to my usual bowl of stewed wheat berries from the stove—no salt, no sugar, no dairy, just grains and sadness—she circled and prodded and poked my father until he looked ready to turn back into smoke just to get away. If she'd been anyone else, I was certain she'd have been a pile of cinders, lack of fire notwithstanding. But unlike my first meeting with Dr. K, my father clearly saw right off the bat that she was the face of a god. Even if he'd been his old full-burn self, he wouldn't have been a match for her, and from the looks on their faces, they both knew it.

"This is just marvelous," Dr. Kowalski said excitedly, dragging her kitchen stool over so she could climb up onto it and peer into my father's eyes. "You used his own curse as an entry point. It's absolutely brilliant! Did you think of that yourself?"

"The Spirit of Dragons helped," I said, piling as many blueberries as would fit into my bowl in an effort to make my breakfast taste less like boiled paste. "But the general idea was mine."

Dr. Kowalski sucked in a proud breath. "*So* good," she said delightedly, working her fingers into my dad's mouth to check his teeth. "But how did you mimic dragon fire? It's a completely different form of magical expression."

I was dying to tell her all the details if only for a rare chance to brag, but the Spirit of Dragons had been *very specific* that what had happened with my dad's fire was privileged information. "I just sort of fudged things around until it felt right," I said instead.

"You *fudged* the essence of a dragon?" My teacher's face split into a smile so wide, her eyes vanished into her wrinkles. "I *knew* you were a natural!"

That wasn't exactly what had happened. I wouldn't have been able to do anything if the spirit hadn't given me a spark to copy. Even with her help, though, I was the one who'd figured out how to turn city magic into dragon fire, so I felt justified accepting the praise. But while I was preening under Dr. Kowalski's impressed noises, my father looked confused.

"Opal," he said when Dr. Kowalski finally took her hand out of his mouth. "What is she talking about?"

"Didn't you know?" I replied with twenty-six years of pent-up righteousness. "I'm a natural-born Shaman."

Yong looked unimpressed. "A what?"

"A natural-born Shaman," Dr. Kowalski repeated, grabbing a handful of his long black hair to check its strength. "Someone who understands instinctively how to work magic in its free form. She has the potential to be the talent of the age if she keeps improving at the rate she has been. Of course, she'd already be there if her early training hadn't been so *grossly* mismanaged."

"It wasn't mismanaged," Yong said angrily, jerking his hair out of her grasp. "She had the best tutors in the world!"

Dr. Kowalski scoffed. "Best according to whom? A bunch of academic Thaumaturges too blinded by their own prejudices to notice when their methods are failing them? *Bah!* Whatever they were, they were fools to try and teach a child. There's a reason mages don't start training until age ten. Magic of any stripe requires the individual to have reached a certain stage of mental development and self-awareness. Starting too early risks harm to the child's still-developing soul. It's ridiculous."

"Opal wasn't at risk," my father argued. "She was bred to be a prodigy. Other children—"

"Just because she was born with a naturally super-high draw doesn't mean she had the capacity to control it. She told me you started her training when she was five. *Five!* Frankly, it's a miracle she didn't burn herself out ages ago, though she was certainly close enough when I found her."

My dad looked at me in confusion, but I just shrugged. What could I say? She was right.

"And that's not even the worst of it," Dr. Kowalski said, shaking her finger in my dad's face. "As if your 'best tutors in the world' allowing a five-year-old to handle magic wasn't bad enough, they forced her to learn *Thaumaturgy,* even when she was clearly not thriving in the discipline. A *good* teacher would have adapted the lesson to fit the pupil, especially one as vulnerable as a young child, but your idiots just kept slamming her into the wall and blaming her when she got hurt! What kind of halfwits did you hire?"

Yong took a step back. "I…Everyone said they were the best."

"Well, *you* should have paid closer attention to what was going on in your own home," she scolded. "Being a dragon is no excuse! You adopted a human child, that makes you responsible for her development. You should have seen she was having trouble and worked with her to guide her natural talent, but did you? *No!* You just assumed she was a bird, tossed her in the air, and told her to fly, never even bothering to look and see if she was actually a fish!"

"I didn't know she could *be* a fish," Yong said defensively. And confusedly. "I'm not even sure I know what we're talking about anymore."

"You wouldn't," Dr. Kowalski grumbled. "Foolish dragons, always thinking they know better."

My dad took a step back, and I had to scramble not to choke on my grains. I'd never seen the Great Yong look so flustered, and it was absolutely priceless. But as much as I was enjoying this, I hadn't actually brought my dad here to get chewed out.

"Dr. Kowalski?"

My teacher glowered over her shoulder, and I pointed at my dad. "You're absolutely right about everything, but I don't think he's going to be making the same mistake with another mage child anytime soon, so would you mind taking a look at his magic and telling me if you see any way I can speed up the transference?"

"What's wrong with what you're doing?" she asked, the anger fading from her voice now that we were no longer focused on my father's sins against young mages. "Last I heard yesterday, he was still in a coma. I'd say you've had great success."

"But it's still not enough," I said, quickly telling her about his smoke form and how my soul ached whenever I passed magic to him. "It's the same feeling I used to get when I'd backlash myself, but I'm not backlashing! I'm passing him perfectly safe amounts of magic, which is unfortunately barely enough to keep him functional. I need to be building him up, not treading water, but I'm worried I'll dislocate my soul again if I increase the power."

"First, good on you for listening to your body," Dr. Kowalski said proudly. "Now, as to your problem, the pain you're feeling is probably related less to the volume of magic and more to the fact that you're passing him dragon fire, or a very close approximation thereof. Just like every other form of magic, dragon fire is true to its nature, which unfortunately means it burns. Since you are not a dragon, it's only natural that you wouldn't be able to hold large amounts of it without pain."

"Oh," I said, feeling embarrassed. It sounded so obvious when she put it like that. "So what do I do?"

"I don't know," she said, scowling in thought. "Let me consult a few books and get back to you. In the meantime, why don't you go out and take care of the watering? Today's vegetable is on the counter."

There were a lot of vegetables on the counter, but only one she could be talking about. "You mean this?" I asked, picking up a butternut squash the size of my arm.

"That's the one," Dr. Kowalski said, walking down the hall toward her library. "Make sure you drench everything. We've had a long dry spell, and autumn gets hotter every year."

I assured her I would, but I didn't think she heard me. She was already climbing up the built-in bookshelf to pull down some huge academic tome with a title so long, it took up the entirety of the book's spine. Satisfied that my problem was in good hands, I grabbed my squash and headed outside, taking care to fill the gourd properly with magic before I pulled the power right back out and shaped it into a giant hand big enough to grab the fifty-gallon rain barrel under the downspout at the house's corner. Filling the squash with magic again, I shaped the diffuser next, lifting my hand over my head to create a shimmering barrier of magic poked full of tiny holes.

The finished product was kind of like an upside-down sieve big enough to cover the entire garden. When I had the magic shaped just the way I wanted it, I upended the first spell over the second, pouring the rain barrel over the diffuser so that the water inside trickled over the barrier, falling through holes onto the garden below exactly like rain.

It was a pretty neat trick if I said so myself. One I'd perfected over weeks of having to do this chore nearly every morning. When I finished emptying the first barrel and turned to grab the next one, I saw my father watching from the cottage's back door with an expression of wonder.

"That was incredible, Opal."

I shrugged, embarrassed he was so impressed over such a small thing. I mean, the rain-barrel-giant-sieve combo was a big deal for *me*, but any real mage could have watered this garden in no time. "Dr. Kowalski's a good teacher."

"So I've been made aware," Yong said, sitting down on the back step with a bitter sigh. "I really did think I was doing what was best for you, you know."

"I know," I said, upending the next barrel over my rainmaker. "You were still wrong, but I know you didn't do it on purpose."

"I only wanted you to live up to your potential," he said, clearly desperate to defend himself. "Even when you failed, I didn't want you to give up, or to think I'd given up on you. That's why I had your teachers push you so hard."

"I know you meant well, Dad," I said irritably, focusing on my work. Watching him get reamed by Dr. Kowalski had been fun, but I really didn't want to have this conversation. The old Opal might have relished telling him how badly all that pushing had messed me up, but I'd been enjoying *not* being furious with my dad for once. We'd made really good progress yesterday, and I didn't want to backslide. Also, yelling at him about past mistakes had never done any good for either of us. Sure he'd been wrong about almost everything when it came to me, but I wasn't a little girl blowing up pumpkins anymore. I was a mature mage with my own talents, and I was getting better every day. That was good enough. I was ready to let it go and move on when my dad opened his mouth and said the one thing I'd never thought he'd say.

"I'm sorry."

I froze. Literally went stone-still right there on the garden path. I'd heard of people being "shocked still" before, but I hadn't realized it was a legit physical phenomenon until this moment. When I finally did manage to turn around, my father was sitting on Dr. Kowalski's back step with his head lowered, his sharp, too-thin shoulders slumped inward like an old, defeated man.

"One of the greatest dangers for a dragon is living in the past," he told the gravel path between his cheap sandals. "It was that weakness that was my father's downfall. He was nearly ten thousand, old enough to know better, yet he still saw humans merely as prey to be chased down and devoured. He did not see what I saw, didn't notice their leaps in intelligence, tenacity, and creativity. He had failed to adapt, which was why he suspected nothing when I worked with the ancient mortals to lure him out into the deep water where I was waiting."

I knew where this story was going. "You killed him."

Yong nodded, flexing his human fingers as if he were remembering the way it felt. "He deserved to die. He was rigid and prideful and weak. An old snake too stiff-necked to look up and see that the world had changed, and that the son he'd taken for granted was not like him. When I ate his fire, I swore that I would never be so stupid. Never repeat his mistakes. But I did."

He looked at me then. I stared back nervously, too unsure of what was happening to even set down the empty water barrel I was still holding suspended in the air. My father talked about the past all the time, just not his. He could tell you the complete history of any country in the world, but he'd never told me this.

"I thought I knew what was best for you," he went on, his voice so quiet I had to strain to hear it over the wind in the trees. "You were such a ridiculous, emotional creature. You needed guidance. I thought I was giving that to you. Thought I knew what that was. When I look at you now, though—what you've done, what you're capable of—I realize I don't know you at all."

He sounded so sad it made me uncomfortable. All of this did, which was strange because this was exactly what I'd wanted. I *wanted* him to realize that I wasn't that bumbling girl anymore. I just hadn't been prepared for how upset it would make him.

"It's not that you don't know me," I said, setting down the empty barrel at last. "I'm just not a child anymore. Mortals change. We grow up."

"I know that," he replied angrily, fisting his bony hands where they rested on his knees. "I am Yong of Korea! I've had more mortals than most dragons have gold. I've grown and defended an empire on my own with no clan for over a thousand years purely by understanding and harnessing just how fast humans can change. I know perfectly well how mortals grow, I just…." He sighed. "I didn't see it in you. The same stubborn blindness I despised in my father was in my own eyes all this time, and I didn't even notice because I didn't want to see. I wanted you to stay forever as you were: a happy, foolish little puppy, rolling at my feet."

"But I never was that," I said, frustrated. "You were always calling me 'puppy' or 'dog girl,' but I'm *not.* I'm not your pet!"

"I never saw you as such."

"Then why do you treat me like one?"

My father sighed again. "Because it was safer."

I scowled in confusion, and my father ran his hands over his face. "I never saw you as lesser," he said, his voice patient and sad. "From the moment your mother handed you to me after you were born, I've considered you my own child. Better than my own, for my offspring would have been dragons like me. Born backstabbers forever after my lands, my fire, and my head. It is *because* you were human that I was free to care for you, to treasure you as much as I wanted without fear of betrayal."

"Then you *did* see me as less," I argued. "You only 'treasured' me because you thought I was too weak to hurt you. Because I was *safe*. How is that not looking down on me?"

My father's eyes widened in surprise, and then he shook his head in disgust. "As I said," he muttered. "I was blind. Blind and stupid, so much so that I'm still discovering how far my willful ignorance reached." He looked down at the ground again. "How fitting that you should be the one who brought me down. Karma truly does flow in a circle."

I rolled my eyes. "Now who's being ridiculous?" I said, walking over to plop down on the step beside him. "I didn't 'bring you down.' You tried to cage me, and I fought back. I'm not going to apologize for defending myself, but that doesn't mean we're fated to be enemies. If there's any karma involved in this, it's that your bad actions came around to bite you in the tail. Fortunately, there's an easy solution to that. If you don't want me to keep fighting you, stop forcing me to do things I don't want to do. Let *me* decide what's best for me, and maybe we can stop biting each other's heads off every time we're in the same hemisphere."

A smile ghosted over my father's lips. "That would be a pleasant change."

"It would," I agreed. "I don't like fighting you all the time, either, but I can't be the only one who moves on this. I already grew up, but if this is going to work, then you have to grow up too. If I'm your daughter, you have to *treat* me like a daughter. That means treating me like family, not a 'puppy' or a 'treasure' or anything else you own."

My father frowned. "Are you sure you want that? My history with family is not a happy one."

"Family is what you make it," I countered, looking him in the eyes. "I don't care about White Snake or whatever patricidal nastiness you pulled a thousand years ago. I care about *us*, right here, right now. Me and Mom, we're the family you chose. But if you're going to call yourself my father, then I need you to act like a father. Not a dragon throwing a fit over his missing gem."

I expected him to get pissy over that last comment, but my dad was full of surprises today, because he smiled. "Never thought *I* would need a lecture about adapting," he said wryly. "Though I suppose one is overdue. After all that has happened, I'd have to be an idiot not to see that you're no longer the same girl who ran from Korea, but that's what I am, apparently. An idiot. I made myself blind because I needed to believe that nothing had changed. That we could still go back to how we were if I could only rein you in. But there was no going back, and in my foolish attempts to keep you with me in the past, I just pushed you further away."

"But not out of reach," I said, scooting closer. "Just because we can't go back to how things were when I was a kid doesn't mean everything's lost. Look at us right now! We're talking like normal people. That's a good start, and if we keep it up, it could get even better. I'm sure it won't actually be that simple, but I'm ready to try if you are."

He looked at me in wonder. "*You* would try?"

"Of course," I said, punching him lightly on the arm. "You're a royal pain in the ass, but you're the only dad I've got."

Now he looked insulted. "Glad you consider me worth the effort."

I smirked at him. "Come on, you know how much I like refurbishing things. You can be my grime-covered painting everyone else thought was trash until I dug you out, cleaned you up, and auctioned you off for millions."

My father glowered at the unflattering comparison. Then, suddenly, he started to laugh. Not an ironic chuckle or a superior smirk, but actual double-over, shoulders shaking, "that's hilarious" laughter. The sight left me dumbstruck. My father was always so proud and formal, always a proper dragon. It had never even occurred to me that he *could* laugh in a way that wasn't sardonic evil-overlord chuckling before this moment, which was proof that Yong wasn't the only one who needed to update their worldview.

If I was going to demand he treat me as a daughter rather than an opal, then it was only fair that I stopped treating everything he did as draconic manipulation. Just as I wasn't a pet, he wasn't actually the monolith I remembered from my childhood. If I was going to get to know the real Yong, I needed to stop knee-jerk reacting to everything he did and start paying attention to what was actually in front of my eyes. And right now, what I saw wasn't so bad. I mean, this whole mess was still his fault, but at least now we both understood that his attempts to control me were wrong. That was a huge change, and while there was no way twenty-four hours' worth of positive interactions could outweigh decades of horrible behavior, for the first time in my adult life, I felt as if we could be all right again.

Stupid assumption, I know, but I've always been an optimist. Trusting my dad not to be terrible was a big gamble, but if we could actually keep this up, the payoff—getting back the kind father I'd loved instead of the controlling one I'd feared—was too good not to go for.

"You know, I think we just had a breakthrough," I said, rising to my feet. "Unfortunately, I need to get back to work before my god-slash-teacher catches me slacking."

"I understand," my father said, standing up as well. "Would you like some help?"

I stared at him, not comprehending. "You mean with the garden?"

"I know great dragons don't usually stoop to manual labor, but it has been a humbling few months," he said, looking around the yard. "What would you like me to do?"

And that's how I ended up pulling weeds with the Dragon of Korea. For all his grousing about manual labor, he was astonishingly good at it. While I dug around and mangled things, my dad pulled the little errant shoots out of the packed soil with a lifelong farmer's skill. When I teased him about it, he told me how, at the age of thirty—which was apparently a baby by dragon standards—he'd protected his favorite mortal village by living among them as a farmhand and telling his father he was practicing maintaining a human form to aid in hunting. The previous Yong, pleased that his son was showing initiative, agreed to spare the village for as long as he needed it for practice, which was how my father wound up "practicing" being a human farmer for the next ninety-seven years.

"Really?" I said, gaping at him. "You were a Stone Age farmer for *ninety-seven* years?"

"It wasn't the Stone Age," he said dryly. "We had iron tools. But yes, I was a farmer, and it wasn't so bad. The land was cleaner then. Things grew well, and the cattle were delicious. Also, it was the first time in my life I wasn't under my father's control."

"Can't imagine what that must have been like," I said sarcastically.

"You can't," Yong replied in all seriousness. "My father was very traditional. He treated his children in the old way: as servants and soldiers. If we did well, he gave us a share of the plunder. If we got out of line, he killed us."

"Us?" I repeated, no longer laughing. "How many of you were there?"

"Fourteen to start," he said, resuming his weeding. "But by the time I killed my father, White Snake and I were the only ones left. I because I was the eldest and strongest, and my sister because she was a coward who was skilled in bribery." His eyes narrowed. "Our father was excessively bribable."

"Sounds like a classy fellow," I said, fisting the pulled weeds in my hands. "Did you…Did you mourn for any of your siblings?"

"No," Yong said without missing a beat. "They were all vipers who would gladly have eaten me alive. If my father hadn't killed them, I would have. It was the only way to be safe. I was foolish enough to let White Snake live, and look how that turned out."

I shook my head. Man, no wonder my dad had such screwed-up ideas about family. Dragon clans sounded *terrible.* But at least this explained why he'd been so confused by my reaction to his control. Compared to the way he'd been raised, my dad's parenting style had been indulgent to a fault.

"So what happened to your village?"

"After I ate my father and became the Great Yong, I made it my stronghold," he said proudly. "Our current mountain villa stands in the same place, and some of my household are actually descended from those first farmers."

Considering how crazy loyal his people were, I totally believed that. "So do I have any ancient farmer sisters or brothers?"

"No," he said. "My consorts have had children before, but you are the only one I've claimed as my own."

"Why?"

He stared at me, and my cheeks heated. I hadn't meant to blurt it out like that, nor had I needed to. He'd told me I was his only child many, many times. But the more I learned about my dad—*actually* learned from him, not the pro-Yong propaganda my mom had taught me—the more incredible that felt. Yong was famous for his mortals. Or infamous, depending on who you asked. Point was, he'd never made a secret of the fact he vastly preferred human company to his own kind, so it didn't make sense to me why he'd waited this long to have one of his own. He'd pretended to be a farmer for almost a century! I'd expected he'd have had a whole stone hut full of kids over the years, but apparently that wasn't the case, so...

"Why?" I asked again. "Why did you decide to make me?"

"Because your mother wanted you," he said simply. "And I wanted her to be happy."

I couldn't believe it. "You did all of this for Mom?"

"Yes," he said, brows furrowing. "You have to understand. Up until a century or so ago, most human children didn't survive their first five years. Why should I risk investing myself in something that was so likely to die? Also, I find babies disgusting."

"You're really selling it."

Yong shrugged. "It's the truth. But with this century's advances in health care and gene editing, I decided it was finally time to take the risk. I've had humans since I can remember, including many treasured consorts, but I'd never had a daughter. I thought it would be a unique experience, something to remember and improve upon over future generations. I didn't expect to love you."

The weeds fell from my hands. "What?"

"I know," he said, scowling at the nettle he was working out of the ground with practiced precision. "It was ludicrous, a dragon growing attached to such a helpless, illogical little thing. It's caused me more trouble than any other decision of my life. It's *still* causing me trouble, but foolish as it was, knowing what I know today, I would still make the same choice."

I couldn't believe my ears. No, scratch that, I *totally* believed I'd caused my father no end of consternation, but the rest of it caught me completely off guard. I'd always known deep down that my father had affection for me, but I'd always assumed it was for a treasure. An object. I hadn't realized he'd treasured me in the normal way too.

"You love me."

The sentence came out sounding more like a question, and my father glowered. "Of course I love you. Why else would I put myself through so much suffering for your sake?"

That was a good point, but, "You never said it before!"

"Why should I say it?" he grumped. "I just told you it was a weakness, and who likes to harp on those? I also saw no point in stating the obvious. It's tedious."

I supposed it was obvious when he put it like that, but I was still too shocked to speak. All this time, I'd thought my dad had been fighting to possess me or punish me because I didn't grovel like his other humans did when the truth had been so much simpler. My dad loved me, and he was embarrassed about it.

I could absolutely see why. I was everything a proper dragon should despise: a weak human of unremarkable beauty who couldn't give him anything. A *disobedient* human whose magic had always been a grave disappointment. I was what his entire culture said he should cut loose, but he never had. For all my faults and rebellions, he'd never stopped calling me his own. And for the first time I could remember, that didn't seem like a bad thing.

We weeded in silence for a long time after that. We'd finished the vegetable beds and were moving on to the annuals when Dr. Kowalski finally came out to join us.

"Well?" I said, looking up excitedly. "Did you find anything?"

She shook her head, and my spirits fell. "I'm sorry, Opal. I've read every entry on magic conversion that I can find, and they all agree there's no way to convert normal magic into dragon fire. Trust me, it's been tried. Dragons have been bullying mages into looking for ways to beef them up artificially since the dawn of human magic, but it's never worked. Not once. Until you."

That was gratifying, I supposed, but it didn't help with our current problem. "So you're saying there's nothing that can show me how to do this better than I'm already doing it?"

"Considering that what you're doing is supposed to be impossible, I'd say you're doing amazingly," the doctor said. "But no. Unless you're willing to feed him another dragon, I couldn't find any other way to build him up. You're just going to have to keep transferring the fire yourself, I'm afraid."

Damn. It wasn't that I minded feeding my father now that I was no longer desperate to kick him out of my life, but dragons needed a lot of magic, and I'd had some *very* bad experiences with taking in too much power. Every transfer I'd made so far had left me exhausted, and that was barely a drop in the bucket. At this rate, I'd be shoving magic into my dad for the rest of my life. It looked pretty hopeless, but when I turned to ask my dad what he wanted to do about it, I was shocked to see him smiling.

"We can manage."

"Are you crazy? What about Korea? You can't defend it as you are, and I can't get you back into fighting shape fast enough on my own!"

That sounded pretty bleak to me, but my father just shrugged. "You brought me back to life when I was supposed to be dead. That's one miracle already. Now we just need a second."

"I'm flattered you've developed so much confidence in my abilities, but 'hope for a miracle' isn't a plan."

"I have faith," he said, lips quirking. "And you have a knack for doing the impossible. Every time I thought I had you cornered, you found a way to wiggle free, even if it meant moving the world. I'm hoping that insanity will work for me rather than against me this time."

Technically, I'd moved the world twice to save him so far, but I didn't want to encourage this madness. "It's not going to work," I said firmly. "I simply can't feed you fire fast enough on my own. If you want to get back on your feet before someone snatches your territory out from under you, we should look for a dragon. Surely there's someone you can pay for a fire donation?"

Yong snorted. "No dragon worth the name would ever trade fire for *money*. Power must be won, and unfortunately I'm too weak right now to defeat anyone worth eating." He shook his head. "We'll just have to keep going and see what happens. If you continue pouring fire into me as you have been, I should build up past my base replenishment rate eventually. Until then…"

He stepped out of his body, which keeled over at my feet, making me yelp.

"Little warning next time, please!" I yelled at his smoky ghost.

"I thought this was the obvious move," my dad said with a shrug. "This form is weak and unable to interact with the outside world, but it costs me almost nothing to maintain and is invisible to humans. That makes it superior for our present circumstances."

"You're not invisible to dragons," I reminded him. "The Spirit of Dragons specifically said—"

"If one of my enemies sees us, I'm no more dead in this form than I would be in that one," he replied, his lip curling in disgust as he passed his smoky foot through his physical form's bony rib cage. "I'm barely stronger than the human I resemble. I couldn't fight a hatchling, let alone a full-grown dragon." He shook his head firmly. "No. If I must be diminished, I'd rather be in the form that saves my strength and draws less attention."

"Can't argue with that logic," Dr. Kowalski said, turning to me. "I can stash his body in one of my spare bedrooms if you like. This place is even safer than your apartment, and the DFZ wants him out for a while so she can clean your bedroom."

"Why is the DFZ cleaning my bedroom?" I asked. "I thought scrubbing was mortal work."

"Normally yes, but this is a matter of security," Dr. Kowalski replied. "Now that you've called the Spirit of Dragons to your place, she can find her way back anytime she likes. Since your apartment is currently floating inside the DFZ's magic, that means she can *also* find her way into our god. Our great city enjoys dragons, but she isn't stupid enough to leave a back door open for one, so she's going to do a bit of rearranging. Don't worry, I'm sure you'll like the result."

I wasn't worried about losing my bloodstained bedroom, but I *was* worried about my dad. It was his body, so I guessed it was his choice, but his smoky form looked way too much like a ghost for my liking. I hadn't been able to handle the thought of my dad dying before we'd made our truce. I *really* didn't want to be reminded of it now that I finally had hope things were getting better.

"Are you sure about this?"

"No," Yong said. "But sometimes you have to make the best of bad options, and it's only temporary. The more magic you feed me, the stronger I'll get. Even if you don't come up with a shortcut, which I'm certain you will, I'm sure I'll be myself again in no time."

"And how long is 'no time,' exactly?"

He thought a moment. "A few centuries."

I knew it. Damn immortals! But other than some general cursing, there was nothing I could say. My dad's fire had taken two thousand years and one devoured sire to reach the size it had been before I'd drained it. Of *course* it couldn't be rebuilt in a few days, or weeks, or months, or reasonable human lifetimes. I just wished I shared my father's faith that I'd figure something out.

"It'll be fine," Dr. Kowalski said, patting me on the shoulder. "You're a fantastic mage! Even if you don't come up with a solution for rapid dragon refill, you're bound to get better at the transfer process. In fact, let's work on that right now."

"What?" I looked around at the sun-drenched garden. "You mean here?"

"This *is* your practice time," she said, sitting down on a stump that had been left artistically in the middle of a bed of crawling violets. "So let's practice! You haven't done any difficult casting all morning, and the DFZ tells me you're off this afternoon for some kind of sporting event."

I nodded as much for myself as to her. In the craziness, I'd almost forgotten that tonight was Nik's fight. Remembering made me even less eager to give my dad a transfer that would leave me exhausted. I didn't know much about it, but the Gameskeeper's arena definitely didn't sound like a place I wanted to walk into empty. That said, I *did* need to feed him, and Dr. Kowalski was right here…

"Okay, let's do it."

"Excellent!" my teacher said, rubbing her hands together. "Do it slowly, please. I want to see exactly how you transform the magic."

I nodded and lifted my hands, focusing on my father's real body since his smoke one made me twitchy. Our connection was in my mind, anyway, so it didn't really matter where I pointed my hands, but it was the principle of the thing. I wanted to feel like I was healing my father for real, not putting a bandage over a wound that I was starting to worry would never actually close.

But those sorts of thoughts only made an already hard job harder, so I forced them away, reaching for the warm magic of the garden instead as I closed my eyes and embraced the memory of fire.

Chapter 7

I ended up transferring magic to my dad three times over the next two hours. I didn't think I had it in me to be honest, but as Dr. Kowalski had predicted, the process got easier the more I did it. It was still exhausting, but knowing that Dr. Kowalski was watching encouraged me to keep my form perfect, which helped to mitigate the strain. She also praised me extensively, which—not gonna lie—was a *huge* factor.

What can I say? Praise from authority figures was a new experience for me. One I was apparently willing to exhaust myself for, because even after the second transfer left me ready to fall over, I dug down deep and somehow managed to pull off a third.

It worked too. By the time I flopped over in a heap, my dad was doing much better. His physical body no longer looked like a cancer patient's, and his smoke form was fully opaque and much less susceptible to wind. His mood had improved as well. I hadn't realized just how maudlin and droopy he'd gotten until he started pulling himself up straight and looking down his nose again like the proud dragon I remembered. That was a mixed bag for me since, in hindsight, I was pretty sure his weakness and vulnerability was what had enabled us to actually work on our problems, but it was still comforting to see my dad not looking like he was on death's door.

His new vigor also made him *much* more helpful. Not only did he get back into his body to finish weeding the garden while I panted on the ground between sessions, he even walked himself up the stairs to Dr. Kowalski's spare bedroom-slash-storage-room in the attic. Good thing, too, since I'd had no idea how Dr. K and I were going to carry him over all the boxes she'd stacked in front of the bed. Thankfully, my dad was back to his old nimbleness. He hopped right over the obstacles and stretched out on top of the dusty twin mattress with only the barest minimum of snooty looks.

"There," he said, rising in a smoke cloud from his chest the moment his body was settled. "I should be fine for the evening."

"Your body will be perfectly safe up there," Dr. Kowalski assured us from down the ladder, which was too narrow and rickety to hold more than one person at a time. "No one comes here without the DFZ's explicit permission except the Great Seer of the Heartstrikers, and he only shows up on Tuesdays for his vegetable order."

My father scowled at that unwelcome information.

"You don't have to leave your body here if you don't want to," I whispered.

"No," Yong said, shaking his smoky head. "I'm better than I was, but everything I said before remains true. Until I'm strong enough to hold my own against another dragon, this is by far the safest form. It's also a good opportunity to practice."

I blinked. "Practice?"

My father grinned, the smoke doing nothing to soften the predatory display of teeth. "I've never heard of a dragon who was able to leave their body before. If I can survive this trial *and* maintain my ability to dislocate myself, I'll have gained a new strategic weapon that none of my enemies will know to expect."

I snorted. "Leave it to a dragon to weaponize being turned into smoke."

"Let no defeat go to waste," Yong replied in a sage voice, flitting through the stacked boxes. "Anything you survive makes you stronger. That's why old dragons are the most dangerous."

I rolled my eyes. Yep, my dad was definitely back in business. But if he was comfortable, then we were done here. It was already two thirty, two and a half hours past the end of my typical morning training window. Usually the DFZ would have shown up by now to check on me, but I hadn't heard so much as a whisper from my god, so I guessed she wasn't coming. Odd since she'd specifically requested I bring her along for tonight's fight, but whatever. She was a spirit, so she could do what she wanted. Meanwhile, I was going to stuff some food in my face and get out of here.

It felt callous to be so excited. As stressful as watching Nik fight for his life in an arena was bound to be, though, this was my first afternoon off in eight weeks. I'd lost two and a half hours already, like hell was I wasting another second. I ate the kale salad Dr. Kowalski had made for me as fast as physically possible and bolted, racing back to my apartment to change out of my jeans and into…well, another pair of jeans since DFZ-provided work wear was all I had right now.

My bedroom door was closed when I arrived. After what Dr. K had said about renovations, I didn't dare open it. Fortunately, the DFZ had moved the door to my bathroom to the living room, so I wasn't cut off from my necessities. I washed up and started digging through my plastic drawers to find the pair of jeans that looked the least like I was wearing two denim sacks on my legs. I didn't exactly have a lot to choose from, but after thirty minutes of trying things on, I'd identified the nicest version of my usual uniform of thick jeans, plain T-shirt, and work boots. Not exactly fashionable, but I had no idea what you wore to a death arena. For all I knew, this *was* the look.

In the end, it didn't even matter. I could have gone naked and no one would have known thanks to the giant magical security poncho I dug out of my closet. I shook out the dust and tossed it over my shoulders, covering myself from neck to calf in voluminous spellworked plastic sheeting that, while even less stylish than my jeans, at least had the benefit of looking expensive.

My father nodded approvingly when he saw it. "Nice to know you kept something we gave you."

"I'm not that petty," I said, petting my poncho lovingly. "This baby has saved my bacon more times than I can count. I didn't need it when I was working in the DFZ's controlled areas, but like hell am I going into an Underground arena without covering my butt. And most of the rest of my body."

"The poncho does make it much more likely that you'll get pickpocketed, though," Sibyl said in my earpiece. "Expensive protections imply you've got something worth stealing."

"They're welcome to try," I said haughtily, sliding my goggles down over my eyes so I'd have the full benefit of my AR and cameras. "I'm a priestess of the DFZ. So long as we're inside the city, anything they steal will just end up right back in my pocket."

"You sure about that?"

I wasn't, but the DFZ had told me numerous times she took care of her own. To be honest, I almost wanted someone to try. I wasn't the desperate, slapdash mage I'd been before. If someone put a gun in my face this time, I'd slam it right back into theirs.

"I love the confidence," Sibyl said, flashing a map of Rentfree into my AR field. "But we're going into the part of the Underground with the highest homicide rate in the western hemisphere, so maybe tone down the violent urges?"

The map she was showing me did look alarmingly red. "Is this up to date?"

"*Everything's* up to date!" my AI said delightedly. "Once you okayed my internet usage, I patched and updated everything that could be patched or updated. We are once more fully compliant and backed up to the cloud, baby!"

"Good for us," I said, reaching out to grab my doorknob. "Ready?"

"Depends," my father said. "Are you talking to me or one of the voices in your head?"

I shrugged. "It was a general query. But since you didn't say you *weren't…*"

I turned the knob and pushed my door open, holding a location rather than an image in my head since I didn't actually have a picture for where I wanted to go. It was the most open-ended request I'd ever used for this spell, but after last night's adventures and opening a door straight into Nik's car, I was feeling much more confident about my city-bending abilities. Sure enough, my door opened straight into Rentfree. Onto the main entry bridge specifically, which was a surprise but really shouldn't have been since the bridge suspended over the chasm was *exactly* what I'd pictured in my mind.

Stupid choice in hindsight since there were no doors on the bridge, but it was the part of Rentfree I'd remembered best. And anyway, it had worked! Despite all impossibility, my door opened directly out of the back of one of the welded iron struts that kept the suspended stretch of asphalt from plummeting into the abyss. Below us, the pit of Rentfree stretched down even deeper than I remembered, its steep walls made of stacked buildings grinding slowly against each other like rotors in a giant machine.

My father must not have expected the sudden verticality, because he grabbed the metal cable that served as the bridge's railing with a jerk, nearly falling over the edge when his smoke hand passed right through it. "Where is this place?" he asked when he'd scrambled back to my side.

"The bottom of the Underground," I replied, looking around at the pedestrian bridge my spell had plopped us in the middle of. "And it's *packed*."

Rentfree had been busy when Nik and I had come here for the Night Lot, but that was nothing on what I saw now. The bridge was so crammed with people, I feared for its structural safety even more than usual. The teeming crowd looked to be evenly split between gawking tourists and Rentfree denizens making money off them, but it was hard to tell for sure through the mass of AR advertisements that started blanketing my vision a few seconds later.

"*Sibyl!*"

"Sorry, sorry," my AI said in a rushed voice. "I installed the latest ad blocker, but the bots down here are the most aggressive in the city. I just need to—there!"

The wall of pop-ups vanished from my vision, and I breathed a sigh of relief. But while offers for discount massage parlors and too-cheap-to-be-trusted firearms were no longer flying at my face, Sibyl couldn't do anything about the projected billboards floating in the shared AR above our heads, many of which featured Nik's scowling face.

"Huh," I said, craning my neck back for a better look at the flickering images. "Guess this fight is a big deal."

"Huge," Sibyl confirmed. "Campaigns are running on every platform, and just look at the crowd! According to DFZ CrowdWatch, this is big even for a Saturday, and Saturday is Rentfree's biggest day."

I'd actually forgotten that it was Saturday—that's what happens when every day is a workday—but it made sense to put your biggest fight on the night most people could attend. The tourists here also looked more international than the ones in Loveland. Most of the gawkers there had been Michiganders hopping the border for a night of debauchery, but Rentfree was famous all over the world. Tourism companies marketed it as the place you went to experience the DFZ Underground at its most concentrated, and it certainly lived down to its reputation. The businesses here were so seedy they bordered on parody. One strip club even had a huge neon sign offering a free gun for every hour you spent in the VIP room.

"Charming," my father said, turning away from the blinking lights to arch a smoky eyebrow at me. "*This* is the god you serve?"

"It's not all like this," I said angrily. "The downside of being a city of free will is sometimes people use their freedom to do shitty, destructive things. Nothing the DFZ can do about it."

Even as I defended her, though, I wasn't sure I believed my own words. Every city had bad neighborhoods, but Rentfree was the worst. I'm no prude, but there's a level of seediness where it stops being dirty fun and starts feeling abusive. Rentfree had always been on the wrong side of that line for me. Case in point, some of the prostitutes working the crowd in front of us looked *really* young and hella drugged out, and while sex work was a personal choice in a city which held that sacred, that didn't seem like a good thing.

I paused a moment to see if my god was going to comment, but the place in my head where the city usually spoke remained silent. Frowning in disappointment, I put a hand in my pocket to protect my phone and started working my way into the crowd. Nik's fight wasn't due to start for several hours, but you never knew how long travel in a mess like this was going to take. Fortunately, all of the foot traffic was flowing in the same direction, which was the one I wanted.

Good thing, too, because once I was in the mix, I couldn't have turned around if my life had depended on it. The sweep of excitedly babbling tourists and street hawkers caught me up like I was a leaf in a river. The only choice I got to make was whether I took the elevators or the stairs down to the bottom of Rentfree's giant urban canyon where the circular arena was nestled like a pearl, its domed surface lit up with giant moving advertisements showcasing the extreme violence that would soon be taking place within. Unlike the flashing ads that still danced at the edge of my vision despite Sibyl's valiant ad blocking, these images were projected in actual light on a real physical surface, which meant my dad—who, as a floating spirit made of smoke, had no AR—could see them too. From the look on his face, though, he'd rather not.

"Blood sports have always appealed to the masses," he said as we walked down the brightly lit metal stairwell because there was no way in hell I was trusting my life to a Rentfree elevator. "But this is ridiculous. They just showed a man being decapitated."

"That's how it is here," I replied quietly, suddenly far more worried about what was in store for Nik. "Pretty much anything is allowed in the DFZ so long as both parties consent, up to and including fights to the death. It's what gives the Underground arenas their competitive edge internationally."

"Arenas," my father said, his voice surprised. "You mean there's more than one?"

I nodded. There were plenty of places you could pay to watch people kill each other in the Underground, but none were as famous or as big as the one we were climbing down toward. I generally stayed away from the industry because yuck, but after Nik had mentioned his past the last time we were here, I'd done a bit of research, and apparently the Gameskeeper's Arena was an institution. It was as old as Rentfree itself, and its fights were broadcast all over the world, or at least to the countries where livestreams of people being disemboweled weren't illegal.

That international appeal was one of the biggest reasons anyone down here made money. The arena crowds dwarfed the Night Lot's pull, and according to the numbers Sibyl had just pulled up in response to my curiosity, they spent a *lot* more. Standing in the middle of a fight-night rush, I could totally see why. Everyone down here, no matter their age, was acting like a college kid on Spring Break. I was pretty sure my dad and I were the only sober ones in the whole place, including the street vendors. Seriously, *everyone* we passed looked drunk or high or both.

Given our run-in with Maggie last time, that shouldn't have surprised me. Even Nik had said he'd been on a lot of stuff when he'd lived here. I didn't know if that was just the culture or if being high was necessary for coping with life in Rentfree. Maybe it was both.

At least the view was interesting. The enclosed spiral staircase leading down to the arena was as plastered with advertising as everything else here, but there were still plenty of gaps I could look through to see the cliff-wall of moving buildings we were walking past. They were *really* moving, too, their constant grinding causing the metal staircase to vibrate like a bandsaw under my boots.

"Why do they move so much?" my father asked, sticking his smoke head through the grate to get a better look at the buildings whirling by.

"This is the DFZ's staging area," I explained authoritatively. "The place where she stashes all the buildings that are due to move into or out of the wider city, but which aren't quite ready for final placement yet. It's a place of constant instability and change, but she still wants people to live here, so she doesn't charge rent. Hence the name 'Rentfree.'"

"I knew that much," Yong said, which was a shock. I'd thought my father had steadfastly avoided learning anything about the DFZ. "I meant, why do they move *all the time*?" He pointed through the wire mesh at the wall buildings that had been shifting constantly since we got here. "See? If it was really just staging, you'd expect the buildings to move off to their final locations, but they don't. They just spin in circles, like teeth in a giant gear. They're not going anywhere." He scowled. "It makes no sense. Even for the spirit of a city, moving something as huge and immobile as a building has to be prohibitively difficult, so why is she doing it? What's the point?"

I didn't know. The staging area thing was just what I'd always heard. Now that my dad mentioned it, all that movement did seem pretty wasteful, not to mention obnoxious. I couldn't imagine living in a building that never stood still. Apparently I was in the minority, though, because every window that went by us had something inside. Sometimes it was a family eating dinner, sometimes it was a bunch of squatters passed out on cardboard boxes, sometimes it was a nest of wire bats chewing on electrical cables, but there was always *something*.

Clearly, the lure of free rent was stronger than the inconvenience of living in a place that spun like a top. Hell, for a lot of people, having an eternally shifting address was probably a bonus. If you were looking to disappear, sleeping in a room that was never in the same place twice definitely gave you a leg up, which might have been why she did it. The DFZ did prize herself as being a place where anyone could start over, after all.

That was the sort of thought that usually prompted a response from my god. When I turned my attention her direction, though, the place where the god spoke in my head was quiet. So much so that I was starting to worry she wasn't there.

"Is something wrong?" my father asked. "It's not like you to be quiet."

"I'm fine," I said, pushing up my goggles to rub my suspiciously empty temples. "Just nervous."

There was certainly plenty to be nervous about. After what had to be a hundred spirals, we were finally nearing the bottom of the stairs, stepping out of the enclosed mesh tunnel into a huge, brightly lit, hawker-filled ticketing yard.

The chaos down here was even thicker than it had been at the entrance. We were standing at the very bottom of the Rentfree chasm, which was *much* bigger than it had looked from the bridge. Beside us, the Gameskeeper's Arena rose like the humped back of a giant sleeping animal, its huge rows of doors thrown open to accommodate the ocean of people who were already swarming inside. In front of those were the ticketing booths, their snaking lines caged in by a labyrinth of street carts and food stalls. People were running everywhere, jumping from line to line as they searched desperately for the one with the shortest wait.

This seemed silly to me since surely everyone had reserved their seats through the online interface already. When I sent Sibyl to ping Will Call for the ticket Nik had said he'd save me, though, my AI informed me that there was no online interface. All arena tickets were *paper* and sold *in person* the *night of*.

"Physical tickets only?" I repeated in disbelief. "What is this, the Dark Ages?"

"That's just how they do things here," Sibyl said mournfully. "I told you this place was terrible!"

Cursing under my breath, I got up on my toes to try and find the Will Call booth over the crowd, but all I could see were heads. I was taking off my goggles to hold them up so Sibyl could find it using my cameras when my father's voice spoke over my head.

"It's that way."

I glanced up in surprise to find him floating several feet off the ground. An unnecessary move since his inhuman height already put his eye level well above the mortal crowd, but one he was clearly extraordinarily pleased with.

"Show-off."

"One makes use of what one has," Yong replied as he floated even higher, hovering above me like a smug dragon cloud as I elbowed my way through the never-ending wall of promoters, scalpers, and T-shirt sellers to the end of the Will Call line.

By the time I made it to the actual window, I'd been pitched everything from a private lap dance to boxing lessons to a condo in the flooded ruins of what was left of Florida. The hawkers were pretty good about taking no for an answer once you said it three times, but there were so damn many of them. The digital sellers were bombarding Sibyl as well, leaving my poor AI struggling to fend off the sales-bot stampede.

The only good thing I could say about the experience was that at least there was no hassle getting my actual ticket. The lady at the window didn't even check my ID. I just told her my name and she handed me a bright-red strip of paper with a barcode on it and told me to head on in. When I finally made it out of the crush of the ticketing area, though, I realized "heading on in" was going to be a lot harder than it sounded.

"Whoa," I said, tilting my head back.

Looking down from the bridge, I'd known the arena was big, but it was hard to appreciate *how* big until I was standing in front of it. I'd assumed it would be the size of a normal sports dome, but the Gameskeeper's Arena was actually bigger than any stadium I'd seen. Not only was it ridiculously tall, its white-domed center was surrounded by a fat ring of external buildings that appeared to house an entire miniature-Rentfree's worth of restaurants, clubs, bars, strip parlors, VR arenas, smoking dens, overpriced clothing shops, and anything else you could sell to a trapped audience in the mood to spend.

There were certainly enough customers. As soon as I got out of the ticketing area, I was shuffled into a new line of people waiting to go through the massive wall of doors that ringed the arena's bottom floor. At least this line moved much faster than the first, mostly because no one was checking bags or scanning tickets to prevent fraud. The doorman didn't even scan my barcode. He just ripped my ticket in half and waved me inside, shouting over my head for the group behind me to step up.

Eager to get out of the way before I was trampled to death by blood sports enthusiasts, I ran forward. When my foot crossed the threshold of the door into the actual arena, though, something hit me in the face, stopping me cold. It happened so suddenly, my father actually floated several feet ahead before he realized I was no longer beneath him.

"What is it?" he asked, floating back.

"Yeah, what's going on?" Sibyl said in my ear. "Your heart rate just went into overdrive."

I didn't reply, mostly because I didn't know. I had no idea how to describe what I was feeling, but the moment I'd stepped into the arena, something had shifted. Something wrong, but not with me. It was the city.

I hadn't left the DFZ since I'd become a priestess. I certainly wasn't outside it now, but there was something about magic in this place that didn't feel right. The normally chaotic city magic was gone, replaced by something harsh and jagged and not at all friendly. Whatever it was, though, I was clearly the only one who noticed. The rest of the crowd didn't even pause when they stepped through the doors. If anything, they sped up, hurrying excitedly toward the neon-lit maze of bars, food stands, and souvenir shops I could vaguely make out through the haze of wrongness.

You feel it too, huh? the DFZ said. *I thought you would.*

I jumped a foot. After being silent all day, the god suddenly sounded as if she were right behind me. "Where have you been?" I demanded, too discombobulated to remember to think the question instead of speaking out loud. "And what do you mean 'I feel it too'?"

I have a theory, the spirit replied, ignoring my first question. *But I don't want to color your perception. Just pay attention and know that I am with you. I may not be able to do much, but you are not alone.*

Between her, my AI, and the smoke ghost of my father, I wasn't worried about that, but the rest of what she said definitely put me on edge. "Why wouldn't you be able to do much?" I asked, slightly panicked. "This is your city, isn't it?"

There's a lot of things who call me home, the DFZ said cryptically. *Some are stronger than others, but you haven't been noticed yet, so everything should be fine. Just keep swimming. I'll tell you if the water gets too deep.*

That was *not* comforting, but it was pointless to keep arguing. No wonder my god had been so happy to let me skip work. I was apparently her submarine into some deep shit. There was nothing I could do except keep going, though, because like hell was I missing Nik's fight. I just hoped we hadn't wandered into some unknown dragon's den. Dealing with the DFZ was bad enough. If I had to worry about my dad, too, I was going to worry myself to pieces.

"It's not a dragon," my father assured me when I mentioned this. "Or, at least, if it *is* a dragon, he's exceedingly good at hiding himself. He would have to be good to run a place like this under the Peacemaker's nose, of course, but I don't think there's another dragon here."

"You want to bet on that?" I asked as the crowd carried us forward. "Because you just made a pretty good argument for why this could be a dragon's lair and we wouldn't notice."

"I don't smell a dragon," Yong said stubbornly.

"You have no nose," I reminded him.

"Scenting dragons has nothing to do with a physical organ," my father explained. "It's about power. I can feel other dragons just as they can feel me. The perception just happens to manifest as scent. It doesn't have to do with the actual olfactory sensors. But weak as I might presently be, there's no way I wouldn't know if we were walking into someone's lair."

"Unless they're hiding like you said."

Yong furrowed his smoky eyebrows at me. "Why are you so determined to believe the worst? It's not like you."

"Just trying to justify my sense of impending doom," I said, clutching my spellworked poncho tight around my body in an effort to keep out the janky-feeling magic. "Let's go find our seat."

As I'd noticed from the outside, the Gameskeeper's Arena was divided into two circles: an outer ring where all the bathrooms, walkways, and concession stands were located, and an inside circle where the actual stands and the arena itself were. In true Nik style, my seat was the cheapest possible, way up in the nosebleed section. Getting there was going to require a lot more stairs, but at least the walk wouldn't be boring.

In a normal arena in a normal city, walking to your seat would have meant passing through a gauntlet of cotton candy, pretzels, and overpriced beer. But this was a death arena at the bottom of the DFZ Underground. Just getting to the right floor, we passed ten brothels, fifteen strip clubs, and more drug vendors and VR sex parlors than I'd seen in all of Loveland. Even the bathrooms were pay per use and lined with fliers for call girls who'd come meet you at your seat. Maximum skeeze.

Ironically, the only vice I didn't see much of was gambling, which was shocking until I realized I just hadn't walked far enough. The moment I turned off the main circle and into the wide cement hallway that would take me to my actual seat, my AR was inundated with bookie-bots. When Sibyl cleared them out enough for me to see where I was walking, I noticed there were physical betting kiosks as well, both digital touch-screen booths and actual windows with people at them for the truly old-fashioned.

Even by the DFZ's slot-machine-on-every-corner standard, it was an impressively comprehensive set up. I also understood now why security at the gate had been so lax. This place didn't make its money off ticket sales. That was just to get people in the door so they could get caught up in the *real* shakedown matrix of gambling, booze, and sex services, all priced at triple what you'd pay anywhere else. If I hadn't been stuck in the web myself, I would have been impressed by the world-class money-funnel the Gameskeeper had created. Even up in the cheap seats, my chair came equipped with a full digital display that let me order food, booze, and party drugs delivered right to my seat. There was even an option to buy a direct connection to the drone camera network so I could watch the action up close.

I actually did spring for that last one. Like I said, the arena was *big*. If I didn't pay for a better camera, I wasn't sure I'd be able to tell which of the tiny dots was Nik and which was his opponent.

It was still early, so the seats next to me were empty, but I had a feeling they wouldn't be for long. Going by the crowds outside, it was going to be a packed house. I was perversely proud that Nik had drawn such a big turnout when Sibyl informed me that wasn't exactly the case.

"Saturdays are always sold out," she said, throwing a colorful schedule into my augmented vision. "This is a bit more than usual, but he's hardly the only thing on show tonight. Nik's the headliner, but there are four undercard events before his."

I groaned. "You mean I've got to sit through *four* other fights before Nik even comes out?"

"That's the schedule," Sibyl said cheerfully. "A hotly anticipated one, too, if the comments are anything to go by."

Imagining what sort of person commented on a death arena schedule, I didn't take that as a good sign. "Is it going to be bloody?"

"The program just says the show will be 'thrilling beyond your wildest dreams.' But there's a big graphic of splattering blood, so I'm guessing yes."

I slumped down in my plastic chair. Great. Apparently being here for Nik also meant being here for an entire night of carnage courtesy of the Gameskeeper, the same guy who'd told Kauffman to buy my cockatrices because their capacity for suffering created good on-stage drama. Just thinking about what that implied made me sick to my stomach, which sucked because the horrible wrong feeling from earlier *still* hadn't gone away. The combination was seriously making me want to dry heave, so I decided to try an anti-nausea spell. Nothing fancy, just my own lazy variation of the anti-hangover spell every mage learns in college. When I reached for magic to give it a shot, though, the power slipped right back out of my fingers.

"What the?"

I tried again, scowling as I grabbed a handful of the ambient magic that was always floating around in the DFZ, except for some reason, the magic here wasn't cooperating. I could grab it just fine, but the moment I tried to shape it into anything useful, the power snapped out of my grasp like someone was yanking it away.

"Did you feel that?"

The question was meant for the DFZ, but strangely, my dad was the one who answered. "Yes. The magic is odd here."

"How do you know that?" I asked, genuinely curious. "Dragons don't use human magic."

"Just because we can't shove it around like you do doesn't mean we aren't aware of it," he said, his shoulders hunched as he floated above the empty seat next to mine. "Also, it's hard *not* to feel changes in the ambient power when you're made of magic yourself."

I could see that. "What does it feel like?"

"Like I'm floating in the ocean and the tide is going out," Yong said, shifting his transparent body uncomfortably. "I don't know what's causing it, but all the power in this place is definitely pulling to the left."

I frowned. "Pulling to the left?"

My father nodded. "It is most uncomfortable."

I still wasn't following, and Yong sighed. "Imagine this place is a bowl," he said, waving his hand at the huge arena with its rings of seating going all the way down to the actual fighting circle at the center. "Now imagine it's filled with water that someone is stirring very quickly, making all the water spin in the same direction. That's what it feels like."

I wrinkled my nose, trying to envision it. Not the image itself—I could picture an arena-sized bowl full of water swirling to the left like a flushing toilet just fine—but magically speaking, what he was describing made no sense at all. Even in a city as magical as the DFZ, ambient power always rose from the ground. Some spots were more animated than others, but even in places were the magic danced, it never all danced in the same direction. Natural magic was chaotic and mushy, moving in jerks and swells and hitches, never solid flows, which was why most mages put it into a circle before trying to do anything with it. Even Shamans had to squeeze the power tight before attempting to use it.

The only time you ever saw large amounts of magic flowing together was inside a spell, and there was no way that was the case here. I mean, it was technically *possible*, but if someone were casting a spell using an arena-sized circle, every mage in the city would be freaking their shit.

"Are you *sure* it's circling? You're not just caught in a draft or something?"

"I know what I'm feeling," my father snapped. "The magic is moving left and downward in a spiral. It's also getting stronger. I didn't notice something was off when you stopped in the doorway, but now I can't feel anything else. Look."

He held up his arm, and I cursed under my breath. The smoke of my father's transparent body was trailing off him as if it were caught in a stiff breeze. He wasn't getting smaller that I could tell, but I didn't think there was any way that could be good.

"What the hell is going on?"

That's what I'd like to know, the DFZ said, her disembodied voice shifting through my head until I had the distinct impression that she was peering out through my eyeballs. *Let's see if it gets bigger as the night goes on.*

I didn't want it to get bigger. Just knowing that the already suspect magic here was all moving in the same direction was sending my sense of impending doom skyrocketing. I understood the DFZ keeping information from me to ensure my observations tonight were free of prior bias, but I was starting to get really freaked out.

You'll be fine, the god assured me. *You're my priestess, remember? Nothing bad can happen to you so long as you are mine.*

That mollified me a little, but I was still on the edge of my seat. It was actually a relief when the speakers kicked up with pumping music, signaling the crowds to head to their seats. My dad made an exasperated sound as hordes of people started pouring into the bleachers around us. The seats next to me ended up being taken by a group of six German tourists. The middle-aged men were very friendly, but also very drunk. One of them actually tried to feed me his popcorn before I switched to Korean, waving my hands as if I had no idea what they were saying. They stopped paying attention to me after that, turning their attention to the arena floor where spotlights were swinging wildly.

After all that buildup, I was expecting a circus ringmaster to appear out of thin air, but the spotlights actually went up to focus on one of the sky boxes hanging below the second tier of bleachers. Inside, behind a wall of bulletproof glass, was a very ordinary-looking man. The crowd went wild when they saw him, but I didn't see what the ruckus was about. The man in the spotlight looked like a typical businessman. He wasn't even dressed like a gangster, the usual go-to for people who wanted to be taken seriously in the Underground.

I couldn't make out his face at this distance, but he didn't appear supernaturally handsome or tall or anything like that. I was wondering if he was just some rando who'd paid to be in the spotlight for his birthday when a deep-voiced announcer came on and told us to pay our respects, because this was the man who made it all possible: the one and only Gameskeeper.

My frown deepened as the arena exploded into applause. *This* was the infamous Gameskeeper? The Underground kingpin Nik was so afraid of? Not that you could measure power from appearances, but dude seriously looked like a mattress salesman. He waved and nodded at the screaming crowd as if their frothing was his due, but he didn't say anything, and eventually the spotlights moved to focus on the arena's huge metal gates, which were rolling up so slowly that either the motor was broken or someone had set the speed to maximum drama.

I squinted at the Gameskeeper's box for a few more seconds, but it was impossible to see through the glass now that the spotlights were gone, so I sighed and turned my attention to where the lighting technicians so obviously wanted it to go.

"Okay, Sibyl, what are we in for?"

"Looks like manticores," my AI replied after checking the program.

I blanched. "Aren't those super endangered? And intelligent?"

"Yes to both," Sibyl said.

My mouth pressed into a thin, angry line as the achingly slow gates finally opened enough to allow two creatures to be dragged out into the sand by teams of handlers. Morbidly curious, I switched on the drone-camera feed I'd purchased, and my vision was suddenly filled with a dazzling close-up of two fantastic creatures the size of cars: beasts covered in burnished red fur with the bodies of lions, big black scorpion tails, and the faces of terrified men.

The crowd's screaming got louder as the armored handler teams dragged the manticores to opposite ends of the arena. My still-churning stomach clenched in a knot when I saw it. Even without my drone cameras, it would have been obvious from anywhere in the arena that these creatures did not want to fight. They looked absolutely terrified, scraping their huge claws through the sand as they tried to run away. Watching them, I couldn't understand why the DFZ allowed it. Couldn't she see that this was happening against their will?

I do see, the DFZ whispered, her voice stricken. *But despite their intelligence, they're not human. That means they're not my citizens, and manticores are not one of the magical species protected by the Peacemaker's Edict.*

Forget the Peacemaker! I thought back frantically. *What about* you? *This is your city, isn't it?*

The spirit didn't answer. A few seconds later, I forgot all about her when the handler teams unhooked the choke collars from the manticores and ran back to the gates. Both creatures were so terrified, they didn't even give chase. When the handlers were safe and the gates were closed again, a horn sounded, presumably to signal the start of the fight. I say "presumably" because neither manticore budged from their terrified crouch against the arena's curved wall. At this rate, it didn't look like there was going to be a fight at all. I was wondering how the crowd was going to take that when something shifted in the magic.

If I hadn't been so paranoid about it already, I never would have noticed. The twitch was tiny, barely more than a jerk, but the moment it happened, everything about the manticores changed. Their terrified expressions vanished, and their postures switched from cowering to aggression. Even their muscles looked bigger under their rust-colored fur as they leaped at each other, claws and tail barbs extended for the kill while the arena roared.

Things went south fast after that. I had no idea what had caused the shift, but the manticores now seemed determined to rip each other to pieces. The fight rapidly got so gruesome I had to disconnect my camera feed to avoid being sick. I'm not normally squeamish, but it was a *lot* of blood. Unnecessary, pointless, cruel blood that made me happier than ever I'd talked Nik out of selling our baby cockatrices to this horrible place. The only good thing I could say about the fight was that at least it didn't last long. Both manticores looked dead by the end, but I guessed there must have been a winner, because the horn sounded again, and an announcer came on to tell people to go to the windows to collect their money.

"Barbaric," my father said as the people who'd bet on the winning manticore hurried down to the bookie area to receive their payouts. "Manticores are incredible scholars with photographic memories. I once met one who'd worked in the long-lost Library of Alexandria. They are ancient and wise, and not many are left. What a waste."

I was angry, too, but not about the waste. I was furious that this had been allowed to happen. What was the point of living in a "free" city if a stronger person could just come and take your freedom away? But while that thought was dangerously close to blasphemy, my god didn't answer. Meanwhile, the show went on.

After that first bloodbath, I was braced for the worst, but the next fight turned out to be a vehicle battle between two tricked-out cement trucks, one of which had been equipped with a flame thrower. If I hadn't been so upset, I would have eaten it up. Truck battles were exactly the sort of cheesy, over-the-top fun I'd come to love after a childhood of nothing but tasteful, educational entertainment. But I *was* upset. I was also still distracted by the magic, which definitely seemed to be growing stronger just as the DFZ and my father had said. After the trucks, the next fight on the program was listed as a ten-on-ten brawl between two teams of surgically augmented women in bikinis, so I felt safe closing my eyes and letting the magic flow through my hands to try and get a better feel for its nature.

By the time all the ladies had lost their tops and were rolling in the dirt pulling each other's hair, I'd determined that, whatever this magic was, it was *not* part of the DFZ. The city's magic felt like city: all wet cement and car horns and chaos. But while this power was definitely still frenetic, everything else was different. Where the DFZ's magic was soft and soupy, this power was sharp, stiff, and hot to the touch. I also noticed that, in addition to flowing in a circle, the power here rose and fell with the crowd. Specifically, it seemed to spike whenever people were calling for blood.

That last detail was particularly noticeable during the bikini fight. Though it had been rising all night, the circling magic actually slacked while the women were fighting. It couldn't be the lack of violence or blood because there was plenty of both, but unlike with the manticores or even the trucks, no one in the audience was screaming for the women to kill each other. While they were definitely giving it their all down there, their battle was ultimately just an excuse to rip each other's clothes off. No one was actually in danger of dying, and the crowd was more amused and titillated than frenzied. All of that changed, though, when the next fight was announced.

People must have been looking forward to this one. They yelled so loudly when the announcer came on, I couldn't actually hear what he said.

That turned out not to matter, though, because before he could finish speaking, the whole arena began to chant.

"Bum fight! Bum fight! Bum fight!"

"What's a 'bum fight'?" I asked the German tourist next to me, completely forgetting that I wasn't supposed to speak English.

"It's the best," he told me excitedly, his flushed face lit up in a huge grin. "They get a hundred bums in the arena and send them at each other! Last one standing gets ten thousand dollars. It's hilarious!"

I didn't believe my ears. I mean, I knew what I'd heard, but he couldn't be serious. All these people couldn't *really* be cheering for homeless people beating each other to death, right?

"Actually, it's a very popular event," Sibyl said in response to my shocked thoughts. "There's always a bum fight of some sort on Saturday nights. Last week they had fifty homeless men take on a single US army battle mage. All the homeless had boxing gloves soaked in colored dye while the mage was wearing a white suit. Anyone who could put a mark on his suit got a thousand bucks while the mage tried to keep them all away with walls of fire. Reviewers called it 'brilliant' and 'the funniest thing I've ever seen.' One man claimed it was 'like watching a grown man fend off waves of toddlers.'"

That didn't sound *so* bad. Dyed boxing gloves weren't lethal, and you could tone down magical fire pretty hard if you knew what you were doing. "Did anyone get hurt?"

"Oh, absolutely. The official death toll was seventeen with twenty more hospitalized for third-degree burns. Do you want to see the pictures?"

I cringed all the way to the back of my seat. "*No!* Why would anyone agree to do that?"

"The arena paid all participants," Sibyl reported. "And the Gameskeeper is covering all medical bills, so—"

"This isn't about money," I said angrily. "Seventeen people got *burned to death* in front of a live audience! How is that even legal?"

"Because they weren't forced," my AI explained, flashing up a highlighted section of the DFZ's extremely short legal code along with an advertisement calling for contestants from the back of the arena program. "See? All participation is voluntary and compensated. There's actually a waiting list since, in addition to the prize money awarded to the winner, every combatant gets five hundred dollars just for signing the contract. It's all on the up-and-up."

I couldn't believe it. I'd lived in the DFZ for years now. I'd Cleaned closet communities, illegally furbished shipping containers someone had bolted to the underside of the skyways and tried to pass off as condos, and on one very poorly thought-out occasion, a single-wide trailer someone had dumped down a storm cistern. I'd thought I'd seen the worst the city could offer, but this took the absolute cake. If a hundred men and women dressed in tattered vending machine clothes carrying pipes and bricks and other improvised weapons hadn't been shuffling out into the sand before my eyes, I'd have said this whole thing was anti-DFZ propaganda made up by a sensationalist news team to use as clickbait. It felt too insane to be real, yet here it was. Here *I* was, sitting in the bleachers while the crowd roared around me, shouting creatively violent suggestions to the thin, bent figures as they took their positions. When the air horn sounded, the audience's excitement grew to a fever pitch, and I turned off my camera feed in disgust.

I didn't want to watch this. I understood *why* it was happening, I just hated that it could. I hated the crowd around me as they laughed and jeered at the desperate people clobbering each other for their amusement. It was barbaric. It was cruel. It should have been criminal, but this was the DFZ. Everyone down in the ring was technically acting under their own free will. A sacred act in this city, which meant there was nothing the DFZ could do. Nothing *I* could do.

And I hated it.

I hate it, too, my god whispered in my ear.

I knew that, but these were her citizens. They weren't fighters. They were just hungry and desperate. The Gameskeeper was taking advantage of that. There had to be something she could—

There isn't, the DFZ said, her sadness so vivid in my mind that tears appeared in my own eyes. *I'm not like you, free to choose who you want to be every day. I'm the spirit of a city, the embodiment of how the world perceives the DFZ. I can only be what humans make me, and you made me like this.*

I sighed. Her other priests had told me the same thing several times. She'd told me herself, but that didn't make it any easier to swallow. It just felt so wrong that a city who could move entire buildings and snatch dragons out of the sky was somehow powerless to stop something as stupid and cruel as a bum fight. What was the point of being a god if you couldn't use your power to do what you wanted?

That's what priests are for, the DFZ whispered through me. *We spirits are just reflections, the faces of what humanity deems important, but this has always been your world. Humans are the ones who move magic. The ones who change things.*

Perhaps, but I couldn't change this.

Yes, you can, my god said fiercely. *Why do you think I let you come here?*

My eyes flew wide. *That* was why she'd given me the afternoon off? I should have known it wasn't so I could see Nik. The DFZ didn't even *like* Nik because he took my attention away from her. But this made sense. It was painfully obvious that there was something seriously wrong going on here, morally and magically. I wasn't sure how, but some force had pushed all the city magic out of the arena and replaced it with something awful. Something that smelled of blood. Again, I didn't know how that was possible, but if what I'd felt before was actually true, if the magic here really did grow every time people screamed for blood, then we were in trouble. Because if there was anything this place had in endless supply, it was bloodlust.

As if to prove me right, the magic chose that moment to spike again, rising with gleeful screams of the crowd like a wave in the sea.

When I opened my eyes to see why, my purchased camera feed cut back
just in time to show me the last of the homeless falling to his knees in slow
motion, his bandaged hands clutching the gaping hole in his chest. I didn't
know if he was going to survive that wound or not, but shot or no, he was
the last man standing. The hideous spectacle of homeless combat was
finally over, which meant it was time for the main event.

Nik's fight.

Chapter 8

Even if the program hadn't told me what to expect ahead of time, I would have known this was the headliner fight from the crowd. They'd screamed and jeered at every act, especially the last one, but when the lights went down to let the army of stagehands clear away the beaten homeless, the arena went absolutely nuts. The German tourists next to me were screaming at the top of their lungs and pumping their arms in the air. They'd cheered for the other fights, too, but this was clearly why they'd come. This was the main event, the *real* fight, and the guys in the control booth were making sure everyone knew it. I could barely see through all the kerosene fog and lasers, and the music was pumping so hard, the cement floor was vibrating in time with the bass beat.

But while the intense sensory cues had everyone else in a froth, I was more terrified than I'd ever been in my life. This morning I would have bet on Nik to win anything. Now, though, after seeing the cruelty and unfairness this place was capable of, I was so afraid for him I was shaking in my seat.

Things only got worse when the giant ceiling fans kicked in, clearing the air to reveal the pictures that covered every jumbo screen and AR field in the arena. It was the same two face-shots from the posters that had been plastered all over Rentfree when we'd arrived. The first picture was of a huge, terrifyingly pale man with stringy white hair, a gruesome facial scar leading up to a fake eye, and a jaw so square he could have sharpened the points.

I studied his image because I felt I should, but I couldn't focus enough to even read his name. My real attention was on the picture beside his, an extreme close-up of Nik's scowling face above huge glowing letters that read "Mad Dog."

That was it. His real name wasn't even listed. Just his fighting moniker, the same one Kauffman had taunted him with in the Gnarls. Nik had hated it then, and from the scowl he was wearing in all his giant pictures, he still did. For my part, I didn't understand how he'd gotten the nickname. Nik was the calmest, most patient, least "Mad Dog" person I'd ever met. It must have fit him on some level, though, because the moment his image appeared in the arena's collective Augmented Reality, the crowd started chanting.

"*Mad Dog! Mad Dog! Mad Dog!*"

"Your criminal is quite the favorite," my father observed from his perch in the air above me. "I knew from the dossier I ordered on him that he'd been a professional fighter, but I didn't realize he'd been so infamous."

Normally, this was where I'd get mad at my dad for ordering a dossier on Nik. Now, though, it just felt like a waste of time. The Great Yong was a wealthy and suspicious dragon. Of *course* he'd paid someone to check Nik out. I was far more interested in the rest of what he'd said, because I'd assumed the same thing.

The way he'd talked about it last night, Nik had made it sound like his previous turn in the arena was a part-time gig. Something quick and dirty he'd only done when he'd needed the money. But this was not a part-time reaction. Just seeing his photo was enough to make the crowd scream like he was a rock star back from the dead, which didn't make sense to me. How the hell was he this famous?

"Because he's a legend," Sibyl said, jumping in with the explanation the moment her surface-thought reader picked up my question. "Nikola 'Mad Dog' Kos is the only undefeated champion in arena history. He won seventeen matches in a row five years ago before disappearing at the height of his career. Naturally, people went nuts. It got so bad, the Gameskeeper offered a million-dollar bounty to anyone who could get him to return, but he never did."

My lips curved into an O. That certainly explained a lot about Nik. I'd assumed it was growing up in Rentfree and his previous life of crime that made him change addresses every few months and constantly look over his shoulder. If the Gameskeeper had been hunting him, though, his behavior made a lot more sense. It wasn't paranoia if they really were out to get you.

Given the cruelty I'd seen tonight, I was shocked we hadn't had more trouble in hindsight, and even more surprised that the Gameskeeper had only asked for five fights. If I'd been a crime lord and the escaped champion I'd been hunting for years had come crawling back for help, I would have put him on the hook *forever*. Five seemed a pathetically low number for someone who could command this sort of turnout. Sure, the other guy probably had fans here, too, but going by the screams, the majority of tonight's packed house was for Nik. The odds on the betting boards were heavily in his favor as well. That should have made me feel better, but after all the weird magic, the tragedy of the manticores, and the bum fight, I didn't trust this place as far as I could throw it. If this turned out to be a fair fight, I'd eat my goggles.

"Please don't," Sibyl begged.

I waved her concern away and scooted forward, pressing my goggles tight against my face as the extra camera feeds I'd paid for showed me a movie-style close-up of the combatants as they marched across the sandy—and gruesomely bloody—arena floor.

Given where we were, I'd expected Nik to be wearing a costume of some sort. The guy walking next to him was decked out in full death gladiator regalia. We're talking black spikes, chrome plates, rubber shoulder pads that looked like they used to be tires, the whole nine yards. Nik, by contrast, was still dressed in the same high-necked black armor and guns he'd left my place in this morning. At least he looked better. The rejuvenation bath must have done wonders, because the bruises on his neck were gone and he was no longer walking with the stiff-legged hobble of someone soldiering through pain.

Seeing that made me feel better until the arena camera feed started flashing the fighter's stats up beneath them. Since he was undefeated, Nik's win-to-loss ratio was obviously superior, but that was where his advantage ended. While the big, scary dude did have a few losses under his giant belt, he'd been in more fights, won more championships, and he was packing holy shit amounts of cyberwear. His gear list was literally three times as long as Nik's, which I took as a very bad sign. I might not be an expert in professional arena combat, but even I knew that the guy with the fewest fleshy bits usually won. I tried to remind myself that this was Nik we were talking about, and he always came out on top, but it was hard to be optimistic when his opponent was a foot taller and two-hundred-pounds-of-metal heavier.

"He'll be fine," Sibyl assured me. "The betting boards favor Mad Dog two-to-one. If professional gamblers think he's a safe bet, surely you can believe in him!"

I wanted to, but it was hard to keep the faith when my eyes were telling such a different story. The big pale guy didn't even look nervous, grinning and waving at the screaming crowd like he had this in the bag. By contrast, Nik was staring at his feet, his dark brows furrowed in what could have been worry or thought. I wanted to believe he was planning his victory, but he could have been scared senseless. His stoicism made it impossible to tell.

By the time the announcer finished the introductions, the crowd was going apeshit. The guys around me were jumping up and down in their seats, making me doubly glad I'd sprung for the good cameras, because my actual view was nothing but hairy, waving, middle-aged-man arms. There was a short interlude while everyone was invited to place their final bets, and then the lights lowered, and a hush fell over the arena.

I held my breath same as everyone else, waiting as the spotlights narrowed on the two men standing alone in the center of the circular arena. I didn't know if we were waiting on a shot or a horn or if they were just going to start killing each other right then and there. I was still waiting breathlessly for something to happen when the whole arena began to shake, and everyone in the audience started going crazy again.

"What's going on?" I yelled over the racket.

"Looks like they're changing the arena," Sibyl replied, placing an arrow on my video feed. "Look there."

Sure enough, the ground directly underneath the fighters' feet was moving, the bloody sand sliding out of the way to reveal a circular platform that suddenly began lifting into the air. It must have been a planned development, because neither Nik nor his opponent looked surprised. The crowd, on the other hand, lost their damn minds all over again.

"I knew it!" one of the guys next to me yelled to no one in particular. "They're doing the pillar! They can't let Mad Dog have a clean fight!"

The moment he said it, I saw exactly what he meant. The rising platform the two men were standing on did indeed look exactly like a pillar. The top had risen so high that the two fighters were only a dozen feet below the peak of the domed arena roof, practically level with my cheap seat. The height plus the relatively small size of the circle—no more than thirty feet across—did indeed put Nik at a disadvantage. Unless his arena style was wildly different from the way he usually fought, Nik was a guns guy. Not that he couldn't get up close and personal, but every time we'd gotten in trouble, he'd seemed most comfortable when he could keep at least a little range between him and the enemy.

No chance of that anymore. Unless they were willing to jump off the edge and fall a hundred feet to the ground, both men were trapped on the platform, transforming what should have been an open-ground battle into an aerial cage match. That sucked for Nik and his guns, but going by the two giant axes the other guy was pulling off his back, his opponent was clearly an in-your-face melee fighter, which meant he'd just gained the advantage. If this had actually been the open-ground arena fight it had looked like at the beginning, Nik could have just stayed out of reach and fired from afar. Up on that tiny pedestal, though, there was nowhere to run, putting Nik in a very bad spot. A turnabout which, going by the loud boos that were starting to fill the dome, all the audience members who'd put money on Nik were just now realizing.

"Clever of them to do this *after* betting closes," my father remarked, looking interested despite himself as he studied the scenario. "Does your criminal have anything other than guns?"

"Would you stop calling him a criminal?" I snapped, covering up the waver in my voice with anger. "And Nik will be fine. He's resourceful."

"Even the most resourceful need something to work with," my father countered, pointing at the tiny circle. "There's little room to run up there, and with the ground compromised as well, I don't see how he has a chance."

I'd been so busy watching Nik, I hadn't even looked at the ground. I did so now, cursing when I saw that my dad was right. While the pillar had been going up, hordes of stagehands had been pouring out of the side doors, dragging what looked like giant metal fishing nets behind them. When they started spreading the nets on the ground, though, I realized they weren't nets at all. They were spikes.

The entire arena was being covered in an octagonal grid of what was basically giant barbed wire, except the wire was steel cable and the barbs were two-foot-long metal spears. The spikes weren't so close that you couldn't walk between them, but anyone who fell off that pillar was pretty much guaranteed to get skewered. Add in the hundred-foot fall, and getting knocked off was pretty much guaranteed insta-death. A fact Nik's opponent was obviously intending to take full advantage of.

"Looks like your streak ends today, Mad Dog!" he yelled, pointing down at the grid of spikes. When the crowd hissed and booed in reply, the huge pale man flashed them a rude gesture. "Should have made the smarter bet!" he taunted them, his scarred face pulling into a sneer. "Your champion's fleshy legs couldn't take that fall even without the spikes! And his weapons are useless against this." He beat his armored fists against his chest, causing the metal under his shirt to ring like a gong. "Hear that? My entire torso's covered in ballistic steel! Your dog never had a chance!"

Taunting an audience in the DFZ was always a terrible move. Sure enough, gun shots rang out from the stands as the angry crowd took offense, but the one bullet that actually hit its target just bounced off the man's chest, proving his point. Seeing the bullet crumple made me wince again, because the giant man was right. I'd known it wouldn't be a fair fight, but this entire situation seemed designed to get Nik killed. I wanted to believe they were just making it *look* like Nik was guaranteed to lose so it'd be more dramatic when he didn't, but all I could think about was how surprised I'd been that the Gameskeeper had only asked for five fights. I'd thought the number sounded low, but that was assuming the Gameskeeper's goal was profit. If he just wanted Nik dead, then five fights would be plenty, especially if they were all like this.

"He's going to die," I groaned.

"Don't be defeatist," my father scolded. "You picked this man. The least you can do is have faith in your own judgment."

"But the space is so small! And that guy's axes are like four feet long *each*! There's no way Nik can dodge both of them while firing back, and if he trips, he's toast."

"The same goes for his opponent," Yong said, floating down to hover at my eye level. "Look."

He pointed at the cybered giant, who was grinning at the booing crowd as if he couldn't get enough of their hate. "The obvious move would be to let the bigger man charge and then trip him at the last moment so that his own momentum would carry him over the edge. But while that would be enough against a normal opponent, this man is an experienced fighter. Despite his boorish behavior, he clearly makes his living doing this, which means obvious moves won't work. Your human is the same, which puts them on much more even footing than is immediately apparent. They both already know all the obvious moves and counters, which means they're going to have to try something *non*-obvious to win. That's what makes fights between experts fun to watch. They have to be creative."

I stared at my dad in horror. "Don't tell me you're *enjoying* this."

Yong shrugged. "I've been watching humans fight for thousands of years. It's hard to find something I haven't seen before, so naturally I'm interested when I do." He frowned. "It's a pity this place is so low-class. Whomever is running the fights here clearly has an exceptional understanding of what makes combat interesting. Any two idiots can kill each other, but it takes expertise to make it dramatic."

I made a disgusted sound. The last thing I wanted to hear was anything resembling praise for this horrible, violent place where Nik's life could be thrown away for drama. As distasteful as I found my father's commentary, though, his words made me feel better. My dad hated Nik, so if he thought he had a chance, then he must actually have one.

It helped that Nik didn't look nervous in the slightest. He mostly just seemed embarrassed, standing at the edge of his half of the tiny circle with his shoulders hunched up like he couldn't wait for this to be over. It definitely wasn't the posture of a man who thought he was about to die, and I tried to take comfort in that as the horn sounded.

Despite what my father had *just* said about him knowing better, the very first thing the big guy did when the fight began was charge. He ran at Nik with both axes, practically begging him to dodge. That was what I would have done if he'd been running at me. Just step out of the way and let the oversized idiot plummet to his death.

But that was why Nik was the professional and I wasn't. He didn't move an inch, and a second later, I saw why. The big man *looked* like he was charging, but as I'd seen listed on the screen earlier, practically all of his body was cybernetic. Including his feet, which—thanks to the drone camera's suspiciously well-timed zoom-in—I could now see had retractable spikes in the heels that allowed him to dig into the platform's surface. If Nik had tried to sidestep, the bigger man could have simply dug in his spikes and pivoted to slam his ax into Nik's open back.

Nik clearly realized all of that way before I did. Not only did he not move, he actually hunkered down, dropping into a crouch and grabbing the edge of the platform behind him with one hand. His other went for the giant shotgun on his back, yanking the weapon over his shoulder.

From his posture, I thought he was planning to shoot the charging man in the face. Again, though, I got it wrong. Nik didn't even point his gun at his opponent. He aimed it at the floor instead, clenching his fingers tight around the platform's edge as he fired into the metal under his feet.

The shot exploded into the sand left over from when the platform had been hidden beneath the arena, blowing up a huge cloud. The billowing dust obscured the cameras for several seconds before their automatic particle filters kicked in, but even when I could see again, I still had no idea what had happened.

Thankfully, unlike every other time I'd watched Nik fight, this time I had the benefit of professional commentary. Seconds after the shot went off, a breathless announcer came on to inform us that Mad Dog's shotgun wasn't loaded with normal shells. He'd fired a fist-sized anti-armor drill slug straight into the motorized platform, which apparently used a gyroscope for stabilization. I figured out that last part on my own, because the gyroscope was what Nik's bullet had just ripped through, sending the whole platform tilting crazily to the side as its ability to balance the two fighter's weights vanished.

The unexpected tilt proved to be more than ax-dude's heel spikes could handle. When the platform tipped sideways, so did he, his spikes sliding right out of the false ground to send him hurtling past Nik. He made a final grab as he flew by, but Nik was holding on to the platform with both hands, and he twisted his body out of the way, leaving the huge man windmilling his arms helplessly as he slid off into nothing.

For a sickening moment, I thought he was going to land face-first in the field of spikes and that would be that. But replacing most of your body with cyberwear comes with more advantages than just being bulletproof. Nik's opponent was only in free fall for a few seconds before his body folded nearly in half, moving in ways no natural bones could to right his trajectory midflight.

He landed safely on his feet between the spikes a heartbeat later, his limbs folding in on themselves to absorb the impact of his fall just like a cat's. I still heard a few things crack that probably shouldn't have, but it looked as if he'd survived mostly unscathed. He was actually straightening up to get back into the fight when the rest of the blasted-out pillar landed on top of him.

The whole arena went dead silent. You could actually hear people holding their breath over the groan of the platform's metal skeleton as bits of it broke off and fell to the ground. Nik dropped down a second later, letting go of the ledge he'd ridden all the way to the ground to land next to his opponent's prone body. He grabbed his shotgun from where it was dangling by its chest strap at the same time, racking the pump-action one-handed to reload it before pressing the huge barrel into the back of the groaning man's skull.

"Your armor can't stop this," Nik said, his calm voice shockingly loud in the stunned silence. "I win."

There was a long pause while everyone processed what he'd just said, and then the announcer came back over the speakers, his booming voice sounding genuinely excited. "Ladies and gentlemen, we have a new record! Eight point two seconds! Mad Dog wins!"

We'd all seen it happen, but the official announcement must have made it real, because the second the words were out, the arena exploded, and not in a happy way. Given how many of these people had bet on Nik, I'd thought they'd be delighted, but the shouts drowning out the announcer as he attempted to read back the blow-by-blow were enraged. There were too many yelling voices for me to make out any actual words, but I caught the gist loud and clear. Despite Nik's record-setting victory, that wasn't the fight they'd paid to see. It was too short, too clean, too bloodless. This wasn't what they'd wanted, and they were *furious*.

"*Shoot him!*" they cried. "Don't stop! *Kill!*"

"Uh-oh, looks like the crowd isn't happy," the announcer said, doing his job of stating the obvious. "Will Mad Dog finish what he started? Will he—"

Nik responded before the announcer could pose any more overly dramatic questions. There was nothing he could have said that would have been heard over the shouting, but he didn't need to say a word. He simply lifted his gun off the still-dazed man's skull and walked away, stepping carefully through the field of spikes as he made his way back toward the arena door.

The reaction was immediate and ugly. The announcer was screaming into his mic, but I couldn't even hear him over the full-throated roar of the crowd. Their anger was so loud, I could feel it in my chest. It was in the magic, too, turning the sharp, spinning power into a buzz saw as their cry of rage transformed into a chant.

"Kill him! Kill him! Kill! *Kill!* **Kill!**"

I curled over in my seat, palms pressed hard against my ears, but it didn't help. The arena magic was surging with every word, the force building until my head felt like it was going to explode. Given just how much magic was spinning around this place, I was amazed more people weren't doubling over. Being a mage wasn't exactly rare these days, and the DFZ had more magical professionals than anywhere else on the planet. There had to be thousands of other mages in the arena, so how was I the only one getting hammered?

Because you're tied to me.

I took a gasping breath. The DFZ was always in my head, but now I could feel her in my body as well, her magic humming under my skin as she took control of my muscles and forced my head back up to look through my eyes.

This is deep magic, she said, her divine voice speaking through me bone and blood. *Too deep for normal humans to feel, but you're experiencing it as I do.* She looked up at the swirling power, which was so thick and fast that I could almost see it flying by in a red haze over my head. *I suspected something like this was happening. I've felt echoes of these chants for years, but I hadn't realized it had gotten this big. This bad.*

"This might be a special circumstance," I whispered, turning our shared vision back to Nik, who was still striding away. "I don't think this place is used to being denied."

And I was so damn proud of him for doing it. Proud and terrified. I knew almost nothing about the Gameskeeper as a person, but I'd seen enough of how he ran his business to know there was no way he'd let the night end like this. Something was bound to happen, and the moment I realized that, it did.

All at once, the overwhelming magic flying past me twisted. It was the same jerking motion I'd felt during the manticore fight, but while that one had been almost imperceptibly tiny, this one hit like a car crash, and as it landed, Nik stopped in his tracks.

As I'd said before, Nik was the calmest, most thoughtful person I knew. He was patient, he was thorough, he was practical, he was kind. He was in no way, shape, or form a "mad dog." This was why, when the cameras zoomed in, my first thought was that they'd cut to the wrong person, because the face on the giant screens looked nothing like the Nik I knew. With that horrible, dead-eyed, bloodthirsty expression, he scarcely even looked human.

"God," I whispered since she was right there. "What's wrong with—"

I didn't get to finish. My throat had squeezed too tight to speak as Nik—or at least the thing wearing Nik's body—turned and leaped back on top of his downed opponent. The poor man didn't even see it coming. He was still pushing up out of the wreckage of the fallen pillar when Nik crashed into him from behind, slamming his face back into the sand with an animal roar.

The crowd roared back, the repeating chants of "Kill!" melting into a single scream of giddy, gory delight.

"Looks like we're not done yet!" the announcer yelled over the chaos. "It's the moment you've been waiting for, folks! He's gone *Mad Dog!*"

"*Mad Dog!*" the people screamed in reply. "*Mad Dog! Mad Dog! Mad Dog!*"

And he was. The horrible magic was pounding harder than ever, washing over me in huge waves that got bigger with every chant. Each one felt like an icepick through my head, but I barely noticed the pain this time. My complete attention, my eyes and brain and everything else I had, was locked on the man in the arena. The man who looked like Nik, but who was doing things Nik would never do. Things like grabbing a defeated man's head and slamming it repeatedly into one of the broken steel bars from the fallen pillar until the poor man's face looked like it really had been chewed by a dog.

He must have passed out at some point, because he didn't move when Nik finally stopped bashing and tossed him into the spikes instead, hurling the larger man's mostly metal body with a strength I hadn't known he possessed. Or maybe Nik didn't possess it. Maybe this wasn't Nik at all.

It certainly didn't fight like him. In addition to the very un-Nik-like brutality, which was both cruel *and* inefficient, he didn't touch Nik's guns or use any of the zip ties or other tools I knew Nik was hiding in his armor's bulky pockets. Nik *always* had something tricky up his sleeve. He never attacked head-on if he could avoid it, but this creature seemed to have no plan at all. His opponent was long defeated. For all I knew, the big man was already dead, but Nik didn't stop.

Even after he'd thrown the body onto the spikes, skewering his metal torso in three places, he just kept going, jumping over the huge barbs to pummel the poor man again. There was no purpose to the violence. No point, no victory to win. Just the mindless attack of a mad animal who keeps chewing at its victim long after they've been chewed to bits.

It made me sick to watch. What had started as a brilliant fight was now a bloody mess. This meant that, unlike Nik's actual victory earlier, it fit right in with the rest of tonight's sad spectacles, so, naturally, the crowd *loved* it. They cheered at every wet smack of Nik's fists, their screams rising to the rafters until they were all I could hear.

"Disgusting," my father said, looking down his smoke nose at the roaring people. "They didn't come to see a fight. They came to watch a slaughter."

I nodded blankly, putting my hands over my ears again, not that it helped since the magic was still pounding into me. I didn't want to think that anyone could cheer for this disgusting, pointless murder. I didn't want to believe *anyone* could enjoy this, but I couldn't deny what was happening all around me. Even the German tourists—men who'd seemed perfectly nice when we'd sat down—were spellbound by it, their transfixed faces red and puffy from all the screaming. Staring at their transformation, it suddenly struck me that this was just as wrong and alarming as what had happened to Nik. Why were otherwise normal people so into this horror? What the hell was wrong with everyone?

It's the magic.

The power and noise were pounding through me so hard, I had to close my eyes to concentrate enough to hear her. "What do you mean?"

The magic here isn't just spinning, the DFZ explained. *Something in this place is seizing their bloodlust and amplifying it. Humans have always taken their cues for what is right and wrong from those around them. That's how genocide and other atrocities are possible even though humanity as a whole abhors such things. People fall into temporary insanities when the environment encourages it, and this place has been designed to do just that.*

"But how?" I asked desperately. "How are they doing this? And why? What's it all for?"

I don't know, the DFZ said, and from the tone of her voice, that *really* bothered her. *There's way more magic here than I thought. Whatever's going on, it's much bigger than it should be and greater than any human mage can control.*

That went without saying. If I tried to move this much power this fast, I'd disintegrate. "You're not human, though," I pleaded. "Can't you stop it?"

No, the spirit said, her voice despairing. *Despite being in my city, all of my magic has been forced out of the arena. You felt that for yourself earlier.*

"So force it back in!"

Don't you think I would if I could? There's something in there keeping me out. That's why I had to sneak in with you.

I scowled, confused. What could keep a god out of her own city?

That's the question, isn't it? As I said before, I have my theories. I hope I'm wrong, but in case I'm not, I want you to stay there and watch what happens as things calm down. These surges have been happening every weekend for the past month, but I still know almost nothing about how they actually work. The more we understand about how this magic behaves, the better our chances of breaking it.

I was all about breaking. After what I'd seen tonight and what they'd done to Nik, my blood was boiling to smash this place to bits. I couldn't do it yet, though. With all that magic pounding down the god inside me, I could barely lift my head to see what was happening in the arena.

Down in the sand, Nik was standing over the pile of bloody chunks and broken cyberwear that had been his opponent. He was red-splattered and panting, clearly exhausted, but his body was still tensed for attack. A few moments later, I saw why as a team of arena guards carrying riot shields stormed out of the gate. Nik charged them the moment they came into view, but the men had obviously done this before. He didn't make it five feet before I heard the gas-powered *pft* of canister shots, and then Nik pitched forward as six red-tufted needles landed through the gaps in his armor with laser precision.

Tranq darts, I realized dumbly. They'd *tranquilized* him like he was an actual mad animal. The crowd loved this as much as they'd loved everything else, laughing and cheering as Nik slammed face-first into the sand, and my hands curled into fists.

The DFZ had said this had been going on for four weeks. This was Nik's fourth fight. I didn't think that was coincidence. Nik had been put through this—tortured, enraged, treated like an animal—for four straight Saturdays. Forget magic, forget priesthood, there was no way I was letting any of this happen to him again. Curse or no curse, I was getting him out of here, and I was bringing this whole horrible place down with us.

Glad to see we're on the same page, the DFZ said, sliding further back into my mind. *Keep watch here until the arena closes. The more we can learn, the more we'll have to work with. If anything happens, run back to the city as fast as you can. I'll be waiting at the border if you need me. Good luck.*

I nodded, shifting with new wariness as I realized that I was without divine backup for the first time in eight weeks. Not that that mattered, of course. I'd lived for twenty-six years without a god to watch my back. I could handle a few hours. It was almost over, anyway. Now that the riot-shield team was dragging Nik's drugged body off the field, the crowd was starting to pack up and leave. I watched them go with stewing fury, attempting to remind myself that they might well be victims of this just as much as Nik. That said, there hadn't been any weird anger magic working on them when they'd decided to spend their evening here. Nothing had forced them to buy that ticket except their own willingness to enjoy the suffering of others, and though it probably made me a bad person, I hated them for it.

"You're mad, aren't you?" my father said.

I rolled my eyes at this brilliant deduction. "What was your first clue?"

"You don't normally breathe through your teeth like that," he replied, completely missing the sarcasm. "I don't understand what's made you so upset, though. You knew what this place was before we entered, and horrible things happen every day in this city. You didn't get this mad when your boyfriend was attacked by thugs in a parking lot."

"That was different," I said, too pissed off to wonder how he knew about that. "Every city has criminals, but this is an arena full of supposedly *normal* people." I waved my hand at the crowds lining up to exit the giant stadium. "This isn't like going to a boxing match! You said it yourself: these people didn't come to see a fight. They came for a slaughter, to see others brought low. Nik, the manticores, those poor homeless people, none of them wanted to fight! They were forced into violence, either by magic or to get the money they needed to live. These people *knew* that, and they still ate it up! They *enjoyed* the suffering, and they screamed like spoiled children when Nik wouldn't give it to them."

My father shrugged. "Humans can be terrible."

"Not this terrible," I grumbled, looking up at where I could still feel the horrible magic spinning under the bright lights like a bloated river. "The DFZ thinks it's because of the weird magic here, but no one would come here in the first place if they weren't already eager to watch someone die. It's not like the extent of the violence is hidden. They brag about how many people died last week right there in the program!"

"If you're surprised by that, you haven't been paying attention," my father said sadly. "I'm fonder of mortals than most dragons, but no amount of civilization or culture can change the fact that you're all still animals at heart. No offense."

"You should say that to the animals," I replied sourly. "At least actual predators eat their kills. They don't just torture things for fun."

"Cats do," Sibyl piped in.

"And it's not as if I don't know what humans are capable of," I went on, ignoring her. "Do you know how much gross stuff I've found in people's apartments?" I shook my head. "Honestly, I wouldn't be a quarter so mad if it was just the violence. If two dudes want to rip each other to pieces for the love of the crowd, that's their bad decision to make. It's the exploitation I can't stand. You felt how the magic forced those manticores to fight just like it forced Nik. And while they didn't need magic for the bum fight, using the homeless's desperation isn't any better. It's not a choice if your options are 'starve in the street' or 'fight for cash.' The DFZ says she can't stop it because there's no violation of free will, but there's nothing free about what's going on here! This whole arena is built on people who've been cornered, and you know how I feel about that."

It wasn't until I said it out loud that I realized how *personally* I hated this place. It wasn't just Nik. *All* the fighters tonight had looked the same way I'd felt when my dad was closing in: helpless, cornered, *desperate.* I despised what I'd seen tonight with every fiber of my being, which meant that for once, the DFZ and I were in complete agreement. I might not be a real priestess, but tonight I felt like Joan of Arc. I didn't know how, but was there going to be some divine retribution when I figured out how to crack this place.

First, though, I had to check on Nik.

"Come on," I said, standing up. "Let's go see how much it costs to get backstage."

"What makes you think they sell access?" my father asked, floating down to walk beside me as I joined the crowd filtering down the aisles toward the arena's outer circle.

I shrugged. "Everything else here is for sale, and selling access to gladiators after fights is hardly a new thing. The ancient Romans did it for centuries. You can't tell me the Gameskeeper isn't going to be in that market given how hard he's exploited every other."

"All good points," my father admitted. "But Mad Dog's case seems—"

"Don't call him that."

"What am I supposed to call him? You object to everything I use."

"I've objected to 'criminal' and the arena label he hates. If you need to call him something, how about his *name?*"

Yong lifted his nose as if the very suggestion offended him, but I wasn't playing around. My dad wasn't allowed to disrespect Nik any more than he was allowed to disrespect me. When he realized I was serious, the dragon heaved a put-upon sigh. "As I was saying, *Mr. Kos* seems a special case. He's hugely popular and clearly not under management's control. If he were my mortal, I would severely limit access to him to prevent unfortunate incidents."

I supposed he would know. Still, I kept my hope all the way through the crowds and down five flights of stairs to the arena's lowest publicly accessible level.

It was a thoroughly depressing walk. The moment we got out of the vice-drenched tourist ring and into the actual business part of the arena, everything got a million times dirtier and even more crowded. Sibyl hadn't been kidding about there being a waiting list for homeless fighters. A good fifty people were camped out in the filthy cement tunnel that led to the back offices. None of them looked at me as I passed. They just stared numbly at the ground, clutching their little number tickets as if the scrap of paper might be the last thing they ever held. Seeing that made me even angrier, which I wouldn't have said was possible, but it was hard not to be angry with the crazy magic still beating on me like a drum.

Since it seemed to be tied to the crowd's bloodlust, I'd assumed the power would go down now that the fighting was over. No dice. While the pressure had definitely fallen from its crazy peak during Nik's fight, the magic was still hammering hard enough to make my ears ring.

By the time I made it to a door with an actual guard, I had a splitting headache. I played it off as best I could, batting my eyelashes shamelessly as I tried to convince the man that I was a rich fangirl willing to pay through the nose for "alone time" with the infamous Mad Dog. It wasn't even a lie. The DFZ had specifically told me to investigate, which meant her expense account was fair game. I had six figures I could drop if necessary, and I was absolutely ready to do so, but in a triumphant return of Opal's Horrible Luck, I'd apparently gotten stuck with the one security guard in the entire DFZ who couldn't be bribed.

"I don't care how much you fork out," he said after I offered to just give him my card and let him pick the number. "No one sees Mad Dog. Gameskeeper's orders."

"Oh come *on*," I begged. "You can't give me five minutes?"

He glowered through the glowing AR display of his headset—which was clear unlike mine, probably so people could see his scary face—and pushed me away. "Get lost."

I stumbled back with a squawk. When I'd recovered my footing, I flicked him off and stomped back up the hallway-turned-homeless-shelter, hating this place more than ever. Seriously, why did the Gameskeeper—of all people!—have unbribable guards? We were at the bottom of the Underground. Everything was for sale down here!

"That's probably your answer," my father said when I tried to complain to him. "If you live in a place where no one is trustworthy, you can't afford to take on people you don't fully control through means stronger than money. Also, if the Gameskeeper truly is as well-connected as Mr. Kos suggests, he's undoubtedly bribed every security guard, doorman, and shift manager in this city already. Why would he risk the same weakness in his own people?"

"I hate it when you're right," I groaned, pausing at the door that led back into the tourist area to figure out what I was going to do next. Bribing a guard had been my best option. I was good at breaking into abandoned apartments, but well-guarded facilities were a whole other animal. If Nik were here, I was sure he'd have a solution, but he wasn't, and I didn't know what to do.

"It isn't fair!" I cried, kicking the filthy wall. "I *finally* have money to throw around, and it's not good for anything!"

"It's not a huge loss," my father said. "Even if you did get in to see him, you saw how many darts he took. He probably won't even wake up until tomorrow, so you're not out anything."

"Just because he can't see me doesn't mean I don't want to see him! If Mom got knocked out, wouldn't you still want to go to her?"

"I would never allow your mother to be harmed," Yong said reflexively. Then he sighed, reaching up to pinch the bridge of his smoky nose. "If it's *really* that important to you, I can go and see."

I gaped at him. "How?"

My father gave me a flat look. "I'm a ghost, remember?" he said, waving his transparent hand through my face. "And unless there's another dragon hidden in there, you're the only one who can see me. I don't think it's boasting to say I can walk through a door and check on an unconscious human."

I totally hadn't even considered that. "*Thank you!*" I cried, jumping up to hug him.

My arms passed right through him, but my father looked touched just the same. So much so that it took him a frustratingly long time to get moving, but I wasn't about to push. My dad had just offered to walk into the lion's den for me. I wasn't going to be an *actual* ungrateful daughter by complaining about his speed.

Once he finally did leave, it took him forever to get back. To avoid suspicion, I waited for him in the tourist wing, sitting impatiently at a bar where I could watch the door to the back area while pretending to drink an overpriced, watered-down beer. It got so bad that the bartender eventually asked me point-blank if I'd been stood up. When I told her I was just waiting for someone, she gave me a pitying look and offered me a free refill, which was really nice of her.

I probably did look horribly pathetic. It was now an hour after the fight. Most everyone was gone, and the raging magic was finally starting to drop back to where it had been when I'd first come in, robbing me of my legitimate work-excuse to be here. Even so, I hung on as long as I could. When the cleaning staff had turned up every chair but mine, I finally gave in and left, tipping the nice bartender a fifty as I shuffled out to the deserted ticketing area to keep waiting. I'd just sat down on a bench next to an overflowing trash can when my father suddenly appeared beside me.

"Finally!" I said, hopping back to my feet. "How is he?"

"Exactly as I said he would be," Yong replied irritably. "Out cold. There was a metal woman tending to him."

I nodded rapidly. "That must be Rena. She's his cyber doc."

"She was doctoring a lot more than his cyberwear." My father's face grew dour. "Mr. Kos's status is…not good. Apparently, whatever they did to force him into his 'Mad Dog' state took an enormous toll on his body. Not surprising considering he was performing inhuman feats of strength, but there's a lot of tissue damage. His doctor did not seem optimistic."

I sat back down on the bench. That was worse than I'd been expecting. I knew I needed to thank my father for investigating, but it was hard to speak. Of all my worries, the idea that Nik had been actually, physically hurt hadn't even entered my head. Why should it? He hadn't taken a single blow, which made all of this even worse in hindsight. Nik hadn't gotten hurt because of any lack of skill on his part. They'd hurt him deliberately as part of the show. He was suffering for no reason at all.

"There's more," my father said, making my head snap back up. "When I was inside, I smelled another dragon."

"Which one?"

"I couldn't tell," he growled, frustrated. "It was too faint, and my senses aren't what they should be yet. But there is definitely a dragon somewhere in that arena."

That was news to me, but I couldn't be totally surprised. The arena was a horrible place, and dragons and horrible tended to go hand in claw. "I bet it's the Gameskeeper."

"That was my thought as well," Yong said. "But we both saw him, and he didn't look like a dragon. No dragon has a human form that old and plain looking."

"It has to be him, though," I said. "Can you imagine a dragon taking orders from a human?"

From the look on his face, Yong could not. "Dragon or no, there's little point in pushing further," he said glumly. "They're already locking up, and I'm too weak to keep scouting unless you feed me more fire, which you look too tired to manage at the moment. For what it's worth, though, I feel that Mr. Kos is in the best possible hands. They need him in shape for next week's fight, after all."

That was cold comfort, but I wasn't in a position to be choosy. "He'll be all right," I said, more for myself than my dad. "He'll call me when he wakes up. Meanwhile, I'm going to make sure I've got some good news to tell him."

"What more can you accomplish tonight?" Yong asked, floating after me as I strode across the huge, empty ticketing area back toward the stairs. "It's two in the morning. Even the criminals are closing shop and going home to sleep. *You* should be asleep."

"I'm too angry to sleep. And two a.m. is actually the best time to find what I'm after."

My father looked skeptical. "And that is?"

I flashed him a grin in the dark. "I'm going to get someone to break Nik's curse."

Chapter 9

My address book had a lot of curse-breakers thanks to my crusade to remove my father's bad luck curse. Most of the places I'd found were scams, but I'd saved the legit ones just in case. Some were even open twenty-four hours. Any of the non-scammers could have answered my questions well enough, but there was only one I trusted with Nik's life, and in a rare stroke of good fortune, two a.m. was smack in the middle of his business hours.

"Come on," I said, tapping my foot impatiently as my phone rang. We were back up on the main bridge that spanned the chasm of Rentfree, which was still bustling with traffic even at this late hour thanks to the Night Lot. We probably should have moved somewhere less public, but I didn't actually know where I was going yet, and I was in a hurry.

"Oh thank god," I said when the call finally picked up, but the elderly female voice on the other end wasn't the one I'd been expecting.

"Office of the Forgotten Dead, Carol speaking."

I froze, too thrown off-balance to reply. In hindsight, my shock was completely ridiculous. It was an office. Of *course* there'd be other people working there.

"Is Peter available?" I asked after an embarrassingly long pause.

"Sorry, hon, it's his night off," Carol said in a warm, kind voice that was so like Peter's, I wondered if the Empty Wind coached his people to speak that way. "Would you like to leave a message?"

"Sure," I said, because why not? "Can you please tell him that Opal Yong-ae called? He should already have my number."

"All right," Carol said, then she paused. "Wait, did you say your name was Opal? Like the gemstone?"

"That's the one," I said. Then, because this was the part people always had trouble with, I added, "My last name is spelled Y-O-"

"Oh, I know you!" she cried, dropping the calm, wise priestess voice. "You're the one Peter's been looking for!"

My chest clenched. "He looked for me?"

"He's been worried sick! He told all of us to contact him immediately if you turned up. Let me give you his home address."

"No, no," I said reflexively, waving my hands. I mean, I *did* want to see Peter, and it *was* kind of an emergency, but Nik wouldn't actually be in mortal danger again for another seven days, and it felt horribly rude to bust into Peter's private home on his night off. "It can wait until tomorrow."

"Nonsense," the woman scolded. "I don't know what your situation is, but Peter wouldn't have been this insistent if it wasn't important. He'll bite my head off if he finds out I had you on the phone and didn't send you over."

I couldn't imagine Peter biting anyone's head off. I'd never even heard him raise his voice, but she was clearly serious because an address appeared in my texts a second later.

"There," she said. "I've already sent him a message letting him know you're on your way. I have to get back to work, but I wish you the best of luck with whatever you're going through, Opal."

"Same to you," I said awkwardly, but she'd already hung up, leaving me staring at Peter's home address.

"What do you want to do?" Sibyl asked. "Should I try cross-referencing the address for a home phone?"

"Don't bother," I said with a sigh, pushing my goggles up on my face. "He's already expecting us. It'll be rude if we don't show up now."

Sibyl's icon flickered in the AI equivalent of a shrug. "Up to you. I've put the address on your map. Shouldn't be hard to get to. It's not far away."

It was *quite* close, actually. If I'd had a car, Peter's house would only have been a ten-minute drive from our current location. My auto-car contract was still good till the end of the year, and I was tempted to order one up just to give him a few minutes to prepare. That said, I didn't think my car service provider sent vehicles to Rentfree, and politeness notwithstanding, I didn't actually want to waste the time. I'd already inconvenienced him. Might as well go all the way.

Pulling my goggles back down, I pushed my way through the obstacle course of vendor carts that covered the Rentfree bridge at all hours of the day and night to the line of actual in-a-building stores on the other side. My father floated silently behind me, his smoky face scowling.

"I hope you're going back to your apartment," he said when I grabbed the door to a twenty-four-hour vending machine restaurant, which was just a fancy name for a temperature-controlled room with a table and a bunch of machines that dispensed pre-packaged food-like substances. "You look tired."

"I'm not tired."

"Don't lie to me. We're magically connected. I can feel your exhaustion as if it were my own, and while I'm proud of you for soldiering through, there are limits. You can't do anything if you're falling over."

"I just need to check off this one last thing," I said, staring hard at Peter's address before closing my eyes. I'd never been to that particular area, so I had zero mental image to work with, but I'd been getting better at moving through the city, and I needed this to work. "It won't take long," I promised, trying my best to sound confident as I pulled the door open, reaching out to the city at the same time to ask for passage.

I clearly hadn't been giving myself enough credit. Even with only an address to go by, the magical portal opened immediately, letting me into—not the brightly lit cubby packed with vending machines that I could still see through the door's smudged glass—but a quiet, well-lit street sheltered under a ceiling of higher-than-normal Skyway bridges.

Smiling at my unexpected success, I hurried through, shutting the door quick before anyone on the street behind us noticed, or decided to follow. The racket of Rentfree vanished the moment the door closed, as did the door itself, leaving us standing in a small park across the street from an older but still charming block of townhomes.

"Where are we now?" my father asked, looking up at the night sky, a triangle of which was visible through a gap in the Skyways above our heads. Probably why there was a park here.

"Uh…" I replied, squinting at the swoopy, almost-too-elegant-to-read letters on the metal sign. "Looks like Laurel Grove." I smiled at the cluster of well-maintained, uniform-but-just-different-enough-to-have-character townhomes. "Looks like an old boom community. Nice to see one that's been kept up."

My father arched a smoky eyebrow. "Boom community?"

"Thirty years ago, before the DFZ woke up and took back her city, there was a real estate explosion in the Underground," I explained, striding across the park's trimmed grass toward the street. "A bunch of developers came in from the US and Canada and started trying to gentrify the areas under the richer parts of the Skyways. This was back before the city moved around all the time and you could actually plan where you wanted a community to be. They built dozens of these compact luxury communities priced for people who wanted the Skyway lifestyle but couldn't afford the rent. Business was booming until the DFZ kicked Algonquin out and seized all the land. With nothing left to sell, the real estate moguls fled, the rich people went back up to the Skyways, and all the units they left behind became housing for the Underground's middle class."

My father looked more skeptical than ever. "The Underground has a middle class?"

"Of course it does," I said, insulted. "We might not be anyone's dream location, but we've got managers and shop owners and office workers just like everywhere else. Those people have to live somewhere, and developments like these are pretty nice spots." I smiled over my shoulder at the obviously well-loved play equipment in the park behind us. "Really nice, actually. I don't get to go to places like this often."

"Because they're so rare?"

"Because they don't come up at Cleaning auctions. The waiting list for places this nice is usually a year or more, and people patient enough to wait that long for a quality apartment generally don't skip out on their rent."

My father scowled. "How do you know so much about this city? Is it part of your priesthood?"

"No, it's part of living and working here for years," I said with a grin. "The DFZ isn't all death arenas and tourist traps. There are nice places and normal people too." And man, after tonight, it was damn good to remember that.

We crossed the quiet street without incident. When we were safe on the opposite sidewalk, I pulled out my phone to see which of the neat little townhouses was Peter's. I was sure Laurel Grove didn't meet my father's definition of "nice," but I thought it was charming. All of the developer's luxury signifiers like decorative tile and ornate metalwork were long gone, but the buildings themselves looked sound and well lived-in. There were bikes on the sidewalk where kids had abandoned them and free-standing sunlamps people had put up so they could grow gardens even in the shadow of the Skyways. The whole place just reeked of wholesomeness, and while that wasn't normally my scene, I was loving it after the violent depravity of the arena.

"It is…quaint," my father admitted as we walked toward the townhouse whose number matched the one on Peter's address. "Though it hardly looks like the sort of place a professional curse-breaker would do business."

"Oh, Peter's not a professional curse-breaker," I said quickly. "He's a priest of the Empty Wind."

Yong stopped in his tracks. "You're going to the home of a *death priest?*"

I opened my mouth to launch a full-throated defense of Peter's profession but thought better of it at the last second. There was nothing to defend. Peter *was* the priest of a death god, and proudly so. If he wasn't ashamed of it, why should I be?

"He's my friend," I said instead. "And an experienced Shaman. He's actually the one who sent me to Dr. Kowalski, and he knows a lot about curses. He's also someone I trust, so don't say anything mean."

My father looked offended by the very thought. "I am never uncouth."

I rolled my eyes and opened the iron gate that separated Peter's little yard from the sidewalk. The area inside was just big enough for a foot-wide strip of grass and a tiny tile patio, but there was a glass wind chime tinkling musically and some decorative glazed pottery placed at thoughtful intervals to make the cramped space more colorful. There was also a rangy orange cat lounging on the mat in front of the door, putting to rest any worries I might have had about this being the right house.

Peter answered his door like he answered his phone. I'd hardly finished pushing the ancient doorbell's squishy button before the door burst open and Peter appeared. He was dressed far less formally than usual in an old T-shirt and what were clearly his around-the-house jeans, which made me feel guilty all over again. Before I could apologize for interrupting his day off, though, he grabbed me in a huge hug.

"*Opal!*" he cried, squeezing me tight. "I'm so happy you're safe!"

I hugged him back, too shocked to speak. I'd been so worried about dragons and gods, I hadn't stopped to think how my normal friends would react to my disappearance. Nik I'd expected to be upset, but Peter's emotional reaction caught me totally off guard. I knew I was awful for making him worry, but it was hard to feel properly bad about it when the rest of me was so touched. Selfish as it was, it felt good to know I'd been missed, and I let myself enjoy it for a few moments while I hugged him back.

"Sorry I didn't call."

"I'm just happy you're not dead," Peter said, letting me go with a relieved smile. "Please come in."

I stepped into his house gladly. Like the front yard, his living room was small but neat as a pin and bursting with color. There was a bright-red couch and a worn leather chair covered in a striped Navajo blanket. The walls were decorated with textured multi-media pieces from local artists. Not always talented ones, admittedly, but the colors were fantastic. Lots of the stuff in here looked local, actually. There was more of the pottery I'd seen out front and a cloth bag from a popular weekly farmer's market on the breakfast bar that separated the living room from the equally tiny white-tiled kitchen.

"Can I get you anything?"

"Coffee would be great," I said, closing the door behind me.

Peter nodded and strode into the little kitchen, pouring me a cup from the pot that was already waiting. "I put some on as soon as Carol told me you were coming," he said with a smile, handing me the mug.

"My vices are well-known," I replied, accepting the caffeine with the same care I would a sacred talisman. "Thank you."

"Thank *you* for not being dead," he said in all seriousness, resting his elbows on the breakfast bar that separated us. "I was worried sick when you disappeared. I knew you weren't Forgotten Dead, but that would have been obvious even if I wasn't a priest given how much Nik was freaking out. I heard a few weeks ago that you'd become a priestess of the DFZ, but we both know that doesn't necessarily mean you were alive."

"The DFZ doesn't let little things like death get in the way of recruitment," I agreed, sipping my coffee, which was freaking delicious. "But how did you hear I'd become a priest?"

"The Empty Wind told me."

My face must have been a sight, because Peter rushed to explain. "My god and the DFZ have always been intertwined. This city is where the Empty Wind first rose, called by all the people who'd perished in Algonquin's flood and all those who still die here with no one to mourn them."

It could be a very lonely city. I totally understood why the Empty Wind would call it home. "I'm not a full priest yet," I explained, eager to head off any misunderstandings. "Not like you, anyway. The DFZ made the offer, but there's still too much of my old life left to deal with before I can decide if I'm ready to dedicate myself fully."

That felt like a very proper, priestly answer, but Peter's reply caught me totally by surprise. "Does it have to do with the ghost that's following you around?"

I narrowly avoided spilling my coffee all over the counter. "You can see him?"

Peter gave me an incredulous look. "You remember what I do for a living, right? Of *course* I can see him. The only reason I haven't greeted him yet is because I don't want to cause alarm. Ghosts get used to being invisible. Being noticed often makes them upset, so I've learned to play it casual."

I stood there for a moment wondering just how many ghosts Peter saw on a daily basis that he'd developed a protocol for approaching them. I was boggling over it when I realized he was still waiting for an answer.

"You don't have to worry about him," I said, pointing over my shoulder at Yong, who was examining the art in Peter's living room with a critical frown. "That's just my dad, and he's not actually a ghost."

Peter's dark eyebrows shot up in surprise. "What is he, then?"

"Not sure, to be honest," I told him with a helpless shrug. "He was in a coma, but then the Spirit of Dragons helped me wake him up, and he ended up like this. We're currently working on getting him back into his body full-time."

"You *met* the Spirit of Dragons?" Peter asked with a look that was equal parts terror and envy. "I've heard so many stories. What was she like?"

"Scary," I replied. "And drunk."

"That sounds about right," he said. Then his eyes flicked back to my dad. "So what would you like me to do? Not that I'm not happy to see you, but you're not normally one for casual visits in the middle of the night. I'm happy to help however I can, but I've never worked with a dragon ghost before."

"No, no, no," I said quickly. "I'm not here because of him. I came to ask for your help with Nik."

Now Peter just looked confused. "What's the matter with Mr. Kos? I talked to him several times a month ago when he was looking for you. He seemed perfectly fine then, other than being greatly upset about you, of course."

Hearing how much Nik had worried over me sparked that selfish happiness again. This time, though, I squashed it mercilessly. "He *was* fine," I said. "But he got himself into some trouble on my account and ended up with a curse. I'm hoping you can help me remove it."

"I'm certainly happy to try," Peter said. "Where is he?"

"Out cold somewhere we can't reach," I replied despairingly. "I realize that makes things difficult, but I thought if I described the curse to you, maybe we could work out a plan."

That was a good spin on what had happened, but it wasn't the truth. I hadn't "thought" about anything. I'd panicked and run to Peter because Nik was in trouble and I couldn't save him. I probably could have slipped that detail by a less observant person, but this was Peter.

"How bad is it?"

"Bad," I said quietly, clutching my mug. "He's got a black mark running around his neck like a noose. Nik says it'll cut off his head if he doesn't do what the person who put it there says."

Peter's mouth pressed into a thin line. "Do you have a picture?"

I did not, which was incredibly stupid. How did I think Peter was going to help me with no Nik and no picture?

"It's okay," he said when I started to shake. "Can you describe the black marks? You said they ran around his neck. Was it all spellwork?"

I nodded rapidly. "Tons of it. All Thaumaturgical in really small, fine text. There was too much for me to read all of it, but I'm garbage at deciphering spellwork equations anyway. What really bothered me was that the markings were burned into his skin in a way I've never seen before. It almost looked like a brand."

Peter's expression turned grim. "I was worried about that," he said, scowling at the countertop. "It's impossible to say for certain without seeing the curse myself, but it *sounds* like Nik is under a Sword of Damocles."

"Okay," I said. "What is that?" Because I didn't think Nik had been cursed with a famous historical anecdote from Cicero's orations.

Peter sighed. "One of the strongest curses there is, I'm afraid. It appears as a black mark on the victim's skin. Typically around the neck, though it can be placed anywhere on the body. It's a very flexible curse with countless iterations, but the basic gist is that the spellwork is tied to a set of mutually agreed-upon conditions. If the victim meets those conditions, the curse does nothing. If they don't, the magic will slice through their body wherever the curse was placed."

"So through his neck," I finished shakily. "How do we remove it?"

"That's the problem," Peter said grimly. "You can't. Unlike other curses, the Sword of Damocles is voluntary. The victim has to allow the curse to be placed on them, otherwise the most important sections of the spellwork won't stick. Unfortunately, allowing a curse into your magic means the Sword of Damocles is able to dig in much deeper than other spells, even in a non-magical person. This depth renders the curse completely unbreakable."

"Unbreakable," I repeated, my voice shaking. "You mean we can't get it off him?"

"Not unless you're willing to rip out his soul in the process," Peter said, shaking his head. "That's why the Sword of Damocles has remained so popular for so many years. It's basically a magical contract. Once both parties agree to a set of terms, the magic enforces those rules to the letter. But it's not all bad news! Despite its sophistication, the Sword of Damocles is still just a spell. It's not smart or adaptive. The spellwork can only do exactly what it was written to do, so while the curse can't be removed, it *can* be circumvented. If you can find another way to satisfy the spell's requirements, the black mark should vanish on its own. You just have to be clever with the interpretation of the language."

"You mean obey the letter, not the spirit?"

"Exactly," Peter said, smiling at me. "Back when I was selling curses, before the Empty Wind found me, I was hired by a loan shark to put a Sword of Damocles on a guy who owed him a lot of money. I wrote the conditions of the curse on the victim's neck exactly as I was told to, but the loan shark neglected to specify that he wanted to be paid in *US* dollars. The cursed man caught the slip, and the next morning he dumped a crate of Fiji dollars—which were worth one one-thousandth of a US dollar at the time—on the loan shark's front step and drove away scot-free. That's what I'm talking about when I say you get around it. A Sword of Damocles is the hardest line in magic, but it's not a flexible one. If you can figure out a clever way to satisfy the rules, the curse will remove itself."

I let out a breath. It wasn't as good as hearing Nik's curse was breakable, but still, I could work with this. Finding loopholes in doomed scenarios was my specialty, after all. Nik had told me the magic would cut off his head if he didn't give the Gameskeeper five fights, but did it say he *actually* had to fight, or just that he had to show up? I didn't know, and without Nik's neck in front of me, I couldn't check, but I was certain I could find a way around. I knew how much legalese it took to make an airtight contract, and there wasn't *that* much text on Nik's neck. I could do this.

"Thank you," I said, reaching out to squeeze Peter's hand. "I don't know what I'd do without you."

"I didn't do much," Peter said self-consciously. "This is all information you could have gotten without me, but I'm glad you found it helpful." He looked back up. "I can still examine him if you want. Just to be sure."

"If I can get a hold of Nik, I'll bring him over," I promised. "But he's kind of unavailable at the moment."

"What's he involved in, if you don't mind my asking?"

My jaw clamped tight. It felt foolish to keep the secret since tens of thousands of people in the arena and probably millions more online had already seen Nik fight, but he'd looked so ashamed. I wanted Peter to think of Nik as the clever, thoughtful man we knew him to be, not that barbaric thing from the arena. So even though it would have made all of our lives easier to just tell him, I shook my head.

"I'll bring him to you if I can," I said. "Even if I don't make it, though, I think I can manage from here thanks to you. The Sword of Damocles can't be removed, anyway, so it's not as if I can make things worse."

"I don't think you'd make it worse," Peter said with a smile. "Your magic looks completely different than the last time I saw you. *Good* different." He smiled wider. "Dr. Kowalski is a miracle worker, isn't she?"

"She is, indeed," I agreed, downing the last of my coffee before standing up. "Thanks a million, Peter. You are a lifesaver."

"That has yet to be proven," he told me sadly. Then his smile returned. "But I pray it works. I don't know him as well as you do, but even I could see that Nik wasn't himself after you vanished. The two of you have been through a lot between this and—" He tilted his head pointedly at my father's shade. "You deserve a break."

"Man, tell me about it. If I can pull this off, the first thing we're doing is taking a vacation."

"You'll save him," Peter promised. "As I said to Nik when he came here searching for you: no one can be truly lost when others look for them so diligently."

"Such wise, priestly advice," I said, laughing. "I should take notes."

"Many years of practice," he replied beatifically. "Is there anything else I can do for you?"

I shook my head and pushed my empty coffee cup across the table. "You've already given me more than I could ask. Thank you again."

"You're welcome," Peter said, standing up to see us out. "And good luck."

I thanked him several more times as we made our way to the door. Peter bore it well, but I could tell that I was making him uncomfortable, so I made myself shut up and just let him say goodbye, promising to keep him updated as I closed the gate behind us.

"He was very pious," my father said as we stepped back onto the sidewalk. "Priests are always priests, it seems. Only the gods change."

"He's a good man and a good friend," I said warningly. "Leave it."

Yong scowled. "I was *trying* to pay him a compliment."

"Yeah, well, you might want to try a less condescending tone the next time you…." My voice trailed off. Peter's prosperous street was as empty and quiet as ever, but I suddenly had the feeling we were being watched. Not that you weren't *always* being watched by someone in this town. If one of the millions of private security cameras didn't pick you up, the DFZ herself saw everything. This was different, though. There was no one on the road, but I could feel the predatory malice sliding over my skin like teeth. My father must have caught it, too, because he stopped in his nonexistent tracks.

"Opal."

"I know," I whispered, striding quickly across the road toward the park where we'd come in. It probably would have been smarter to run back to Peter's, but I didn't know what this was yet, and Peter had done enough for me already. Leading an unknown attacker into his lovely little house would have been a fine thank-you for all the help he'd given me, and I could handle this on my own. I was a (temporary) priestess of the DFZ, dammit. I would not be intimidated in my own city.

"It's probably just a rat," I said as we stepped onto the grass that was thriving under the tiny spot of open sky.

My dad shook his head. "Sounds a lot bigger."

I snorted. "Have you *seen* a DFZ rat? Bastards can be the size of Dobermans."

"Don't exaggerate."

"I'll take you to one of the unlicensed Underground zoos, and *then* we'll see who's exaggerating," I replied, but I was only half-arguing. The feeling of being watched had lessened for a moment when we'd crossed the street, but it was back stronger than ever. Fortunately, we were almost safe. The park we were in had a playground with several structures, one of which was a toy house whose plastic door—though sized for a five-year-old and covered in stickers—would work splendidly for my purposes. I was stepping off the grass onto the woodchips to grab the handle when the dragon appeared in front of me.

I wished I knew how they did that. Dragons couldn't actually teleport, but you'd never know it from how they acted. Even my dad used to pop into hallways unexpectedly, nearly giving me a heart attack every time. I think it was because they were so much faster than the humans they pretended to be, they never actually moved the way my brain assumed they would. However they did it, though, this one clearly had the trick down pat.

He wasn't quite as tall as my father, but he still towered over me by a good ten inches. That was pretty average by dragon standards, though. I was much more interested in his eyes. Eyes always told the dragon, but this one's silvery-gray color didn't match any of the clans I knew. His human form looked like a Viking with thick red hair, a full beard, and a pale sneer. A Nordic dragon, perhaps? Last I'd heard, the Arctic seas were ruled by White Witch and her sisters. They would never tolerate a male this aggressive in their territory, which might explain why he was here. Or I could be totally wrong. Only one way to find out.

"Who are you?"

"It's not your place to ask such questions, mortal," the dragon sneered, taking a threatening step forward. "But I know who *you* are. You're Yong of Korea's brat."

"How *dare* you," my father snarled, but I waved a hand through him. The Spirit of Dragons had said my father's smoke form would be visible to other dragons, but this one didn't seem to have noticed him yet. I didn't know if that was because the Spirit of Dragons was wrong or if this idiot was just dense, but it was a lucky break on our part, and I didn't want my dad ruining it by getting all huffy.

"That's me," I said with a shrug, using the motion to hide my pointing finger as I directed my smoke father into the shadows under the wooden playset. "Brat Yong-ae, at your service."

"Don't be cute," the dragon growled, though not deep enough to make me wince. Whoever this guy was, he was too young to give off the predatory terror my father radiated off like heat. Malice, sure, but no more than the average murderous human stalking you through the night. *Very* young, then, maybe not even older than the mid-twenties he appeared. Not that that meant he wasn't dangerous—*all* dragons were dangerous— but when you were used to dealing with wyrms in their thousands, a whelp was a welcome change.

"Everyone's saying Yong of Korea is dead," the young dragon went on, his silver eyes narrowing. "But I can smell him on you." His nostrils quivered, and a hungry smile spread over his face. "Tell me where he is, and maybe I'll let you live."

I crossed my arms over my chest. "No."

The dragon jerked in surprise, and I rolled my eyes. "Those lines might work on a normal human, but if you know who I am, then you should also know that I was raised in a dragon's household. I've understood since I was a kid that anyone who says 'Do X and maybe I'll let you live' has absolutely no intention of actually letting you live. If you want to threaten me, you'll have to do better than that."

"Fine," the dragon snarled, raising his fists, which were the size of my head. "Tell me where Yong is, or I'll kill you right here."

"If you do, you'll die next," I warned him, digging down deep to summon all the bravado I had. "This is the Peacemaker's city, and 'no murdering humans' is his number one rule. You won't like what happens if you bring the Peacemaker's Edict down on your head."

That was enough to give the dragon pause. I kept my glare locked on him, clenching my fists to show I wasn't afraid. It was a total act. Young or not, being threatened by a magical predator who could roast you in one breath was terrifying. If my father hadn't been here, I probably would have been shaking in my boots, but he was. Yong of Korea was watching me from the shadows, and I'd rather be eaten by a random dragon in the street than give him any ammunition to call me weak.

"I could take you to Canada," the dragon said at last, his bushy eyebrows shooting up in excitement. "No one will care if I kill you there!"

"You're missing the point," I told him flatly. "It doesn't matter where you threaten to kill me because I don't know where Yong is. I haven't seen him in two months."

"Lies! You were seen riding on his back when the city swallowed him!"

"Yeah, two months ago, like I *just* said, but that doesn't mean I've seen him since," I explained patiently. "The DFZ took him because I begged her to save his life, and I've been working for her ever since to pay back that debt. Today's the first day I've had off in eight weeks. I don't even know what's going on in the outside world, much less where my dad is, so tough luck, buddy."

Out of the corner of my eye, I saw my father step closer, but I didn't dare look straight at him or shake my head. I was lying through my teeth, mixing in just enough of the truth to make it believable. But while dragons couldn't smell lies, they *could* smell fear, and despite best efforts, mine was starting to leak through.

"If you really don't know where he is," the dragon said, moving closer, "why are you so afraid?"

"Because you're threatening to kill me," I replied, stepping back. "Helpless mortal, remember?"

The dragon shook his head. "The Dragon of Korea wouldn't claim a coward as his child." He took another step, closing the distance I'd just made. "I think you need to be taught a lesson about what happens to liars." His silvery eyes dropped to my clenched fists. "The Peacemaker won't mind if I take off a few fingers."

"Maybe, but the DFZ will," I warned, stepping back again. "Did you miss the part where I belong to the spirit of the city? She's going to hit the roof if you damage me, and then the roof will hit *you.*"

"Perhaps," he purred. "But the DFZ isn't here."

Frightened as I was, that was too stupid to let slide. "Not here?" I snorted. "Where do you think we are? This is the living city. The DFZ is *everywhere,* and she's always watching." I took a big step back, putting several feet between us this time as I raised my hands defensively in front of me. "Last chance to be smart and leave."

He didn't. Of course he didn't. Dragons *never* thought humans could hurt them, and I didn't exactly look like a mighty dragon hunter. I was, however, a Shaman and priestess of the DFZ. If he thought I was going to stand here and let him torture information out of me, he was sadly—and soon to be painfully—mistaken.

With that, I forced myself to stop shaking and concentrate. The dragon was stalking toward me across the grass. I had maybe five steps before he grabbed me, which wasn't a lot of time given how fast dragons moved. But while I'd never tried this particular trick before, it was basically the same thing I'd been doing every day for the last two months. All I had to do was picture what I wanted and drop down, letting my fingers curl around the long, cool blades of grass like I was grabbing a rope.

Or a door handle.

The moment that image popped into my head, the ground beneath the dragon's feet swung open, and he dropped into the dark. A second later, he reappeared from the second door I'd opened in the bottom of the Skyway bridge above our heads, plummeting a hundred feet to crash into the street behind me.

"Why didn't you drop him into the void?" my father hissed, running over.

"Because it's one of her private places," I hissed back. "She gets mad when people litter on the street! I don't think she'd appreciate me dropping a *dragon* into her personal space!"

I'd hoped the hundred-foot fall onto asphalt would be enough to knock him out. But while young dragons were weaker than old ones, they were still frustratingly tough. This one must have had an even harder head than average, because he was already pushing back to his feet. He wasn't even bleeding when he turned to face me again, his teeth bared and sharp and suddenly too big for his human face.

"*I'll kill you!*"

I eeped and grabbed as much magic as I could. We're talking State-Fair-winning-watermelon levels that I rolled into a ball and hurled into his chest. The blast was enough to make the dragon stagger, but it was uncontrolled and soft. My next attempt was much better, knocking him several feet down the street, but still not far enough.

"You can't keep that up forever!" he taunted, grinning as he dodged my next shot. "It's funny, White Snake's mortal claimed you were a terrible mage. Seems that was a lie too."

"You should know better than to listen to anything involving White Snake," I said, forming the magic into a spear this time before hurling it at him. It was a beautiful shot, catching the dragon right in the chest. He must have been getting used to my magic though, because he got back up a second after I knocked him down, brushing the dirt from his hands as if this was just a bit of fun.

"I take it you're working with White Snake, then," I said, trying to buy myself some time. "How much is she paying you?"

The dragon laughed. "Nothing. I'd never partner with a defeated coward! Everyone saw the DFZ smack her into the river like a gnat. Any reputation she had is mud, and she knows it. No one's seen her any more than her brother. Even her humans abandoned her. I bought your info off one of her men in exchange for a plane ticket out of town."

I shared a quick look with my dad, but there was no time to discuss this new development. The young dragon was closing in fast, his silvery eyes glowing in the dark.

"All of Korea is without a dragon," he said excitedly. "One of the world's richest territories, ripe for the taking! Every clan in the world is at the Dragon Consulate right now arguing over who should get it, but if I show up with Yong's head, everyone will know that *I* defeated him, and all that land will be *mi—*"

He cut off with a grunt as I slammed a fridge-sized lump of hardened magic into his chest. It was my best shot yet thanks to all that talking giving me time to prepare. Sadly, even that was still only enough to knock the dragon back. As he rolled to his feet yet again, I had a new idea. A *much* better one. It would be risky, but this was clearly going nowhere, so I decided to take a risk, closing my eyes and dropping to my knees as the dragon began to run.

It's a terrifying thing, being charged by an apex predator. Even with my eyes closed, I could feel his feet pounding toward me through the ground. If I couldn't make this work, they'd pound me into paste, so I forced myself to ignore what was coming and focus on what I was going to do about it. Focus on pulling the rich magic of the city into me, and not in pumpkin-measures this time. This was going to take all the power I could hold. After how badly I'd hurt myself last time, the thought of using my full draw again terrified me. But it was that or lose to this cocky idiot, so I stomped my fear down and did it anyway, sucking in magic until my soul felt like it was about to explode.

It hurt just as bad as I remembered. Now that I knew what I was doing, I could feel just how dangerously overfull I was, how thin the part of me I thought of as myself was stretched. Thankfully, I only had to bear it for a moment. That was the beauty of Shamanic magic. I didn't have to draw a circle or write out spellwork. All I had to do was not lose control, riding that lightning for the split second it took me to whip all that magic into the shape I'd already envisioned.

The instant I had it, the magic ripped out of me. As it left, I worried I'd pushed too fast, that my vision wasn't strong enough to actually hold all that power together. But all those weeks of practicing must have done something, because even though I'd been working in a terrified rush, the shape the magic took was exactly the one I'd had in my head. Not a spear or a ball, but the streaking silhouette of a train running down the tracks at full speed as it crashed into the dragon who was now less than a foot away.

What happened next I will treasure for the rest of my life. The train I'd conjured was no more physical than anything else I shaped with magic, so I had an unobstructed view of the dragon's surprised face when my spell slammed into him. The moment it hit, he went flying. He would have crashed into the townhouses across the street, but there was no way I was sending a dragon through Peter's front door. There was also no way I was leaving this would-be dad-murderer so close to us on the off-chance this wasn't enough to kill him. The moment the magic left me, I dropped to the ground for the next part of my plan, grabbing the grass again to open a door in the wall of Peter's front courtyard just in time for the dragon to fly through it. I slammed the portal shut the moment he was through, cutting off his startled scream as the bricks snapped back into place.

"Are you all right?" my father asked, his smoke hands sliding through my shoulders as he tried and failed to help me up.

"Am I all right?" I repeated, chest heaving as I grinned up at him. "I'm a freaking *boss*! Did you see him go sailing?!"

"I did," my father said angrily. "That was very dangerous, Opal! Why didn't you run?"

"Because I didn't think I could get away," I told him honestly. Then I scowled. "And because I'm tired of running. I'm sick of being afraid all the time, especially now that I don't have to be. I mean, I just punted a *dragon!*"

My father's jaw clenched, but he couldn't argue. "I hope you punted him far," he said instead. "I'm not sure which clan he belongs to, but he's definitely a European dragon. They're all scales. Tough to kill." He frowned. "Where did that door go, anyway?"

"Lake Erie," I replied, brushing the dirt and grass off my jeans as I stood up. "Given how fast he was going, though, he might end up in Cleveland."

"A punishment indeed," my father said drolly, then his scowl melted into something a parental-approval-starved nutcase like myself *might* have been able to interpret as a proud smile. "That was ably handled."

"Thank you," I said, savoring every second.

My father nodded and turned around, scanning the dark street as if he expected more dragons to jump out any second. "Now let's get back so I can reclaim my body."

"I thought you were staying in this form to conserve energy?"

"I was, and that's still the most efficient strategy, but I'd rather turn to ash than be forced to watch helplessly while you do anything like that ever again."

My father groused about my safety all the time. Normally I found it annoying and condescending, but this was different. This time, I understood he spoke out of love. Grumpy, prickly, dragon love, but that was how we'd always been, and for the first time in decades, I was okay with that.

✳✳✳

There were no more whammies on our trip back to Dr. Kowalski's house. I was eager to talk to my mentor about the Sword of Damocles curse and how we might get around it, but by the time I got my dad back into his body and gave him the dose of magic needed to keep him in it, I was exhausted.

No wonder since it was four in the morning on my second late night in a row. Dr. Kowalski hadn't even materialized yet. Despite being a ghost who technically didn't need sleep, she kept old-lady hours, vanishing when it got dark and reappearing at sunrise. I probably could have gotten her to pop out for an emergency, but no dragons could jump us here, and Nik's head probably wasn't going to get chopped off in the next three hours, so I didn't want to play that card just yet.

"Couldn't play it" was closer to the truth. Now that my dad was fed and we were safe, I was having trouble staying upright. I would have been hard-pressed to follow a conversation about croutons, let alone curses. Even opening a door back to my apartment suddenly felt like too much work, so since my dad had gotten his body out of Dr. K's spare bed, I flopped mine into it, falling into a deep sleep the moment my head hit the dusty pillow.

The next time I opened my eyes, sunlight was streaming in through the attic windows. Shielding my face against the blinding light, I hauled myself out of bed with a curse, grabbing my phone off the floor where I'd dropped it to see that it was almost noon. I'd slept through my entire practice session.

"Why didn't you wake me?" I cried, tossing my phone on the bed so I could grab my boots.

"Because Dr. Kowalski turned off my alarm," Sibyl replied angrily. "I would have told her no, but you left me in open mode and we're back in this internet-less hellhole so I couldn't ping my security server for an automatic permissions update!"

I was too groggy to parse most of that, but I did catch the important bit. "Dr. Kowalski turned you off?" I said, pausing my frantic shoe-shoving. "Why?"

"I suppose because she wanted to let you sleep," my AI said grumpily. "She didn't explain her motives to me. She still thinks I'm just a *phone*."

The disgust in her voice was palpable even through her auto-tune, but I was touched. Dr. Kowalski wasn't a cruel teacher, but she was demanding, and like the god she served, ever vigilant against any perceived slacking. Sleeping in was for the lazy and the weak. If she'd let me do it this time, I must have looked truly dreadful.

I was up now, though, so I finished putting on my boots and headed downstairs to find my teacher sitting at her kitchen table peeling potatoes.

"Hey, Dr. K," I said cheerfully as I sat down next to her. "Thanks for letting me crash."

"You're welcome," she said, sliding her knife skillfully under the smooth red skin of a new potato the size of my fist. "But it wasn't my decision. *I* believe the best cure for a night out is a hard morning's work, but the DFZ said you'd been on city business all night and to let you rest."

I said a quick prayer of thanks to my god for looking out for me. "Where's Dad?"

"Outside doing your chores," Dr. Kowalski replied, nodding at the window.

My eyes went wide in shock.

"I know," the old woman said with a grin. "Not every day I get a dragon to pull my weeds. But he said you needed to recover your energy so you could give it to him. He's also much more thorough than you are, so who am I to complain? Maybe the beans will be properly weeded for once."

Still numb with awe, I got up from the table to get a bowl of wheat berries. I wasn't even that hungry, I just wanted something normal in this crazy upside-down world where my dad did my chores and the city who never rests fought for my right to sleep in.

"Oh, I almost forgot," Dr. K said as I grabbed the kettle to pour some hot water over my raw grains. "You have a visitor."

I jumped, nearly pouring scalding water all over my hand. "A visitor? *Here?*"

I hoped to the DFZ it wasn't a dragon. That would make the most sense given how last night had ended, but I couldn't deal with that level of talking so soon after waking up. When Dr. K pointed down the hall at the front parlor, though, it wasn't the Peacekeeper or the Great Seer of the Heartstrikers or anyone else so huge and troublesome.

It was Nik.

At least, I thought it was Nik. The heavily bandaged man sitting on Dr. K's cluttered couch wasn't wearing any of the stuff Nik usually did. His arm was in a sling, and he was dressed in what looked like pajama pants and a white bathrobe over a pair of muddy combat boots, the only remotely Nik-ish thing about him. But even with his face wrapped in gauze and his shoulders hunched up to his ears, I'd know him anywhere. It was my Nik, and he looked absolutely miserable.

"He showed up in the woods just after dawn," Dr. Kowalski informed me, taking the steaming kettle from my hands before I burned myself. "I had the trees give him the usual run-around, but he wouldn't give up, so I took pity and let him in before he collapsed from exhaustion."

I could have hugged her. "Thank you!"

"Yes, well, unconscious bodies are a lot of trouble," she said, but she was smiling. "But since you're already taking the morning off, you might as well go see what he wants."

I didn't wait to be told twice. I tore out of the kitchen like a shot, racing into the parlor to throw my arms around Nik.

"Ow," he said when I grabbed him, but he didn't make me let him go. "Glad to see the old lady wasn't lying."

"Not as glad as I am to see you up," I replied, pulling back so I could look him over.

It wasn't good. Literally every part of Nik was wrapped in some kind of bandage or cast. Even the thing I'd thought was a bathrobe turned out to be a hospital gown, making me reevaluate my previous statement.

"*Should* you be up?"

"Probably not," he admitted. "But I'd rather die in the woods than spend one more hour in that damn hospital bed." He turned to look out the window, which had a nice view of the front garden where my father was tending the kale bed. "Is this where you've been hiding?"

"Here and my apartment," I said, nodding. "Dr. Kowalski's the one who's been teaching me not to suck at magic. But how did you find this place?"

Nik's face grew supremely annoyed. "I almost didn't. When I woke up after the fight, I tried to call you, but your phone was off. I called Peter next because he's the only other person I know that you talk to, and he told me about this place. He neglected to mention it was a goddamn million-mile walk, though."

"That's not his fault," I said quickly. "The woods around here are…variable. It took me hours my first time."

"I'm just happy the old lady let me wait inside," Nik said, reaching up with his left hand to rub his bandaged shoulder. "I thought your dad was going to yank my head off like he's doing to those weeds when I first walked in."

A week ago, Yong probably would have. I should have been happy that wasn't the case now, but I was too distracted by what Nik was doing with his hand to be properly appreciative. "Holy crap," I said, grabbing his wrist and snatching it away from his shoulder so I could be sure. "Nik, where's your *arm*?"

Nik's right arm was entirely gone. The robe's sleeve had been hanging normally, so I hadn't noticed it was empty until he'd reached up to rub his shoulder. Now, though, the loss was all I could see.

"It's being fixed," Nik replied casually, shrugging off my look of horror. "Apparently I didn't regulate the force properly when I…" His eyes dropped suddenly, and he took a shaky breath. "Anyway, the artificial tendons got shredded. Rena's replacing them."

I nodded, unsure what else to do. "Does it hurt?"

"No, it's a fake arm. The other stuff hurts way worse, but I'll deal."

He didn't look like he was dealing. "How bad is it, really?" I whispered, reaching out to touch the back of his bandaged palm.

"Not as bad as it looks," he said, turning his hand over to lace his fingers through mine. "I mean, everything feels like shit, but it's nothing I haven't dealt with before. It's just…" He closed his eyes with a sigh. "I wish you hadn't seen that."

He didn't have to tell me what "that" meant. "It's okay."

"It's *not* okay," he said, jaw clenching. "I swore I'd never be like that again. I sure as hell didn't want to do it in front of you."

"It wasn't your fault," I told him firmly. "It's the curse that's—"

"It's not the curse," he said sharply, reaching up to press his fingers into the black marks encircling his neck. "I didn't have this shit when I fought five years ago, and the Mad Dog thing happened then too. I don't know why I get like that. I never go crazy anywhere else. Only there."

My eyes went wide. Good god, he didn't know.

"Nik," I said, grabbing his hand as tight as I dared. "You didn't do that."

"Of course I did it. I don't remember anything that happens when I get like that, but I saw the video. That's me in there bashing a man into paste."

"But it's *not*," I said frantically. "I mean, it was you physically, but I was there when it happened. I felt the magic twist."

Nik looked at me like I was nuts. "What magic?"

"Awful magic," I assured him. "I don't know what's going on with that arena, but it's full of the angriest, bloodiest power I've ever felt. You're not the only one who lost it. Everyone in there went nuts. You think people cheer for that sort of horrific violence normally?"

"Yes," Nik said flatly. "Because people are shit."

"Not that much," I argued, getting frustrated. "I'm not saying people can't be jerks, but there's a big, fat line between being a callous asshole and being a bloodthirsty psychopath. Just like you don't normally black out and turn into a mindless killing machine, I bet those people don't normally cheer for grisly murder. There's something in that arena that makes people terrible. I was there, Nik. I felt it!"

He scowled, thinking that over. "It is a horrible place," he said at last. "But it doesn't matter. The Gameskeeper told me when I woke up that he's already got next week's match set. He didn't tell me who I'd be fighting, but he made it clear that he doesn't expect me to survive. If I skip out, though, my head pops off and I die anyway."

"That's not going to happen," I said. "Let me see your neck."

Nik dutifully leaned over, pulling the bandages down with his sole remaining hand to reveal the entire noose of the black marks. "I don't know what you're looking for," he said in a heavy voice. "Peter already warned me that the curse wasn't removable when I talked to him this morning."

"He told me the same thing last night," I said, pulling out my phone since my goggles were still upstairs on the bed. "But he also said there might be a way to get around the rules, so that's what I'm going to look for."

Nik chuckled. "You *are* good at finding loopholes."

I was, and dammit, I was going to find this one. As I'd noted yesterday, the spellwork branded into Nik's skin was dense and complicated. Now that I was staring straight at it, I recognized Kauffman's work. He hadn't signed it or anything, but the pin-neat handwriting was a dead giveaway, and given where the curse had come from, he was the only mage that made sense.

That was bad news for me. Loath as I was to say anything nice about him, Kauffman was a damn good mage. I looked up all the functions in my phone's spellwork dictionary anyway, just to be sure, but as usual, Kauffman hadn't left any dangling threads. The core of the curse was simple and clear: Nik had to fight five opponents of the Gameskeeper's choosing in the Rentfree arena. If he tried to run or cheat or otherwise get out of the agreement in any way, the curse would cut off his head.

"No dice, huh?" Nik said when he saw my face.

"He's a thorough bastard, I'll give him that," I said, sliding Nik's bandages gently back into place. "But just because I couldn't find an escape on first glance doesn't mean one doesn't exist. We'll figure it out. I am *not* letting you die in that stupid arena."

"I don't want to die there, either," Nik assured me, but his eyes were lowered. "It's just…maybe this is it. I've been running from the Gameskeeper for a long time. He said I'd never get out the first time, but I did. I thought I could do it again. Thought I knew what he wanted and how to play him, but…" He heaved a defeated sigh. "All runs come to an end eventually, you know?"

"No, I don't know," I said, grabbing his shoulders. "We're going to do this. I'm not giving up on you!"

The way he looked at me then was something I couldn't describe. He still looked like Nik, but I'd never seen his face like that before. He was clearly killing himself to hide it, but even when he'd been lying on his couch drunk with backlash, he'd never looked so scared.

"Oh, Nik," I whispered, wrapping my arms around him. "It's okay. I won't leave you. You don't have to face this alone."

"You should leave," he whispered, burying his face in the crook of my neck. "I did this to myself. I was so stupid to go back there. I deserve whatever I get, but I don't want to take you down with me."

"You won't," I promised, ducking down to make him look at me. "And *no one* deserves what's been done to you. The Gameskeeper isn't bringing either of us down, I promise."

"You can't keep that," he whispered, his eyes scared. "All the other crazy stuff we did, you always had a plan. Maybe a nuts one, but it was always there. You don't have anything this time."

"I've got you," I said. "I've got the DFZ. I've got my dad. None of us are alone. We can figure this out together."

Nik's answer to that was to press his face back into my neck. He stayed there for a long time, just sitting with his body pressed into mine. I secretly suspected he was crying, but I wasn't about to check. I'd never seen

Nik get like this before, but I was determined to make sure he didn't feel bad about it. Half of him might have been metal, but he was still human, and humans broke down. I'd been falling apart since we met, but Nik had always been there for me no matter how much trouble I caused him. Now it was my turn, and I was determined not to fail him.

"Sorry," he said at last, pushing himself off me.

"There's nothing to be sorry for. Feel better?"

"No," he replied flatly. "But I'm out of time. Rena's putting my arm back on this afternoon. If I miss my appointment, the Gameskeeper will send someone to fetch me, and that's not something anyone wants."

I didn't want to let him go back to that horrible place, but until I figured out how to make good on all my wild promises, there was nothing I could do except help him back to his feet. At least I could make his trip shorter, using the parlor door to open a portal through the forest to the dead-end street at the edge of the woods where he'd left his car. I knew from my own first visit that the walk back wasn't nearly as long as the journey in, but I didn't want Nik standing on those injuries any more than he already had.

I watched from the doorway as he got into his car and drove away, staring down the road long after his red taillights had vanished around the corner. Only when I saw other cars stopping to gawk at the door that was suddenly standing at the edge of the woods did I finally close it, collapsing the portal I'd made through the city. When I opened the door again to step through it normally and head back to the kitchen, my father was standing on the other side.

"Jeez!" I cried, jumping a foot in the air. *Don't do that!*

A normal person would have apologized for scaring me, but this was Yong, so all I got was an exasperated look.

"How long were you eavesdropping?" I asked, crossing my arms over my chest.

"The whole time," he replied without a trace of shame.

I sighed, too battered down by all of this to even roll my eyes. "Then you heard about the curse," I said, leaning tiredly on the doorframe. "I don't suppose your twisty dragon brain came up with anything?"

"To get around the curse's criteria?" He shook his head. "But I did think of something else we could try."

My face lit up. "What?"

"You won't like it," he warned.

"Who cares? I'd eat an entire pumpkin patch raw if it'd get us out of this mess."

My father smiled at that, then his face grew serious. "It will take some preparation, but your god is in on this as well, correct?"

I nodded. "The DFZ doesn't care about Nik, but she wants that arena taken down as much as I do."

"Excellent," Yong said. "Because we're going to need her expense account."

Now I was *super* curious. "What are you planning to do?"

"What we do best," he replied with a haughty look. "Go for the head."

Chapter 10

It was a good thing the DFZ considered this arena stuff top priority, because completing the setup for my dad's plan took a huge chunk out of my cash card and the rest of the afternoon. In a perfect world, we would have gone to the Skyways for everything, but the upper levels were way too risky after last night's attack. Fortunately, you could find anything in the Underground if you looked hard enough, and by the time we returned to my apartment for final preparations, we were all set. I just wished I could say the same for myself.

"Are you *sure* this is a good idea?" I asked nervously, staring at the ridiculously ruffled—and ridiculously *expensive*—dress I'd just pulled out of its garment bag. "It seems reckless, and that's saying something coming from me."

"'Good' and 'bad' are meaningless distinctions," my father replied, tying his deep-blue tie perfectly without even looking in the mirror. "It's a practical idea with a good chance of success. That's what matters."

I bit my lip. Despite the staggering number on the price tag still dangling from his sleeve, my dad's severe black suit was a lot cheaper looking than his usual. It was a huge upgrade from his vending machine clothes, though. My dad looked so much more like himself in a suit and tie, it was actually making me nervous. That said, there was definitely something different about him. Something very not "Great Yong of Korea," and that worried me.

"It just feels crazy," I pushed, picking up my own costume, a pale-pink dress that looked like something you'd see on the "classy" kid at a child's beauty pageant. Just looking at it made me feel ridiculous, which was why we'd picked it. The dress was the exact type of thing I used to wear all the time to all my father's various parties and events. If his plan was going to work, we both had to look the part.

"We've been working so hard to keep you hidden," I went on. "Now we're going to walk into the Gameskeeper's office like nothing's happened? Not to be a doubter, but I don't see how that's going to end in anything other than catastrophe."

"It's a calculated risk," Yong said, carefully biting the tag off his jacket with his sharp teeth. "Last night's attack proves we're out of time to be timid. Up until last night, I considered White Snake to be our primary concern. As my sister, she has the strongest claim to my territory, but no one would accept her as Dragon of Korea without proof that I was dead. In that scenario, staying out of sight until I recovered was the most logical strategy. Now that we've learned she's run away with her tail between her legs, though, we're in an entirely different situation. With White Snake out of the picture, Korea is fair game for whomever is strong enough and bold enough to claim it. Assuming the whelp was telling the truth last night, the vultures are already circling. My humans in the Korean government and the Peacemaker's firm stance against claiming territory by conquest will keep them occupied for a while, but we're already two months down, which means time is running out. If I want a home to go back to, we can't keep hiding. I need to return to the global stage and show the world that I'm not dead, and this meeting with the Gameskeeper is a perfect opportunity to do just that."

I gaped at him. I knew he was a dragon, but that was a *lot* more plotting than I'd expected. "I thought we were doing this to free Nik!"

"We are," my father said, brushing his long black hair with his fingers, which somehow made it fall around his face in a perfect shiny waterfall rather than in stringy clumps as mine would from the same treatment. "But what kind of dragon would I be if I couldn't do two things at once? From what we saw in his arena, this Gameskeeper is clearly a man of business, so I'm going to make him a business proposition to buy out Mr. Kos's contract. I don't normally go after fighters, but the world already knows me as a human collector, so he shouldn't suspect an ulterior motive.

He's also only human himself, which means he won't be able to notice if I smell weaker than I should."

"But what if he's *not* human?" I pressed anxiously. "Remember the dragon you smelled before. What if that's the Gameskeeper?"

"Then I'll fake it," my father replied, turning to give me a haughty look. "If he *is* a dragon, I haven't heard of him, which means he must be very young. As you saw from that idiot last night, youth in dragons is the same as blindness. I plan to play on that blindness by showing him exactly what he expects to see: the Great Yong of Korea, purchasing a human to please his spoiled daughter."

"But what if he doesn't sell?"

"Then we'll raise the number until he does," Yong replied, turning back to his reflection. "Dragon or mortal, everyone has a price. Once we find the Gameskeeper's, you'll get your precious Mr. Kos back with head still attached to body, the arena your god hates will lose its champion, and the world will know that not only am I not dead, I'm back in business and doing deals same as ever. This sort of thing never stays secret. By tomorrow morning, news that I bought the Gameskeeper's Mad Dog will be all over the city. Once those snakes at the Dragon Consulate realize they're no longer fighting over an empty throne, they'll slither back to their holes without me having to lift a claw." He smirked. "We get three birds with one stone, and all on someone else's money. How's that for a twisty dragon plan?"

It certainly was twisty. But while I agreed with all of my dad's logic, I couldn't shake the feeling that this was a horrible idea. No one who'd set foot in the Gameskeeper's arena could possibly argue that its master wasn't a greedy man, but I'd felt the magic he'd stirred up. I still didn't know what it was for, but anyone who could harness enough power to push out a god was someone to be reckoned with. Even if it wasn't flowing to him personally, it just didn't seem logical that the Gameskeeper would give up magic like that for boring old cash.

That said, it wasn't as if I had a better idea. If my dad's plan worked, we'd neatly avoid all my worst-case scenarios *and* get Yong back on track to not being my dependent anymore. Those were all good things I wanted, and I hoped rather than believed this was the way we got them.

"Okay," I said, pulling the ridiculous dress over my head. "Let's see if I remember how to do this."

***

Thirty minutes later, my dress, shoes, and makeup were on, and we were in a hired car on our way to Rentfree. It was weird to actually drive somewhere after two months of teleporting wherever I wanted, but not as weird as being dressed up next to my dad. I felt like I was thirteen again, going to some big society shindig where my only jobs were to smile and not embarrass anyone. That last bit never applied to myself, of course. It was impossible *not* to be embarrassed when you were a grown woman dressed like a toddler.

"I feel ridiculous," I announced, brushing my hands over my multi-tiered skirt in a vain attempt to make it lie something resembling flat.

"But you look lovely," my father said, smiling at me. "As your mother discovered years ago, voluminous dresses with high necks always look best on you. The extra fabric and elongated lines help to balance out your head."

I gave him a deadly look, and his smile slipped. "What?" he asked, genuinely confused. "You have a strong jaw, so you look best when you wear clothes that counter that. It's an observation, not an insult."

"Just because it's true doesn't mean you have to point it out," I grumbled, reaching up to rub my chin, which did *not* feel square to me. "Haven't you heard of tact?"

"Tact is for strangers. Family deserves the truth. How can you master your flaws if I don't help you find them? Would you rather I lied?"

212

I looked down at my lap with a huff, digging into the endless ruffles to find the small purse where I'd stashed my phone. Sibyl's earpiece was still in my ear, hidden by a curl of my over-styled hair. I didn't actually need to touch it, but grabbing it gave me something to do with my hands that wasn't wringing my father's neck.

It was more important than ever that I keep my temper tonight. I hadn't played the docile mortal in a long, long time, but even I remembered that glaring and back talk were strictly not allowed. I just wished I could remember the rest of it. Being a beautiful, silent attendant who responded instinctively to her dragon's every whim wasn't as easy as it looked. Even back when this had been my full-time life, I'd never been anywhere near as good as my mom. She could tell what my dad wanted from a single look. I had to rely on hand signals.

"Remember, let me do the talking," Yong said as our car started down the long spiral ramp that served as both the VIP and service entrance to the bottom of the Rentfree chasm. "If this is going to work, the Gameskeeper has to believe you're mine, and kept humans—"

"Don't speak," I finished with a sigh. "I know."

"I was going to say, 'are deferential,'" he replied, handing me the briefcase we'd prepared earlier.

I sighed again as I hefted the hard leather case into my lap, looking warily out the tinted window at all the limos that had been crammed into the arena's underground parking deck. "Did you make an appointment?"

"Of course not. Dragons don't make appointments."

"*What?* How do you know he'll even see us, then?" According to Nik, the Gameskeeper was the biggest deal in the Underground, and important people didn't see anyone without a prior request. I knew that my dad understood that because he was the one who'd taught it to me, but while I was starting to panic, my father just smiled.

"We don't need an appointment because we're not going to see *him,*" Yong said, reaching down to straighten the points of the pink ribbon at the base of my high collar. "I'm allowing him to see *me*. Our visit is his privilege, puppy. That is what it means to be great."

I was so boggled, I didn't even flinch at the hated nickname. I simply could not understand how my dad—reduced to a tiny fraction of his former strength, wearing an outlet-store suit, relying on a briefcase full of money that wasn't his—could be so cocky. It must have been an inborn draconic superpower, because when our car rolled to a stop at the curb in front of the arena's red-carpeted VIP entrance, the weariness that had clung to him since he'd woken up fell away like a shed skin. I'd driven down here with my dad, but it was the Great Yong, Dragon of Korea, who stepped out of the vehicle, looking down his nose at the armored humans guarding the VIP door with a sneer that made me feel like a lowly worm just for being in the same vicinity.

"I have come to speak with the Gameskeeper," he pronounced, his voice rumbling with a predatory menace no human throat could copy. "Inform him that the Dragon of Korea has arrived."

That was it. No explanation, no please, just wild demands out of the blue. Typical dragon behavior, in other words. If guarding that door had been *my* job, I'd have been pulling my gun and calling for backup, but the poor men in front of my father did no such thing. They looked as if they were having trouble staying on their feet, actually, their hands shaking so badly that their guns were rattling.

The reaction struck me as odd. Given the place they were guarding, I'd have thought they greeted monsters all the time. Then I remembered dragons didn't usually deign to visit the Underground, which meant these men had probably never seen one in person before.

That explained it. Your first dragon was a unique experience, and not one you could prep for. Even Nik had gone to his knees the first time he'd seen my father. These poor babies were clearly new to the phenomenon as well, because the magical predator-induced terror was reducing them to jelly before my eyes.

And I *loved* it. After so many years of being on the receiving end of dragon bullshit, it was incredibly satisfying to have all that power on my side for once. So much so that I fell into my part without thinking, standing behind my father with his briefcase in my gloved hands and a smug smirk on my made-up face that I'm sure made me look just like the little spoiled doll I was dressed up to be.

"I-I'm sorry, sir," the guard on the left stammered when he'd finally recovered enough of his wits to string words together again. "But the Gameskeeper isn't seeing anyone at the—"

"I did not ask what he was doing," my father said, his glowing eyes narrowing to slits. "I am here, therefore, he *will* see me."

"Yes, sir," the guard whimpered, surrendering the fight at once. "I'll show you to the Game Room where you can be entertained until—"

"No," Yong snapped, causing both men to flinch as if the word had been an actual bite. "I did not come here to be entertained. I came to speak with your master. He is in the building, yes?" When the human nodded, my father lifted his chin. "Then you will take me to him. No stops, no stalling. Is that understood?"

He punctuated the order with a growl I felt all the way to the pit of my stomach, and I wasn't even in his direct line of fire. The guards were, though, and the sound set both of them scrambling. There was no more back talk after that. They simply opened the armored doors and stood aside, cowering in the alcoves as they waited for my father to pass.

He did so like a cold front, sweeping down the red carpet and past the security cameras as if he owned the place. I followed at a respectful distance, keeping my eyes sharp as we walked out of the parking deck and into a very different part of the Gameskeeper's arena.

When I'd come in through the front gates last night, everything I'd seen had been designed to suck as much money out of the tourist crowd as possible. The room we entered now served the same purpose, but at a much higher price point. Instead of VR parlors, digital bookies, and slushy-machines full of alcoholic drinks, I saw polished-wood floors, marble-topped bars staffed with impossibly handsome black-tied waiters, and elegant brass betting windows where affable bookies were taking wagers by hand.

But despite the posh, old-world, "I can buy and sell you like cattle" vibe, it was still basically a casino. Even late on a Sunday night with no fight scheduled, there was still a good crowd of fancy-dressed people lining up to empty their pockets at the felt-covered poker tables and red-curtained VIP rooms. I was scanning the crowd to see how many washed-up celebrities I could spot when a new security officer—this time dressed in a tux rather than armor—darted in front of us.

"Great Yong," he said, clearly panicked but still bravely positioning himself between my father and the other guests. "The Gameskeeper has been informed of your presence. Please follow me."

I blinked in surprise. Despite how easily we'd bowled over the guards at the door, I hadn't actually expected my father's plan to work quite this smoothly. Clearly, I'd underestimated the power of an angry dragon. The guard in the suit wasn't even trying to distract us with free drinks or gambling vouchers. He was doing exactly as we'd asked, leading us toward a door at the back marked "Private" at slightly less than a terrified run. The surprise victory made me feel a lot better about our endeavor. When he led us through the door, though, the hallway on the other side was not what I'd expected.

In my experience, wealthy people liked nice stuff. Given how much money he made and how fancy the arena's VIP area had been, I'd expected the walk to the Gameskeeper's personal office to be wall-to-wall gold plating, naked models, and piles of coke. What I *got* was a cement maintenance tunnel lined with electrical cables. There was barely enough room for the three of us to walk single file, and my dad had to duck several times to avoid banging his head on the flickering fluorescents.

In hindsight, I should have suspected something like this. The arena was huge with multiple different facilities and levels. All those different parts demanded an expensive back-end infrastructure to support them. Manticores and teams of homeless gladiators didn't just pop out of nowhere. All those kitchens for the restaurants and medical areas Nik was constantly being sent to had to go somewhere, not to mention the plumbing needs of thousands of drunk people. There was a *lot* to the arena we didn't see, in other words, and we'd just stepped into it. But while that explained all the electrical wires, hissing pipes, and fiber-optic cables, what stopped me in my tracks was the writing.

The narrow hallway our terrified escort was hurriedly leading us down was absolutely jam-packed with spellwork. Magical instructions had been carved into the cement walls from floor to ceiling, running down the hallway in small, neat lines that—after staring so hard at Nik's curse this morning—I instantly recognized as Kauffman's handwriting.

The equations were so long and complicated, and written so *tiny*, I couldn't make out what they did without leaning my face right up to the wall and giving myself away. Sibyl could have done it using text recognition, but my phone was buried under my dress, and I wasn't about to blow our ruse by digging it out, especially since it wouldn't do any good. Even with Sibyl looking everything up for me, I couldn't have deciphered this much Thaumaturgical jibber-jabber if I'd had a month to work on it. But while I couldn't read what the spellwork here actually did, I had a pretty good guess.

From the moment my dad had shown me that all the magic in the arena was moving in a circle, I'd known there had to be something making it happen. At the time, I'd had difficulty believing anyone could create a magical circle capable of controlling so much power. Walking past the endless spellwork, I realized I hadn't been thinking big enough. There had to be a thousand lines in this hallway alone, and every time we passed a fork, I saw the functions running down the other halls as well. If these tunnels ran beneath the bleachers all the way around the arena, that would *definitely* form a circle large enough to channel the roaring magic I'd felt last night. The only part I still didn't understand was what the spellwork was telling all that angry, bloody magic to *do*.

It had to be something big. There was enough spellwork in here to launch a mission to Mars, and it was all active. As we walked closer to the arena's center, I realized I could still feel the angry magic from last night pulsing in the air. It wasn't nearly as overwhelming as it had been, but considering the arena was closed tonight, the fact that the magic was still here almost twenty-four hours later felt significant. As did the fact that the deeper we pressed into the arena, the thicker it got.

By the time the hall we'd been following dead-ended at an unmarked security door, I felt like I was swimming through syrup. Even my dad was starting to look uncomfortable, shifting his feet as our guide knocked on the security door's steel surface, nodding to the camera on the wall as he did so. There was a heavy *click* a second later as the magnetic latch decoupled, and the door slid open just enough for our guide to squeeze his head inside.

"Master?"

I held my breath. From his stillness, I knew that my dad was doing the same. I hoped his dragon ears caught more than my human ones, because I didn't hear a thing. Something must have been said, though, because our guard nodded like a bobbleheaded doll before scuttling back into the hall.

"The Gameskeeper will see you," he announced, his face so relieved he looked close to tears.

My father nodded as if this were the only possible outcome, but I had to fight not to drop my jaw. Of all the ways this could have gone, the idea that the Gameskeeper would just *see* us—no traps, no stalling, no gotchas—had barely made the list. Even if he wasn't actually busy, making us sit in a waiting room for half an hour would have been the minimum acceptable power move. My dad would have made him wait for days if the situation had been reversed. But apparently the Gameskeeper didn't play that way, or maybe he actually did want to see my dad, because when the guard opened the door the rest of the way, there he was.

I hadn't gotten a good look at him during the fight, but what I had seen had been so unremarkable that I'd assumed it must be a front. There was just no way that the Gameskeeper—the richest man in the Underground, owner of the world's largest blood sport arena—was *actually* the plain-faced, middle-aged man I'd seen waving placidly to the cheering crowd. Assuming we actually managed to get to him, I'd expected full gangster: flashy suit, tiger on a chain, suited thugs with sunglasses, that sort of thing. But the man sitting at the desk in front of us was the same one I'd seen last night, and now as then, he looked entirely, almost aggressively, average.

He was neither tall nor short, neither fat nor thin, no longer young but not yet old. His face was perfectly symmetrical with no memorable faults, but so plain that it could never be called handsome. His hair was short and peppered with gray, but no matter how much I stared, I couldn't tell if it was black or just dark brown. Even his race was ambiguous. You could have told me he was a mix of anything, and I probably would have believed you. He was *so* nondescript, *so* unremarkable, I was having trouble keeping my eyes from wandering off him to the rest of the office, which was far more interesting.

The room was much larger than the narrow security door had suggested. I'd expected a broom closet, but the reality was roughly twelve by twelve feet with a high ceiling. The only light came from an old-style green shaded lamp on the Gameskeeper's equally old-fashioned wooden desk. These plus the chair the Gameskeeper was sitting on were the only actual furniture in the room. The rest of the space was taken up by hundreds of flat LCD screens mounted to the walls showing security footage from all over the arena, parts of Rentfree, and several other areas in the Underground.

The only wall of the office that *wasn't* filled with screens was the one directly behind the Gameskeeper, which was taken up by a floor-to-ceiling window that looked out over the empty arena. This must be his skybox, I realized with a start. We were inside the glass VIP box where I'd seen him waving to the crowd last night.

Considering how obsessed he clearly was with fighting, the fact that the Gameskeeper worked out of his box seat didn't surprise me. I was more astounded by his setup. Spartan aesthetics were one thing, but what kind of boss watched his own security cameras? That was next-level paranoid. Or, at least, that was what I assumed. When the Gameskeeper stood up to greet us, though, the absolute lack of fear in his eyes threw me for yet another loop. Even if it was just a front, anyone capable of acting like having a dragon walk into your office unexpectedly was nothing to get worked up about was someone to be taken seriously.

"Well, well," the Gameskeeper said, nodding to my father with a placid smile. "The famous Dragon of Korea. It seems rumors of your death have been greatly exaggerated. To what do I owe the pleasure?"

His words were perfectly polite, the exact sort of inoffensive greeting you'd expect from a professional, but I still took an involuntary step back. His plain face might look boring and nonthreatening, but his voice was anything but. Hearing it, my first thought was dragon. We'd already suspected that might be the case, and while I'd never met one who'd be caught dead with a face that plain, their human shapes were just masks at the end of the day. Most dragons chose to be handsome because they were vain and because humans were drawn to pretty things, but a boring mask could also be useful if you were trying to hide.

But while all of that made perfect sense, I rejected the idea as soon as it popped into my head. The Gameskeeper's voice was deep and resonant and terrifying in a similar way to my father's, but the power rolling off him wasn't sharp like a dragon's, nor did he smell of smoke. Now that I was all the way inside, the only thing I could smell was blood.

I planted my feet as a wave of nausea rolled over me. The air in the office was even more saturated with the strange magic than the hallway outside. It pulsed like a heartbeat, thrumming in my ears until I could almost hear the screaming from the stands my eyes could clearly see were empty through the window. The sensory disconnect was so disorienting, I had to look down at my feet to keep steady, which was how I saw that the spellwork from the hallway continued in here.

No, not continued. *Culminated.* The lines that had run straight outside started to curve the moment they crossed the security door's threshold, twisting into a spiral that ended beneath the Gameskeeper's chair as if he were a spider sitting in the middle of a giant, arena-sized web.

Not a comforting thing to realize about the man you were standing in front of, but it was too late to back out. The guard had already closed the door behind us, trapping us in the dark room with the man who smelled overwhelmingly of blood. The combination of pulsing magic and the coppery stench made it hard to breathe. Thankfully, I didn't have to say anything. That was my dad's job. I was only here as his mortal, and for once I was more than happy to shut up and let him take the lead, which he did in classic dragon style: with an insult.

"I see you believe in doing things yourself," Yong said, sneering at the camera feeds covering the walls as if their presence insulted him. "Can't the most powerful man in the Underground afford to hire competent help?"

"You don't get to be the most powerful man in the Underground by trusting others to handle what's important," the Gameskeeper replied, seeming completely unfazed by the predatory menace that was rolling off my father so hard that even I was starting to sweat. "But let's not waste each other's time. You wouldn't have come here if you didn't want something, and I wouldn't have let you in if I didn't want to hear it, so…"

He sat down after that, spreading his fingers above his desk in invitation. My father obliged.

"I'm here to make a purchase."

Yong's arm twitched as he finished, but I was so nervous it took me several seconds to remember that was my cue. When I did, I stepped forward in a rush, fumbling the latch as I struggled to open the briefcase I'd been carrying. My mother would have been mortified, but in my defense, it'd been a long time since I'd had to be my dad's hench-mortal, and briefcase latches were bullshit. Thankfully, the Gameskeeper was too interested in what was inside to notice my lackluster performance.

He leaned forward, his dark eyes lighting up when he saw the direct-uplink crypto-bank terminal we'd convinced the DFZ to loan us. Personally, I thought the flat gray box with its yellow-green entry screen looked super boring. Not to be tacky, but this was a backroom deal with an Underground kingpin. Surely it deserved something flashier like gold or diamonds.

But those sort of frivolous thoughts were why I was a Cleaner and not an international criminal. Gold and gems *looked* impressive, but you could only pack so much of either into a briefcase. A portable, anonymous bank terminal, on the other hand, implied infinite funds, and from the way his mouth was curving upwards, the Gameskeeper got the message loud and clear.

"I appreciate that you've arrived prepared," he said, sitting back in his worn leather chair. "But what makes you think I have something to sell? I'm an entertainer, not a shopkeeper."

"Entertainment is still a business," my father said, his deep voice as smooth and deadly as a silk garrote. "If you know who I am, then you know I'm a collector. Like any good collector, I'm willing to pay for quality, and you've got something I want."

I had to fight not to flinch. When we'd gone over this part earlier, I'd argued that line was coming on way too strong. Typically in a negotiation, coming straight out and saying "I want this" was the worst possible move. When I'd pointed this out to my father, though, he'd told me I was missing the point. We weren't here to get a good price. We were here to save Nik, and stating our intention directly showed we weren't screwing around. Dad's logic was "if you can't walk away, go in strong." I still wasn't sure I agreed with that, but at least the Gameskeeper was listening.

"You must want it *very* badly to come to me in person," the blood-smelling man said, his creepy voice purring with anticipation. "I have a guess, but I'd like to hear you say it. What do I have that you want?"

"The human, Nikola Kos," my father replied without hesitation.

That was clearly not the answer the Gameskeeper had expected. "Kos?" he repeated, his plain face going slack with surprise. Then his eyes flicked to me, and his smug smile returned. "Ah."

I didn't like the way he said that one bit. I didn't like anything about this man or this place, and if Nik's life hadn't been riding on me pretending to be a dragon's obedient mortal, I would have told him so in words he'd never forget. It was through true heroic effort that I kept my expression passive and my mouth shut. A Herculean task that got even harder when my father reached back to pet me on the head like I was a dog.

"My daughter has taken a fancy to him," Yong said, his tone making it clear that he thought this was utterly ridiculous, but what could one do? "Fortunately, I have the means to indulge her. I want to buy out Kos's contract. Name your price."

"There isn't one," the Gameskeeper replied. "Mad Dog is not for sale."

Yong flashed him a predatory smile. "Everything's for sale."

The Gameskeeper chuckled. "Don't feed me that line. I know your story, Yong of Korea. You're your daughter's puppet. Everyone in the DFZ knows how you nearly killed yourself over her. Kos made the same mistake, which was how he fell back into my hands after years on the run." The Gameskeeper's gaze slid to me. "What is it about you, I wonder? You're not *that* pretty."

I wanted to roll my eyes so bad. Why did they *always* go after my looks? It was just so lazy, not to mention ineffective. My dad had said as much and worse all my life, but for some reason hearing someone else insult my face got him riled.

"My daughter is a jewel," Yong snarled. "The opinion of a bottom-feeding scavenger like yourself means nothing."

"It must mean something to make you snap," the Gameskeeper replied with a grin. "But thank you for proving my point. Everyone has something money can't buy. Your 'jewel' is obviously yours. Kos is mine."

"That is different," Yong said, still growling deep in his throat. "Opal is my only daughter. Kos is a dog by your own admission. You can get another champion, one who actually *wants* to fight."

"I've got plenty of champions," the Gameskeeper said, seemingly completely unconcerned at being growled at by a dragon. "But there's only one Mad Dog." He leaned forward on his desk. "Do you know what he did?"

My father's eyes flicked to me, but I wasn't sure what the Gameskeeper was talking about, either. I knew Nik had worked for him doing all manner of dirty work before actually fighting in his arena, but he'd never told me any of the details, and frankly I didn't want to know. I didn't like hearing about Nik getting hurt or doing horrible things. Fortunately, it didn't look as if my lack of knowledge mattered. Despite being the one who asked the question, the Gameskeeper seemed determined to answer it himself.

"He *left*," he said, eyes flashing in the dark. "I rescued him from the street. Gave him his gun and his implants and his training. I made him what he is today, and he turned his back on me. Just when he was starting to build a name for himself, he abandoned his contract, stiffed his fans on fight night, and vanished without a word. When I sent people to bring him back, he killed them. He very nearly killed my best mage Kauffman earlier this year just for crossing his path."

I took a shaky breath. Nothing he'd said was actually news, but I hadn't thought about it all together like that. Hearing him say it, Nik sounded like a monster. Fortunately, my father wasn't so easily swayed.

"I wouldn't have thought that would bother you," he said, tilting his head. "You run an arena where people trapped in contracts fight to the death. Surely *you* don't expect loyalty."

"I don't expect it," the Gameskeeper said sharply. "If Kos had tried to kill me or take over my operation, I'd have accepted that as life running its course, but he didn't. He did worse. He *ran.* His cowardice is a mockery of everything I built this arena to be! My ring is a shrine to the strong, a place where warriors embrace their power and crush all who stand in their way. Every champion falls sooner or later, but that's why champions exist. They're the goal, the bar for new challengers to strive against. That's how the cycle works. If the man at the top can simply *leave* before he is defeated, it undermines the entire operation!

"I've been trying to make Kos pay for that for years. Now he's finally back on my leash, and you want me to sell him for money?" He scoffed. "I can make *money* anywhere, but what Mad Dog gives me, nothing can buy. He gives me purpose. Every time he walks into that arena, I win. I win over him, I win over this city, I win over all the people who lie and say they don't want to see a fight. I give the blood-hungry crowds what no one else will, and they worship me for it, for I am the Gameskeeper! King of the arena! *No one* is too good for what I offer, and no one escapes me without a fight."

With every word the Gameskeeper spoke, the magic in the room grew thicker. It was the exact same bloodlust magic I'd felt in the arena when the crowd was yelling at Nik to kill, but there was no crowd here. Just me and my father and this strange person who smelled of blood. The man I was starting to realize wasn't a man at all. It was so obvious in hindsight, I felt like an idiot for not seeing it sooner. The Gameskeeper wasn't a dragon or some other alien creature. He was one of us, a monster of our own creation.

He was a Mortal Spirit.

"And you're slow on the pickup for a priestess of the DFZ."

I snapped my head up to see the Gameskeeper staring down at me, his eyes glowing blood red in a face that was no longer benign or ordinary, but as blunt and cruel as a bloody fist.

"Did you really think I wouldn't know you?" he asked, staring into me. "The moment you set foot in my domain, I knew. The dragon and his ruffled doll threw me for a little while I'll admit, but there's no way I wouldn't ferret you out in the end. How could I not? We're the same magic, you and I." He leaned closer. "Sister."

"Don't call me that."

The ringing words spoke through my mind and lips, but they weren't mine. I hadn't even felt her lurking, but suddenly the DFZ was there wearing my body like a suit, glaring down my nose at this little upstart who dared raise his head in *her* city.

"Do not address me so informally, monster," the DFZ said through my gritted teeth. "We are not family, and you are not welcome in *my* domain."

"But there's nowhere else I could be," the Gameskeeper said, facing the god of the city as fearlessly as he'd faced my father. "I was born here, same as you. We're both the natural products of a city where anything can happen. Sometimes, that anything is me."

The DFZ's disgust washed over me like storm surge down a gutter. "You are *nothing* like me."

"Of course I am," he said, pointing at me. "That's why you sent her. If we really weren't related, you wouldn't have to bother sending in your mortal eyes. You don't spy on the Empty Wind or Papa Legba or any of the other gods who share your city because you don't overlap with them. But we do."

"Enough," the city said.

"*No!*" the Gameskeeper yelled. "You sent your agent into my arena after years of pretending I didn't exist! You will not ignore me to my *face*. You brag and brag about being the city of freedom, but when people

226

exercise those freedoms in ways you don't approve of, you push them down into the gutters. What did you think was going to happen?"

"I didn't—"

"You come in here like an angry landlord," he said over her. "But I'm not your tenant. I'm your logical conclusion, the place where all your unrestrained violence and greed and spectacle meet in one glorious, gory package! That's why I keep growing despite everything you've done to stop me, including shoving me to the very bottom of your city. But you can't root me out, DFZ. You're the reason I exist."

"And I'll be the reason you go down!" the DFZ cried in my voice. "You abuse my people and splatter my name with blood! The world sees your barbarism and thinks it's the same for all the DFZ! But my citizens are not your playthings, and this city deserves better than you!"

The Gameskeeper sneered. "Please. Your citizens are why I'm still here. It's mostly out-of-towners who buy the tickets, but it's the people of the DFZ who profit and worship me. I've brought steady income to the lowest points of your precious city. For the people of Rentfree, I'm a better god than you've ever been."

The city's rage roared through me. "*You fight my homeless for sport!*"

"And who let them be homeless?" the Gameskeeper asked, glaring at the god behind my eyes. "*You* let them sink. All I did was give them a way to climb back out. You think all those 'desperate people' you moralize over would flock to me if I didn't give them a better deal? No. They fight in my arena because dying to the screams of the crowd for a chance at a better life is better than dying on your streets alone, forgotten and hopeless."

"That's not true," the DFZ said desperately. "You take advantage of those who have nothing and turn them into a mockery! That's not freedom!"

"It's their choice. Don't you hold that sacred?"

The DFZ flinched inside me, and the Gameskeeper went in for the kill. "You go on and on about how you're a city of free will, but you only support those who use that freedom in ways *you* approve of. You're always trying to change, always shuffling neighborhoods and teaming up with soft-souled weaklings like the Peacemaker in a vain attempt to be what you're not. To be *better*. But you can't change what you are. You're the DFZ, the city where the strong survive and the weak get crushed, just like they do in my arena. Look at it that way, and we're one and the same."

"I'm nothing like you!"

"But you are," he pressed. "That's why you're so scared of me. While you hide and shift and try to bury your nature, I embrace this city for what it is: a giant arena, a constant fight for supremacy. I'm the pure expression of what you are too cowardly to accept, and in a city where only the strong survive, that makes me the winner." He grinned. "Face it, I'm a better DFZ than you are."

The city began to tremble. "You're not!"

"Deny it all you want. I'll happily build an empire on your rejects. I've already taken Rentfree, and look how well that's gone for me." He tilted his head at the arena behind him. "I'm well established, and the more I show people what this city is *really* about—power, ambition, the triumph of the strong—the bigger I get. *I'm* the god they want. You're nothing but a bunch of shuffling buildings."

My god was panicking by the time he finished, her frantic thoughts washing over mine until her fear and doubt was all I could feel. He was right, wasn't he? She *was* a terrible city. She'd always known she was. Everyone thought so. Even when she strove and changed to be better, she couldn't stop people from suffering. No one was happy here. Her streets were always washed in tragedy and violence and dog eating dog. What if the Gameskeeper *was* the true face of the DFZ? What if she was nothing but a—

"He's wrong."

The city jumped. The words had come from my lips, but unlike everything else I'd said over the last five minutes, these were actually mine.

"You don't know anything about the DFZ," I told the Gameskeeper, stepping in front of my dad since the jig was up. "Sure, she's a hard city where people fight each other for every inch, but she's also a place where they succeed *without* shanking their neighbors. For every terrifying underpass and back alley, there's bright places full of wonder and opportunity. That's why so many people move here despite the slums and the giant rats and the blood-soaked commercials you're constantly running: because the DFZ *is* a city of free will. It *is* a place where anything can happen and anyone can start over. You say people use their freedom here to do terrible things, and that's true, but it's *also* true that they use it to lift each other up. The difference is that the DFZ encourages the good and strives to be better while you do nothing but amplify the bad."

The Gameskeeper narrowed his bloody eyes at me. "What do you know? You're the pampered daughter of a dragon. You know nothing about survival."

"I know because I did it! You think my dad *let* me move here? I ran to the DFZ for the same reason everyone else does: because I wanted to live free. This city gave me that, and I've fought tooth and nail to keep it. And before you say that proves your point, my struggles were nothing like the tragedies you put on. Your shit isn't even real!"

"You think *that's* not real?" the Gameskeeper spat, pointing at the bloodstained sand behind him.

"Not a bit," I said. "I've been to your fights, and every single one is a setup. How could they not be? You're an arena god, a self-professed entertainer, and entertainment's all about putting on a show. But don't confuse your manufactured conflict with real life. All those people you *claim* you're giving a fighting chance? They're not chasing their dreams. They're jumping for the bait you're dangling just out of their reach while the audience laughs. That's not the DFZ. It's not even survival of the fittest. It's cruelty. Good, old-fashioned, school-bully meanness. And while that is part of humanity, it's not a part we should celebrate, and it's *definitely* not something we should worship."

"So they should worship your DFZ instead? Prostrate themselves before a god who can't even accept what she is?"

I shrugged. "I'll be the first to admit the DFZ isn't perfect, but I'll take my chances with her over you any day. So would everyone who fights in your arena, I'll bet, which is why you have to trap them with curses that chop off their heads. If fighting in your ring was really so great, Nik wouldn't have run away. Even your audience isn't real. I've felt the magic pumping through your arena. The only reason those people are cheering instead of screaming in horror is because you whip them into a murderous frenzy!"

"I push back the veil civilization has draped over their true selves!" the Gameskeeper roared. "*They* are the ones who cry for blood, and their cries are prayers to me!"

"Then why don't you show them what you really are?" I yelled back. "What kind of *god* hides himself behind a face so bland that no one can remember it? Or forces his 'champions' to do all his fighting? If every human wants blood, why do you have to turn Nik into Mad Dog to get it?"

"Enough."

"*Why?*" I demanded again. "If you really were the unapologetic god of this city's true face, then hearing this stuff wouldn't make you uncomfortable because it wouldn't be true. But it is, so it does, 'cause you're *not*. You're not the real DFZ. You're not even a god. You're a magical parasite leveraging the worst of human nature to feed on its weakest."

"So what if I am?" he asked, the room going darker as he walked out from behind his desk to loom over me. I took an involuntary step back as he did so, because the figure in front of me was no longer small or innocuous, but as huge and terrifying as an angry mob.

"You call me a parasite, but do you think this arena would be here if the people didn't want it? Humans are violent, panicky animals. Savages who delight in inebriation, fornication, and any bloodshed that doesn't involve them. That's not my fault. I'm just a spirit, a reflection of what you humans value. If you have a problem with what I do, look in the mirror."

"I do look," I said, my hands balling into fists. "Why do you think I hate you so much? You're everything that's wrong with us! I know *exactly* what you are because I've had boots on my neck. I've been desperate and broke and backed into a corner and done stupid things because of it. I've had my back against the wall same as all those people who sign up for your fights! Unlike them, though, I was lucky enough to have people around me who didn't take advantage of that. *Good* people who were willing to help me even when I could give them nothing in return. The DFZ could have held me over a barrel to save my father, but she didn't. Nik could have left me to rot a million times over, but he didn't. That's why they're worth fighting for, and you're not. You're just another spirit, another human flaw made flesh, but that doesn't make you divine. We made you, we can unmake you. If we couldn't, you wouldn't need all of this."

I stomped my foot on the floor where the spiral of spellwork was glittering like fresh blood. The Gameskeeper was glowing, too, his eyes shining with a cold light that made the dark room even darker.

"You're very cocky, aren't you?" he said at last, lips spreading to show his teeth, which were sharp and jagged as the jaws of a bear trap. "I like that. Fighters need to be cocky, so why don't we make a deal?"

He waved his finger between the two of us, pointedly leaving out my father, who I'd just realized hadn't said a word this whole time. When I looked to see how that was possible, I saw that he was trapped, wrapped up in a cocoon of bloody, screaming magic.

"*Let him go!*"

"Why would I do that?" the Gameskeeper asked with a jagged smile. "We've already established that I'm unfair, and as your father was unwise enough to blurt out earlier, I've got what you want. I'm holding all the cards, so let's talk about what you can offer me."

My blood ran cold. In my head, the DFZ was silent, leaving me way too much space to imagine all the horrible things the Gameskeeper could do to my father while I watched helplessly. Now that I knew he was a Mortal Spirit, I could feel how much smaller he was than the DFZ, but a god was still a god. Even a little one was way too much for us to handle alone, especially since my dad was already neutralized. As was fitting for an arena god, he had me down in the sand and put a sword at my throat, and as much as I hated to say it, I had no choice.

"What kind of deal did you have in mind?"

"One that's good for both of us," the Gameskeeper promised in a voice that made me certain it was no such thing. "As I'm sure you saw last night, my Mad Dog's not cutting it anymore. He's always been a brilliant fighter, but he's not a very entertaining one. He's too efficient, not dramatic enough, and I can't keep pushing his button at the end of every fight much longer before people start getting bored."

"What does that matter?" I scoffed. "I thought you were the god of champions. Not the god of keeping idiots entertained."

The Gameskeeper shrugged. "In the arena, the crowd *is* the champion. Their screams are prayers to me, so it's in my best interest to make sure they stay on the edge of their seats." He spread his hands benevolently. "What god doesn't wish for his followers to be happy?"

I didn't think happiness gained through the suffering of others deserved protection, but I'd already made my opinion of his divinity clear, so I just motioned for him to get on with it.

"I've got a killer final match lined up for Mad Dog next Saturday night," the Gameskeeper continued. "Something that will *really* make people sit up and take notice. It's just the sort of spectacle a rising god like me needs to break into the big time."

I arched an eyebrow. "And why would I help you do that?"

The bloody god's smile grew crueler. "Because between you and me, it's not going to be much of a fight. As good as my Mad Dog is, especially when I…encourage his underlying talents, he's still only human, and that's not going to count for much against *this*."

He pointed over my shoulder at one of the dozens of security monitors bolted to the wall behind me. I'd ignored the video feeds since we'd arrived because I was focused on the threat in front of me. When I turned around to see what he was talking about, I saw something I *really* should have noticed sooner. A total game changer, hidden in plain view.

It was a dragon. A long, snaking white dragon inside a cage of glowing spellwork. She was curled into a miserable ball with her head tucked under her tail, but I still recognized her immediately. It was my father's sister, White Snake.

"*You* have her!" I cried, whirling back around. "She didn't run away in disgrace. You kidnapped her!"

"I didn't kidnap anyone," the Gameskeeper said, insulted. "I rescued her from the river after the DFZ struck her down and offered her a deal, just as I'm doing for you. See, for some reason, humans *love* dragons. Anything involving one of those snakes is guaranteed to be a hit. Just ask Marlin Drake. The First Dragon on Television has been making millions off the 'put a dragon in it' business model for almost a century. I've been trying to get one for my arena for years, but I've never been successful thanks to their famous egos and the Peacemaker's ridiculous rules. But White Snake was in a, shall we say, 'unique' position."

"You mean she couldn't say no."

The Gameskeeper chuckled. "Considering she was struck down while trying to kill you, I don't see why you should care."

"Just because she's awful doesn't mean you get a free pass to abuse her!"

"It's not abuse if she agrees," he replied with a grin. "At least in the DFZ. I'd originally planned to fight her against another animal, but I couldn't find anything spectacular enough. Then I heard about poor Nik Kos, bereft of his dragon's princess. He was so desperate for help finding you, he was ready to agree to anything, so I set him up for greatness. The undefeated Mad Dog, going toe-to-claw against the most feared monster in humanity's history!" His eyes flashed with delight. "The crowd would eat it up, and Nik would be just plain eaten. All upsides."

I opened my mouth to tell him Nik would kick White Snake's scaly tail, but the angry words fell flat before I could get them out. Even I wasn't *that* naive. Nik was good, but White Snake was a dragon. A small, cowardly one, but still way more than a single human could handle alone without an anti-dragon weapon, which I was *sure* the Gameskeeper wouldn't allow.

"Why do you want Nik dead so bad?" I asked instead, trying another angle. "Isn't he your champion?"

"He is," the Gameskeeper said. "And that's why he has to die. As I told you before, champions exist to be defeated. A winner who wins every time gets boring, and boring is bad for my reputation. That might not sound like much, but for a spirit, reputation is everything. As you saw last night, Mad Dog's shine is already wearing thin. It's time for him to go out in a blaze of glory, and what's more glorious—or more blazing—than a dragon? It'll be the biggest event in my arena's history, the fight of the century! The only downside is that everyone knows he doesn't have a chance. They'll still show up to watch him get eaten, but it takes a bit of the wind out of a fight if the ending's a foregone conclusion. Still, one must work with what one has…unless you can get me something better."

His blood-colored eyes slid to my father, and my whole body clenched. "No."

"But this gets you everything you want," the Gameskeeper cooed. "White Snake told me all about your strained relationship with your father. I know how badly he's treated you, and what you've done to him in return. Kos is different. He *loves* you. All I had to offer him was a chance at rescuing you, and he bared his neck to his most hated enemy. Surely that selfless act warrants some favoritism? And it's not as if your so-called 'father' actually cares about you. To him, you're just another collectible, and he and White Snake have been enemies for centuries. Their battle was always inevitable, so why shouldn't I make a show of it? And meanwhile, you get to save your loyal knight who loves you with all his heart."

The spirit held out his hand. "This is your chance, Opal," he whispered as a pool of blood formed on his palm, the thick liquid trickling across his roughened skin to form a circle that was an exact miniature replica of the spell looped around Nik's neck. "I can let him go right now. One flick of my finger, and poor lovesick Mad Dog will be free to run back to your side, and all it will cost you is your tyrant. The whole world already saw him fight his sister in the sky. If I can bring them back together, even those who normally scorn what I do will be driven to come and watch, and unlike poor Mad Dog, Yong might actually win. There's literally no downsides. Just say 'yes' and it's done. I'll even throw in box seats for you and Kos on the house."

The thought of watching from a box seat while my dad fought his sister in a stadium full of people screaming for his death made me sick with rage. We'd come here to buy Nik's life, but there was no way I was trading my father—my *family*—for anything. Even if Yong had been at full strength and capable of crushing his sister in one blow, I would have refused on principle.

The only reason I didn't tell the Gameskeeper to shove his deal up his spellwork and walk away right then was because I didn't understand why he was bothering to bargain in the first place. He had my dad and Nik by the throat, *and* he was a god. So long as I was on his turf, there was no way I could fight him, so why were we doing this? Why wasn't he just taking my dad already?

Because you have him, the DFZ said. *And I've got you.*

I jumped. Her space in my head had been so quiet and empty, I'd thought she'd left. An assumption that drew great ire from my god.

I would never abandon you! I was only holding back because you were doing such a good job on your own. What's the point of having priests if you can't trust them to speak for themselves?

Thanks for the vote of confidence, I thought at her. *But what do you mean 'I have him'?*

Instead of answering my question, the city spirit twitched my hand, and I looked down to see something glowing wrapped around my clenched fist. When I uncurled my fingers, I saw it was a silver thread. A brilliantly glowing line of magic was running between my father and myself.

It's a bond! the DFZ said excitedly. *Just like the one that connects a mage and a bound spirit! I don't know how you managed to form one with a dragon, but nothing about you and your father has followed the normal rules since this started, so who am I to say?*

I nodded, still staring in wonder at the glowing line. I'd never met a mage crazy enough to bind a spirit, but I'd read about it at school. I hadn't realized the link was so thin. The thread in my hand looked as delicate as spider silk, but I could feel its strength down to my bones.

There's nothing stronger, the DFZ confirmed. *So long as that thread exists, the Gameskeeper can't touch a scale on Yong's snout without your permission unless he kills you first, and he can't do that because I'm here.* She moved inside my body as she spoke, lifting my other hand to show me how my skin was shining with a rainbow of neon colors as bright and varied as the lights of the Underground. *You are my priestess. My domain. Just as I can't enter his arena, he can't touch you so long as you are mine.*

I nodded, staring at the wild colors shimmering under my skin. It was pretty trippy, but my life had been off the deep end for a long time now, so I just rolled with it.

How do we escape?

My god made a worried sound. *That's a trickier issue. You dad belongs to you, and you belong to me, but this place belongs to the Gameskeeper. So long as we're on his turf, I can't do anything outside my domain, which currently ends at your epidermis.*

I sighed. Just like last night, her powers were useless, which meant that—despite having a god nestled inside me like a Russian doll—I was essentially on my own. No doors, no throwing buildings, nothing. The Gameskeeper must have known my dilemma, because he was grinning like a cat with a cornered mouse, which *sucked* because I was so tired of being the small, helpless creature in these metaphors. But what could I do? The bloody magic was so thick it was choking me, but all the spellwork around us was keeping it locked up tight.

That was why I couldn't grab the magic here. It was already in use, tangled up in a million lines of Thaumaturgical code. I *still* didn't know what the spellwork did, but so long as it was there, the magic here was out of my reach.

I tried anyway, just to make sure, but the power snapped back out of my grasp just like every other time I'd attempted to cast in this cursed place. I couldn't even make an old-fashioned run for it since the Gameskeeper had my dad tied up like a mummy. I was scrambling to think of something brilliant—hell, I'd take something stupid so long as it got us out of here—when my dad's stiffened body suddenly went slack against the Gameskeeper's magic.

I froze. Oh no. Oh crap crap *crap*. My dad must have been fighting his hold this whole time and exhausted himself. Now he was unconscious, which meant our chances of escaping had gone from terrible to nonexiste—

"Opal."

I jumped a goddamn foot. You'd think I'd be used to disembodied voices by now, but there is simply no way to normalize ghosts whispering your name in your ear.

"Don't turn around," the smoky phantom of my dad ordered when I instinctively moved my head toward him. "He can't see me."

I didn't understand how that was possible. My dad was invisible to humans and little idiot dragons, but the DFZ could see him just fine. The Gameskeeper was also a spirit. *Surely* he'd be able to…

I trailed off, fighting not to grin like an idiot. Yong had been standing next to me when the Gameskeeper had grabbed him. But when he'd manifested his smoky self, he'd done so *behind* his own tied-up body. It wasn't that the Gameskeeper couldn't see him because he was invisible.

The Gameskeeper couldn't see him because my dad was using himself as cover, literally hiding in his own shadow. Clever dragon.

"I'm going to make a distraction," my father whispered. "While he's busy, you free my body, and we'll run for it."

Easier said than done. The bloody cocoon the Gameskeeper had wrapped around my father was the thickest version of his magic I'd seen yet. I couldn't grab and move the normal stuff. How the hell was I going to shift bloody coils the size of my arm? And on that note, what did my dad think he was going to do for a distraction? So far as I'd seen, his smoky body went straight through everything. How could you cause a distraction when you couldn't touch anything?

I was still worrying my way through all the reasons this wouldn't work when my dad blew through me. His shape changed as he moved, the smoke wavering until he no longer resembled a human, but a dragon. A huge dragon made of billowing ash-colored clouds that slid through me to fly straight at the Gameskeeper, ghostly fangs open wide.

It's not every day you get to watch a god freak out. From the Gameskeeper's perspective, it must have looked as if I'd just launched a huge smoke-dragon spell that did who-knew-what out of nowhere. Divine or not, that's not the sort of thing you want flying at your face, and he leaped back with a yelp. It sounded *hilarious.* I just wished I could have watched more, but I was already wrestling with the magic trapping my father's body.

As I'd feared, it was pretty much impossible to grab. But while I couldn't actually get a hold on anything, I *could* slam the coils around. So that was what I did, punching the magic this way and that until, at last, I'd loosened the wraps enough for him to slide free.

Yong was back inside his body before it hit the ground. "*Go!*" he yelled, grabbing me around the waist and throwing us both at the exit. Before I could catch the breath he'd knocked out of me, he'd smashed through the metal security door with his shoulder, carrying me under his arm like a sack as he leaped over the crumpled metal to charge down the spellwork-covered hall back the way we'd come.

Chapter 11

Since running straight down a hallway away from your enemy was a universally terrible idea, my dad took the first turn he came to, then the next, then the next. This process got us rapidly lost in the depths of the arena, but at least it got us out of the Gameskeeper's line of sight. For all the good that did.

"Put me down," I ordered when I'd gotten enough breath back to speak again.

My father shook his head. "You can't run in that dress."

I rolled my eyes. "Dad, we're lost in the back tunnels of a huge arena crammed full of cameras, security guards, and professional murderers. We're not getting out of here by running."

"Then how are we getting out?" he snapped, gripping me tighter as he charged ahead, turning a corner just in time to avoid a group of armed men coming down the hall we'd been following from the opposite direction. "Your god can't do anything here. We're on our own, but this place is still a giant public arena. There has to be more than one way out."

There undoubtedly was, but our chances of reaching it before the Gameskeeper's people found us were getting smaller by the minute. The cement hall was already echoing with the shouts of guards working together to corner us. My father's supernatural speed had kept us ahead of the trap so far, but the longer this went on, the worse our options got.

"Put me down," I said again. "I have an idea."

My father didn't look happy about it, but he did as I asked this time, setting me back on my feet. The moment I was safe on the ground, I kicked off my stupid heels and grabbed my phone out of the little bag hidden in the ridiculous ruffles of my skirt.

"Sibyl," I ordered, pointing her at the wall beside us, which was covered in spellwork just like everywhere else in these tunnels. "Highlight the variables."

"Right-o, boss!" my AI said cheerfully, whirring the cameras on the front and back screens of my AR smartphone as she tried to scan both walls at once.

"What are you doing?" my dad asked.

"Looking for a lucky break," I replied. "With all this spellwork, there has to be something."

My father frowned. "Aren't you terrible at spellwork?"

"Absolutely awful," I assured him, smiling as Sibyl's photo recognition filled my phone's screen with red circles, showing me where all the variables were located in the carefully balanced spellwork equations. "But that's the idea. A good Thaumaturge would never do *this*."

I grabbed my dad's hand and lifted it up, using his claw-like nails to scratch a big fat zero over the elegant notation carved into the concrete. Kauffman's spellwork was so complicated, I wouldn't have known that particular set of quasi-Greek symbols *was* a variable if Sibyl's spellwork helper hadn't identified it for me. I still didn't know what it was a variable for, but that didn't matter. The moment I wrote over it, I moved on to the next one then the next and the next, replacing the meticulously written magical notation with zeroes as fast as I could.

"Opal," my father said nervously.

I heard it. We'd stopped in the middle of a long tunnel, and the straight walls provided excellent acoustics for the shouting men I could hear closing in on us from either side. One group was already rounding the corner ahead of us. When they raised their guns to fire, though, the armored man at the front of the pack went down with a shattered helmet. His teammates backed off at once, and I looked back in surprise to see my father tossing something in the hand I wasn't currently using as a cement chisel.

"Hex bolt," he said, opening his palm to show me the fat ring of metal. "They're all over the floor here. Throw one hard enough, and it makes a decent bullet."

"Nice job," I said, legitimately impressed.

"A patch job," my father replied grimly, his glowing eyes focused on the corner where the enemy was regrouping. "There's another pack of guards behind us as well." He clenched his sharp teeth. "We should have kept running. If I had my fire, it wouldn't matter, but I can't hold a hallway with one hand and a bunch of spare bolts."

"Almost got it," I assured him, pressing his clawed finger back to the wall as I drew and drew and drew. I knew it was going to take a lot. Huge spells like this always had a bajillion fail-safes to prevent exactly this sort of tampering. But no fail-safe held up forever, especially against a brute-force attack that wasn't actually trying to change the spell's nature. I wasn't trying to redirect the magic or change the prescribed outcome. I was simply setting everything I could reach to zero, because nothing important in a spell was *ever* set to zero.

It was a stupid hack and an embarrassment to professional magic, but if there was one part of Thaumaturgy I'd always been good at, it was breaking shit. Sure enough, after I'd zeroed out half the variables on the wall to our left, all the spellwork in our immediate vicinity began to short out. It didn't smoke or spark or anything like that—much as I hated to admit it, Kauffman was a *really* good mage, which meant his spells didn't explode—but I could feel the normally taut power around us going slack. Grinning, I reached out to grab it, my smile going even wider when the power didn't snap back this time. It still felt absolutely dreadful, like grabbing a handful of screaming blood, but at least all that terrible power stayed *in* my hands this time, which meant we were back in business.

And not a second too soon. I was so excited about what I'd done, I didn't even hear the gun go off until my dad pushed me out of the way. He dragged us both to the floor, covering my body with his as a hail of automatic fire sailed over our heads. Snarling like the monster he was, he ripped a pipe off the wall and hurled it at the guards who'd flooded into the hall behind us. The two-foot length of metal hit the tallest of the men right in his bulletproof face-shield, dropping him like a stone and sending the others scurrying back. But not away.

My father growled low in his throat. He didn't even have to say it. I knew as well as he did that we had enemies ahead and behind, which meant we were trapped. At least, that's what *they* thought.

"Cover me," I whispered as I scrambled back to my feet. "I'm going to make us a way out."

"Can you open a door out of here?" Yong asked hopefully, ripping another piece of pipe off the wall and hurling it at the guards to keep them scattered.

That was my plan, but not the way he meant it. Shorting out the spellwork had released the magic, but we were still deep in the Gameskeeper's domain. Way too deep for me to reach the DFZ's power that allowed me to tunnel through the city. That was okay, though, because I wasn't just a priest. I was also a mage. One that didn't suck at magic anymore.

I reached out to grab a huge armful of the slack, sagging arena magic. The bloody power screamed when I grabbed it, but that just made me clench down harder, holding the picture of what I wanted it to become like a beacon in my mind.

"Fire in the hole!"

I slammed all the magic I'd just grabbed into the cement like a battering ram. As it hit, the spellwork-covered cement wall exploded, shattering all the zeroes I'd drawn and everything else to open a gaping hole. I jumped through the moment the jagged pieces stopped falling, diving into the next room, which turned out to be an electrical closet.

"Good job!" my father said, jumping through after me. "But where are we going?"

I didn't know, and I didn't care. My whole brain was occupied with gathering up enough magic to do it again. Fortunately, supply wasn't an issue. Now that I'd cracked the spellwork holding it in place, the soup-thick magic of this place was practically shoving itself down my throat. All I had to do was give it an opening and the power rushed in, filling me with blood and screams as I stepped forward to slam my magical hammer into the next wall. The blast sent up an even bigger cloud of dust than the first one, making me cough and blocking my vision, but I didn't need to see where I was going. The shortest distance between two points was always a straight line, so that was what I made: a razor-straight tunnel of destruction between "us" and "out."

I had to punch through ten walls, one bar, and a ticket office, but it worked. We jumped through each hole as it opened, my dad keeping my back safe as I pounded whatever was in front of us into dust. The Gameskeeper's security teams tried to stop us. There were more guards than ever, all of them fanatically shooting, but while my dad wasn't at full strength, he was still a dragon. An old, experienced one. He kept the hordes back using nothing but broken pieces of cement wall and steel rebar, cracking face plates, breaking guns, even knocking bullets out of the air while I cast and cast and cast until, at last, we broke out into the open air of the arena's ticketing yard.

"Opal!"

Coughing out dust, I looked up to see a door rising from the filthy, gum-covered pavement. It opened the moment it was clear, and Dr. Kowalski burst through. "*Come on!*" she yelled, holding out her calloused, wrinkled hand.

I didn't wait to be asked twice. I threw my whole body at her. If she hadn't been so stocky, I would have knocked us both to the ground, but Dr. Kowalski was an immovable object of a woman. She caught me without so much as a stumble, hauling us both out of the way just in time for my father to rush inside, punting the guard who was trying to grab him off our tail before slamming the door behind us.

Silence fell like a sandbag. I hadn't realized just how many people had been yelling for our blood until they fell silent. As I thought about that, though, I realized I was wrong. The deafening screaming hadn't been coming from the guards. It had been inside me. The arena magic I'd been using to hammer the walls had been roaring through me like an angry mob. I could still feel the echo of it bouncing around inside my soul, making me feel bruised and dirty from the inside out.

"Hey," Dr. Kowalski said, squeezing my shoulders. "Are you okay?"

I nodded, not trusting myself to speak yet for fear that I'd start screaming too. I was still working my way though it when my teacher's concerned face shifted, and suddenly I was looking into the delighted, orange-glowing eyes of the DFZ.

"That was amazing!" my god cried, throwing Dr. Kowalski's stocky arms around me. "*I'm so proud of you!*"

I could feel it. As the screaming magic drained away, the DFZ's joy flooded in clear and strong to fill the void. The city magic felt like heaven after all that bloody rage, but also slightly maddening. I was so used to being a failure, I didn't know how to act when someone thought I wasn't one, especially when my success was so small. I'd gotten us away from the Gameskeeper, sure, but everything else about our situation was much, much worse.

"What were you thinking?"

My god jerked back like I'd bitten her. "What do you mean?"

"You know what I mean!" I pointed at the empty space where the door had been. "You *knew* he was a spirit! Why didn't you warn me? You let us go in there blind!"

I was screaming by the end. In my defense, it had been a very stressful night, but even I was shocked by how angry I was. I just couldn't believe that the DFZ—the god I'd started to think of as *my* god—had left me to dangle so bad. If I hadn't thought as fast as I had, I could have lost everything tonight, and from the look on her face, she knew it.

"I wasn't trying to keep secrets," she said, her glowing eyes locked on the ground. "As I told you before, I had my suspicions, but I didn't actually know for sure that the Gameskeeper was a spirit until I went in there with you."

"How could you *not know*? He runs a murder arena below your city! And not a secret one, either. He has *billboards.*"

"Blood sport isn't illegal if everyone involved agrees," the god said in a small voice. "He's done everything by the book, so—"

"He kidnapped Nik off the street as a child and trained him to be a teenage hitman!" I yelled at her. "He has his own magic that feels like screams and *blood*! Even if you didn't know he was a god, you should have done *something*!"

"I know!" she yelled back. "But I couldn't! How many times are you going to make me say it? The Gameskeeper followed all my rules. I hated what he was doing, but unless I was ready to go against myself, I couldn't stop him. And before you accuse me of lying again, I really didn't know for certain he was a spirit before tonight!"

"How is that possible? You're a god too! Can't you recognize your own?"

"I should have," she muttered, scrubbing a hand through Dr. Kowalski's curly gray hair. "But I'm not an ancient power like the Empty Wind. I only woke up twenty years ago. I don't know everything yet, and the Gameskeeper doesn't behave like any other spirit I've met. I share my city with plenty of gods, and none of them have ever tried to hide from me or take my territory. Not to push stereotypes, but I was actually leaning toward him being a dragon. At least that would explain his greedy behavior."

"Dragons aren't the only ones who want more than what they have," Yong said dryly.

"Yeah, gods can be assholes too," I agreed. "That's basically all of mythology. But I *still* don't see how you didn't know."

The DFZ shrugged helplessly. "In my defense, he has convoluted himself pretty hard."

Couldn't argue with that. In the short time we'd been trapped in his office, the Gameskeeper had named himself the god of arenas, champions, the strong, the DFZ, and a whole bunch of other stuff I couldn't remember. He'd claimed so many domains, I didn't know which one he actually came from.

"He's the god of the arena," Dr. Kowalski said.

I blinked, looking up just in time to watch my teacher take her body back over, which was still pretty damn creepy even though I'd seen it happen dozens of times.

"I did some research while the DFZ was in there with you," she said, taking on the lecturing tone that was apparently an inborn trait of all professors. "There have been many gods associated with arenas from dozens of cultures all over the world. The current Gameskeeper is an amalgam of these older powers, which explains his plain face. Gods who have to be many things to many people are always blank slates. But while his worship was ancient and widespread, he's never been a big god. Not like death or war or the concept of a city. That's why he's bending himself around so hard to link his arena to the idea of the DFZ. He's looking to upgrade."

"An arena god doesn't seem the type to ever be content with his lot," my father agreed. "Makes sense he'd be gunning for someone else's territory, especially if he saw them as weak."

"Can he do that, though?" I asked. "I mean, gods are gods of what they're gods of, right? Life in the city can be hard, but the DFZ isn't *actually* an arena. He can't just come in and take over, can he?"

"I don't know what he can do," the DFZ said quietly, inhabiting Dr. Kowalski's body again as she sank down to sit defeated on the garden's upturned dirt. "Mortal Spirits are made by humans, and if there's anything humans are good at, it's changing their minds. I've been using that same talent to try and change myself. That's why you're here, don't forget."

She lifted her head briefly to smile at me before sinking back into her slump. "But I don't think it's working. I've been trying so hard to be a better city, but social improvements don't get nearly as much attention as death arenas. You've seen the tourists. The Gameskeeper is famous all over the world, and he's only getting bigger."

"But he can't get bigger than you," I said. "I mean, he's just a venue. You're an entire city! The city he's inside, I might add. That makes you bigger by default."

"Geographically yes, but I'm not a Spirit of the Land. I'm a human god, the face of how people see the DFZ. Everyone who lives here knows me, but the world's a lot bigger than Detroit. If the Gameskeeper's arena is the first thing the rest of the planet thinks of when they hear my name, then he's the spirit of the city, not me."

I couldn't believe what I was hearing. "You mean he can actually replace you? Shouldn't you have done something about this *earlier*?"

"What could I have done? I don't exactly have a lot of laws, and he followed all of them! He's also someone who came to the DFZ to go up in the world, which is what I'm all about. I don't know if that was his plan all along or if he just lucked into my perfect blind spot, but he's played my own nature against me. I can't crack down on someone for chasing their dream, even if that dream is replacing me. It goes against everything I am!"

I ground my teeth so hard my jaw ached. Goddamn gods. Why were they never powerful when you needed them to be? Seriously, what did it take to get some good old divine retribution?

"Why can't you fight back?" my dad asked, voicing my thoughts. "It's not your nature to block someone's dream, but it's also not your nature to give things away. An invader has built a fortress in your territory. Why can't you smash it down?"

The god sighed in frustration. "You think I haven't tried? Why do you think that arena's at the very bottom of Rentfree under a ring of constantly moving buildings? I've been shoving him down as hard as I can for years, and he still sells out every night!"

"Then move a building *into* him," Yong suggested. "Aren't you the city where only the strong survive? If he's taking your land, collapse the Rentfree chasm on his head. That's what I would do."

"Yeah, well, you're a dragon," she grumbled. "And I'm trying not to be that type of city anymore. Equal enforcement of the law is the line between a free city and a corrupt one. If I ever want to be a good place where people are free to chase their dreams, I have to follow my own rules. That means no dropping buildings on someone just because I don't like them."

"He trapped my dad in a blood cocoon and then tried to kill us both with a pack of armed guards," I reminded her. "Surely that's cause for some divine punishment?"

The DFZ made a face. "*Technically*, it wasn't entrapment because you never actually asked to leave. Also, you began the physical altercation when you broke his door, so all the shooting afterward could be classed as self-defense."

My father snorted. "Are you a god or his lawyer?"

"Cities are all about laws!" she cried. "Seriously, what part of 'defined by my domain' do you not understand? If you wanted to stick it to the Gameskeeper by ruining his view with a parking deck or burying him in exorbitant water bills, I'm your metropolis, but I can't take him out directly. I fought Algonquin for my city because if I didn't, I wouldn't exist. I fought for *you* because you were my priest and White Snake was very obviously breaking my laws, but the Gameskeeper situation is *complicated*. Fighting him requires fighting part of who I am, because he's not entirely wrong. I *am* a city where things like him can thrive. If I crush him, I crush myself, and I can't do that."

I heaved a long, frustrated sigh. It wasn't that I didn't understand her point. I was actually proud of my god for sticking to her laws instead of acting like the corrupt, chaotic city so many accused her of being, but her insistence on taking the high road was *seriously* biting us in the ass, and it was only going to get worse.

"I understand what you're saying," I said, striving to keep my voice patient and even. "But we have to do something. The Gameskeeper's already taken a bite out of Rentfree. If he actually pulls off his dragon fight, who knows how much bigger he'll get? Also, Nik's going to die. I can't let that happen."

"I know," my god said, pushing back to her feet. "And I didn't say I wasn't going to do anything. Just because I refuse to drop a building on him doesn't mean I'm going to stand around twiddling my thumbs while the Gameskeeper steals my city. Being the DFZ is my dream too. I'm not just going to roll over and let him take that away."

"Great," I said, hopes rising. "So how are we going to stop him?"

The garden fell silent.

"Could you close off Rentfree for that day?" my father asked. "The Gameskeeper draws his magic from the crowd. If Kos fights, but no one's there to see it, he gets nothing."

"I could try," the city said. "But Rentfree's got a million ways in, and the Gameskeeper controls enough of them that there's a good chance he could get around any barriers I put up. Also, there's still the TV audience to think about. There's more viewers at home than he could ever fit in that arena, and I can't do anything about a satellite feed."

"And Nik would *still* get eaten by a dragon," I added angrily.

Neither my father nor the DFZ looked as if they particularly minded that part. I was fuming about that when a new idea popped into my head. "What about the Peacemaker?"

My father made a disgusted face. "What about him?"

"Spirits aren't the only power in this city," I said, turning to face the DFZ since Yong was clearly a lost cause. "The Gameskeeper might not be breaking *your* laws, but there's no way the Dragon of Detroit will tolerate a dragon being caged and forced to duel a mortal in his territory. This fight spits in the face of everything he stands for. Once he knows what's going on, he'll have to do something, so let's go tell him! I bet we can get him to trash the entire arena for us."

"He and his followers certainly excel at trashing things," my father said. "But I don't think bringing in the Peacemaker is a good idea."

"Of course you don't. You've never liked him. But we can't let your prejudice—"

"It's not prejudice," Yong said stiffly. "It's fact. The Peacemaker is a terrible excuse for a dragon, but even he has limits. He might not like what's been done to White Snake, but she's never been part of his alliance, so he has no obligation to fly to her rescue. Also, if the Gameskeeper is to be believed, then White Snake signed a contract to fight in that arena just like everyone else, which means her battle is perfectly legal according to the laws of the DFZ. I'm sure the Peacemaker would still try something because that idiot's never met a situation he wouldn't meddle in, but if he rolls in there fire blazing, the Gameskeeper will be able to—quite rightly—call foul. If things go wrong enough, we could end up in a situation where the DFZ is forced to defend her enemy against her ally, which is the opposite of what we want."

"Oh yeah," the DFZ agreed glumly. "Major suck."

I threw my head back with a groan, hating that they were right. The Peacemaker might call himself the Dragon of Detroit, but he and every other dragon in this city were only here because the DFZ allowed it. If he broke her laws, even for a good cause, she'd have no choice but to come down on him same as anyone else. A situation I'm sure the Gameskeeper would *love.*

"Okay," I said, rubbing my aching temples. "So calling in the dragon cavalry is a no-go. What else have we got?"

Silence fell again, which only made me angrier. We were a god, a dragon, and a mage. There had to be *something* we could do, but I couldn't think of what. The Gameskeeper had us blocked at every turn. I couldn't even bribe White Snake to throw the fight because a) her pride would never allow her to be defeated by a human on international television, and b) the curse would probably count that as cheating and cut Nik's head off. Even if I smuggled Nik an anti-dragon gun, that would only give the Gameskeeper a better fight and make him even *more* powerful. I was struggling to imagine an outcome where that hateful arena spirit didn't come out on top when my father's eyes lit up.

"We could free White Snake."

I stared at him in wonder, feeling like an idiot for not thinking of that myself. All this time, I'd been worried about how to stop the fight without killing Nik, but the Gameskeeper had already admitted that Mad Dog wasn't the star. All of those people were coming to see a *dragon* fight, not him. Remove the dragon, and you killed the whole act.

The DFZ was clearly thinking along the same lines, because her face lit up. "That is a *fantastic* idea! How do we do it?"

"The first step is to find her," my father said, looking at me. "I was bound up at the time, but the Gameskeeper showed you where she was being held, correct?"

I nodded rapidly, then shook my head. "He showed me a video, but I don't know where the camera was. From the picture on the screen, it looked like she was underground, but there's a lot of that in this city."

"Not where I can't see," the DFZ said, turning to my dad. "He must be holding her under the arena itself. It goes down deep, and it's the only place he could put her that I wouldn't be able to get her out."

"Then that's where she has to be," Yong said. "I can pass through walls and don't show up on cameras, so I'll go and sniff her out. If I can locate her tonight, we can set her free tomorrow. Moving quickly is key. No one expects a fresh attack so soon on the heels of a defeat, and by the time he notices what we've done, it'll be too late. It's not as if he'll be able to get another dragon to replace her, and no dragon, no fight."

"It sounds good when you put it like that," I said. "Just one problem."

My dad looked at me curiously, and I sighed. "White Snake hates us, remember? If we set her free, the first thing she's going to do is try to kill us. We also don't know her situation. Even after we let her out and she burns us to a crisp, she still might go up and fight Nik anyway to satisfy whatever deal she's made with the Gameskeeper. Or maybe she'll just do it out of spite. I wouldn't put it past her."

"It's absolutely something she would do if she had the chance," my dad agreed. "But there's something you must understand about my sister:

before she is a dragon, she is a coward. She hates me as much as I hate her, but her first loyalty is to herself. I'm sure her need for revenge burns as bright as ever, but if she's as trapped as I think she is, then there's nothing she'd take—not even a chance to kill me—over her own freedom."

I bit my lip. "You sure about that?"

"Positive," Yong said, drawing himself up to his full height. "Trust me. If we give her the chance, she'll run. She always does."

He would know, I supposed, but I still didn't like it. I could see my dad's logic, but freeing a dragon who'd *just* been trying to kill us was reckless even by my low standards. It also didn't help that this was the one dragon we absolutely couldn't bluff. There'd be no tricking White Snake into thinking my father wasn't a shell of his former self because she was the one who'd made him that way.

Even if by some miracle she *didn't* immediately try to eat us, I wasn't sure this plan would actually make a difference in the long run. Sure Nik wouldn't have to fight a dragon next weekend, but I was certain the Gameskeeper could find something else equally horrible to kill him at a later date. Meanwhile, White Snake would be free to plot against us, and the arena would keep selling tickets and growing in popularity, just as it always had.

Thinking about that made me feel defeated all over again. No matter what we did, the Gameskeeper was always a step ahead. It didn't even matter if my dad's plan worked. The crowd would cheer just as hard watching Nik get eaten by a yeti or a cockatrice or a polar bear. And while I felt a lot better about his chances versus any of those, the end would be the same. The Gameskeeper had made it clear that Nik wasn't going to survive his final fight, because this wasn't about the fight at all. It was about the drama. That's why the people had booed Nik's actual victory and cheered his pointless rage: they were there to see a bloody show, not an actual struggle. God of champions my ass. The Gameskeeper was a god of *pandering.* So long as he gave the people what they wanted, they'd scream his name until the whole city sank into the cesspit he was—

I stopped, eyes flying wide. That was it!

"What is it?" the DFZ asked, looking painfully confused. "Sorry, your thoughts are too crazy for me to—"

"We're focused on the wrong thing," I said over her, too excited to care that she'd been digging through my mind again. "Going for White Snake is our best plan yet, but even if we pull it off perfectly, it won't ultimately change anything. The Gameskeeper will just find something else to whip people up about, and the cycle will continue. But! But but *but!* If we don't do anything, if we stay away and let him hype this thing to the sky like he's planning, we'll give him enough rope to hang himself."

"I'm sorry," the DFZ said, scratching Dr. Kowalski's curly gray hair. "I can read your mind and I'm still not following. How does letting the Gameskeeper get what he wants help us?"

"Because we won't actually give it to him," I replied, grinning like a mad woman. "What makes the Gameskeeper powerful?"

"The roar of the crowd," my father said.

I nodded. "Exactly. And crowds are famously fickle, which is why the Gameskeeper has to put on crazier and crazier spectacles to keep them coming back. Spectacles like a dragon. Doesn't get bigger than that, right? But imagine what would happen if all those people actually showed up. If the arena was crammed to bursting with millions watching at home. Imagine if everything the Gameskeeper wished for that night came true, and then, when the lights came up and the doors opened, there *was no dragon.*"

"That's what *I* said," my father grumbled.

"No, you just wanted to free her. I'm talking about timing. They haven't even announced the fight yet. If we followed your plan and busted White Snake out tomorrow, the Gameskeeper would just find something else for Nik to fight, and no one would ever know what they'd missed. But if we wait until the last possible second—I'm talking minutes before White Snake is due to go on—the Gameskeeper won't have anything to put on in her place. All those people he worked so hard to pack into the arena, the masses who bought the tickets and fought the crowds and maybe even flew in from other countries to see the fight of the century will be left staring at an empty stage, and they'll *hate* him for it."

By the time I finished, the DFZ's orange eyes were shining as bright as stars. "You're going to make him look like a cheat! That's perfect. Everyone hates a cheat!"

"I'm going to make him look worse than that," I promised. "The Gameskeeper's entire shtick is based around presenting himself as a god of champions and winners, the master in the dog-eat-dog world of the DFZ. But if he sells the world on the spectacle of a lifetime and then doesn't deliver, he's going to look worse than a cheat. He's going to look like a failure, and no one worships those."

I could already see how it would go down. The Gameskeeper was right about the draw of a dragon. I'd seen the crowds my dad could summon just by showing up. Add in the blood sport element, and you had media gold. You wouldn't even have to advertise. The news channels would do it for you, breathlessly reporting on the gruesome spectacle and playing up the controversy for ratings. It would be the train wreck the whole world couldn't look away from, but just like the Sword of Damocles, that enormous power cut both ways. The bigger the hype got, the more people there'd be to watch it fail. A flop of that magnitude would be a devastating blow to any business. For a god who relied on the crowd's opinion for his power, it could be fatal.

"We *have* to do it," the DFZ agreed, grabbing my hands.

"It was my plan to start, so obviously I'm in agreement," my father said. "The most difficult element will be the new timing. If we're going to remove White Snake fast enough to leave the Gameskeeper empty-handed, everything has to go like clockwork." He frowned. "I'm still going to go in and find out exactly where she is tonight. That way we have as much time as possible to plan our assault."

I stared at him in wonder. I'd been so caught up in solving the problem, I hadn't stopped to think about how strange it was that my dad was just…helping. Anger at the Gameskeeper aside, I'd have thought he'd be all down with the idea of a fight to the death between his sister and Nik. But he seemed totally on board, crouching in the dirt with the DFZ to sketch out how far down they thought the arena went.

"Are you sure about this?" I whispered, crouching down next to him. "I know you've got the smoke thing, but this is still really dangerous. Even if the guards and cameras can't see you, the Gameskeeper can. He couldn't get you before because of our connection, but I don't know how far that protection stretches. If he traps you, I might not be able to get you out."

"It's a calculated risk," Yong agreed, brushing the dirt off his hands. "But a necessary one. Not only is it a father's duty to fight for his children, White Snake is my only living relative. A hated one, admittedly, but that doesn't mean her actions don't still reflect upon me. If I allow the Gameskeeper to fight my sister in a ring like a dog, our clan's good name will be forever stained. Especially if your human wins."

He shuddered at the thought, but I smiled. "You think Nik can win?"

"I think people around you have a proven habit of doing the impossible," he replied. "I've seen Mr. Kos fight, and though she has the natural advantage, my sister is a backstabber, not a warrior. Let's just say Kos is the underdog I wouldn't bet against."

I smiled wider at the rare words of praise, and my father's scowl deepened. "Don't look like that. It doesn't matter who would win. The fact that this is happening at all is a disgrace. White Snake has already shamed us enough by agreeing to participate in this monstrosity. I don't care what it takes, this fight *cannot* be allowed to take place. If my sister fights a human on pay-per-view, I'll never be able to show my face to the clans again."

That was very my-dad reasoning, and it made me feel a *lot* better. Yong fighting for me was a new and untested development, but Yong fighting for his pride was a force I'd bet my life on. But just as I was starting to think we might actually be able to do this, Dr. Kowalski fought her way back to fore.

"Wait!" she cried, shooting up from the ground where the DFZ had crouched their shared body. "Before we make any more plans, there's still one element we haven't considered."

I groaned. "How many elements of this stupid thing can there be?"

"When your enemy is a god? Infinite. Before we do anything to the Gameskeeper, though, we have to figure out how we're going to handle his funnel."

"Funnel?"

"His magic-channeling apparatus," Dr. Kowalski clarified. "The DFZ showed me your memories of the Thaumaturgical spellwork on the arena's maintenance hallways, and I think I've figured out what it does."

"What?" I asked, too eager to be insulted that the DFZ was showing people my memories like vacation highlights. "Other than keeping me from grabbing magic, of course."

"Actually, I think that element might be a byproduct," she said. "Obviously, it's impossible to know all of a spell's functions from looking at a single portion of the spellwork, but between the functions you saw and the magical circling we observed last night, I'm ninety-nine percent certain that the whole arena is one giant circle dedicated to capturing and amplifying the crowd's magic."

I'd known something had been making people go more nuts than they should, but, "Is that all it does?"

"All it does?" my teacher repeated incredulously. "We're talking about a magical amplifier on a municipal level. Haven't you wondered how the Gameskeeper is able to generate so much power despite being such a small god? An arena's worth of people is nothing on the spirit scale. The DFZ is a city of over nine million, and her name is common knowledge all over the world. She's the setting of countless movies, novels, and shows. She's the subject of songs and stories, even legends! *That's* what it takes to make a god. The Gameskeeper's arena isn't even the biggest attraction in the DFZ. He should be a flea compared to our great city, yet he's grown to be a serious threat. How can that be?"

I didn't know. When she put the comparison like that, I felt foolish for being afraid of him.

"It's the spellwork," she said authoritatively. "All the magic you felt swirling around last night wasn't part of a larger spell. It *was* the spell. All that spellwork enables the arena to act as a collection dish, capturing and amplifying the screams of the pumped-up crowds. During fights, the power churns around to build up strength, feeding back on itself to push the crazed fans even further. Then during the off-hours when the arena is closed, it acts as a storage vessel, keeping the magic from drifting away and rejoining the city as ambient power."

"So it's a giant battery?"

"More like a generator that's also a gas tank," Dr. Kowalski said. "The spellwork allows the Gameskeeper not just to catch and hold the crowd's magic, but also to build it up way bigger than it should be. That's why people go so nuts."

I'd known all that spinning magic had to be for something. At the time, I'd assumed it was the spin-up for some monstrous spell that hadn't gone off yet, but now I realized I'd been over-complicating things. All that magic wasn't swirling around because it was being moved into position for some greater purpose. The spinning *was* the purpose! I'd been sitting inside a god's magical reserve tank while it was being filled. That also explained why the magic had still been there today despite the arena being closed *and* why the spellwork had finished its spiral under the Gameskeeper's chair. It had been sending all that magic straight to him.

The setup was pretty brilliant in hindsight. Brilliant and necessary, because unlike dragons and humans and manticores and every other magical creature, spirits had no physical body. They were sentient magic, and the more they got, the bigger they grew. But while I was certain Dr. Kowalski was right on the money with this, I still didn't see how it was a problem for us.

"What does that matter, though?" I asked. "So he's got a magical engine feeding him power, so what? It won't save him when we turn his great fight into a giant flop."

"Maybe not," Dr. Kowalski said. "But it will make executing the plan infinitely more difficult. If we wait until the last moment to free White Snake, excitement for the fight will be at its peak, which means the Gameskeeper will be at the height of his power. With so much magic at his fingertips, he'll be functionally omnipotent within his domain, which would make stealing his star dragon out from under his nose practically impossible."

"Fair point," I said. "So what can we do about that? Break the spellwork?"

"You can't break that much spellwork," Dr. Kowalski scoffed. "We don't know how many spellworked tunnels there are, but for the arena to work as a circle, there has to be at least one ring of spellwork going all the way around. Given the size of the arena and the density of the functions you saw, I bet there are *miles* of spellwork down there, and all of it carved into cement. It'd be easier to collapse the entire arena, which our god has already declared she will not do. But just because we can't physically smash the spellwork doesn't mean we can't destroy it."

She gave me a knowing look, but I wasn't following.

"Remember when you first came to this place," she coaxed. "How you couldn't even use spellwork without blowing it up?" I nodded, and my teacher smiled. "Well, I think the most effective way of eliminating the Gameskeeper's advantage is for you to go back to your old bad habits, but on a much bigger scale."

My eyes widened in horror as I realized what she meant. "You want me to blow out the *entire* arena?"

Dr. Kowalski nodded, and the blood drained from my face. It wasn't that I couldn't do it. Before I started training here, I'd overloaded pretty much every circle I'd touched. I was confident I could do the same to

Kauffman's giant ring. I just didn't see how I was going to do it without blowing myself—and the rest of Rentfree—to smithereens in the process.

"We've already thought of that," Dr. Kowalski assured me, guessing my worries before I could put them into words. "I know this is a hard thing to ask. Blowing out spells is what drove you here to begin with. I can understand why the thought of going back to that pain is terrifying, but we're not asking you to die for this, and the DFZ *definitely* doesn't want you blowing up one of her neighborhoods. You're a much better mage now, and you've got us."

"No offense," I said shakily, "but how are *you* going to keep *me* from blowing myself up?"

Because with me in here, you won't be able to, the DFZ answered in my mind. *So long as you're my priestess, your soul is my domain, and I'm much, much bigger than you are. When the backlash comes, you won't have to bear it alone. All you'll have to do is pass the power to me. It's the exact same thing you've been doing for your father all week, except I'm even bigger. I've got a city's worth of space to fill! Pass it to me, and you won't even feel a twinge.*

"You'll also need the DFZ's help to initiate," Dr. Kowalski added in a practical voice. "You have the strongest draw I've ever seen, but even you can't grab enough magic to overload a circle built to handle the blood-frenzied energy of thousands. If you want to smash things built on a divine scale, you need another god. Fortunately, you've got one. All you have to do is get her inside, and she'll do the rest."

Once the Gameskeeper's circle is smashed, everything else should be easy, the DFZ assured me. *Depending on how distracted he is on fight night, we might not even need to break things on the way in! We will* definitely *need it to get out, though. Even after we ruin his fight, his circle's still going to have all the magic generated during the run-up, and you'd better believe he's going to use that power to crush you. If we don't break his ability to hold magic before that point, even I won't be able to protect you from his rage. If you're inside his domain, he'll flatten you like a pancake.*

"Then we'd better make sure he's hamstrung before then," I said, but I still wasn't feeling great about this. Not about the plan, I understood the logic there perfectly. I just didn't know if I could do it.

You'll do great, the DFZ said with divine certainty. *You're a genetic super mage, remember? You also shouldn't need to push hard. If the hype for this is as big as we think, then the Gameskeeper's circle should already be close to capacity by the time you arrive. With so much power under pressure, all you'll need to do is give it a shove, and the whole thing should pop.*

It sounded so easy when she said it, but I still didn't see how I was going to survive a stadium-sized backlash. That said, I'd survived a lot of stuff I shouldn't have, and I had a god on my side this time. It also helped that I wanted to wreck the Gameskeeper harder than anyone. This was the guy who'd abused Nik as a child and tried to fight my baby cockatrices, who'd taunted me to my face and tried to force me to sell my dad. I wanted him gone for good. *Forever.* Wrecking his fight of the century was a killer start, but if we took out the spellwork that kept him supplied with magic at the same time, we'd deliver a one-two punch he'd never get up from. It would also let us escape the arena alive, a combination of long- and short-term benefits that, even with my fear, definitely seemed worth the risk.

"Okay," I said with a shaky breath. "Let's do it."

"Are you sure?" my father asked.

"Why hit them once when you can hit them twice?" I said, trying not to sound as panicked as I felt. "If we're going to do this, we might as well get everything we can out of it."

"Spoken like a true citizen of the DFZ," Dr. Kowalski said proudly, slapping a heavy hand on my shoulder. "I can't guarantee it'll be safe—big magic never is—but I believe you can do it. When you first came here, you couldn't fill a potato without cooking it. Now you're throwing around magic like you've been a Shaman all your life. You even figured out how to make dragon fire!" She slapped her hand down again, making me grunt. "You've made better progress than any student I've ever had. It's still going to take practice—we're going to be dealing with magic on a divine scale, which is a lot more than the handfuls you've been passing your dad—but if anyone can make it work, it's you."

As always, her praise went through me like wildfire. I didn't know if having a teacher who thought I wasn't garbage was ever going to lose its shine, but if I hadn't been on board before, hearing Dr. Kowalski say she had faith in me would have had me jumping the ropes to get in.

"When do we start?"

"Right now," Dr. Kowalski said, yanking me toward the house. "DFZ, Yong, you're coming too. If we're going to practice transferring magic, we need a donor and a receiver."

"Delighted to oblige," my father said with a hungry smile.

The spirit inside me seemed nonplussed at his enthusiasm, but she didn't protest. When Dr. Kowalski looked at me, though, I put up my hands.

"Can I have a moment first? There's someone I need to call before I vanish again."

My father lifted a suspicious eyebrow, but Dr. Kowalski just smiled. "Take all the time you need," she said, ushering my dad toward the kitchen. "Just make sure 'all the time you need' is no more than five minutes. We've got a lot to do."

I gave her a salute, and my teacher led my dad away, leaving me alone in the dark garden to dial up the one person who was even more involved in this mess than we were.

***

Shocker, Nik was *not* happy to discover he was going to be fighting White Snake.

"Are you shitting me?" he asked, his incredulous voice weak and raspy from his ordeals. "*That's* their super-secret guest star? A *dragon?*"

"It gets worse," I warned. "The Gameskeeper's not a man. He's a spirit."

I paused to let that bomb explode, but Nik just sighed. "Yeah, I know."

"Wait, you know? *How?*"

"Well, I didn't know he was a spirit specifically," Nik said. "But I knew he had to be *something*. I've known the man since I was eight, and he's never aged a day. He also never leaves his office, which doesn't have a bathroom, by the way. I just sort of put two and two together."

I closed my eyes in frustration. "You could have warned me."

"I did warn you," Nik said angrily. "I told you countless times that the Gameskeeper was dangerous and murderous and powerful and you should never go near him. How much more warning did you need?"

I sighed.

"Besides, don't you work for the DFZ? She should know all about other spirits in her territory."

"You'd think that," I muttered, rubbing my face. "But it doesn't matter. We know what he is now, and Dad and I have a plan."

"The fact that your dad's involved makes me *more* worried," Nik said. "But go ahead."

I smiled and flicked my finger over my screen, pulling up the arena calendar Sibyl had been forethoughtful enough to download for me. "There hasn't been an official announcement yet, but unless the Gameskeeper changes his mind, you're fighting White Snake next Saturday night. There was nothing going on today because it's Sunday, but every other night this week has something scheduled. They're already hyping some big reveal during the 'Dog Fight Madness' event on Wednesday, so I'm betting that's when the world will learn about Mad Dog versus Dragon."

"Probably," Nik said. "I'm guessing you have a plan to stop it?"

I shook my head. "Just the opposite. I want eeeeeeeeveryone to hear about this, and I want you to help."

"*What?*"

"Hear me out," I pleaded. "I know you hate the arena, but I need you to play the celebrity fighter for the next few days. Give interviews, go on talk shows, throw a diva fit and punch a fan, whatever it takes to make sure as many people are watching your fight this Saturday as possible. Then, right before you're scheduled to go on, Dad and I are going to sneak in and free White Snake. No dragon, no dragon fight! The whole thing will be a disaster, and since we're doing it at the very last second, the Gameskeeper won't be able to reschedule. This is where it gets good for you, because the curse on your neck only dictates that you have to show up for your fights. It doesn't say you have to have an opponent."

"That's nuts."

"No, it's our loophole," I said proudly. "If we can get the timing tight enough, you should be able to walk out there and instantly win because your enemy ran away. Once that happens, the five-fight requirement will be complete, the curse will fall off your neck, and wham-bam you're free!"

That was the part of the plan I hadn't told the others, mostly because it didn't involve them. This was between me and Nik, part of my fight to pay him back for everything he'd done for me. But while I heard his breath catch in excitement, his voice was still worried.

"Are you *sure* you can get White Snake out? Not that I doubt your breaking and entering abilities, but the arena goes deeper than you'd think, and security at the bottom is tight."

"I don't have to get her out," I said confidently. "She's a dragon! The only reason the Gameskeeper was able to trap her in the first place was because the DFZ punched her into the river. But she should be recovered now, which means all we have to do is open the door and she'll bash her own way to freedom. It's *perfect.*"

"It's risky," Nik said. Then he sighed. "So a typical Opal plan, then."

I shrugged. "No risk, no reward."

"I get that," he said. "But I don't think you realize how much you're asking. The Gameskeeper's been after me to do PR since the first time I fought for him, but aside from mandatory stuff like photos, I've always avoided it like the plague. It took me years to live down being his champion the last time I quit, and that was with the Gameskeeper actively burying my involvement because he was embarrassed I'd run away. Now his reach is even bigger with millions watching his fights all over the world. I know you wouldn't ask if it wasn't vital to the plan, but this isn't a small thing. If I let the Gameskeeper turn me into the arena star he's always wanted, I'll never have a moment's peace again. Idiots will be chasing me to 'fight the champion' for the rest of my life."

When he put it that way, I could see why he was reluctant. Paranoia notwithstanding, Nik was a very private person. Having his face splashed all over the Underground alongside the nickname he hated must have been painful enough already, and here I was telling him to make things even worse. It *was* a lot to ask, but I stuck to my guns.

"It'll be worth it," I promised. "I'm not just doing this to save you. If we play our cards right, the Gameskeeper will feel this blow for years, maybe for*ever*. This is our chance to take him down, and the odds get a lot better if you help."

"It *would* be nice to hit back for once," Nik admitted. "I owe him for a lifetime of bad shit."

"He's done bad shit to everyone. That's why it's so important that we don't mess this up. The Gameskeeper doesn't leave many openings. If we flub this, we may not get another shot. Also, you'll be eaten by a dragon."

"Hard to argue with that," he said, sighing into the phone. "All right. If you say we need hype, then I'll hype. But if we *do* pull this off and I'm still alive when it's over, you have to help me hide. You have no idea the crazies being an arena fighter attracts. I might have to spend all of next year in my apartment."

"I will absolutely help hide you," I promised. "You could use some time off, anyway."

He snorted. But while Nik was playing it cool as usual, I could hear the fear he was desperately trying to suppress with every breath.

"Do you really think it'll work?" he whispered.

I wanted to tell him of course it would. Everything would be fine! But Nik deserved better than that from me. Also, he could always tell when I was lying. But as I opened my mouth to explain the plan and all associated risks in full, Nik cut me off.

"You know what? Never mind. I don't want to know the odds. You already told me what you need me to do, so I'm just going to go for broke and worry about the fallout later. I was the idiot who panicked and put himself back under a blood god's boot. Can't complain if I have to do crazy stuff to get out again."

"You weren't the idiot," I said fiercely. "I was. This happened because I was rushing ahead so fast, I didn't think things through. I kept secrets and let you assume the worst, and everything went to shit because of it. But that's never happening again. If we get through this alive, I swear I'm going to be the best possible partner to you from here out."

"You already are," he said, the words so warm I could hear the smile in his voice. I was smiling back when I heard someone yelling in the background.

"Crap. I gotta go. I'll do my part."

"I'll keep you updated," I promised.

"Don't," he ordered, his voice tight. "If I'm actually going to act like an arena star, then I'm about to put myself deep in the Gameskeeper's world. The less I know about what you're planning, the less I'll have to hide. I trust you to do your best, and if it works, I'll see you on the other side."

"See you soon," I whispered, clutching the phone, but the connection had already gone dead. I hung on a moment longer out of sheer stubbornness, but eventually I let my arm drop, staring up at the golden glow of the city lights bouncing off the low night clouds until Dr. Kowalski came to drag me back to work.

Chapter 12

I'd thought Dr. Kowalski and the DFZ had worked me hard before, but the last two months were a vacation compared to the next five days. We trained every waking hour, including during mealtimes, which is how I learned to move magic and eat at the same time. I worked until my insides felt like goo, transferring huge amounts of magic from the DFZ to my dad, but also into a cornucopia of vegetables, circles, and across various magically charged areas of the DFZ.

Sometimes Dr. Kowalski and the city would take turns tossing me armfuls of power just to see if I could catch it. If I did, they'd make me hold all that magic until I thought I was going to burst. Other times they had me transfer power so fast I felt like a human wire. Some days I didn't even know what I was doing. I just followed instructions and tried not to self-destruct as the magical load went up and up and up.

If I hadn't had two months of brutal magical labor under my belt already, it would have broken me. Unlike everyone I was working with, I was only human. The only edge I had going was that I couldn't have been more motivated. It was rare in life that you got a clear path to what you wanted, and I wanted to take down the Gameskeeper *bad*. If that meant learning to move godly amounts of magic without cracking, then I'd make myself an indestructible human pipeline.

I just hoped it would be enough. Contrary to what the kid shows preach, trying hard doesn't always guarantee success, and the Gameskeeper wasn't my only enemy. He was the god feasting on the crowd's magic, but Kauffman was the man who made it possible. The last time I'd gone up against his spellwork in the Gnarls, I'd won by out-crazying him and nearly died. I couldn't be that sloppy this time. Nik was counting on me. The DFZ was counting on me. *I* was counting on me.

For the first time in my life, I felt like I was doing something that mattered, something that would make a difference. I felt powerful, like I was in control of my own destiny. That was a heady feeling for someone who'd always lived in someone else's shadow. I still wasn't sure I could pull it off, but I was determined that, if I failed on Saturday, it would not be from lack of effort.

It helped that I wasn't the only one working hard. The DFZ and Dr. Kowalski were right there with me, but the real shocker was my dad. Obviously he was more than happy to let me practice shoving magic into him. Given the size of the power I was moving, you'd think I'd have pumped him back to full in the first few days. But even dumping the DFZ's magic into him as fast as I could, restoring the Great Yong felt like trying to fill the Great Lakes with a fire hose.

Watching all that power vanish into the void, I understood for the first time the true difference in scale between humans and everything else. I'd known my father was a powerful dragon, but I hadn't known—*couldn't* have known—just how much he'd lost until I tried to replace it. Looking back, I couldn't believe he'd let me burn all that magic up with my stupid gold-market trick. I was also starting to worry that I'd never get his fire back to what it was. I was simply too small, and he'd been building his flames for two thousand years, plus whatever he'd eaten from his father. The best I could say was that at least he was no longer in danger of snuffing out.

But while I was getting bowled over by the harsh realities of our situation, my dad was more energized than ever. Not only did he stay right by my side through every grueling hour whether he was needed for the exercise or not, he even found time to go looking for White Snake in the bowels of the arena during the brief periods when I was allowed to sleep. Thanks to his smoke body, he was able to pass through guards, cameras, and walls unseen. Wards gave him more trouble, but he always wiggled through eventually.

In the end, the only barrier he couldn't get past was the one surrounding White Snake herself. I thought that was perfectly reasonable—a dragon ward that didn't stop dragons wouldn't be much use, after all—but it seemed to bother him enormously. So much so that, on Friday morning, he asked the DFZ to give me thirty minutes off from training so we could talk about it.

"It just makes no sense," he said as I collapsed on the floor of Dr. Kowalski's living room.

"What about it doesn't make sense?" I panted, too tired to even lift my head. "It's tuned to stop dragons, and even when you're made of smoke, you're still a dragon. Seems obvious to me."

"That's not what I'm talking about," my father snapped, sitting down beside me with his dark brows furrowed so tight they made a V on his face. "It's White Snake. I *know* she knows I'm there. Even if the barrier blocked all sight, sound, and smell, I know she can sense me, but she doesn't react at all."

I shrugged. "Maybe she's drugged. If I was keeping a dragon prisoner, I'd load her down with as many handicaps as possible."

"She's not drugged," Yong said with absolute certainty. "There are only a dozen substances on this planet strong enough to incapacitate a dragon. I've learned to identify all of them by taste, scent, and symptom because to not do so is asking to be poisoned, and I didn't detect anything."

"Maybe the DFZ punched her harder than we thought," I suggested. "Or maybe she *has* picked you up and just knows better than to let you know she knows. She *is* famously suspicious."

"That last one is more likely than anything else you've suggested," he said, scraping his hands through his long hair with an exasperated sigh. "But it's so *frustrating*. I'd hoped to talk to her in advance since we likely won't have much time to explain anything during the extraction, but I couldn't even get her attention. I thought perhaps the prison acted as a sensory block, but she saw and spoke to the guards who came down to feed her." His eyes narrowed. "She's up to something."

I laughed out loud. "Of *course* she's up to something. She's a caged dragon! If she wasn't spending every waking moment plotting her escape and revenge, I'd worry she was dead."

That seemed obvious to me, but my dad just kept shaking his head. "It just feels wrong," he muttered. "I've never been close to my sister, but I've still known her all her life. This isn't how she usually behaves. I don't like it."

I sighed. I'd been so busy practicing to make sure I could break the Gameskeeper's magic, I hadn't had time to think about all the steps that came before that. Assuming the plan worked and we could get to White Snake without the Gameskeeper noticing, I was reasonably certain that I could crush whatever spellwork Kauffman was using to hold her. After that, I was hoping freedom would make its own argument, but I should have known it was never that simple with dragons.

"We'll figure it out," I said, letting my tired eyes droop shut again. "Whatever else she's got going on, White Snake's not going to say no to a no-strings-attached prison break. I'm way more worried about how we're going to stop her from eating us the second she's out."

"She won't eat us," Yong said confidently. "Even in this compromised state, I can still put up too much resistance, and if the guards stick to the same just-in-time schedule they've used for all the arena's other acts, we'll be setting her free minutes before they come to fetch her for her fight. She's too selfish to waste that precious time fighting us instead of saving her own skin. If we give her the chance, she'll run. She always does."

That was comforting, I supposed. Honestly, I was just happy my dad was the one worrying about this, because I didn't have a brain cell to spare. There was so much to do and so many ways it could go wrong. It was good to have a dragon to help me keep track of it all. More specifically, it was good to have a father I could trust. A miracle I hadn't had time to fully appreciate yet.

"Thank you."

My father scowled. "For what?"

"Everything," I said, forcing my eyes open again. "Staying. Helping. Working so hard. This isn't your fight or your city, and you've got plenty of your own problems to deal with. I wouldn't have faulted you if you'd gone back to Korea the moment your magic stabilized, but you're still here and working as hard as anyone, and I'm grateful for it." I smiled at him. "Thanks for sticking it out with me, Dad."

Yong stared down at me, his perfect face appalled, which was not the reaction I'd expected. "Do you think so little of me?"

"What?" I cried, pushing myself up. "*No!* I was trying to give you a compliment!"

"Opal," he said in his sternest voice. "I am your father. From the day I first called you 'daughter,' I accepted a sacred obligation to defend your life and your happiness. I don't always understand why you make the decisions you do, but I will never leave you to face them alone, for you are my child. My daughter, my joy, and my treasure, forever and always." He glared at me. "You should know this by now."

I did. He'd said it in such a stern, lecturing tone of voice, it would have been easy to miss, but I didn't. I didn't even care that he'd slipped back into the old possessive language, because I understood that my father wasn't trying to control or own me anymore. He was trying to tell me how precious I was to him. How important. For the first time in twenty years, I felt like we were finally speaking the same language, and it felt like coming home.

"I love you too," I whispered in Korean, leaning over to rest my head against his shoulder. "Thank you."

"Do not thank someone for doing their duty," he scolded, but there was no more harshness in his voice. Yong sounded as close to giddy as dragons got, enough that I felt comfortable teasing him.

"Well, it's not as if you're doing it for free. I've dumped how much of the DFZ's magic into you so far?"

"The side benefits are quite nice," he admitted, looking down at his hands, which were finally no longer skeletal. "But I would have helped you even without them. From the moment your mother handed you to me, you became my greatest treasure. What sort of dragon would I be if I didn't defend that to the death?"

It was a sign of how far we'd come that I didn't even get mad at that. "I'm just glad you're getting better, and that I didn't *actually* kill you with currency markets," I said. "If we can get through this Gameskeeper business alive, you'll probably be good enough to go home."

I'd thought he'd be excited about that. My dad loved Korea more than anything, but the moment I said the word 'home,' the smile slipped off his face.

"No," he said, shaking his head. "Not until I'm stronger."

"That might be a while," I warned. "I've been dumping magic into you for days, and it's barely a drop in the bucket. There's no way we're getting you back up to your old power anytime soon, and we're running out of time. The other dragon clans are dividing Korea between themselves as we speak, *and* we're about to free White Snake. Just because we're pretty sure she'll choose running over killing you this time doesn't mean she won't come back to finish the job later. She'll talk if nothing else, which means the whole world's about to know that you're alive for sure, not just rumors."

"I am aware of the situation, but I'm not going home until I can defend it. If I go back to Korea now, all it will do is invite war to our shores. If I stay here, though, any battles I fight will be on the Peacemaker's lands. It's bad hospitality, but I'd rather risk the Dragon of Detroit's anger than my people's lives. The farther away I stay, the safer they'll be. That's all I can do for them in my current weakness."

I supposed that made a certain sort of proud-dragon sense, but, "Can you at least call Mom? You don't have to tell her where you are, but you should at least call and let her know that you're not dead in person. It's important. Trust me, I know from experience."

"I'm sure you do, but your mother is the last person on Earth I'd call."

"Why not?" I asked angrily. "Isn't she your First Mortal?"

"That's precisely why I can't tell her. I'm her dragon. She's dedicated her life to me. I'm stronger than I was, but I can't appear before her like *this*. Weak and dependent." He shuddered. "I'd rather be eaten by White Snake."

I rolled my eyes so hard I hurt something. All this time I'd thought my mom was the crazy one, but I saw now that Dad was just as bad. He'd rather be eaten than risk losing the admiration of his consort. It would have been cute if it hadn't been so obnoxious, not to mention totally *wrong*.

"Dad," I said with an exasperated huff. "Mom loves you with cultish devotion. You could get turned into a turtle and she'd still coo over you and hand-feed you lettuce for the rest of her life. She's not going to care about your fire."

"But *I* care about keeping her safe," Yong replied stubbornly. "Mortals are fragile, and my affection for your mother is well-known. She's got enough of a target on her back as it is without me limping back to make things worse."

There was undoubtedly some truth to that, but it still sounded like an excuse to me. The more time I spent with my father as an adult rather than as a child, the more I realized that, while Yong of Korea was definitely not your typical dragon, he still had the idiot parts of draconic pride in spades. But as much as I wanted to tell him he was a fool for thinking Mom wouldn't die for him no matter what shape he was in—or that being separated from him wasn't killing her with worry—it didn't matter. There was no one on the planet more single-minded about anything than my mother was about her dragon. Whether he called or not, she'd track him down eventually. Given all the times we'd been outside this last week, she was probably already closing in. She'd find him soon enough, and then they could work out their problems on their own time. Meanwhile, we had bigger things to worry about.

"I have to get back to practice," I said, crawling back to my feet. "Can I leave White Snake and the rest of the dragon stuff to you?"

"Of course," Yong said, rising much more gracefully. "I wouldn't have suggested freeing her if I didn't think I could handle it. Leave the management of my cowardly sister to me, and when this is over and the DFZ is in our debt, we'll see about increasing the rate of my recovery."

This was the first I'd heard about a debt, but I should have expected he'd come up with something like that. Dragons never did anything for free, and honestly, I didn't think the DFZ would mind. She was the city of nothing-for-free. If my dad demanded payment for his part in our operation, she'd probably just whip out a boiler-plate contract and start negotiations right then and there.

I didn't quite know how I'd ended up in a life where cities bargaining with dragons over fair payment for a hit job on a god counted as normal, but here we were. I was far more surprised that I'd somehow ended up being the least mercenary person around. Truly, wonders never ceased.

Shaking my head at the strangeness of it all, I walked out into the garden to find Dr. Kowalski, who, sure enough, had my next exercise already lined up.

***

Since all this training would be for nothing if I was too exhausted to use it, I was given the daylight part of Saturday off to sleep and prepare. That was the idea, anyway, but I actually spent most of the time lying in bed checking on what Nik had been up to.

True to his word, he hadn't contacted me since our call last Sunday, which was good for the mission but bad for me. It had been a hard, hard week, and I missed him terribly. I would have given a kidney to drive around the city with him in his car again, windows down and no worries other than what kind of treasures we'd find in our next apartment. Not that we'd ever been that carefree, but the nostalgia was nice, especially given what I was seeing now.

Nik had clearly been working just as hard this week as I had. My internet search turned up a media blitz of trailers, interviews, and a risqué photo shoot I would have loved if they hadn't gone out of their way to make Nik look like a total psycho. There were pictures of White Snake as well. Mostly shaky-cam shots from when she'd been chasing Dad and I over the river, which definitely made her look scary. I'd almost forgotten how big she was, which was crazy considering those truck-sized jaws had almost bitten me in half, but it was hard to keep something so much larger than you in the proper scale in your memory.

I had to hand it to the Gameskeeper, though. Dude knew how to stir up buzz. He barely even needed the paid advertisements. Nik's fight was the talk of every media channel. Even serious international news organizations who'd normally never cover something this sleazy couldn't seem to stop talking about the guy who was going to fight a dragon to the death on live TV. Add in the Peacemaker's strong objections and vows to investigate, and you had the type of viewer-gluing drama reporters lived for.

The firestorm was *so* big, I was surprised the DFZ had stayed with me through the entire training. I knew she could be in multiple places at once, so I wasn't shocked when I saw her on camera, but some of those interviews looked *hard.* The Peacemaker had to be grilling her behind the scenes, too, but other than looking a bit distracted on occasion, she'd never made me feel like I was anything other than the sole subject of her attention.

I didn't know if that was because she was really good at doing lots of things at once or if she actually was concentrating on me and giving everyone else the brush-off, but I appreciated her dedication. She might not be able to bodily go into the arena with me, but no one could say she hadn't done her part. Even lying in bed, I could feel her city magic humming through the bond between us, ready for me to use the moment I needed it.

I just hoped I could pull it off. At the rate this thing was building steam, Nik's fight really was going to be the event of the century, and we'd helped make it happen. If we didn't break the Gameskeeper tonight, we were going to make him, and I wasn't sure I could live with myself if that happened.

"You'll be fine," Sibyl assured me. "Remember your positive mindset! Also, this is your thirty-minute alarm."

"Time to get going," I told the picture of Nik's scowling face on my news feed. "Hang in there. It's almost over."

That went for me as well. Maybe not sleeping was a bad idea, because my whole body ached when I hauled it out of bed and forced it into clean clothes. Dark ones, because the first part of the plan involved sneaking, and while I wasn't exactly a ninja, even I knew that my preferred neon palette wasn't going to fly.

When I was dressed in my darkest pair of jeans, my old knee-high Cleaning boots, and the cheap long-sleeved vending machine T-shirt I'd bought for my dad—which hadn't been made to be worn twice, but was the only black top I owned—I dug my poncho out of the closet and tossed it over my shoulders. The poor thing was looking a bit ratty these days, but the protective wards still worked, and if there was ever a time I needed a get-out-of-being-shot-free card in my pocket, it was tonight. I was putting the last items I felt I'd need into my bag when my dad knocked on my door.

Since he was up and about, I'd moved back into my bedroom, which was all nice and unbloody again thanks to the DFZ's redecorating job. This arrangement put him on the couch, but seeing how he needed pretty much no sleep and I was the one paying for the apartment, I didn't feel bad about it. He hadn't complained in any event, and he actually knocked before barging in on me, which was huge progress. When I opened the door to tell him I was ready to go, though, the sight of him left me speechless.

"What the *hell* are you wearing?"

Where I was dressed for intrusion, my dad looked like he was going to a black-tie dinner. Not only did he have on the suit we'd bought to go to the Gameskeeper's, he'd somehow also managed to score a new tie, slick new shoes, and a pair of silver cuff links, none of which were appropriate for what we were about to do.

"We're not going to a party, Dad," I said, looking him over in disbelief. "Where did you even get this stuff?"

"Here and there," he replied cryptically, brushing a speck of nonexistent lint off his tailored shoulder. "It's not armor, but I feel more comfortable dressed like this."

He did look way more like the old Yong in this getup. Even with his long hair pulled back—his one concession to the fact that we were going to be sneaking through enemy territory—my dad looked closer to how I remembered him than he had since this mess started. That would probably come in handy when we talked to White Snake, but getting to her was another matter entirely.

"Okay, James Bond," I grumbled, shoving the last of my equipment into my shoulder bag. "I just hope you can run in those shoes, or this is going to be a very short night."

My father shrugged. "If we have to run, we've already failed."

That was the damn truth. There was no backup waiting for us tonight. Nik was busy, and the arena was the Gameskeeper's domain, which meant there'd be no DFZ rising to our rescue this time. If we got caught, we'd be on our own, and while my dad was looking a lot better, I didn't like our odds against the Gameskeeper or his hordes of hired guns.

"Guess we'd better make sure we don't get caught, then," I said, double-checking to make sure I had everything. When I was satisfied, I slid my shoulder bag on under my poncho and reached up to pull my goggles down over my eyes. "Sibyl?"

"I'm ready," my AI said in my earpiece.

I am, too, the DFZ whispered in my mind. *I'll be with you the whole way. You are not alone.*

I was never alone these days, but I took the words as the comfort she meant.

"The DFZ doesn't publish maps for Rentfree since it changes so much," Sibyl continued, oblivious to the other conversations going on in my brain. "But I've had a script scraping the city's contractor forums for updated utility maps, and I think our best starting location is here." She threw up a sewer map with a big red arrow blinking at a center junction. "That should get you closest to where your dad said White Snake's cell is located."

I wasn't the one to ask about that, so I pulled out my phone to show the map to my father.

"Looks good," he said, nodding. "The place they're holding her is very deep, so the farther down we can start, the better."

"Sounds like a plan," I said, stepping out into the living room with him so I could use my bedroom door. "Ready?"

The moment he nodded, I grabbed the knob and turned it hard, staring at the map Sibyl had projected in my AR until the lines were burned into my eyeballs. This was the most I'd ever asked of my city-traveling abilities. As always, though, the magic worked just fine, and a second later, we were stepping out of my apartment into a reeking pitch-black tunnel with a six-inch layer of lumpy, sludgy water flowing at the bottom.

"Ugh," I said, lifting my boots high to keep them out of muck. "Did you *have* to pick a sewer?"

"It was the only place big enough for you to stand up," Sibyl said apologetically. "Would you have preferred a two-foot-square electrical shaft?"

I shuddered and flipped on the LED light attached to my goggles. Not that light made things better since it meant I could see the thousands of insects scurrying along the sewer pipe's greasy walls instead of just hearing them, but I figured if I was going to step in something regrettable, I'd rather know ahead of time.

"Lovely," my father said, hopping nimbly over the disgusting water to land with his feet braced against both sides of the curved tunnel only to immediately start slipping as his fancy shoes lost their grip in the slime.

"I warned you not to wear those," I said as he started to scramble, turning my attention back to my map. "Where are we going?"

"Dead ahead," Sibyl replied, placing a blinking target icon on top of the green-tinged cement wall directly in front of us. "Not sure how you're getting through, but that's where the DFZ ends and the arena's underground complex begins."

Unbelievable, the DFZ whispered. *He kicks me out, but he's still using my sewers! The nerve.*

There were indeed several pipes coming out of the wall ahead of us, each one dumping a prodigious amount of waste into the channel we were wading through. "You should plug them up," I suggested. "Add to the chaos."

An evil laugh filled my head. *You have the best ideas,* the DFZ said as the pipes in front of us started wriggling like snakes. A moment later, they'd bent back on themselves, sending the flow of sewage back up the pipe from whence it'd came.

"Nice," I said, grinning. "Backflowing toilets aren't an emergency you can ignore. That should keep someone distracted, at least. And speaking of distractions, did you do the thing?"

A few days ago, when we'd planned tonight's timing in detail, one of the roadblocks I hadn't known how to get around was the Gameskeeper's ability to feel when the DFZ—or specifically, someone carrying the DFZ inside them—stepped into his territory. Kind of hard to sneak into a place when the owner can feel your presence. The DFZ had said she'd handle it, but I'd been too busy to follow up. A choice I was regretting right now.

Relax, I've got it covered, my city assured me. *I've called in priests from all over the city to help out. They're entering the arena with the rest of the crowds as we speak.*

I blinked. "The Gameskeeper's letting them in?"

Of course, she said. *They're paying customers.*

My shock must have come through loud and clear, because she hurried to explain. *I'm not the only one who's subject to her domain. The Gameskeeper is the god of the arena. It goes against his nature to deny anyone a seat, especially on a night like tonight. I paid top dollar for those tickets, and my money is as good as anyone's. He knows they're spies, but he can't deny me any more than I could deny him. Meanwhile, his arena is filled with false positives. I'm going to be in their heads even more than yours to keep things nice and confused,* so unless you do something really *obvious, he shouldn't be able to track you specifically.*

That was great news! "Does this also mean we'll have backup if things go bad?"

Uh...no, the DFZ said. *My other priests aren't what you'd call "Good in a fight."*

The only other priests of hers I'd met had been Dr. Kowalski and the person called Nameless who lived in the Wandering Cathedral, who were definitely both oddities. I'd assumed she had more normal people as well somewhere out in the city, but apparently "normal" didn't apply to the DFZ.

They're normal for me, the city grumbled. *I'm not a war god! The sort of people who dedicate themselves to a living city don't tend to be commando types. Or "go outside" types. But they're putting it out for me tonight, so let's respect their efforts.*

Hey, if they were willing to risk the Gameskeeper to help us pull this off, they were all amazing in my book.

They are *amazing!* the DFZ agreed excitedly. *I've got a literal financial wizard of an accountant, a rat-whisperer who champions my rodent population, a doctor who treats people in the back alleys with the flip of a coin, and...well, that's it actually.*

My eyes went wide. "You only brought three other people?"

Cut me some slack, I'm a young god! My priesthood is a work in process, but three should be more than enough to keep the Gameskeeper from zeroing in on you. Trust me, my people are very *distracting.*

It would have to do. I had my own problems, starting with how we were going to get inside. Aside from the pipes sticking out the bottom, the wall in front of us appeared to be made of solid cement. Not exactly an easy in.

"Can you open a door for us?"

Negative, the DFZ said. *The pipes were just over the line, but the wall itself is his domain. I can't move it.*

"I can," my father said when I explained the situation to him. "Stand aside."

There wasn't much room to stand anywhere in the narrow tunnel, but I scooted back as far as I could, pulling the hood of my poncho tight to cover as much of my face as possible.

"Clear!"

The moment the word was out of my mouth, my father hit the wall in four places. Each strike went faster than my eyes could follow, but when he was done, there was a neat rectangular crack in the cement. One more kick was all it took to bust open a perfectly Yong-sized hole.

"Nice," I said appreciatively, grinning at the broken, startlingly thick cement. "You *must* be feeling better!"

"Not that much better," he said, shaking his right hand, which had bruises all along the knuckles. "That should have been easier."

Rolling my eyes at ridiculous dragon standards, I stepped through the hole he'd made into what appeared to be a storage room full of dusty stage crates and huge stacks of plastic stadium seating. Nothing looked particularly dangerous, and—better still—there were no cameras on the walls. It was also dark as pitch, but that was fine with me. Dark rooms were rooms no one was looking in, and I had a solution built in.

"Okay," I said, flicking off my headlamp as I activated my goggles' night vision. "Where next?"

My father scowled in the dark, turning his head this way and that.

"Do you need me to turn the light back on?"

"No," he said irritably. "My night vision is as good as it ever was. I'm just trying to get my bearings. When I was scouting this place earlier, I came in through the door, not a wall."

Fair enough. While he looked around, I took the opportunity to check my news feeds. I wasn't stupid enough to get on the arena's WiFi, so I had to use regular DFZ municipal, which—surprise, surprise—was slow as balls down here. I had to turn off images before it would load, but eventually I read that the arena was already filling with people. Reports listed the crowd as massive, not that it could have been anything less after all that media coverage.

It's gigantic, the DFZ confirmed. *All of Rentfree is packed. Mostly out-of-towners, but there's plenty of locals in the mix too.* I felt her frown in my mind. *I have no idea how they're all going to fit.*

"Not our problem," I said as my images finally loaded, filling my vision with ads for T-shirts, posters, and other commemorative paraphernalia with Nik's face plastered all over them.

The sight made me wince. Poor Nik. He was never going to live this down. If we survived tonight, I was going to take him on a vacation. Somewhere nice and tropical and very far away.

"Opal."

I looked up to see my father standing across the room with his head sticking out the door. "Are you nuts?" I hissed, banishing my news feed as I ran over. "Don't open the door!"

"I checked for guards first," he said, insulted. "We have to go out sooner or later, and the hallway's empty at the moment. See?"

He opened the door wider so I could see the wide cement hall outside was, indeed, empty. Judging by the dust on the floor, it had been that way for a long time.

"About time we had some luck," I said, poking at the thick layer of grit with the armored toe of my boot. "Have you figured out where we're going?"

Instead of answering, my father stepped into the hall, leaving me to scurry after him.

The lower levels of the arena were very different from what I'd imagined. I'd expected a typical backstage full of bustle and chaos with supplies and props packed to the ceiling. This actually reminded me more of a military installation. As Nik had warned me over the phone, it went *very* deep. We'd come in through the Rentfree sewers, the lowest point in the whole DFZ, but according to my dad, we weren't even halfway down. I was wondering how the Gameskeeper had dug all of this out without anyone noticing when the DFZ popped into my head with the answer.

It was already here, she said, directing my eyes toward the faded paint on the dusty walls. *This used to be part of the old Detroit Salt Mine. I closed off the entrances ages ago, but I couldn't move the mine itself since most people don't know about it and therefore it's not considered part of my city. I suspected the Gameskeeper had taken it over when he built his arena right on top of it, but I didn't worry too much. I mean, what was he going to do with a giant hole in the ground?*

A lot, apparently. The Gameskeeper must have been as much of a pack rat as I was, because every storeroom we passed was filled to the ceiling. Most of it looked like props for the arena—old hollowed-out cars, fake building fronts, lion cages, and so on—but there were plenty of weapon vaults as well, including some major military hardware.

"Whoa," I said when we passed a room full of guns big enough to take down a dragon.

That's exactly what they're for, the city confirmed. *Those are anti-dragon weapons.*

"Are you kidding? Where did he get those?!"

They're leftovers from when Algonquin ruled the city. I sold all her stuff after I kicked her out.

I pressed my palm over my face.

What? I needed the money! All my buildings were wrecked, and steel doesn't come cheap. What was I supposed to do, hold a bake sale?

I saw her point but selling off the Lady of the Lakes' armory seemed like a spectacularly bad idea. One that was currently being highlighted in bold as we walked by another room marked "Anti-dragon/Anti-aircraft Launchers. Live Ammunition: Keep Out."

Okay, so maybe I was a tiiiiiiny bit reckless, the god admitted. *But it's all locked up in warehouses, and we're about to take the Gameskeeper down anyway. I'll just take it all back when he falls. No blood, no foul, right?*

That had yet to be seen, but I didn't have time to argue with her. We'd reached the end of the hall and were now facing the central freight elevator. My dad hadn't said anything yet, but I presumed our target was the flight of emergency stairs set into the far wall. Unfortunately, to get there, we were going to have to cross a wide loading area watched by at least three security cameras.

"What do you want to do about those?" I asked, nodding at the cameras.

My father shrugged. "You have a top-of-the-line AI. Can't she take them over?"

"Uh, no," I said with a snort. "Sibyl's a social support bot. She doesn't hack."

"I can ask about their work satisfaction," Sibyl offered helpfully.

My father sighed and reached into his pocket to pull out a small steel ball bearing. "Guess we do it the old-fashioned way, then."

I knew what he was planning the moment he hefted the metal sphere, but before he could throw it like a bullet at the closest camera, I grabbed his wrist.

"I've got a better idea. One that won't result in dead cameras that might tip off security."

My dad shrugged and slipped the ball bearing back into his pocket. Meanwhile, I dropped into a crouch and slowly leaned down the wall, edging my head around the corner until the tiny camera on the corner of my goggles had a good view of the entire freight elevator lobby. When I was certain I had a good mental image of all three cameras, I pulled my head back and closed my eyes, reaching out to grab a handful of the arena's slippery magic.

The power fought me as always, but there was no spellwork on the walls down here. It still didn't flow like normal DFZ magic, but it was the loosest I'd felt inside the arena. I'd also been working my magical muscles all week, and between those two factors, I was able to wrench free enough power to do what I wanted to do.

"Okay," I said, gripping the magic tight. "When I say go, run for the stairs."

I waited for my father to nod, and then I closed my eyes again, this time picturing a hand reaching out to grab each camera. As Dr. Kowalski had taught me, I focused on the image until it felt as real as any memory of an actual object. Then I pictured it again, doing the motion so many times in my head that I could have done it in my sleep. Only then did I let the magic actually slide out of me, reaching across the empty space to grab each camera and wrench them away from us.

"*Go!*"

We bolted forward, my dad shooting ahead to open the stairwell door for me. Above us, the cameras were straining on their automated arms, fighting my hold. But while I hadn't been able to grab much, it didn't take a strong hand to beat such a tiny engine. I maintained control no problem, keeping the cameras pointed firmly at the opposite wall until we were both inside the stairwell with the door closed.

"One in here too," my father warned. "Just below us."

Panting more from the running than the magic, I did the same spell again, jerking the camera toward a blind corner so we could slip past it. When we were a flight down, I let it go again, and the camera went right back to its usual position, meaning anyone watching the feed would only see a brief blip that would look like a temporary malfunction. That was my hope, anyway, but we didn't hear any alarms, so it seemed I'd done well enough.

We had to repeat this song and dance for every floor. Despite this, we still made good time. All of the cameras were identical in model and position, so I was able to process them quickly, and the farther we got from the spellwork in the arena, the easier it was to cast. The arena magic was still awful to work with, but I knew what to expect now, and I managed the screaming all right. I was far more concerned about the actual voices I could hear talking on the other side of the metal doors every time we passed a landing. No one came into the stairwell, though, so we just kept going, moving swiftly and silently down, down, down the circling stairs until, at last, we reached the bottom.

"Hold up," I gasped when we were safely past the last camera. "Let me…catch my…breath."

My father scowled. "It was only ten flights."

"I don't…exactly get time…to do cardio…these days…" I panted. "Cut me…some slack."

He did, though not without reminding me that he'd been basically dead not a week ago, and he'd managed the stairs just *fine*. I didn't have the breath to waste pointing out that he was a supernatural creature while I was merely human, so I saved myself the trouble and looked around instead.

Just as the DFZ had said, we were standing inside a mine. Unlike the floor we'd come in on, there were no cement hallways or rooms full of random storage down here. Just dark, rough-cut tunnels through the stone big enough to drive a tractor down. The lights were few and far between and so old they hummed like pitch-pipes. The rock floor was even dustier than the one upstairs, and while I could see a few footprints going down the cave ahead of us, it didn't look as if anyone had been down here in a long, long time.

"Are you sure this is the right place?"

"Positive," my father said. "I saw her with my own eyes just this morning, and you couldn't ask for a better place to lock up a dragon." He nodded approvingly at the rough-cut stone. "Nothing to burn, too tight to use our wings, and too much rock for us to break through. It's perfect."

"I'm sure the Gameskeeper has imprisoned all manner of creatures down here," I said bitterly, remembering yet again that this was the monster who'd wanted to fight our baby cockatrices. That thought got me riled up again, and I pushed off the rock wall. "Okay, I think I'm done dying. Which way to White Snake?"

My father pointed down the tunnel and off we went, keeping to the shadows even though there seemed to be no cameras at all down here. I knew there had to be at least one because that was how the Gameskeeper had showed White Snake to me, but the tunnels themselves appeared completely unwatched and unguarded. Also unmarked. We passed so many forks and turns that I was soon hopelessly lost.

Thankfully, my dad seemed to know exactly where he was going. He led us unerringly down tunnels and around corners until, at last, we dead-ended at a huge steel security door set deep into the stone—an old Algonquin Corp one according to the logo stamped into the upper corner—and I broke into a grin.

"I got this."

"You do?" my father asked, looking surprised. "I thought we'd have to break it down."

"We still might, but let me try first," I said, digging into my bag for my pliers. "These old doors are everywhere in the city. I don't think you can be a Cleaner for more than two weeks without coming up against one. Fortunately, they're all made exactly the same way, so I've gotten pretty good at cracking them." My father's eyebrows shot up at that last part, and I grinned wider. "My job required a lot of breaking and entering."

"I see why your mother despised it," he said dryly, but he didn't get in my way as I switched my usual metal-lined safety gloves for my full-rubber, anti-electrical set and started digging my pliers into the door's punch-code box.

I knew the moment I popped the panel that this was going to be a standard model. I didn't consider that an oversight on the Gameskeeper's part, though. This door was the best security you could get for the price, which was why everyone used them. But when everyone uses something, the knowledge of how to break it also becomes widespread, especially among Cleaners. I'd looked up how to crack these things so many times I had the process memorized, and barely a minute later, I had us in.

"There," I said as the last latch popped. "I know there's at least one more camera inside, but I'm going to let you get it this time. I don't want to have to hold it with magic the whole time we're in there, and I'm going to need my attention for the ward."

"Right," my father said, tearing his eyes away from the metal door I'd just processed like a pro-burglar. "One moment."

He pulled the ball bearing out of his pocket again and grabbed the door's handle, leaning his body inside. He must have already spotted the camera during his scouting, because he didn't even have his head around the corner before his arm lashed out, sending the steel ball flying with sharpshooter precision. There was a sharp crack followed by the clatter of glass as the camera's metal casing shattered, and then my father pushed the door the rest of the way open.

"After you."

I dropped a fake curtsy and hurried inside, taking a breath to ready myself for what I knew was waiting. But even though I'd seen it myself already, cameras were terrible at capturing scale, and the memory of the little picture on the Gameskeeper's monitor did nothing to prepare me for the monster waiting inside.

I stopped cold, clamping my teeth tight to stop the alarmed yelp. The room we'd stepped into wasn't a room at all, but a huge cavern. And at its center, surrounded by a warded metal cage the size of a three-story building, was White Snake.

As I'd seen on the camera, she was in her dragon form, but even curled into a ball to fit inside her prison, the sheer size of her was shocking. You'd think growing up with my dad would have gotten me used to dragons, but while I didn't even notice Yong's predatory menace when he was in his human form anymore, it was impossible *not* to be intimidated by an actual, in-the-scales dragon. She may have been only half my father's size, but White Snake was still hundreds of times larger than myself. Bars or no bars, under the ground or in the sky, dragons were terrifying, and being in the same room with one who'd been trying to kill me not two months ago was almost more than I could take.

"I wonder why she hasn't woken up," my father said, politely ignoring the near-panic attack I was having beside him. "It was like this when I was here before. She's breathing, but her eyes aren't open."

I'd been too busy staring at her teeth and claws to notice her eyes, but I took his word for it. "It's probably the ward," I said, pointing at the glowing lattice of spellwork that covered her cage. "If I was crazy enough to imprison a dragon, I sure as hell wouldn't leave her awake."

My father nodded in agreement, eyeing the ward with malice. "Can you break it?"

I was sure as hell going to try. I'd actually been looking forward to using this as my practice run. There were tons of safe ways to break a ward, but none of those let me practice blowing up one of Kauffman's circles. Dr. Kowalski thought I was ready, but if I couldn't overload this thing without hurting myself, then blowing the arena was a pipe dream. It was time to see if all my practice had paid off, so before I could lose my nerve, I strode into the room, walking straight to the edge of the glowing spellwork surrounding the still, seemingly sleeping dragon.

It was one of the scariest things I'd ever done in my life. Objectively, I knew I was perfectly safe, or at least as safe as I could be down here in the belly of our enemy. We'd already taken out the camera, and if the Gameskeeper or White Snake could have attacked us, they would have done so already. This was actually the *least* dangerous part of our entire plan, but there was just something about walking toward the thing every survival instinct I had was begging me to run away from that turned my muscles to water. By the time I actually reached the cage, I was shaking so badly my teeth were chattering.

Don't be afraid, the DFZ ordered, her voice reverberating in my rattled mind. *You are my priest, and I smacked her out of the sky like a fly. We beat her once. We can take her again if it comes to that.*

I yearned to remind her that we were not in the DFZ this time, which meant no punching with buildings, but there was no point. Freeing White Snake was the most critical element of our plan. If she decided to eat us on the way out, there wasn't much we could do to stop her. We just had to hope she wouldn't bite the hand that freed her, because it was waaaaay too late to turn back. Her fight with Nik was starting in less than an hour. We actually only had about ten minutes left before the guards would arrive to take her upstairs to the arena. It was now or never, so I took a huge breath and knelt on the ground, pulling off my rubber safety gloves to place my bare palms down on the glowing spellworked bars that contained her.

The moment I touched the ward, I knew it was Kauffman's. Just like every other bit of his work I'd touched, the spell holding White Snake down was perfectly tuned and neat as a pin. This time, though, instead of despairing at how much better he was, I focused on my own talents. I'd never be a good Thaumaturge with perfect spellwork, but I'd become a pretty decent Shaman, and we rocked at stuff like this.

"Okay," I whispered to the DFZ. "Let's blow it."

Magic bubbled up inside me in answer. Even after days of training, the sudden surge of power I hadn't put there caught me by surprise. I compensated by focusing on the parts I *was* used to: namely throwing all of that magic into Kauffman's perfect circle as hard and fast as I could. Just like the one I'd destroyed in the Gnarls, I knew it was going to take a lot. Kauffman's circles always had multiple fail-safes. Unsurprising for a dragon prison, this one was even sturdier than usual, but I had something he'd never thought to plan for: a direct magical link to a god. I didn't even bother trying to get around his spellwork. I just bulldozed straight through it, shoving magic into the circle as fast as the DFZ could feed it to me until, with a blinding *pop,* the whole ward exploded.

It'd been so long since I'd been backlashed, the sudden wall of force caught me completely by surprise. For a terrifying moment, the power of the overloaded spell raced through me like lightning, burning and breaking everything it touched. Then my training kicked back in.

All at once, I stopped fighting the lightning and grabbed it instead. I didn't have to hold it, didn't have to endure. All I had to do was pass it on, sending the roaring magic through me into the DFZ like electricity down a wire.

As fast as it had started, the explosion vanished. I didn't even get knocked over. When I opened my eyes again, I was still crouching right where I'd been with my dad right beside me, watching nervously.

"Did it work?" he whispered.

"Hell yeah, it worked," I breathed, looking at the bars, which were no longer glowing, but charred and brittle as old fire logs. "It worked great."

The words weren't even out before I collapsed onto the ground. I'd done it! This was what I'd practiced for, but after so many years of eating backlashes to the face, being able to pass all that horrible, out-of-control magic to someone who could actually handle it felt like a miracle. I still wasn't certain I could manage a circle the size of an entire arena, but we'd just proved the concept, and I was so *happy*! I would have rolled around in sheer joy if there hadn't been an enemy dragon not two feet in front of me. A dragon that, I was suddenly keenly aware, was no longer held down by magic.

I froze, all happy feelings driven out of me by an icy wave of fear. Above my head, the huge form of White Snake began to shift inside her steel cage, the burned-out bars of which were looking flimsier by the second. When I tried to scramble away, though, my father caught my arm.

"Don't," he ordered sharply, his eyes locked on his towering sister. "Show no fear, no weakness. Don't give her an inch."

I nodded, forcing myself to stand back up instead of fleeing like I so desperately wanted to. When I was back on my feet at his side, my father took my hand and squeezed it. "Don't be afraid," he whispered. "I know how to handle her."

I wasn't at all sure that he did, but it was out of my hands. My part was over. All I could do now was stand up straight and trust in my father as the dragoness opened her huge eyes, the black-slitted pupils dilating in confusion before locking onto my dad as she took a hissing breath of pure, smoky hate.

"*You.*"

Chapter 13

I jumped backward. Stupid, I know, since my dad had just warned me not to do exactly that. In my defense, the instinct to keep my soft, easily chewed body as far as possible from those huge teeth was *really* strong. I was still getting myself back together when my father stepped in front of me.

"White Snake," he said in Korean.

The dragon above us blew an angry huff of smoke out of her nostrils, and I braced for the worst. My dad looked a lot better than he had a week ago, but there was no fooling White Snake. She knew exactly how weak he was, because she was the one who'd made him that way. I was already reaching out to the DFZ for more magic to stop…whatever it was she was about to do. Eat my dad. Eat me. Trample us both while laughing on her way to freedom.

All seemed equally likely. In the end, though, White Snake did none of those things. She simply put her head back down, resting her wedge-shaped, sharp-toothed jaw on her folded forelegs with a disgusted sigh.

"What do you want?"

I frowned. That was not the reaction I'd expected. Fortunately, my dad was still on the ball.

"We've come to set you free," Yong replied, pointing at the open security door behind us. "Go. I promise not to follow."

White Snake snorted, sending a cloud of white-gray smoke up to the rough-cut ceiling. "I'm not afraid of you," she grumbled. But she still didn't move, and my father's firm scowl grew confused.

"Why aren't you leaving?" he demanded when it had become clear she wasn't going to budge.

"Why should I?" she replied, turning her huge head away. "There's no point."

"There is *every* point," my father said angrily. "We have been enemies since you hatched, but we are still blood. I will not stand by and allow my sister to be used as mortal entertainment!"

White Snake glared at him through resentful, slitted eyes. "You don't get to tell me what to do. As you are so fond of reminding me, we are not clan." She curled herself tighter, tucking her head under her long tail. "Go away."

My father stared in disbelief. I was right there with him. Of all the ways this plan could have gone south, the idea that White Snake would simply *not want to leave* hadn't even blipped my radar. And that sucked, because according to the timer Sibyl was keeping at the corner of my vision, the guards would be down to escort her to the arena any moment.

"Don't you want to get out of here?" I cajoled, going for a different angle. "The Gameskeeper's planning to humiliate you tonight, but if you run, there's nothing to stop you. You can go back to your humans! I'm sure they're worried sick."

"There's no one worrying over me."

I was opening my mouth to say that wasn't true when her head suddenly snapped back up.

"Don't you get it?" White Snake snarled, pressing her snout against the blackened bars. "You *won.* Thanks to whatever miracle you pulled to get the DFZ on your side, I was defeated in front of the entire world! Do you honestly think my mortals would stick around after that?"

My father's would, but my dad had always been special. White Snake's relationship with her humans seemed far more typical. Considering the dragon who'd jumped us outside of Peter's place had bought his info from one of White Snake's people in exchange for a plane ticket, I had a feeling she was right on the money. But while I could see her predicament, my father looked deeply, *personally* offended.

"So you're just going to give up?" He sneered. "I don't recall you being so *weak.*"

"Don't talk like you know me," she said, baring her huge teeth at him. "You've done everything you could to keep me away for a thousand years. You have no idea what I've been through! You were always strong, and you only got stronger after you ate Father's fire, but I had *nothing*! I had to connive and pander and show my belly to stronger dragons just to survive. The fact that I didn't end up as a head on some enemy clan's wall is proof that I'm more resilient than you could ever be, a sentimental idiot who let himself get drained dry over a mortal!"

My dad and I both flinched.

"But that's all over," White Snake went on, her voice defeated. "I bet everything I had on this plot. After using your mortal to weaken you, I was going to eat what was left of your fire and present your severed head to the Peacemaker as proof. He'd kick me out of the DFZ, but the world would know I was strong enough to defeat Yong of Korea. The real one, not the sad shadow you'd become. That was the plan, anyway, but neither of us can fake it now, can we? Just as the whole world saw me go down, they saw your bleeding carcass get rescued by the DFZ. We were both weak in front of everyone, and that means we're both prey. Even if I ate you right here, you don't have enough fire left to make me a threat to anyone."

She jerked her head toward the open door. "You call it escape, but if I go out there, I'm dead. Every greedy snake on the planet will be hunting me down to eat my fire the second I reemerge. You know that perfectly well, because you hid too. Not that I get much news down here, but you wouldn't still be alive to bother me if you hadn't. But whatever madness you're trying to pull tonight, I'm not stupid enough to go along. The Gameskeeper and I have a deal. He'll let me live down here in safety, and all I have to do in return is fight in his arena."

My father looked more appalled than ever. "So you're going to allow him to humiliate you just so you can *hide in a cave?*"

"Yes," White Snake said, resting her head on her claws. "Because unlike the Great Yong, pride isn't a luxury I've ever been able to afford.

You think life's easy for a dragon living in exile? The only reason I've lived as long as I have is because I'm willing to do whatever I must to survive. This is just more of the same. All I have to do is endure down here for a century or so until this blows over, and then I'll see about rebuilding. It won't be pretty, but I've done more with worse, and I'll do so again. I'll do whatever it takes to stay alive. That is *my* strength, brother. It's not much, but it's all I've got."

"It's a lie!" Yong roared, knocking aside the brittle bars and marching forward until he was standing practically on his sister's face. "This is your victory? To live in a hole like a *worm?*" He sneered. "I respected you more when you were trying to kill me and take my lands! At least then you were living as a dragon should."

"You think that's what this was about?" she asked, her voice despairing. "I never wanted to be Dragon of Korea. All I wanted was to go *home!*"

My father looked disgusted, but I jumped up. "Wait," I said, moving as close to White Snake as I dared. "If that's true, why were you always trying to kill him?"

"Because he'd made it clear that 'over his dead body' was the only way I'd ever get back to Korea," White Snake replied, her resentful eyes locked on my father. "It's the only home I've ever known, the only place in the world I've ever felt safe. All I wanted was to live on my mountain in peace, but as soon as *he* came to power, he kicked me out! Left me to wander alone and clanless, an easy target for any dragon looking for someone to trap under their claws."

I turned to my dad. "Is that true?"

"She tried to stab me in the back the moment our father was dead!" he cried. "What kind of fool welcomes a viper into his house?"

"I only attacked you because I knew what you were going to do!" White Snake yelled back. "You told me to my *face* that you'd kick me out the moment you had the power to do so! Of course I fought. What else was I supposed to do? You never listened to anything I said!"

"Because you always lied."

"Not about this," she said, her slitted eyes pleading. "I've spent a thousand years *begging* you to let me come home. I've bribed you, bargained with you, brought you treasure, promised you eternal service. You never listened to any of it, but there's still no way you couldn't know what I wanted. Not after I came so many times. You knew exactly what I longed for most, and you made it perfectly clear that so long as you were its dragon, Korea would be forever beyond my reach." Her claws dug into the stone. "You say we were enemies from our hatching, but we both know that's not how it was. You *made* me your enemy. I would have done anything you wanted if you'd just let me come home, but I was never good enough for you. You enjoyed watching me suffer while you sat secure on your throne surrounded by your fawning mortals because it made you feel strong. Of *course* I attacked the moment you were weak! You gave me no other choice!"

She was shouting by the time she finished, her huge voice booming off the stone walls. It should have been terrifying, but I wasn't afraid anymore. All I felt for White Snake now was pity, because her description of my father was very similar to what my own view had been barely a week ago. Things between us were better now, but I was still leaning toward White Snake's side in all this. My dad had made his opinion of other dragons—and White Snake in particular—very clear, and while I couldn't remember if I'd been present for any of her visits, I knew she'd come to his fortress in Korea several times bearing gifts. Seeing my father's look of disgust now, I had no problem believing he'd been cruel to her. Not that I thought she'd been a saint or anything, but their bad blood put us in a very poor position. Our plan hinged on removing White Snake from the equation. As things stood currently, it was looking as if she'd fight Nik just to stick it to my dad.

"Enough of this," Yong said, crossing his arms over his chest. "What will it take to make you leave?"

"More than you have." She lowered her head to the stone, pressing her huge body stubbornly into the ground. "You're not the Dragon of Korea anymore. We're both homeless, so take your mortal puppy and leave me alone."

Every word she spoke cut my hopes lower. I supposed this turn of events shouldn't have been surprising. White Snake and Yong never agreed on anything, including apparently what counted as freedom. White Snake was already tucking her head back under her tail, digging her claws into the stone like she intended to stay here for a hundred years. Shaking with defeat, I was turning to my dad to ask if we had a Plan B when Yong said something I never would have expected.

"What if I promised to let you come back to Korea?"

White Snake's head shot up, her eyes going round with shock before they narrowed in disgust again. "I wouldn't believe you," she grumbled. "You might be famous for the strength of your word, but giving me anything goes against your nature. I know I'm fighting your daughter's human lover tonight. You're just playing me so you can give your precious Opal what she wants, just like always." She snorted out a puff of smoke. "You spoil her rotten."

I took offense at that, but Yong barely seemed to hear. "What if I swore on my fire?"

She snorted again. "What fire? You couldn't even singe me with that candle flame you've got inside you. How do you think you're going to take back Korea like that? Give the other clans a stern talking-to?"

"I don't have to take back Korea," Yong said confidently. "Because I never lost it in the first place. I do not accept defeat as easily as you do, and my mortals do not abandon me. They will defend my lands for me until I return, and I *will* return. Just because I have been forced to bide my time while I recover doesn't mean I've lost. I am already exponentially stronger now than I was a week ago, and I will be stronger still, for I am the Great Yong of Korea! And I swear on my life and my fire that if you help us, I will welcome you home and take you back into my clan."

His words rang through the air like golden bells, filling the old salt mine with the scent of fire and the sharp bite of dragon magic. Even among the most treacherous of snakes, oaths made on dragon fire were unbreakable, and my dad had just thrown his down like a gauntlet. Good thing, too, because that bold move was probably the only thing we had left that could have gotten White Snake's attention. Her eyes had already been closing as he spoke, but now they snapped back open, her huge, wedge-shaped head moving toward us until her snout was level with Yong's chest, staring my human-sized father eye to giant eye.

"Do you mean it?" she whispered, her voice quivering with something very close to hope. "You will let me come home?"

"I swore it, didn't I?" Yong replied haughtily. Then his expression softened. "I didn't know you wanted to come home so badly. I assumed you wanted my throne like everyone else, but I can't fault anyone for longing for somewhere as beautiful as our Korea. Had I been less proud and more attentive to what was in front of me, all of this might have been avoided."

His eyes flicked to me as he said that, and then he put out his hand to White Snake. "We have too many enemies between us to waste time fighting each other. I cannot undo the past, but the future is still ours to make whatever we wish. We might just be two weak dragons, but together we can be strong again. I'm willing to try if you are, sister."

"Then swear," she ordered, her sea-blue eyes bright again for the first time since we'd come down here. "If you mean what you say, swear again on your fire that I can come home. Swear that you'll welcome me back as a fellow dragon of Korea, and I swear I'll help you protect our lands from any who'd try to steal them."

When my father nodded, White Snake lowered her nose to his outstretched hand. The moment they touched, dragon magic roared through the cavern like a firestorm. I wasn't even involved, but I could still feel the vow biting down like teeth all over my body. Maybe it was because I was part of their clan too thanks to my connection with my dad, or maybe the ultimate promise between dragons was just that strong. Either way, there was no denying what had just happened. The oath they'd made was dug into all of us as deep as the curse on Nik's neck. Unlike the Sword of Damocles, though, this wasn't a deal with the devil. It was a promise between family. Family I was part of, too, because the moment my father welcomed White Snake back, I felt her fire like an inferno. Felt her happiness like my own, the heady joy of being almost home.

Almost, but not quite.

"That was bigger than I expected," White Snake said when it was finished. Then her eyes went to me quizzically. "But why does the mortal feel like clan too? What have you been doing, Yong?"

"I'll explain later," my father promised, his face suddenly exhausted. "For now, though, you have to leave. They'll be down to collect you for the fight any second, and we don't want to be here when they do."

White Snake must have been serious about only wanting to go home, or maybe she really didn't want to live in a hole for the next hundred years, because she jumped to obey, hopping to her feet so fast the cave shook. "Do you need a ride out?"

That would have been a great plan if getting out was all we had left to do. But while I was already more than ready to leave this place, we weren't done. White Snake's escape was actually a critical part of our strategy, because if I was going to get that curse off Nik's neck, I needed to keep the Gameskeeper distracted, and a rampaging dragon was a *great* distraction. If the Gameskeeper was too busy chasing White Snake to notice when it was fight time, Nik could simply walk out onto the empty sand, declare himself the victor, and the curse would vanish. After that, all that was left for me to do was blow Kauffman's circle so the Gameskeeper could never get this strong again. Or crush us all on our way out.

He certainly had enough juice to do it. Even all the way down here, I could feel the arena's magic building as the crowds piled in. The huge swell worked in our favor since it would push Kauffman's spellwork to its limit, making it easier to break, but it was also a terrifying reminder that we were playing chicken with a god. A smaller one than mine, true, but still huge next to me.

But as scary as things were getting, we were still on target. Despite everything, the plan was working. All we had to do was keep on keeping it together and we'd snatch Nik right out from under the Gameskeeper's nose. But as I opened my mouth to tell White Snake we didn't need a ride, thanks, but would she mind breaking as much stuff as possible on her way out, the growing magic that surrounded us suddenly lurched sideways.

Lurched and *expanded,* the magic crashing over me until it felt like I was back in the arena with the screaming crowd. The change was so explosive, it knocked the breath right out of me, which was why I couldn't shout a warning to my father when the Gameskeeper condensed out of the magic-saturated air right behind him.

***

I didn't have time to scream. I barely managed to choke before the Gameskeeper lifted his hand to point the biggest gun I'd ever seen at my father's head. I was still boggling at the size of it—seriously, that thing had a barrel like a drainage pipe—when the door behind us burst open, and dozens of armored, armed men poured into the cave.

Oddly, White Snake was the first of us to recover. Maybe being drained had slowed my father's reflexes, or maybe years of living on the run had honed his sister's survival instincts to a razor's edge, but the first of the men had barely made it through the doorway before she reared back and blasted them with fire.

The dragon flame passed so close to my head, my hair crinkled from the heat. She caught the first group flat-footed, but the soldiers behind them already had their guns up, a whole firing line of ridiculously oversized arm-cannons identical to the one the Gameskeeper was pointing at my dad. That was all I managed to see before they opened fire.

The barrage was so loud in the enclosed room, I went deaf for several seconds as a fusillade of sharp-pointed shells covered in glowing spellwork split White Snake's plume of fire to land in her open mouth. The explosion that followed was so bright that I lost my vision, too, leaving me clutching the stone floor in a world that consisted of nothing but blinding light and terrible ringing.

By the time I came back to myself, White Snake was a bleeding mess on the ground. She wasn't dead, but whatever they'd shot at her had clearly taken a chunk out. The wounds were already healing before my eyes—classic draconic toughness—but she didn't look eager to eat another barrage. Even after her bloody face had knitted itself back together, she stayed down, watching the Gameskeeper and his men with patient, calculating hate.

She was doing better than me. The moment I could see and hear again, my body had launched into a full-blown panic. I'd never seen anything like those weapons before, but between the old Algonquin Security Force logos stamped onto their huge barrels and what they'd done to White Snake, it wasn't hard to guess that these must be the Anti-Dragon guns my god had foolishly sold to the enemy. The man-portable version, thankfully, not the giant tractor-towed cannons we'd passed on our way down, but this was still a disaster. Normally, a weapon small enough to be lugged around by humans wouldn't do anything but piss a dragon off, but we weren't exactly at our best, and from the smug smile on his face, the Gameskeeper knew it.

"Well, well," he said cheerfully. "Look what we've caught."

"How did you know?" I asked, partially to keep the Gameskeeper talking because talking wasn't shooting, but also because I really did want to know. I'd thought we'd done an exemplary job sneaking down here, and now that I was recovering from my initial panic, the fact that he'd had an army waiting to jump us the second we finished felt supremely unfair.

"I didn't," the Gameskeeper said, keeping his huge gun pressed against my father's skull. "Not specifically. I suspected you were up to something when Mad Dog suddenly took an interest in fight promotion, so I went ahead and armed an anti-dragon team. I'd originally set this ambush up for Kos's room given your past antagonism with my lovely challenger, but then I saw her camera go out and realized I hadn't given you enough credit. Not that it made a difference since we still arrived in plenty of time to catch you, but I have to say I'm disappointed." His eyes flicked to White Snake. "I expected better of you. We had a good deal. What happened?"

"He offered me a better one," White Snake replied, her eyes never leaving the row of guns that was still pointed at her face. "But this is very stupid, Gameskeeper. Your surprise attack may have bloodied me, but those antique guns aren't enough to put my brother and I down, and you are still a small god. You can't stop us."

That seemed like a gutsy thing to say considering neither White Snake nor my father had moved yet. To my surprise, though, the Gameskeeper nodded. "I can't kill you both," he agreed. "But why would I want to? I promised the world a dragon fight, and I intend to deliver. We just need to come to a new arrangement."

His finger tightened on the gun he was holding to my father's head, and my stomach shrank to the size of a pea. It was easy for White Snake to talk a big game; she was still at full strength. My dad was another story. We'd made huge progress, but I wasn't about to gamble that he could live through an anti-dragon round to the head, which sure as hell looked like what was about to happen. The only reason I didn't do something insanely stupid was because my dad didn't look worried at all.

"A gun? Really?" he drawled, turning around to face the huge barrel the Gameskeeper was pointing in his face with a look of supreme disappointment. "What kind of god needs a mortal weapon to enforce his will?"

"It worked for Algonquin," the Gameskeeper replied with a shrug. "The Spirit of the Great Lakes was exterminating dragons with these 'mortal weapons' for decades before the rest of us woke. Who am I to argue with success? And in case you forgot, I'm the god of the arena. Weapons are as much a part of me as the sand and the blood. You should be thankful that I'm not using a barbed spear like the ancient dragon slayers. The gun is much quicker."

The Great Yong looked nonplussed, but I didn't have time to listen to the banter of higher beings. My dad's poker face might be flawless, but I knew the cards he was holding. He was bluffing big time, and if I didn't figure out how to follow it up with something real, real fast, we were all seriously boned.

Don't worry, the DFZ said in my mind, her voice finally breaking through the wall of my panic that she'd clearly been beating on for a while. *This changes nothing. Stick to the plan!*

Which part? I thought back frantically, because the plan as I knew it was totally off the rails.

Nothing's off the rails. We're still inside the arena, and the system that feeds magic to the Gameskeeper is still in place. All you have to do is blow his spellwork like we practiced and everything will be fine.

I didn't see how that could possibly be the case. Yes, we were technically inside the Gameskeeper's domain, but the spellwork that captured and held the crowd's magic was thousands of feet above me. How was I supposed to overload a spell I couldn't even see?

The distance doesn't matter, the DFZ said firmly. *Every part of this place is part of him just as all corners of the city are part of me. There is no near or far, it's all the same magic. The opening fights are happening as we speak, and the place is packed. The crowd's already running near peak. All you have to do is add my power on top of that, and this whole place should blow!*

That was indeed the strategy we'd come up with, but even if I could reach the spell from here, it was too early. Nik hadn't even come out yet. If we blew the spellwork now, he'd still be cursed.

We'll deal with that later! Power surged into me as she shoved magic through our connection. *But if you don't do something now, your dad is dead!*

I took her magic grudgingly, but I didn't like this one bit. This wasn't how the plan was supposed to go. Even if I succeeded in blowing out his ability to catch and hold the crowd's power, it wasn't as if the Gameskeeper would just poof into thin air. There was plenty of magic floating around to keep him manifested, and he'd *still* be holding an anti-dragon gun to my dad's head. Seriously, why hadn't the DFZ destroyed those things?

Because I'm a city of commerce! I can't not *sell something worth that much money! And anyway, it's not my job to keep dragons safe. That's what the Peacemaker is for.*

Yeah, well, it was biting us in the tail now, wasn't it? Thanks to her reckless capitalism, my dad was cornered. White Snake was looking pretty gun-shy, too, which meant we were double screwed. If she couldn't run away, Nik's fight was still on. If we didn't stop that, why the hell were we doing this?

For everything else! the DFZ yelled, her voice frantic. *Remember the horrible things the Gameskeeper has done to my city! I know tonight hasn't gone exactly as we wanted, but if you destroy his ability to catch and hold the crowd's power, that's still a win! Given how things stand, it might be the only one we get. I'm already working on a way to get you out, but right now I need you to do what we trained you to do and blast him while you still can!*

Nothing about this felt like a win to me. I still had to try, though. Even if everything else had failed, something was always better than nothing, so I reached out and grabbed the magic the DFZ was frantically throwing at me, pulling power through our bond until I could feel and hear and smell the city all around me. Until I was—

"Stop."

My eyes flew open. The Gameskeeper's gun was still pointed at my dad, but his bloody glare was locked on me. "I can feel what you're doing," he warned, shifting his finger menacingly on the trigger. "I will not be hobbled on the night of my greatest achievement. Let the magic go, or your father loses his head."

"Don't listen to him," Yong said, his eyes going to me as well. "I can take care of myself."

The arena god laughed. "You can't take care of anything. You might be better dressed, but there's no hiding what you are when you're standing beside a real dragon. You're weak, a shadow of what you should be. You couldn't take a head shot from a normal gun right now."

"Perhaps," my father said, lifting his chin. "But I'd rather die than be the anchor who drags his daughter down." His bright sea-colored eyes flicked to mine. "Do it, Opal! Show this pathetic false god what it means to be a dragon!"

"But she's not a dragon," the Gameskeeper said sweetly. "And yours isn't the only life on the line." Without taking his eyes off me, the spirit tilted his head toward the door. "Kauffman!"

I hadn't actually seen the mage whose spellwork I'd been obsessing over since our fight in the Gnarls, but he looked as smarmy as I remembered. Even the superior smirk was the same as he walked into the room and took his position at his god's right, lifting his hand to show me the black circle twined around his wrist. An exact replica of the one burned into Nik's neck.

"The Sword of Damocles is a very fair spell," the Gameskeeper said, taking Kauffman's arm and moving it closer to me so I could see the markings. "It is equally irremovable for both parties. But while we've upheld our end of the bargain, you're in here trying to rig the fight for Mad Dog, and that's not allowed." The god dropped his lackey's arm with a grin. "You broke the deal, sweetheart. That means his head is mine to take whenever I wish, fight or no fight. One false move from you and I pop him, right after I kill your daddy."

Don't listen to him, the DFZ ordered. *He's just trying to intimidate you.*

He was doing a damn good job.

There's no way he'll kill his champion on fight night. He's just bluffing because he's afraid of what you can do, which means you should do it now!

She was right. I knew she was right, but the entire reason I'd become a priestess was to save my dad, and I was here tonight mostly because of Nik. If I did as she asked, I'd lose both of them.

But you'll gain so much more! Remember what the Gameskeeper is! He's not a god. He's a parasite who feeds on the worst of human nature! Those are your words. Remember what drove you to do this!

How could I forget? Just looking at the Gameskeeper sent bile rising up my throat. I *knew* how bad he was. He was shoving his cruelty in my face, and yet…

Do it, Opal! my god roared, flooding me with power. *Before he kills you too!*

There were a *lot* of guns pointed my direction. While I'd been talking with the Gameskeeper, his goons had completely surrounded us, confirming my suspicion that blowing the spellwork really would be my last chance to hit back before we all went down. My dad would have done it. He would have died with his fangs in the Gameskeeper's throat before he gave the bastard an inch. But despite my upbringing, I wasn't a dragon. I was just me, and no matter how good it would be for the city and everyone else, I couldn't throw away the two people I'd come here to save.

The moment I made that decision, something inside me snapped. All at once, all the magic the DFZ had been pouring into me started rushing back out again. I grabbed for it instinctively, crying out to her, but the city didn't answer. Nothing did. For the first time in weeks, I was alone in my head.

The emptiness hit me like a gut punch. I fell to the ground, too overwhelmed by the torrent of magic gushing out of me like water from a broken jug to feel anything else. When it was all finally gone, I looked up to see the Gameskeeper leering down at me, his bloody eyes glowing with triumph.

"I knew you weren't a real priestess."

His words were a second sucker punch, because they were true. A real priestess put her god first. That's what Peter did, but I wasn't like him.

I'd been happy to use the DFZ's power, but I'd never committed, and so when our bond was tested, there'd been nothing for either of us to hold on to. We'd snapped like the brittle links we were, and now I was alone. Alone and mortal, on my knees at the feet of a god who no longer felt small.

That was my last thought before the Gameskeeper reached down and struck me across the face. The blow sent me flying. I would have crashed into the wall if his magic hadn't caught me. It was the same horrible, bloodthirsty force that had grabbed my father in his office. I'd been immune back then because I'd belonged to the DFZ, but I didn't belong to anyone anymore. I was just another human in way over her head. Change that to "about to lose her head," because the Gameskeeper was starting to squeeze, his magic crushing me tighter and tighter until—

"Stop!"

The voice was so panicked, I didn't even recognize it as my father's until he dove in front of me, shoving his body between mine and the Gameskeeper's. "Stop," he said again.

"Or what?" the god asked mockingly. "You just said you were willing to die. Why shouldn't she go with you?"

"Because she's no longer a threat. Her connection to the DFZ is gone. She's just a mortal now, so let her go."

The Gameskeeper began to laugh. "You haven't been paying attention if you think appeals to conscience work on me. There's no mercy in the arena, but it does sound as if you're ready to talk, so how about we make a deal?"

Oh hell no. I hadn't just blown my connection to the DFZ so my dad could turn around and put himself into this maniac's hands. I struggled as hard as I could against the binding magic, mouthing frantically at my father since the pressure on my throat kept me from yelling, but he didn't even glance my direction.

"What kind of deal?"

"The best kind," the Gameskeeper said greedily. "An upgrade." He pointed a finger at the cut rock ceiling. "I've got a hundred thousand people up there plus millions more watching at home waiting with bated breath to see my champion fight a dragon. Just one problem." He stuck a thumb over his shoulder at White Snake, who was still crouching on the ground. "The one I've got is already a loser. Everyone in the world already saw her get smacked down when the DFZ saved your life. That was good enough when I didn't have anything better, but now I do." He smiled at Yong. "I have you."

My father scoffed. "I thought I was too weak."

"You are," the Gameskeeper said. "But that doesn't mean you have to stay that way. I've heard how dragons get power. You eat it out of your defeated enemies, and you've got a prime candidate right here."

He turned to look at White Snake, who shrank into the bloody ground. "There's your power, Yong of Korea. She's always been your enemy, hasn't she? Eat her and take her fire for yourself, and then go face my dog in the arena. If you win—and there's no way you won't—I'll give you your Opal back no worse for wear, and the two of you can go wherever you want. I'm sure you must have all sorts of problems waiting for you back home. This way you'll be strong enough to deal with those, and I'll be able to give my worshipers an even better spectacle than I promised. We both win, and all it will cost you are the lives of your lifelong foe and your daughter's thuggish boyfriend, whom I'm sure you never approved of anyway. There are literally no downsides for you, but make your choice quick. One way or another, I'm sending a dragon into that arena, so what do you say? Do we have a deal?"

I screamed silently against the magic that was wrapped around my head like a fist. My dad fighting Nik in the Gameskeeper's arena was such a worst-case scenario, I hadn't even thought to be afraid of it. Whichever one of them triumphed, I lost someone irreplaceable. Probably Nik, but his Mad Dog was so deadly and my father was so weak that I couldn't say for sure. Given the way my luck was going tonight, they were *both* going to die, but there was nothing I could do. I couldn't even get my dad's attention as he stood in front of me, his brows furrowed as if he were giving this insanity serious thought.

"It seems I don't have a choice," he said at last, shaking his head as if this were all merely a vexing inconvenience and not the end of the goddamn world. "Very well. Spare my daughter, and I will debase myself by entering your arena, but I'm not taking White Snake's fire."

His sister sagged in relief, but the Gameskeeper looked insulted. "You're not fit to fight without it. My people came here to see a dragon. You can't even get out of your human disguise."

"I don't need to change to beat a mortal," my father said haughtily. "Do you know how many 'champions' I've killed in my two thousand years? This will be nothing, and anyway, I've already sworn on my fire to take White Snake back home with me to Korea. If I eat her, my own flames will consume me for oath breaking, so it's a moot point." He crossed his arms over his chest. "I'm all the dragon you're going to get. Take it or leave it, but I'm doing my part. Now you do yours. Let my daughter go."

As much as I hated every part of this, I was on board with that last bit. I'd been choking for over a minute now, and my vision was starting to go dark. Thankfully, while he didn't look happy about it, the Gameskeeper must have decided Yong's offer was good enough, because his magic dropped me a second later. I fell sprawling onto the ground, my body convulsing with hacking coughs as I fought for air. I was still working on it when a new set of hands dug into my shoulders, and I looked up to see Kauffman's smug face leering down at me. He wrenched my arms behind my back next, securing my hands with one of those horrible plastic zip-ties Nik loved so much.

"I accept your terms," the Gameskeeper told my father as Kauffman yanked me to my feet. "But until you defeat my champion, I'll be keeping your treasure as collateral. I just want to make sure you're *really* fighting out there. My audience deserves nothing less."

Yong growled deep in his throat. White Snake did too. She must have been genuinely moved by Yong's refusal to take her fire, because her whole demeanor had changed. Unfortunately, the anti-dragon guns were all still pointed at her, and despite her talk about them not actually being able to kill her, she didn't look ready to take another barrage just yet.

"You men stay here," the Gameskeeper ordered, handing his own gun to the soldier closest to him. "Make sure our backup dragon doesn't go anywhere. Meanwhile, the new challenger and I have a crowd to greet."

He held out his hand to my father. With a final look at me, Yong took it. The two of them vanished a moment later, riding up the bloody magic to the arena where I could already feel the crowd's anticipation thrumming like a heartbeat.

"You heard the boss," Kauffman told the soldiers. "Stay here and keep the dragon pinned. If she moves, shoot her until she stops, and don't worry about overdoing it. Dragons are nearly impossible to kill. Meanwhile, I'm going to secure this."

He shook me at them like I was a piece of paper and started dragging me toward the door. I fought back as best I could, but it's hard to dig your heels into stone, and in the end I couldn't do anything except bump along behind him, frantically reaching for the bloody magic I was no longer strong enough to control.

Chapter 14

Kauffman marched me straight back through the mine to the elevator. I fought him the whole way, but it was more of a principle thing than a real resistance. I couldn't stop him, and even if I could, I had nowhere to go. My father was gone, my god was gone, Nik was who knew where, and White Snake was pinned down by a firing squad. Even Sibyl couldn't help me. The moment we were inside the elevator, Kauffman ripped my goggles and earpiece off my head and shoved them into my bag, which he'd also commandeered, slinging the huge utility sack onto his own shoulder as we shot up out of the ground toward the arena above.

The magic thickened as we rose. I'd thought it was strong downstairs, but that was nothing compared to the pulsing, screaming power waiting for me when the elevator finally dinged at the ground floor. Kauffman must have felt it, too, because his face was strained with more than just the effort of dragging me as we made our way down one of the narrow, spellwork-covered hallways to a door that looked exactly like the one on the Gameskeeper's office.

I was so turned around by that point, I assumed that was where we were going. When Kauffman kicked the door open, though, the room inside was totally different. The Gameskeeper's office had looked like a command center. This looked like a honeymoon suite.

The only word for it was "gaudy." The carpet was crushed red velvet while the ceiling was so white you could see every smudge and speck of dust. Between these two extremes were walls covered in a golden pattern so busy, it made the room feel half the size it actually was.

The furniture was picked to match, including a white-and-gold couch covered in a designer-logo print, a black marble entertainment center that was way too large for the room, and a solid glass coffee table designed to look like it was floating. Through the far door, I could see a bedroom with more of the same gimmicky, empty-statement pieces. None of it looked practical or useful or even comfortable. Its only purpose was to show everyone how rich you were. I saw stuff like this all the time when I Cleaned Skyway apartments, and I wasn't shocked in the least to see it in Kauffman's rooms.

The only thing that *did* surprise me was that the fake oil paintings (actually textured prints) on the walls were of tigers and cityscapes instead of naked women. I was about to ask if Kauffman had a velvet smoking jacket to go with the rest of his casino vibe when he threw me down on the one spot of carpet that wasn't crammed with ugly furniture.

"*Oof*," I grunted as I landed facedown on the red velvet, which wasn't nearly as plushy as it looked. "Could you not?"

"Given what you and Nikki did to my face in the Gnarls, you deserve much worse," Kauffman said, rising up on his toes to shove my work bag into the gap between the stone entertainment center and the ceiling. When he'd pushed it as far out of my reach as possible, he walked over to pour himself a drink from the laser-cut mahogany sideboard cabinet, his fingers tapping the overpriced liquor bottles in time with the pulses of magic that rolled through the air.

Which gave me an idea.

"Why are you working for the Gameskeeper?" I asked, rolling onto my back. "The spellwork in the hallways is yours, right? Not to puff your head up, but it's incredible stuff. You could get a job at any multinational you wanted with skills like that. Why are you wasting your time down here?"

"Because the Gameskeeper gives me more than a corporation ever could," Kauffman replied, taking care to spill a bit of his drink on my face as he stepped over me to take a seat on the ugly couch. "He found me as a child, same as Nikki. Unlike Kos, though, I knew a good thing when I saw it. *I* never left, and the Gameskeeper rewards loyalty." He waved his hand at the overdecorated room. "I build his spells and keep track of his magical projects, and in return he gives me whatever I want. Money, women, heads on platters, *anything*. That's better than even the DFZ can boast, and I don't even have to become a priest!" He flashed me a smirk. "Jealous?"

"Hardly," I said with a flat look. "The DFZ's not perfect, but at least she's not evil. You work for a dark god of bloodlust!"

"Says the girl who calls a man-eating monster 'Daddy,'" Kauffman replied in a mocking voice, putting his feet up on the glass coffee table above my head so that I was forced to stare at his shoes. "You know, I'm not surprised to hear you ended up with the DFZ. For a city who's supposed to embody survival of the fittest, she has an astonishing love of the untalented and the sloppy. So many *Shamans*." He shuddered. "It's a miracle this whole place hasn't collapsed."

I scowled, but Kauffman had turned his attention away, hitting a button on his remote to open the entertainment center and reveal the giant flat-screen TV inside. Not surprisingly, the screen was already set to the arena feed when it flicked on. The undercard fights were just wrapping up, but while the announcers were frantically hyping what was coming next, my eyes were locked on the crowd.

I'd known it would be huge because we'd planned it that way, but the chaos I saw on the screen was absolutely insane. They must have taken out the seats—and completely ignored the concept of fire safety—because the arena stands were at least twice as packed as when I'd been here last Saturday. People were crammed in shoulder to shoulder, sometimes even closer, screaming at the top of their lungs as the drone cameras swooped by. Now that I wasn't entirely focused on Kauffman, I realized I could feel their stomping through the carpet, the beats hammering in time with the bloodthirsty magic that saturated everything.

I'd never felt anything like it. Even in the Gnarls where magic had been coming up from the dark like a waterfall in reverse, it hadn't been this intense. There was so much power in the air that even a handful would have been enough to blast Kauffman and his stupid couch into confetti, but I couldn't get a handful. I couldn't grab so much as a finger's worth, because even at this enormous size, Kauffman's spellwork had the crowd's magic locked down tight, swirling the power around the arena like a washing machine on the spin cycle.

Just trying to grab it as it flew by was enough to make me dizzy. I kept my mental hand out anyway, feeling the magic as it slid through my grasp in an attempt to gauge how taut it was and therefore how close the spellwork holding it might be to capacity. Before I could get a good measure, though, the crowd on the screen above my head burst into even wilder applause.

When I looked up to see why, all the cameras were focused on the north door into the arena where ten men were dragging what appeared to be a circus cage on wheels onto the sand. Then the cameras zoomed in to show the man behind the bars, and my heart stopped.

It was Nik. Nik was in that cage, and he looked absolutely horrible. His face was pale and he was trembling bad, which was a perfectly natural reaction for someone who was about to duel a dragon to the death. I was far more worried that he didn't seem to be armed.

Nik's pistols and shotgun were nowhere to be seen. Instead, he was wearing a full suit of crush armor, the sort they put on miners who worked way down at the bottom of the ocean. Aside from that, though, he had nothing. Not even a knife.

Considering he was going to be fighting my dad, I was trying to see Nik's empty hands as a good thing when the announcer came on to say there'd been a change in plans. The undefeated champion Mad Dog would *not* be fighting the dragon White Snake as previously scheduled. Instead, he'd be fighting the dragon who defeated her. The powerful, the dominating, the ancient *Yong of Korea!*

There'd been some booing when the change was announced, but it was absolutely destroyed by the roar that followed my father's name. I hadn't realized he was so well-known among arena fans, though it could have been that they didn't know him at all and were just cheering because they were getting the bigger of the two dragons who'd fought over the river. Or maybe they were just caught up in the screaming magic that was pulsing through the air like blood from an arterial wound. Whatever the reason, the crowd went absolutely *nuts*. I thought people were going to start tearing each other to pieces as the doors at the opposite end of the arena opened, and my father walked through.

He was also unarmed. Unlike Nik, though, Yong did not have armor, just the fancy suit he'd been wearing when the Gameskeeper had taken him away. But while I was relieved to see him walking in alert and seemingly free of any pre-fight shenanigans, the crowd instantly began to jeer. Apparently, they wanted to see an *actual* dragon, not a human who was supposed to be a dragon. The ugly turn in the crowd's demeanor made the pulsing magic lurch sharply, and Kauffman jerked on the sofa, nearly spilling his drink.

"What's wrong?" I asked mockingly.

"Nothing," he said stiffly, settling back in. "Pressure's just running high. Nothing you'd understand."

"Even I know all spellwork has a limit," I replied with a grin. "Not that I *want* to die in a giant magical explosion, but it would be the height of irony if the Gameskeeper stopped me only to have his spellwork overload anyway from the energy of his own record-breaking crowd."

"It would also be the height of improbability." Kauffman glared down at me through the glass. "Unlike some people, I'm not a spoiled brat who has to crib her spellwork off the internet. All of my circles are top-notch work with multiple overflow vectors capable of modulating even the sharpest of power spikes. That's how a *real* mage operates."

That jab hit a bit closer than I liked, but I didn't have anything to prove to this man. My magic worked for me, even if it wasn't working right now. I was far more concerned with watching my dad stride toward the center of the arena where the stagehands had already deposited Nik's cage.

He was still standing quietly inside, his eyes closed as if he were meditating. My father looked equally calm, dipping his head to Nik, which was a great show of respect. Together, the pair of them formed a quiet, dignified oasis in the sea of screaming bloodthirsty chaos, and that gave me hope. A warm feeling that Kauffman immediately ruined.

"Ah, this is nice," he said, taking a sip of his drink. "I almost don't know who to cheer for. On the one hand, watching Nikki get eaten has always been one of my fondest wishes. On the other, seeing an arrogant dragon dismembered by a human would also be most delightful."

I rolled my eyes.

"I just wish I didn't have to be stuck in here for it," he went on sourly. "I was going to watch from the Gameskeeper's own box, but *nooooooo*. You had to go and ruin things, so I'm forced to watch the dying on television with the rest of the common rabble."

"No one's going to die," I said stubbornly. "Your Sword of Damocles only demands that Nik be present for the fight, not that he win. If he throws one punch, the curse's requirements will be fulfilled. Once your noose is off his neck, he can just surrender, my dad will accept it, and this whole thing will end in a whimper."

I hadn't actually considered that angle until I said it, but as soon as the words were out of my mouth, I realized I had a good point. Maybe everything wasn't lost after all! Sure I'd only just thought about it, but my dad was a sneaky snake. I was certain he'd already come up with the same idea, if he hadn't thought of something even better. But as my hopes began to soar, Kauffman burst out laughing.

"Oh, you poor little thing! You really think the Gameskeeper is leaving any of this to chance? There's no getting out of this fight. *That* pedal is already pushed down to the floor."

I really didn't want to give him the satisfaction of asking, but this wasn't about me, and I had to know. "What pedal?"

Kauffman pointed at the screen. I whipped my head around, looking up just in time for the camera to zoom in on Nik's eyes. His empty, wild, mad eyes, their gray depths completely devoid of rationality or conscience or anything that wasn't pure animal rage.

"No," I breathed.

"Oh yes," Kaufman purred, savoring the moment. "There's no reversal this time. He's Mad Dog right from the start, which means this is going to be the fight of his life whether he wants it or not."

I didn't want to believe it, but there was no denying what was in front of my own eyes. The crowd clearly saw it, because their booing at my dad was instantly replaced with a scream of pure delight for the violence to come.

Even knowing that they were being egged on by the raging magic, hearing them cheer for this tragedy made me sick to my stomach, though that could also have been from the fear. I knew my dad was a good fighter—you couldn't live as long as he had and *not* be good at keeping yourself alive—but he was still way below where he should be, and Nik would leave him no room for error. He was going to go straight for the kill, which meant my dad would have to fight back for real, and that wasn't going to end well for anyone. Whatever clever plans he might have come up with would never survive Mad Dog's mindless onslaught. Any way you ran this scenario, one of them was going to die unless something stopped them, and as the only card left on the table, that something had to be me.

With that realization, I stopped freaking out and pulled myself together. This was no time to be a victim. As bad as it looked, no one was actually dead yet, and if I could just think fast enough, maybe I could keep it that way. I already had an idea. A terrible, half-baked one that was missing several critical steps, but I'd figure out the rest of the details if I got that far. First, though, I had to get out of here.

I looked up at Kauffman through the green-tinted glass of his tacky table, thanking my lucky stars that the arrogant bastard hadn't bothered to tie anything except my hands. Or get a proper guard. It was just the two of us in here, and while he was unquestionably the better mage, I had more to lose. Also, as he'd so dismissively pointed out, I was a Shaman, which meant I didn't need to set up a circle or write spellwork to cast. I just needed to find some magic I could actually use.

Unfortunately, that was one of the blank bits in my plan. Despite the power shooting over me like a pressure wash, Kauffman's spellwork was every bit as good as he'd bragged. No matter how much or how hard I grabbed, the arena magic always ripped right back out of my mental grasp before I could do anything with it.

It was the same stupid problem I'd had since the first time I'd come in here. Now, though, I didn't have the luxury of shrugging it off. I had to get power from somewhere, so I closed my eyes and forced myself to *think*.

The Gameskeeper was a spirit, and this arena was his domain. That meant all the magic here was his and thus inside the control of Kauffman's circle, but the arena wasn't a pocket dimension. We were still on planet Earth. Still in the DFZ, the city that had been ground zero for *both* mana crashes. The arena's magic might be locked up tight, but the land beneath it—not the city, but the physical ground—should still be radiating ambient power just like every other place on the planet. It would be small and heavily dissipated, but that actually worked in my favor, because the one part of my spellwork courses I'd never had a problem with was the list of all the shit we were free to ignore in our equations.

Whatever mages like Kauffman claimed, Thaumaturgical spellwork notation was hardly comprehensive. There were tons of little, annoying, impossible-to-square factors that simply got glossed over, and ambient magic was one of those. I certainly hadn't bothered to account for it, and while Kauffman was far more meticulous, I bet he hadn't, either. Why should he when multiple studies had shown that ambient magic wasn't strong enough to throw off spellwork? If he *was* ignoring it, though, then that meant there was at least some magic here that wasn't being claimed. I just had to find it.

With that, I squeezed my eyes even tighter and reached out with my mental hand, the one Dr. Kowalski was always claiming was huge compared to normal people's. I got embarrassed every time she said that because it sounded so weird, but I'd never been happier to have a freakishly huge draw than I was now, because that big reach allowed me to grab a *giant* handful of magic.

It was a classic Opal handful too. None of that pumpkin-sized safety stuff Dr. Kowalski had taught me. This search was all about volume, so I scooped up as much as I possibly could. Enough to blow myself up if I'd actually tried to use it, but I didn't have to worry about that here. Just like every other time I'd grabbed magic in the arena, Kauffman's spell snatched it right back, but instead of reaching frantically for the next handful as I usually did, I kept my seemingly empty grasp tight, probing with my mind to find what his spell *hadn't* yanked away.

It was a bit like panning for gold. Unlike the DFZ's syrupy magic or the arena's screaming bloodlust, ambient magic was mild and sedate. Picking it out from all that chaos was like trying to pluck a gentle breeze out of a hurricane. Even when I did manage to find some, it was exceedingly thin. I had to grab three more giant fistfuls of magic before I'd scraped together enough to cast even a tiny spell. Fortunately, tiny was all I needed.

I popped my eyes back open and checked the screen. My magical barrel-scraping had taken longer than I'd liked, but for once the Gameskeeper's need for drama was on my side. They couldn't just pop Nik's cage and let them go at it. Oh no. They had to play the full ten-minute highlight reel of Mad Dog's previous fights spliced together with news footage of my dad as a bloody dragon over the Detroit river. I didn't know what they thought they were going to get out of it. If this crowd got any more hyped, people were going to start having heart attacks. But the dramatic delay gave me the space I needed.

The tiny bit of magic I'd scavenged wouldn't do crap against a mage like Kauffman, but there were other ways to hurt a man. You just had to get creative, so creative was what I got, scooting as quietly as I could across the carpet to press my forehead against Kauffman's ridiculous glass coffee table.

Fun fact about decorative glass: it is very sensitive to heat changes. Especially uneven heat, which can cause one part to expand so rapidly that the rest can't keep up and the whole thing shatters. I'd seen the aftermath of such explosions twice: once in a fancy furniture showroom where some idiot had left a twenty-thousand-dollar glass sculpture touching a heater, and once in an apartment I was Cleaning after there'd been a fire. It was rare, but the physics involved were relatively simple, especially for someone who'd been turning magic into dragon fire all week.

I didn't even need my hands. I just stared at the bit of the table Kauffman was resting his feet on and focused on fire, squeezing the tiny wisp of natural magic I'd gathered smaller and smaller, denser and denser. When I had it down to a focused dot of white-hot flame, I touched it to the glass directly under Kauffman's left heel.

He didn't even have time to feel the heat before the temperature differential grew too great and the whole table exploded. Much bigger than I'd anticipated, actually. All the glass furniture I had experience with was made from safety glass, stuff that shattered into millions of little beads rather than jagged shards so you didn't accidentally trip on your table and die.

But safety was clearly not a concern for whomever Kauffman had purchased his monstrosities from. His table exploded into glass daggers, one of which got me across the cheek. The pain was enough to make me yelp, but I got off easy compared to Kauffman. He had glass stuck through every limb. One shard had actually pierced his leg and come out the other side. It was horrible, way worse than I'd intended, but at least he was too busy screaming and bleeding to chase me when I jumped to my feet and grabbed a shard to cut myself free.

It took some finagling and a lot of sliced fingers, but I eventually got the length of broken glass under the plastic tie trapping my wrists behind my back. The moment my hands were free, I jumped for my bag, using the marble TV stand as a ladder as I climbed up and grabbed it. I ran for the door next, kicking Kauffman's grabbing hands out of the way as I charged into the hall…

…and right into the chest of an armed guard.

"Hey!" the man cried, grabbing my shoulders. "Who are you?"

"Never mind that," I said, thinking fast. "Kauffman needs help! Someone attacked him and he's bleeding everywhere. If we don't get him to medical *stat*, he's going to die!" I jerked my head back toward Kauffman's room. "You go in there and stop the bleeding. I'm going to get a doctor!"

"Right!" the guard said, too caught up in the emergency to realize I didn't belong here. Kauffman gave me a surprising boost as well by choosing that moment to pull himself out of his room, screaming something unintelligible as he flung his bloody hands toward me. It looked like something out of a horror movie, and it worked like a charm. The moment the guard saw him, he forgot all about me and rushed to his superior's side, grabbing Kauffman and pinning him to the ground in an effort to stop the bleeding while I darted in the other direction.

I charged down the hall, feet and arms pumping in time as I flew past the spellwork-covered walls, which were glowing like blood-drenched phosphorous thanks to all the magic pumping through the arena. All that pulsing red light made the warren of cement tunnels even more confusing than the first time I'd been here. But while I had no idea how to navigate this mess, it was impossible to miss the roar of the crowd, so I focused on following that instead, running toward the noise as it grew louder and louder until I burst through a door and found myself standing on the lowest tier of arena bleachers.

It felt like stepping into another world. Even after following it all the way here, the sound of the crowd with no walls to mute was like nothing I'd ever experienced. It was so *loud.* I felt it more than I heard it, a deep, throbbing vibration that rattled my stomach and clenched my muscles. If I hadn't been in such a rush, it would have stopped me cold, but I had momentum on my side. Momentum and fear, because the sandy arena floor was right in front of me.

Sitting up in the nosebleed section, I'd had to rely on cameras to show me what was going on in the actual ring. Down here on the bottom tier, though, I could see everything. Even crammed against a security door with the maddened crowd thrashing around me like a storm-tossed sea, I had a clear view of Nik's cage, which was opening with the same slow *click click click* of a roller coaster going up to its first drop. Across from him, my father was standing ready, his bare hands fisted for what he knew was coming. What I had to stop at all costs.

Still gasping against the sound, I turned on my heel and dove back into the hallway. Slamming the door on the crowd meant I couldn't see what was going on, but I'd already seen enough to know I couldn't stop them on my own. If I was going to do this, I needed help, so I'd gone back to the place where I could hear, frantically opening my bag to dig my earpiece out of whatever random pocket Kauffman had stuffed it in.

"Thank goodness!" Sibyl said the second we reconnected. "I thought you were—"

"Not dead," I told her, digging my phone out next. "But someone will be soon if we don't act fast. I need you to strip all the security off my contact list."

"Your contact list?" my AI repeated, her digital voice confused. "But we spent weeks setting up all those fake accounts and double-backs so that—"

"Don't care. Clear the whole damn list, and turn off my call blockers too. Total open protocols. I need her to know it's me when my number shows up."

"Her who?"

I gripped my phone as the wall of digital security I'd built around myself over these last three years came crashing down.

"It's time to call Mom."

I couldn't remember the last time I'd voluntarily called my mother. The only reason I knew her current number was because I'd worked so hard to keep it blocked. I dialed it now with shaking fingers, praying she'd pick up, which was silly in hindsight. She had just as many programs looking for me as I had to keep her out. I didn't even hear a single ring before the call connected, and my mother's terrified voice sounded in my ear.

"*Opal!*"

"Mom," I said, my body slumping in relief before the shrieks of the crowd through the door behind me jerked me tight again.

"Are you all right?" my mother asked frantically. "What's wrong? Where are you?"

"I'm fine," I said quickly. "But I need your help."

"If it's about your father, I'm already on my way," she said, her lovely voice steely with determination over the *thump thump* of the helicopter rotors I'd just now recognized in the background. "I moved our entire security team to the emergency base in Canada the day after you two vanished. We've been set to scramble ever since the advertising for White Snake's fight began, but when your father walked out instead, that was the last straw. I hope the Great Yong will forgive me for acting without orders, but I just couldn't wait any longer."

If things hadn't been so deadly, that would have made me laugh. Only my mom could worry about Dad being angry she'd come to save his life without permission. I also wasn't surprised she was already on her way. Mom paid more attention to Yong than anyone else on the planet. I was more shocked that she wasn't beating on the Gameskeeper's door already, which reminded me…

"Do you know where you're going?"

"Not as well as we'd like," she said angrily. "Maps are useless in this cursed city! This 'Rentfree' place doesn't even have streets listed. But it's a giant arena, so it shouldn't be that hard to find."

"Seriously?" I yelled at her. "You're flying in blind?"

"Not on purpose! But my last scout vanished, and I didn't have time to send another, so we're winging it. Not my preferred strategy, but what else could I do? My dragon is in danger!"

"Wow," Sibyl said as I dragged a hand over my face. "I see where you get your recklessness from now."

"*Mom*," I said sharply, ignoring my AI. "There's no need for that. I'm already in the arena. Sibyl's sending you my location. Just come to me and you'll find Dad."

"We already traced your call, actually," she said without a hint of shame. "Heading to your location now. How is he doing?"

"Alright at the moment," I reported, checking my video feed. "But I don't know for how much longer."

Even if I hadn't been watching it live, I would have known Nik's cage was almost open from the crowd. The shouting above me was so loud, I could feel it like a hammer in my skull, though that could also have been the magic. At this point, I wasn't sure if the two were separate. The crowd's excitement fed the Gameskeeper, whose bloodlust magic fed back into the crowd, forming a continuous loop of crazy that was getting bigger by the second.

Even Nik was part of it. I didn't know how the magic that turned him into Mad Dog worked precisely, but there was no way he could be at the center of this maelstrom and not be affected. He certainly looked frenzied, bashing his body against the rising bars like the mad animal he was supposed to be.

"How long until you get here?"

"We just crossed the river," my mom reported. "ETA is five minutes."

That was faster than I'd expected, but it still felt like forever. Nik's cage would be open in the next few seconds, and after that, things were going to get bloody. Whose blood, I didn't yet know, and I didn't want to find out.

"Just get here as fast as you can. I'm going to try and stall."

"Opal, *no!*" she cried. "It would kill your father if you got hurt! Trust in our dragon. He can handle this!"

Easy for her to say. She didn't have bloodlust pumping through her skull. But I didn't have time to explain things to her, and it wouldn't have done any good if I did, so I cut the call and shoved my phone back into my jeans pocket, turning around to kick the door behind me open as I plunged back into the crowd.

The moment I was back in the arena, the atmosphere hit me like a frying pan to the face. It wasn't just the noise and the lights. It was everything. The whole throbbing, chaotic mass, and running through it all was the magic.

There was so much power here, I didn't even have to reach for it. The spinning magic was practically shoving itself inside me, a hateful, screaming power that made me feel disgusted and exhilarated at the same time. It was so intense, I actually forgot what I was doing for a second. The only reason I didn't get washed away and start cheering like the rest of the frenzied crowd was the fear. Dread sat like an anvil in my stomach, keeping me grounded as I started shoving my way down toward the ring. I'd barely made it five feet before the cage finished opening, and Nik burst free.

There were so many people crammed into the stands, I couldn't actually see it happen, but I didn't have to. The second Nik got out, the crowd's fever pitch jumped to a full-on riot. The magic followed suit, swelling so hard and fast I had to sit down before it knocked me over, which was the only reason I saw what happened next.

My view of the arena was hopelessly blocked by the bodies in front of me, but my goggles were still hooked into the camera feed. I'd pushed them up so I could see while I elbowed my way through the crowd. When I fell, they'd slid back down over my eyes, giving me a beautiful, slow-motion shot of Nik as he lunged for my dad's throat.

The digital manipulation was the only way I was able to follow it. Nik had always been fast, but I'd never seen a human move like he did now. Even my dad looked surprised, his perfect face going blank in shock as Nik jumped at him like a tiger. But Nik wasn't the only one who was quick. A heartbeat later, the Great Yong got himself back together, stepping gracefully to the side at the last second to let Nik fly past him.

The Nik I knew would have been prepared for that. He would have landed on his feet and whirled around with some new trick already set to go. But this wasn't the Nik I knew. This was Mad Dog. He didn't even bother to check his fall as he soared past, landing face-first in the sand only to throw himself right back up, launching at my father again before Yong could even finish turning his head.

He still managed to dodge—even weakened, dragons were much faster than humans—but it was a closer thing this time. Too close, because Nik wasn't pulling any punches. I saw now why they'd only given him a suit of crush armor. With wild charges like that, a weapon would have only gotten in his way. He needed his hands free to catch and relaunch himself every time my dad slipped away.

Again, my Nik would have stopped and adjusted his strategy when he saw it wasn't working. Mad Dog charged ahead blindly, going for Yong's throat, his chest, his arms, his eyes, anything he could reach. Even with his superior speed, the chaotic assault put enormous pressure on my father, because he was clearly trying his damnedest not to hurt Nik. I wasn't sure if that was for my sake or if Yong's famous pride wouldn't allow him to kill someone who was so clearly not in control of his actions, but I'd never been more grateful to my father in my life.

Also terrified, because refusing to strike back meant that my dad was completely on the defensive, and Nik was showing no sign of tiring out. Quite the opposite. The more the crowd cheered, the harder he went, the curse on his neck burning like black fire as he attacked again and again and again, moving so fast that even the camera drones were struggling to keep up.

Cursing under my breath, I tore my eyes away from the spectacle and started shoving through the crowd more determinedly than ever. With hits like that, it was only a matter of time before my dad slipped up. One mistake, that was all it would take for him to eat one of those full-body punches, and then things would get *really* bad. Maybe he'd get hurt and start to slow, opening himself up to more attacks. Or maybe Yong would decide enough was enough and start punching back.

Either way, I couldn't take it. I'd fought so hard to avoid this. Worked so damn *hard* to keep both of them safe, and it was all dissolving before my eyes. Forget five minutes. At the rate things were escalating, one of them was going to be dead in the next thirty seconds. Maybe both. They were going to die in front of me for the amusement of a blood-drunk crowd who didn't even have the presence of mind to know what they were screaming for. Die so that the worst god *ever* could make his big power play. Die before I got to enjoy the peace I'd finally made with each of them.

My fists clenched so tight, I left bruises on the screaming man I was shoving out of my way. *No.* Even in a city as famously cruel as the DFZ, this was too much. I didn't care how much stronger the Gameskeeper was, I would *never* let him pay for his godhood upgrade with the lives of my two most important people. They were not cheap entertainment. Not things to be used and thrown away. They were *mine*— my treasures, my heart, my future—and I was going to save them. I was going to save them even if I had to bring this whole damn place down on top of me to do it, which was how I got my next idea.

"Idea" was too strong a word. I was too panicked and rushed to think of anything so coherent. This was more instincts acting in a line as I forced my way through the crowd, wiggling and elbowing and kicking out knees, whatever it took to get myself to the edge of the arena.

When I reached the short wall that separated the stands from the sandy circle below, I didn't let myself hesitate. If I waited, doubt might creep in, and I didn't have time for that. I didn't have time for anything, so I just went for it, vaulting over the barrier the moment my hand touched the railing.

The fall to the bottom was a lot farther than I'd thought. It hadn't looked that big from up in the stands, but now that I was hurtling down it, I realized the distance between the bottom tier of seats and the arena floor was closer to twenty feet than ten. If I'd been thinking, I would have grabbed some more ambient magic to cushion my fall. I hadn't been, though, and ambient magic wasn't the sort of thing you could just grab on the fly, leaving me with nothing but empty hands and kicking legs as I landed on the arena floor.

Holy *crap*, did it hurt. As I apparently had to keep relearning tonight, I was just a normal person. I wasn't built to fall twenty feet onto sand-covered cement.

If I'd been less frantic, that probably would have been the end of the line. From the pain in my ribs and arm, I'd *definitely* broken something. But that's the great thing about running on instinct: if it's not stopping you, you don't actually have to care. As soon as I realized I could still move, I was up and running again, charging across the arena floor—which was also much bigger than it had looked from up top—toward the blur that was my father and Nik.

Someone must have finally landed a hit while I'd been falling, because the first thing I noticed as I charged forward was the bright-red blood splattered on the sand in front of me. As I got closer, I saw it was my father's. Yong's formal suit was torn at the shoulder, and his sleeve was dark with blood. He was still moving faster than my eyes could follow, but his chest was heaving with effort, and his expression was grim. He was so focused on dodging Nik's attacks, he didn't even notice me until I grabbed him, wrapping myself around his body like an octopus.

"Opal?" he said, the look on his face transforming from grim concentration to confusion, then to naked terror. "What are you doing? *Get out of here!*"

He struggled against me as he spoke, trying to push my arms away. Trying and failing. All that supersonic dodging must have cost him even more than I'd realized, because he didn't have the strength left to make me budge. Granted, I was a bit crazed at the moment, but it still should have been no contest. The fact that it was terrified me all over again, but not half as much as the shock I got when I turned to look at Nik.

When I'd come up with the half-baked idea to rush in, my decision had been based on a single supposition: that no matter how crazed they made him, Nik would never hurt me. I had no evidence of this, but I'd believed in it strongly enough to throw myself into the fray. Now that I was actually here—standing on the bloody sand under the glaring lights, clinging to my father like a crazed monkey in front of thousands of suddenly silent people—my adrenaline-fueled brain was finally catching up to the fact that I might have just done something terminally stupid, because the man staring me down wasn't Nik at all.

He *looked* like Nik. He had Nik's face and Nik's hair, his scowl and his body. But aside from the obvious physical features, everything else was all wrong. He didn't move like Nik, didn't fight like him. Even the way he glared wasn't right. It was Nik's body no question, but the thing staring at me through his eyes wasn't him, and while he *had* frozen when I'd grabbed my dad, I didn't think it was recognition. He mostly looked confused, as if he didn't understand where I'd come from.

"Opal," my father said, keeping his voice to the low, calm tone best used for spooked animals. "You need to go."

"I'm not leaving you," I said angrily, keeping my eyes on Nik, who was still watching us warily. "Either of you."

"That's not your choice. I—"

I'm certain my father thought he had an excellent argument for why I didn't get a say in a duel he was ostensibly fighting for my sake.

Whatever it was, though, he never got to say, because that was the moment Mad Dog resumed his attack, swinging for my dad's left, the side opposite of the one I'd grabbed.

If my father hadn't been a dragon, he would have lost an arm. Thankfully, he wasn't that far gone yet. He danced out of the way with supernatural grace. When he tried to drag me away with him, though, I let go.

"*Opal!*" he hissed, but I'd already turned my back on him. Dad might be the one on the defensive, but he wasn't the person who needed my help right now. That honor belonged to the man in front of me, the growling animal I still stubbornly believed Nik was inside of somewhere.

"Nik," I said quietly, holding out my hands. "It's me."

Mad Dog growled and hunkered down, but he didn't attack, which I took as a good sign. "This isn't you," I told him, careful to stay very still. "It never was, and it never will be. You got free of this world once. You can do it again. Don't let him turn you back into something you hate."

The monster wearing Nik's face bared its teeth at me and took a step forward. Only one step, though. He couldn't do more than that because his right foot was still dug into the sand. No matter how he pulled, it stayed put, and the longer he struggled, the angrier he got.

Above our heads, I could hear the announcer saying something breathlessly, but it was impossible to make out the actual words over the crowd. The audience that had gone quiet when I'd first run onto the sand had finally found their voice again, and it was a furious one. I was sure no one up there understood what was actually going on, but my presence was definitely *not* appreciated. And as their angry shouting grew, the pumping magic of the arena began to twist and roil like a storm cloud above me.

"That's it!" I told Nik, ignoring the doom hanging over our heads like a sword. "Fight them! I'll help you. I'll *always* help you, just like you help me! We're not alone anymore, and we never have to be again. You can do this, Nik! You can—"

Stop.

I froze, heart pounding. The voice had spoken in my head just like the DFZ's did, but it wasn't my god. Even at her worst, the DFZ had never sounded this cruel, the sound tangling my mind like a barbed whip.

What are you doing? the Gameskeeper whispered. *He can't fight this. His soul's already mine, bought and paid for. All you're doing is making his death more painful.*

As if to prove his point, Mad Dog chose that moment to fall to his knees, clutching his head with a scream that reminded me more of Nik than anything else Mad Dog had done tonight.

See?

"Ignore him, Nik!" I cried, dropping down beside him. "He wouldn't be here telling me to stop if you really had no chance. It's just the stupid curse, not you! You can make it!"

And you call me cruel, the Gameskeeper sneered in my head, which pissed me off to no end. I was so sick of every force of nature in this city getting free access to my brain. Seriously, how were they getting in?

I didn't 'get in' anywhere, the arena god said with a chuckle. *You came into* my *domain. You forced your way into* my *magic with that huge open soul of yours. You might as well be naked.*

I clenched my teeth.

I can see everything, he went on, goading me. *Your life, your past, your choices. You'd actually fit in very well here, you know.*

"Screw you!" I yelled.

See, that's exactly what I'm talking about, he said, his voice getting excited as his bloody magic pounded through my brain. *I thought you were just another of the DFZ's sycophants, but now I see why you couldn't be her priestess. You're like me. The DFZ's greatest flaw has always been that she believes her own propaganda. Despite daily evidence to the contrary, she stubbornly clings to the simplistic fable that anyone can get what they want if they work hard. But you know better. You had everything—wealth, power, your very own dragon— and you threw it away. You saw the dream of the DFZ for the sham it was, but still you fight. I respect that.*

A hand appeared in the magic in front of me, shimmering like heat waves above Nik's head. *Come and fight for me,* he beckoned. *Unlike the*

DFZ, my promises aren't empty. My champions truly do get everything they want, at least before they fall. But we all fall in the end. You know that, so come and live out your brief life here. You've already proved your worth by beating my mage. Come and be a champion, Opal of Korea. Shine in the arena for me. Give yourself to the crowd, and you will finally have the adoration and respect you were always so unfairly denied.

The hand wiggled enticingly, and I made sure to let my disgust shine clear through my mind before I smacked it away. "If that's the conclusion you came to after seeing my life, you're a bigger fool than I thought."

Ignorant girl, the Gameskeeper hissed. *You—*

"No!" I shouted. "You think I'm afraid of you? I've been talked down to by *way* scarier things! You wouldn't be crap if your 'loser' mage wasn't using a blood-drunk mob to pump you up. You act like you're a big god, but everything you've said has been so wrong, I don't even know how you got there." I slapped a hand against my chest. "You think *I* want to be a champion in your little blood show? I *hate* fighting! If you'd actually understood any of the personal info you snooped through, you'd know that the last few years have been the worst of my life! I wasn't 'striving' for more because I saw through the sham of wealth. I was stuck with my back against the wall, and I hated it! I *hated* fighting against my dad and being broke and constantly having to come up with work-arounds just to make it through the next day. The only reason I did any of it is because I hated being trapped even more!"

The god made a disgusted sound, and I lifted my head higher, shouting to the rafters. "All I ever wanted was to be free! To live my own life without having someone's boot on my neck!" My eyes went back to Nik, who was shaking on the ground in front of me. "That's something you clearly know nothing about, so get out of my head, and get out of his. Nik's paid his dues to you tenfold, so I'm taking him back. He's not yours to step on anymore!"

I dropped down to clutch Nik to my chest, and the bloody god sighed. *Your life to waste, little girl,* he said disappointedly. Then his voice grew hard.

Kill her.

The moment he gave the order, the storm magic that had been building above my head dropped like a stone. My whole body clenched as it landed, but it didn't actually land on me. It crashed into Nik, making him go still as a statue. I was looking down to see what had happened to him when a hand clamped down on my shoulder.

Just in time. I didn't know how long my father had been standing behind me, but I'd never complain about his hovering again. His quick reflexes were the only thing that saved me as Nik's metal fist slashed up through the air exactly where my head had just been. But even though I'd dodged death by a hair, all I felt was defeat, because when Nik rolled back to his feet, his eyes were emptier than ever.

Kill her, the Gameskeeper commanded again, his voice booming with the fury of the crowd yelling from the stands for the fight to continue. *Our arena welcomes all comers. If the girl wants to stand on her own so badly, she's free to try. She is your opponent now. Kill her and be victorious.*

Mad Dog bared his teeth in anticipation, and I shrank back against my dad, my brain wheeling as I tried to figure out what I was going to do, how I was going to fix this. I'd thought I could get through to him because he was Nik and I was me and we'd always been able to work together, but there was no way anyone could resist the weaponized bloodlust of so many people. The Gameskeeper's magic was so thick around him I could actually see it shimmering in the air like heat. I was wondering how the hell I was going to get Nik out of that without burning myself to a cinder when I noticed his chest was covered with blood.

I didn't know how. My dad hadn't even touched him. Then I saw that the blood was coming from his neck, and I understood.

It was the curse. The black spellwork of the Sword of Damocles was digging into Nik's throat like a ring of knives, but Nik wasn't budging.

He was fighting back, resisting the order to fight me with everything he had, and the curse was cutting off his head because of it.

"*No!*"

I leaped forward, grabbing the torrent of magic with both hands. The power burned me just like I'd known it would, but I was too desperate to feel the pain. Not that it did me any good. When I grabbed the power to yank it off Nik, Kauffman's spellwork jerked it right back into place, just like always. And it was that, not the pain, that made me stumble. I'd failed. I couldn't move it, couldn't save him. Nik was going to die. He was going to—

"*Opal!*"

My father's voice knocked me out of my panic, and I looked up to see him looming over me.

"Stick to the plan!" he yelled.

What plan? If he meant the DFZ's plot to crack the Gameskeeper's spellwork engine, that ship was way sunk. Without the DFZ inside me, I couldn't get the magic I needed to overload Kauffman's circle, nor could I survive the inevitable backlash that would come after. But just as I was opening my mouth to say it was hopeless, my father held out his hand.

"Use me," he said. When I started to argue, he cut me off. "I know you can do it. You're a talented mage. You brought me back from the dead, you can save him too. Just try."

I didn't know if he'd skipped the part about how there was nothing to lose since we were all going to die anyway in a rare display of tact or if he simply thought it was too obvious to mention, but I was grateful either way. I knew it sounded pathetic, but hearing my critical father say he believed in me made me desperate to prove him right. I'm not sure if it was panic-fueled insanity or plain old wishful thinking, but right then it didn't matter that his plan was nuts. Any chance was better than zero, and if I was going down today, then dammit, I'd die as my father had taught me: with my teeth in my enemy's throat.

With that, I turned and thrust my hand into the pillar of magic surrounding Nik. I grabbed hold of my father at the same time, clutching hard not just to his arm, but to the connection that ran between us, the silver thread I'd seen in the Gameskeeper's office.

I could almost see it, the silver line shining like a sunbeam through the bloody haze of the arena master's magic. More importantly, I could feel it. I'd sent so much magic to my father over the past week, I knew every detail of the path that ran between us. I walked it again now, only this time I wasn't bringing fire in.

I was taking it out.

Moving fast, both for Nik's sake and to stay ahead of my own fear, I plunged my hand into my father's magic and started ripping out everything I'd put in. His fire burned me as I pulled, and I heard Yong roar, but though it must have felt like dying all over again, he didn't fight back. He just stood there and let me suck him dry, pulling out his fire in huge handfuls that I then turned and shoved into the spinning maelstrom of the arena as hard as I could.

I was terrified it wouldn't be enough. Unlike the DFZ, my father wasn't a spirit. He wasn't even a full dragon. I could kill him and still not have what I needed to put us over the line.

For all my worries, though, I wasn't the only one who'd worked on this plan. Nik had done his part, too, and done it well. So had my father, and the DFZ, and Dr. Kowalski. Between all of us, we'd made this the biggest fight night in DFZ history. A wild success, everything the Gameskeeper could have wanted and more, which meant we *had* to be close to the limit of what the circle could hold. As I'd just told Kauffman, all spellwork had limits, and my sudden addition of an entire dragon—even a significantly reduced one—was more than the arena could take.

I felt the break before I saw it. One second I was feeding magic into the chaos hand over fist, the next the whole cyclone of power jolted. The magic was still spinning, but the circle it was spinning inside was no longer large enough to contain it, and like a wheel grown suddenly too big for its wheelhouse, it burst free, exploding outward in a violent torrent of raging, uncontrolled power.

Straight into me

As a lifelong magical failure, I'd been on the receiving end of more overloaded spells than I could count. It was always terrifying and painful, but none of those previous botches came anywhere close to the tsunami of backlash bearing down on me now.

As it landed, I had one of those strange, calm moments when you know you're absolutely screwed, but defeat is so inevitable that it feels like a waste of time to get upset. I was far more worried that all this exploding magic might end up killing thousands of spectators in addition to myself. True, they were terrible people who'd shown up to watch Nik get eaten, but I still didn't want to be responsible for their deaths.

Thankfully, since the Gameskeeper had already centered most of the power on Mad Dog, the majority of the destruction looked like it would happen in the middle of the arena, away from the crowd. I was telling myself to be happy that at least I hadn't accidentally become a mass murderer in my last seconds when I heard someone shouting.

"What are you doing?" My father's face appeared in front of mine, his smoky features so faint I could barely see them. "We're not done! Grab it again quickly, before he takes it back!"

For a horrible second, I had no idea what he was talking about. Then I felt it. I wasn't having a moment of calm before the end. The Gameskeeper had *caught* the exploding magic just before it spun out of control. The power was far too big for him to control safely without spellwork, but he was still wrestling it down, sucking the magic back into himself while the crowd watched in confusion. He'd already wrangled most of it. A few more seconds and he'd have the rest back in hand as well, which meant I'd drained my dad for *nothing*.

Screw that! With a scream that came from the soles of my feet, I reached with everything I had to grab back the magic I'd just sent flying. The Gameskeeper roared in reply, a terrifying cry of divine anger, but for once his nature was working against him. He was the god of the arena, and taking on opponents stronger than yourself was what arena fights were all about. He'd named me challenger, and I accepted it, clawing the roaring magic from his fingers and back into myself.

Where I had no place to put it.

This was the place in the original plan were the DFZ was supposed to swoop in and save my poor mortal soul. But I didn't have the DFZ anymore, and what room I did have was rapidly burning up. I was going to pop like a balloon if I didn't find somewhere to put all this power fast. Thankfully, my salvation was already tied to me.

"Opal!" my father's shade cried, his voice sounding a thousand miles away as he reached out his near-invisible hand where our thread was still floating, silver and whole.

He didn't have to say more. Thanking my god for making me practice this so much, I turned and pushed all the magic that was slamming into me straight into him. It ran down the silver thread like lightning, which was a problem because I was only supposed to send him fire.

Just as I started to panic, though, I saw that it didn't matter. Unlike the first time in my apartment, my father was no longer embers, and he'd been practicing too. He'd been right there with me for all of it, learning as I learned. The moment I sent the magic at him, the smoldering embers of his fire grabbed it and burst back to life, the growing flames hungrily consuming everything I threw into them.

At least, I think that's what happened. I was working so fast to keep the magic moving, I couldn't focus on anything else. All I knew was grab and push, grab and push, faster and faster just like Dr. Kowalski had made me practice until, all at once, I reached for more magic and came up empty.

I jerked, my eyes shooting open despite the fact that I didn't remember closing them. I was still in the center of the arena, but there was no more roaring or thumping or hammering. For the first time ever, the stadium was totally silent. Even the bright lights seemed dimmer, like I was standing in shadow.

No, I realized slowly. Not like. It *was* a shadow. Something enormous standing above me, blocking the floodlights. When I finally looked up to see what it was, I found myself staring into the grinning, sharp-toothed maw of the biggest dragon I'd ever seen. The beautiful red-maned, blue-scaled, sea-eyed, smoke-wreathed face of the Great Yong of Korea.

Chapter 15

He looked even bigger than I remembered. I didn't know if that was because we were crammed into an arena or if I'd pumped even more magic into him than he'd originally possessed, but my dad was absolutely colossal. He was so big that even the crowd shrank back, trembling in their seats at the terrifying, terrible wonder that was a dragon in his true shape.

As always in this place though, the quiet was only temporary. The moment the people got over their shock, they started howling louder than ever, yelling their throats raw as they realized it was actually happening.

A dragon had come to fight in the arena.

Huge eyes narrowing at the noise, Yong snorted in disgust and tilted his head to look at Nik, who was still writhing on the bloody ground with the curse chewing through his neck like teeth. With a sympathetic rumble, my father lifted his foreleg and pressed a clawed forefoot the size of a minivan on top of Nik's convulsing body. When no part of Nik was visible through the cage of claws and scales, the dragon lifted his chin and announced in a booming voice:

"I win."

There was absolutely no denying it. Even if Nik hadn't been busy fighting decapitation, there was no possible way he could defeat something as ancient and huge as my father. Stating the obvious was critical, though, because the moment Yong spoke the words, the fight was over. Its final requirement fulfilled, the Sword of Damocles vanished from Nik's neck, freeing him to collapse into the sand.

I was at his side in an instant, ducking under my father's claws so fast, I sliced a chunk off the end of my ponytail.

"*Nik!*"

"I'm alive," he croaked, his voice hoarse from his wounded, but still intact, throat. The Sword of Damocles must have been designed to cut slowly in order to give him time to change his mind, because Nik's neck wasn't nearly as bad as I'd feared. His skin was chewed to bits and there was a *lot* of blood, but none of the wounds were deep enough to be a true emergency; a realization that left me so relieved it was almost painful.

"I'm so happy you're not dead!" I sobbed, throwing my arms around him. "You have no idea!"

"I think I might," he rasped, looking up at the underside of the dragon's foot shielding us from the world. "Guess I lost."

"No way," I said fiercely, letting go of him just long enough to lift up my poncho and rip a strip off my T-shirt to use as a bandage. "You won! You didn't do what they wanted. You stood your ground even when they were cutting off your head." I wrapped the dark cloth around his bloody neck. "I knew you could do it. I'm so proud of you!"

His body stiffened so fast, I worried I'd hurt him. Then he lurched forward, grabbing and hugging me so tight I could barely breathe.

"I did win, didn't I?" he gasped, his injured voice happier than I'd ever heard it. "I'm free!"

"You're free," I agreed, collapsing into his viselike embrace as all the fear and sadness and pain I'd been desperately holding back finally broke free. It was over. We'd done it. We'd saved him. My dad too. We'd saved everyone!

The mix of relief and joy that came with that was too much for me to handle. I started bawling, sobbing myself into a soggy mess in seconds. I could have kept going like that for an hour at least—it had been a hard end to a *hard* week—but as I settled in to let it out, I realized the crowd was still screaming, their voices pounding in unison like an army of drums.

"Kill! Kill! Kill!"

I froze against Nik. I'd been so overwhelmed by our victory, I hadn't been paying attention to what was building outside. Now that I'd noticed it, it was impossible to miss. The arena's bloody magic was back with a vengeance. I'd thought I'd broken the circle and dumped everything that remained into my dad, but I'd forgotten the first rule of magic: there was *always* more. All I'd done was break the holding tank, but the source of the arena's power was the crowd, and they were still screaming for blood.

"*Finish him!*" they demanded as the magic churned higher. "*Burn him! Eat him! Turn him into—*"

"***Enough!***" my father roared.

His voice cut through their demands like claws through flesh, and the crowd jerked back, their bloodlust overwhelmed by the predatory menace pouring off my father. Even I was shaking, pressed down into the sand by the weight of the Great Yong's displeasure. I'd seen him angry plenty of times, but this was different. When he got mad at me, love was always there to temper it, but there were no softer feelings here. The force emanating from my father this time was a disgust so sharp it soured my stomach, making me retch as he slid his slitted eyes over the trembling crowd.

"There will be no more killing tonight," he boomed, his voice so loud, it rattled the flood lamps. "What is wrong with you? You live in a world that has always been saturated with violence and tragedy. What could possibly drive you to seek out more? Are your own lives so empty you have to fill them with the blood of others?"

He paused as if he expected an answer, but the crowd was cowering too hard to shout back, and eventually my father continued. "I have watched your kind for two thousand years, and yet I am continually amazed by how you never seem to learn. Every time one of you attempts to lift humanity out of its barbarism, ten more fight to drag it back down. Why do you do this to yourselves? You are the masters of magic in this world, the force that creates gods! Why do you insist on rolling in the worst of your own filth?"

He lifted his eyes to the VIP box where I knew the Gameskeeper was watching. "What happens in this arena is not an inescapable truth of the world," he rumbled. "This place and the horrors it celebrates exist because *you* allow it. You cheer for this cruelty because it is not happening to you, never even seeing that you are *all* drowning in blood! But my family will not be part of your self-destructive idiocy. If you want blood, go spill your own, for you deserve none of ours."

With that, my father dismissed the crowd with a snort and looked down, turning his clawed hand over so that Nik and I could climb on. I clambered up the scales like an old pro, but Nik took some cajoling before he would step into the dragon's palm. When we were both finally in position, Yong lifted us into the air. We'd barely made it halfway up his body when the crowd recovered its voice.

Even dragon panic couldn't last forever. The more time that passed without them being devoured, the more the people recovered. As their fear waned, rage rose up to take its place, and they started hurling things at us. Only curses at first, but the harsh language was soon joined by trash and beer bottles.

The anger didn't surprise me a bit. I also hated when Yong lectured me, and he wasn't even their dad. Being dressed down by a dragon you weren't even related to had to be galling to the sort of person who went to a blood sport arena, and the greater their rage grew, the more violent they became.

"Are we going to be okay?" I asked my dad.

"Of course," he replied as he placed us on his shoulder. "One of the benefits of being a dragon is that you don't have to care about the opinions of lesser creatures."

Normally, I took offense when my dad insulted humans, but I understood what he meant this time. These people weren't "lesser creatures" because they were mortal; they were less because they were *here*. These were the people who'd chosen to spend their Saturday night watching Nik get slaughtered, whose thrill at the suffering of others had empowered a dark god. I had no sympathy for them at all.

"Let's get out of here," I said, clutching Nik tight with one hand while gripping my dad's mane with the other.

Yong rumbled in reply, dropping his feet back to the sand in preparation to crash through the ceiling to freedom. Just as he was about to jump, though, a new force swept through the arena. It flew over our heads like a giant hand, grabbing the crowd's fury and transforming it into something that wasn't impotent. Something deadly. My dad must have felt the change, too, because he crouched back on his haunches. I hunkered down as well, squeezing his crimson mane tight as the gate they'd wheeled Nik's cage through rolled open again.

Given what was going on, I was expecting an army, but only one figure came marching out of the dark. A single man with a plain face transformed by rage into something much closer to his truth.

The Gameskeeper.

"Where do you think you're going, dragon?" the god taunted, throwing out his arm toward my father. Magic followed the motion like a whip, wrapping around my father's body and dragging him into the sand. "Can't you hear the people? The fight's not over. No fight can be without *blood!*"

"*Blood!*" the crowd roared in delight. "*Blood! Blood! Blood!*"

The Gameskeeper spread his arms as the chant washed over him. It crashed into us as well, nearly knocking me off my father's shoulder with its strength. "We have to get rid of the crowd!" I cried as I pulled myself back up. "The Gameskeeper's not a big god on his own, but there's no way we can beat him with all those people behind him."

"We could burn them," Nik suggested, grabbing my hand to help me. "Aren't dragons good at that?"

My father turned up his nose. "I'm not a barbarian."

"We're not murdering a whole arena full of people," I said firmly. "Even if they are the worst."

Nik didn't look as if he cared what happened to the crowd who'd cheered for his death, but he didn't argue. "You'd better come up with something else fast, then," he said, pointing over my shoulder. "Look."

I turned back to the Gameskeeper, who'd grown noticeably bigger. Not as big as my dad, but several times larger than a normal human, his form pulsing in time with the screams that gave him power.

"Okay, that's bad," I said, eyes wide. "We have to stop him!"

"I'm open to suggestion," my father replied, lowering his shoulder so we could slide off. "You two get to cover. I'll deal with this."

"No way," I said, clinging to his scales. "You're not facing this alone!"

"I've hidden in your shadow long enough," Yong told me dearly, plucking me off his shoulder with a gentle claw. "Now it's my turn to take care of you."

"But he's a *god*!"

"And I'm a dragon," my father replied as he set me down. "Spirits aren't the only powers in this world, puppy. It's time someone reminded him of that."

I didn't want to let him go, but my dad slid out of my grasp like the slippery snake he was, leaving me next to Nik in the sand.

"*Can* Yong beat him?" Nik whispered as my father walked away.

"Loyalty demands that I say yes," I replied. "In reality, though…"

My voice trailed off, and Nik's scowl deepened. "We should focus on the crowd, then," he said, grabbing my hand to pull me toward the arena wall, as far from my father and the Gameskeeper as we could get. "Their screaming is what's giving the Gameskeeper his juice, right?"

I nodded. "I already trashed the spellwork that lets him catch and hold their magic, so what they're giving is all he's got. If we can get them to stop cheering—or even better, to leave—he should run out of power pretty fast. But how are we going to do that? These people showed up to see a dragon fight, and now they've got a god in the mix as well. This is everything they paid to see and more. How do we get them to give that up?"

Nik didn't answer, and I gritted my teeth, glancing back at my father. He was still huge and terrifying, but unlike the Gameskeeper, his power was fixed. He couldn't grow like his enemy could or replenish his strength from the crowd, which meant time was against him. The longer this fight dragged on, the more disadvantaged he'd be. Clearing the arena would solve that, but how did two people fight a hundred thousand? How could we do *anything* against—

"Opal?" a familiar artificial voice chirped in my ear.

I jerked in surprise. She'd been so quiet, I'd forgotten that Sibyl was still with me.

"I know you're busy," my AI said briskly. "But just a heads-up: you're going to want to find cover in the next five seconds."

"Why?" I asked frantically, looking around. "What's going to happen in the next five—"

My answer was a hail of gunfire through the ceiling above us. The automated shots perforated the peak of the arena's dome like needles through paper. No, I realized when I saw the debris flying from the shots, not *like* paper. The roof *was* paper, or at least very thick cardboard.

That wasn't actually too uncommon in the deep Underground where you never had to worry about rain. But this was an arena, not a cheap warehouse! I'd just assumed the roof was made of metal, but the only solid parts were actually the steel girders that held up the lights. A fact that quickly became abundantly apparent as ten heavy combat helicopters blasted through what was left of the paper covering to explode into the stadium from above.

"*What the—*" Nik grabbed me and hit the sand, shoving my head under the shelter of his freshly repaired bulletproof arm. "What is *that?*"

I wiggled out of his grip, grinning so hard my face hurt as the helicopters descended in formation behind my father.

"It's my mom!"

***

"*Opal!*"

Shielding my eyes from the blowing sand, I got back to my feet just in time to see my mother leap out of the nearest helicopter the moment it was within safe jumping distance of the ground. As befit the situation, she was wearing combat armor. Perfectly fitted combat armor in a lovely shade of forest green that flattered her complexion—never forget who this was—but it was hands down the most practical thing I'd ever seen her wear. I was still gawking in disbelief when she threw her arms around me.

"I was so worried!" she cried, hugging me tight for a split second before she shoved me back to the ground. "Stay right there! I have to go talk to your father."

"Mom, no!" But she'd already run off to join the other hundred soldiers dressed in the same deep-green armor as herself—albeit the far less fashionable version—who'd already formed a blockade between Yong and the Gameskeeper. My mother made her way to the center of the group at once, dropping to her knees with her head pressed into the sand at my father's feet.

"Great Dragon," she said reverently.

"Consort," he rumbled back, his voice proud. "Excellent timing, as always."

"I live only to return to your side," my mother replied, raising her head to look up at him with a worshipful expression. "How may I serve you?"

"Pull back your men," Yong ordered, his voice sharpening to a growl as his eyes returned to the Gameskeeper. "Our forces are not prepared for a battle such as this, and anyway, this is my fight. Take your team and go to Opal. She'll tell you what to do."

"Opal?" my mother repeated, her lovely face utterly confused. A second later, her obedient expression returned. "At once, Great Dragon," she said, bowing again. "As you command."

With that, she hopped back to her feet and retreated. Her army retreated with her like the tide, pulling back to form a black pool around Nik and I instead. When we were completely ringed in, my mother stepped forward to stand before me. "Opal," she said primly. "The Great Yong has placed you in command. What are your orders?"

By the time she finished, my eyes were nearly falling out of my head. I'd heard Dad say it with my own ears, but it still didn't seem possible that my *mother*—the same woman who'd refused to let me wear any clothes she didn't personally select until I left for college—was standing there waiting for me to tell her what to do. I never would have predicted this turn of events in a million years. Then again…this was my mom. If Dad told her she could fly, she'd jump off a building without hesitation. Same went for taking orders from me, apparently, because here she was, her perfect face the picture of attentive readiness as she waited for me to tell her what to do.

"Right," I said at last, pushing my goggles up so I could look at her directly. "The Gameskeeper is a Mortal Spirit who's drawing his magic from the crowd. I'm pretty sure Dad's stronger, but he can't beat an enemy who's constantly healing. If we want our dragon to win, we have to get rid of the Gameskeeper's power source, so I want you to take your men and clear the building. Don't kill anyone if you can help it, just make them leave. Make sense?"

My mother nodded and turned back to her riot-geared unit. "You heard the Great Yong's daughter!" she said in the firm, authoritative voice that seemed to work as well on soldiers as it did on servants. "Our dragon's victory depends on dispersing the locals. Groups one through four, you take the north side. Groups five through eight, the south. Use non-lethals only, but leave no one in this building."

"Yes, First Mortal!" they replied in unison, sliding their guns off their shoulders to replace their live rounds with clips full of rubber bullets. My mother did the same to the weapon strapped across her own back, popping the clip out of the submachine gun and replacing it with a deftness that made me wince. Was there *anything* she wasn't good at?

"We've got the crowd, daughter," she told me as she slid her gun back onto her arm. "You stay here and do whatever you can to help your father."

"On it," I said, but she was already jogging away with her men.

"Is everything good?" Nik asked as they left. "Because I didn't understand a word of that."

I frowned at him, confused for a second before I remembered he didn't speak Korean. "It's great," I reported. "Mom's people are going to disperse the crowd for us."

"Sounds good," Nik said. Then he scowled. "Does your mom always arrive with an army?"

"Pretty much," I said, watching my mom's soldiers use their grapple guns to scale the arena walls into the stands above, where people were already starting to panic. They'd had no problem with a dragon or helicopters so long as they stayed in the arena, but armed troops climbing into their seats was apparently where even the most hardcore arena fans drew the line. Most people chose to run, but a few blood-drunk idiots started throwing things, forcing Mom's teams to shield their faces as they pushed forward.

"Should we go help them?" Nik asked. "Even with armor, there's enough people up there to trample them if the crowd turns."

"She'll be fine," I said confidently. "Mom can do anything. That's why she's been First Mortal for the last thirty years. And she's not alone. Look!"

I pointed up at the top level of the arena stands where people were screaming and fleeing in panic even though Mom's troops were nowhere near them. This was because, while there were no soldiers up there yet, there were several dozen rats. Huge ones the size of sheep all moving together under the direction of a scrawny old man wearing sewer-worker coveralls. He waved when he saw me looking, and I realized that this must be one of the priests the DFZ had sent in to help hide my presence from the Gameskeeper.

I waved back. Someone less familiar with the DFZ would probably have been shocked he'd been able to get all those rats in here, but not me. Honestly, the rats were the most plausible part of all of this. You couldn't keep those bastards out! I was far more astonished that they listened to him. So far as I knew, DFZ rats didn't listen to anyone. These followed their priest's orders gleefully, jumping at the arena-goers with squeaks of glee. The people screamed and fled, dropping their nachos and popcorn and cotton candy, which the rats devoured in greedy abandon before scurrying over to the next tier of seats to repeat the process all over again. They cleared an entire section in the few seconds I was watching, proving that the DFZ had been wrong. Her people *were* good in a fight after all!

Hopes soaring that my god hadn't abandoned us after all, I turned back to my father, who'd planted himself between us and the Gameskeeper. The blood-rage-fueled spirit hadn't gotten any bigger, but I could still feel his magic hanging in the air above me like an iron weight. It wasn't a patch on the DFZ's magic, but it was still way more of a power reserve than my dad possessed, which was going to be a major issue if I didn't find some way to even things out.

"I'm going to help him," I said, sitting down in the sand. "Cover me."

"Opal, he's a *dragon*," Nik said frantically. "What are you going to do?"

"Anything I can. Just watch my back. This is going to take all my concentration."

"I won't let anyone touch you," Nik promised. "But…" He trailed off, gritting his teeth. "You aren't always the most responsible with magic, okay? I'm all for beating the Gameskeeper, but I just got you back. What do I do if things go wrong?"

"Wait for me to make them go right again," I said, lying back. "I've learned a lot over the last two months. Trust me. I can do this."

Nik still looked skeptical, not that I blamed him. I wouldn't have trusted the me of two months ago with this kind of giant magic either. Thankfully, I wasn't that person anymore. There was no way to make Nik believe that except to show him, though, so I gave him a final smile and closed my eyes, focusing all my attention on the magic roaring all around us.

There was a *lot*. It reminded me of the time I'd fallen into the void below the Gnarls both in terms of sheer volume and rampant chaos. At least when it was being channeled through Kauffman's circle, all the magic had been spinning the same way. Now it was just a cacophony of angry screams, panic, and the clenched desperation of a fighter with nothing to lose.

Not the sort of power any mage in her right mind would touch, in other words, but I'd gone way too far to start being sensible now. I dove straight in, grabbing the magic like I was wrestling a sea monster. My plan was to do what I'd done before and channel the roaring power straight into my dad. Unfortunately, while there was actually *less* magic than earlier thanks to the bunch I'd grabbed last time, what was left was locked up so tight in the Gameskeeper's grasp, I couldn't get a finger in.

The reduced magic volume seemed to be working enormously in his favor, actually. The mountain of power he'd built at the start of Nik's fight must have been way too much for him to personally control, which was how I'd been able to steal it, but the level he was at now was apparently perfect. Siphoning magic off him this time felt like trying to pinch sand out of a rock. And that was a problem, because despite everything, the Gameskeeper was still a god, and even though my father was back to his old self, he was still just one dragon, and he was getting hammered.

I saw now why he'd sent Mom and the other soldiers away. The Gameskeeper's magic encircled the area around him like an iron fist, crushing anything smaller than a dragon. Even Yong looked beaten down, his body low and coiled. But a cornered dragon is the most dangerous dragon of all. My father fought back with claws and fangs, blasting the Gameskeeper with gouts of white-hot fire that turned the sand beneath him to glass.

If he'd been anything else, that would have been it, but the Gameskeeper was a spirit. His body was no more physical than my dad's smoke form had been. Every fiery breath and slashing claw passed straight through him, leaving him free to swing the arena's thick magic like a whip, battering my father with invisible blows that sent him staggering. It was a bad, bad situation, but with the Gameskeeper's power surrounding them both like an iron wall, I couldn't do anything to help.

"Crap," I said, opening my eyes again. "I gotta get in there."

"Uh, this might not be a good time to move," Nik's strained voice said from somewhere above me.

I sat up in a rush only to get shoved right back down into the sand by Nik as a bullet whizzed over my head.

"What the hell?" I said when he let me up. "Who are these guys?"

When I'd closed my eyes a few seconds ago, we'd been alone at the edge of the arena. Now, Nik and I were trapped against the wall by a circle of guards dressed in the arena's trademark cheap security armor and carrying guns that, while equally cheap looking, were still doing a good job of keeping us pinned.

"Security team," Nik replied, blocking a bullet on his metal arm while a second *pinged* off the shoulder of the crush armor he'd been given to draw out his fight against Yong. "Didn't think they'd be brave enough for this shit, but apparently the Gameskeeper is still calling the shots, and he still considers you enemy number one."

After all the trouble I'd caused, I could see that. I was more annoyed that an asshole like the Gameskeeper commanded such loyalty from his employees. Once I got a look at their faces, though, I realized I was wrong. This wasn't loyalty. These men were terrified, firing their cheap guns at Nik with a desperation that made me sick to my stomach. I didn't know what the Gameskeeper had on them that could make them this crazy, but it didn't really matter. Whatever it was, we clearly weren't getting out of this without killing him. Or killing them.

I knew my preference. "Can you hold them off?" I asked Nik.

"Probably," he said, ducking a shot without even looking. "Even if their guns weren't shit, they're too scared to shoot straight, and you're wearing your bulletproof tarp." He nodded to my poncho, which I immediately slapped my hand against to activate the anti-bullet ward. "We'll have a problem if they charge us, but until they get the spine for a direct attack, we should be alright. What are you going to do?"

Something crazy. I knew better than to tell him that, though from the grumpy look on his face, Nik already knew.

"Just don't die, okay?"

"Same goes for you," I said, rising up to give him a quick peck on the cheek before I closed my eyes and plunged back in.

And ran right back into the wall of the Gameskeeper's magic.

I beat my mental fists against it, but it was no use. The spirit was locked up tighter than a dragon's treasury, and my dad was trapped inside. I tried reaching out to the DFZ for help next, hoping that shrinking the Gameskeeper's power had also shrunk his domain, but I got nothing. Despite the chaos, the Gameskeeper was clearly still the god of this place. My mom's troops and the DFZ's rat priest were making chaos of the stands, so I knew he had to run out of oomph eventually, but I didn't know when that would be or if my dad would last that long. Yong was already looking bloody, his blue scales soaked with that shimmery, magical dragon blood I never wanted to see again.

I glanced back at the Gameskeeper, cursing as my father's claws slid through him yet again. It didn't matter how strong Yong was. If he kept taking damage while the Gameskeeper didn't, there was no winning this fight. I *had* to get through that barrier and help him before things got too lopsided to fix. I was wracking my brain to figure out how I was going to do that when something sharp cut into my palm.

I gasped in pain. My first thought was that a bullet had gotten past Nik. When my eyes popped back open to check, though, my hand was fine. There was no wound or blood, just the faint silver glow of the thread.

In my panic over saving my father, I'd clenched the silver thread that connected us so tight, it had cut into my magic. Even after I let go, it hurt like crazy, but the pain gave me an idea. *I* might be locked out, but we'd proven over and over that the connection between my father and I was unbreakable, and he was already inside. If I wanted to join him, all I had to do was follow the path.

I took a sharp breath. The plan forming in my mind was nuts even by my standards, but I didn't see anything else that would work, and really, what was the difference between a human and a dragon? Sure, the nature and source and mechanics of our magic were all totally different, but ultimately speaking, we were both just souls stuck inside a physical shell. Connected souls, and if he could leave his body, why couldn't I leave mine? After all, as I'd learned the hard way when I'd nearly broken mine, human souls were just magic. Delicate, unique, irreplaceable magic, but so was everyone else here. I couldn't replace Nik or my father or my mom, and I was going to lose them all if we didn't beat the Gameskeeper soon. There'd be no second chances if I held back, so I did what I did best and went for it, diving headfirst down the thread the same way I'd sent every other bit of magic to my father since I'd first brought him back from the embers.

And sweet fire, did it hurt.

Accidentally dislocating my soul had been painful and terrifying. Intentionally ripping it out and sending it down a magical link was all of that again times ten. If I hadn't had such a solid link to hold on to, I would have torn myself to pieces, but even when I was panicking from the pain, the silver thread held me together. Every time he'd acted out of love for me, every time I'd refused to throw him away no matter how mad I got, every sacrifice, every hardship, every trial we'd passed, it was all there. *All* of it counted, and all of it held, forming a bond strong enough to shield my soul from the chaos as I shot through the arena god's wall of magic to my father's side, appearing on his shoulder with a suddenness that made us both jump.

"Opal?" he panted, his eyes wild with battle rage that was rapidly changing into fear. "What are you doing here?"

Steadying myself against his scales, I looked down my hand, which was now made of the same curling smoke his had been the first time he'd left his body. *Whoa,* I said, breaking into a delighted smile. *It worked!*

"You are not allowed to be happy about turning yourself into a ghost!" my father shouted, blowing another blast of flame at the Gameskeeper before turning his glare back to me. "Get back in your body this instant!"

No way, I said, clutching his scales tighter. *I didn't turn myself to smoke for funsies. I'm here to help you.*

I could tell he desperately wanted to snarl that he didn't need help. But while he had many faults, my father had never been a liar.

"I don't see how you can," he said in a resigned voice, grunting as another invisible blow smacked into his side. "This fool doesn't take damage."

Maybe not in the normal way, I said, pointing beyond the wall of screaming magic at the stands, which were now nearly empty. *But he can't keep this up forever. Mom's breaking the crowd hard, and I've already smashed his circle. There's no more magic once this is gone. If we can just hold tight, he should run himself dry.*

Easier said than done. Now that I was inside the maelstrom with him, I could see that my dad was in even worse shape than I'd feared. He was tough and fast, but the Gameskeeper had him surrounded. Dodging one blow just threw him into reach of the next. Freed from the restrictions of mortal eyeballs, I could actually see the bloody magic coming in like a bludgeon from above to bash my father's skull. He got out of the way at the last second, but the blow still glanced off his back, making him stagger.

Dad!

"I'm not that weak," he growled, lashing back with claws that went straight through the Gameskeeper's smug face. "But if you have an alternate approach, I'm open to suggestion."

That was as close to a cry for help as the Great Yong got. Unfortunately, he wasn't going to like my answer.

You need to stop dodging.

My father growled, almost knocking me off as he rolled through the dirt to avoid a swift strike from the ground. "I fail to see how letting him hit me is going to help."

explained. *He knows that you can't hurt him, so he's conserving his strength, using just enough magic to keep you pinned while he takes you down with a thousand cuts. But this is a bleeding battle on both sides! If we want to win, we have to make sure that he bleeds faster, and the best way to do that is to bait him into a full-power attack.*

"That's what I'm afraid of. He hits *hard*."

Only because your scales don't work against the damage he dishes out, but that's about to change. I balled my smoky hands into fists. *You're not alone, Dad. I got this. Let him swing.*

I knew that my father's trust in me had grown enormously over the last week, but I was still surprised when he actually did as I asked, placing his feet back on the ground where he'd already lifted them in preparation to jump out of the way of the next hit, which was coming in from the left.

I saw it, too, a mass of screaming power coming at us like a wrecking ball. But where my dad had nothing but his reflexes and his scales to protect himself, I was a human mage. Moving magic was my bread and butter. I might not have been able to dig my fingers into the wall he'd built, but even a god couldn't keep away magic he was literally throwing at my face. Stopping so much power would have been suicide, so I didn't even try. Instead, I used the skill set I'd been practicing all week, plunging my mental fingers into the oncoming attack to transfer all that raging force *through* me instead, turning myself not into a wall or a shield, but a lightning rod.

The power transfer was a *lot* easier to manage when I didn't have a body to worry about. There was no resistance, no pain, no mental game of imagining fire running into wires. I was past all that now. All I had to do was grab hold of the magic long enough to redirect it, riding the lightning up one arm and down the other straight into my dad.

Just like before, he ate it up. This was only the second time we'd tried this, but no one could match a dragon for greed. His flames sucked the power out of me as fast as I pulled it in. Within seconds, the huge fist of magic the Gameskeeper had thrown at us wasn't just deflected, it was gone entirely. We'd sucked it dry, and from the way the smug smile was sliding off his face, our enemy knew what that meant.

"*You!*" he cried, his bloody eyes locking onto my tiny smoke figure. "I'll skin you alive!"

My father answered his rudeness with a gout of flame. Unlike my dad's other blasts, the Gameskeeper actually rolled out of the way of this one. Watching the flames, I understood why. When it got hot enough, dragon fire was capable of burning *anything*, even magic. But such attacks were costly. Forming them required breathing out the hottest, purest, deepest part of the flame that created a dragon's life and magic. It wasn't something to be used lightly, or ever. As always, though, my father and I were different. Between the magical buffet the Gameskeeper had put on and my ability to feed him fire, I could fill my dad up faster than he could burn himself down, and he used that new advantage as ruthlessly as I could have hoped.

"Again, daughter!" Yong roared, following the Gameskeeper with a stream of fire so bright, I couldn't even look at it. "Do it *again!*"

He didn't have to tell me. I was already reaching down for the magic the Gameskeeper was lashing at us from the ground in a desperate effort to sweep my father off his feet. With no body to slow me down and the silver thread holding me tight, I caught it before it could even touch his claws, sucking the power into my dad like a magical vacuum hose. As soon as I gave it to him, Yong blasted it back out, forcing the Gameskeeper to retreat or be turned to a crisp under a torrent of all-burning fire.

And just like that, the tide began to turn. Every time the Gameskeeper attacked, we tossed it right back, forcing the god to retreat. The few times the blazing fire dimmed enough for me to catch a glimpse of his plain face, the Gameskeeper looked shocked, as if he couldn't believe this was happening, which was fair. My father was spending his fire at a rate that would have killed any other dragon in minutes, but he wasn't any other dragon. He was *my* dragon. We'd always been a unique situation.

Mostly a nonfunctional one, but when we did manage to find our common ground, nothing could stop us.

I was sure there was a lesson about the strength of family in there somewhere, but I was too busy helping my dad burn a dark god to think about it. Even after the Gameskeeper wised up and stopped throwing his magic at us, there was no putting this dragon back in the bag. Now that I knew how easy it was to channel in this form, I started stealing the Gameskeeper's power straight out of the air, gathering it up in bigger and bigger handfuls until, all at once, there was nothing left to grab.

Yong's fire stopped a second later, leaving me blinking in the sudden dark. When my eyes—or, more accurately, the mental concept that served as my eyes since I was currently disembodied—adjusted, the Gameskeeper was back to his previous size, panting on his knees at my father's feet. I wasn't sure which had been the final straw, my rampant theft or Dad's fire, but the god clearly had nothing left. He didn't even flinch when my father pressed his foot down on top of him, his long claws forming a cage that pinned the defeated spirit onto the smoking, melted sand.

"You are defeated, Arena Master," Yong said, his voice booming through the empty stadium. "And we all know what happens to a defeated champion in your ring."

"It makes no difference," the Gameskeeper replied, his plain face pulling into a defiant sneer. "I am a spirit, a true immortal! You can't kill me. So long as humans lust for blood, I'll always rise again!"

"Then we'll just have to make sure this city is a better place before then," I said, crossing my smoke arms. "You might be part of humanity, but that doesn't mean we have to welcome you. We decide which gods we worship, and now that we know what you really are, I'm going to do my damnedest to make sure you never get a foothold in the DFZ—or any other city—again."

"With what power?" The god scoffed. "You're not a priestess anymore, and now that you've shown your true colors, you never will be."

I shrugged. "I don't have to be a priestess to do what's right. As I've been informed many, *many* times, cities are shaped by their people. If I want to make a better DFZ, all I have to do is be better while living in it."

"No one here will welcome you," my father agreed. "You might not be killable the way we are, but all gods depend on humans for their power, and yours relies on others perceiving you as the lord of champions." His flashed the Gameskeeper a sharp-toothed smile. "Tell me, Spirit of the Arena, what happens to your power when the god of winners loses?"

The Gameskeeper went still, his eyes shooting wide. "A-all champions fall sooner or later," he stuttered at last. "But people forget, and new champions rise!"

My father chuckled and looked up at the flock of drone cameras that were still hovering under the supports of the broken dome. "I don't think they'll forget this."

Before I could ask my father what he meant by that, the Great Yong plucked the Gameskeeper off the sand and ate him. Literally shoved him whole into his mouth and snapped his teeth closed. Since spirits didn't have blood, it wasn't the gory spectacle it should have been, but I still recoiled in horror, backing away so fast that I lost my hold on his scales. The moment our connection broke, something inside me kicked hard, making me double over with a grunt. When I opened my eyes again, I was back in my body, lying gasping on the sand with Nik's nervous face hovering over me.

"Hey," he said as I coughed, his worried expression turning to relief as he reached down to brush the hair out of my face. "Are you okay?"

"Are *you* okay?" I asked, sitting up in alarm.

Nik looked horrible. I mean, he'd looked bad before with his chewed-up neck, but this was even worse. There was a huge bloody gash on his forehead that I swear hadn't been there when I'd lain down, and the bulky plates of his crush-proof armor were riddled with bullet dents and scorch marks.

"What the hell happened to you?"

Nik shrugged. "The usual," he said, scooting over so that I could see past him.

My eyes went wide. The sand around us looked like a war zone. There'd only been a dozen or so terrified security people shooting at us when I'd gone to help my dad. Now, the small stretch of arena that hadn't been taken over by the Gameskeeper's duel was littered with groaning, wounded bodies. Mostly hired muscle in security armor, but there was one unarmored figure I recognized immediately.

"Holy crap, is that *Kauffman?*"

"No other," Nik said with a cruel smirk. "Pro tip: next time you decide to stab someone full of glass, make sure you cut him enough that he stays down. Those cowards were content to make a show of shooting at us until he showed up and started screaming about how the Gameskeeper was always watching and halfhearted obedience wouldn't be tolerated. Things got serious after that."

"I see," I said, looking at Kauffman, who was lying on his back with his face looking even worse than the last time Nik had punched him. "Looks like 'serious' didn't end so well for him."

"Actually, he was doing great until your dad started burning the Gameskeeper," Nik said, reaching up to apply pressure to his head cut, which was still bleeding sluggishly. "I was about to grab your body and make a run for it when the Gameskeeper started going down. Once that happened, Kauffman's company line stopped working. All the guards who could still move broke and ran, and he suddenly found himself all alone."

"You'd think he'd learn," I said, shaking my head at Kauffman's groaning body. "Good on you for not killing him, though."

"I really should at this point," Nik grumbled. "For all his 'just business' talk, bastard doesn't know when to quit. I'd be saving myself a lot of trouble if I offed him. But I don't do that crap anymore, so I guess I've got no one to blame but myself when he shows up with a grudge in a few months."

"When that happens, we'll deal with it," I promised, rising up to kiss him on the cheek. "But I'm proud of you for sticking to your principles." I wasn't sure I would have been that strong. After all the trouble he'd caused us, a dead Kauffman sounded like a lovely turn of events to me.

Nik was grinning when I sat back down. He was leaning in for a proper kiss when a deep growl interrupted him, and we glanced up to see my father towering over us.

"Sorry to interrupt," he said, not sounding sorry at all. "But I need to check on my daughter."

"I'm fine, Dad," I said, too happy that was true to be miffed by his hovering.

Now that everyone was alive, it was starting to sink in that we'd won. *Actually* won this time. The Gameskeeper was gone, and his arena was pretty much destroyed. My mother was leading the last of her troops back over to my father as I watched, bowing before him as she reported that the entire Rentfree chasm was now under their control. My father nodded approvingly and lowered his head to whisper something in her ear. Whatever he said made my perfect mother blush scarlet, and she darted away, practically bowling her guards over as she raced to the nearest helicopter parked on the edge of the arena. When she came back a second later, she was holding a man's dark suit, white shirt, and mirror-black leather shoes in her arms.

"Wait," Nik said as she presented these to my father with a bow. "She brought him a change of clothes?"

"Dragons are naked when they go back to their human shapes," I explained, turning my back politely as my father's scaly body vanished in a poof of smoke. "You learn to travel prepared."

"I can see that," Nik said. "It's just…I mean…is there *anything* your mother doesn't think of?"

"Of course not," said a deep voice behind us.

He must have gotten his old speed back in spades, because when I turned around, there was my dad, already dressed in one of his ubiquitous dark suits and walking toward us with my mother bobbing happily in his wake.

"Did you think I chose her as First Mortal *merely* because she was beautiful?" he asked, looking down his nose scornfully at Nik before reaching out to take his consort's hand. "Mi-yeon is the most accomplished mortal I have ever known. I will treasure her for the rest of her life, and when she departs this world, I will build a shrine to her memory so that all future generations will know of her devotion and skill."

I'd never seen my mom be anything but perfect, but by the time he finished, she seemed ready to melt into a gooey puddle. The situation only got worse when my father brought her fingers to his lips, making her look so happy I worried for her health.

Smart move on his part. Mom might worship the ground he walked on, but that didn't change the fact that Yong had vanished for two months without telling her. Some buttering up was *definitely* in order, because while she could never be angry with him, it was obvious this had been just as hard for her as it had been for us. I actually spotted the beginnings of a wrinkle on her brow.

But all was clearly forgiven now. My mother looked as if she were going to float away as my father led her over to address the soldiers who'd flown to his aid. He'd just launched into an eloquent speech about loyalty living on forever in the heart of a dragon when I felt the magic lurch around me.

"What?" Nik asked as I grabbed him in panic. "What's wrong?"

I didn't know. I'd been tossed around by so many magical shenanigans in this place, I didn't know which way was up anymore. This surge didn't feel particularly alarming, but anything unexpected was not welcome at this point. I was struggling to grab a handful of my own power to defend us when I finally recognized the power surging under my feet. Even so, I'd barely managed to get my fight-or-flight under control when a huge door rose out of the middle of the blasted arena and the DFZ burst through.

"There's my Opal!" she shouted, running at me with arms thrown wide. An alarming sight since she was dressed for combat in the biggest body I'd seen her put on yet and carrying a telephone pole like a club. She grabbed me a second later, sweeping me into a hug that lifted my feet a good foot and a half off the ground. "I'm so glad you're all right!"

"I'm good, I'm good," I gasped, patting her shoulder until she got the hint and put me down. "But I'm a lot better now that I've seen you. If you're here, that means we really killed him!"

"There's no killing a god," she reminded me. Then her huge face split into a grin. "But I don't see how he'll rise again anytime soon after that humiliation. A spirit getting eaten by a dragon on live television!" She whistled. "It was definitely the spectacle of the century, just not the one he wanted."

I didn't see how getting eaten by a dragon was a mark of shame, but I was only human, so what did I know? The DFZ clearly thought it was an embarrassment that could never be lived down, and that was good enough for me.

"Sorry it took me so long to get here," she went on, setting down her telephone pole. "Even after my rat priest and your troops scattered the crowd, the viewers watching at home kept his power riding high. It wasn't until Yong started kicking his ass that people's faith in him finally crumbled enough for me to get through. Man, though, when it fell, it *fell*. I've got everything back from Rentfree chasm all the way down to the mines." She lowered her voice. "Coincidentally, your other dragon downstairs ate her guards and fled. She crossed over the border into Canada ten minutes ago. Not sure where she is now."

I didn't care where White Snake had run. She'd stood by us when it counted *and* she hadn't come up to stab us in the back, which was all that really mattered. It was probably better for everyone that she *hadn't* come up to help. It was enough of a miracle we'd pulled this thing off as it was. I didn't know if we could have managed another complication, even one that was technically on our side.

I was far more concerned about the DFZ in any case. I could see her in front of me like always, but her voice was just regular sound. There was nothing in my head at all, and remembering how that had happened made me anxious all over again.

"Are you mad?" I whispered.

The city blinked at me. "About what?"

"You know…" I twisted my fingers. "The priest thing."

She leaned on her telephone pole with a sigh. "I'd be lying if I said I wasn't disappointed, but I always kind of knew you'd never be my priest. I *hoped* that wasn't the case, of course, but no one sits on a trial for two months if they intend to actually follow through."

I nodded silently, grateful but still horribly guilty. Everything I'd done had technically been within the bounds of our agreement, and no one could say I hadn't worked my ass off in her service, but I still felt like I'd used her. I was trying to think of how to explain this in a way that didn't sound crazy when the god took my hand.

"It's okay," she said with a smile. "I told you from the start: I only want willing servants. If you don't want to dedicate your life to me, that's your choice. I still want you in my city, and you're welcome to keep working in my sorting area because I've got *tons* more that needs to get done."

She turned her smile on Nik, who was watching the interaction warily. "That offer extends to you as well, by the way. You're going to be famous for a good while after this, which I understand from my time in Opal's head isn't something you're a fan of. If you want to disappear, I'd be happy to take you in! I owe you both big time for putting an end to this drama, and I'm seriously shorthanded. Also, you two are going to need somewhere to run in just a few moments, so it's a good deal for everyone!"

"Wait, what was that last bit?" I asked nervously. "Why would we need somewhere to—"

I was interrupted by a smashing sound as several huge somethings crashed through what was left of the arena's roof. For a horrible second, I was certain I was about to be crushed. Then the huge shapes spread their wings, and I realized they were dragons. The entire arena was *filled* with dragons, and even more were hovering in the open space of the Rentfree chasm above. None were anywhere close to my father's size, but they were still enormous, magical, fire-breathing monsters of every breed, shape, and color. Even my dad looked stunned, his face pale as he stared up at the sky full of fluttering wings. I was turning back to the DFZ to ask what the hell was going on when a roar filled what was left of the arena.

"*Yong!*"

I jumped. I knew that voice, though I'd never heard it use that tone. Sure enough, when I turned around, the Peacemaker was stomping toward us across the sand, his normally gentle face more furious than I'd known it could be.

"What do you think you're doing?" he demanded, stopping in front of my much taller father.

Yong lifted his chin and straightened up to stand even straighter. "I don't see how that is any of your concern."

"Not my concern?" the Peacemaker repeated, his green eyes so bright they glowed. "You flew a military convoy into my airspace without warning or permission and crashed it into a sporting arena full of people! You knew fighting was strictly forbidden in my territory, but you dueled and *ate* a god on live TV! How is this *not my concern?*"

"He was forcing my sister to fight," Yong said dismissively. "If you're so concerned about duels, why didn't you bring all this force to free her?"

"I *did* try to free her!" the Peacemaker yelled. "But she refused because, according to her, she wanted to be there. What was I supposed to do, tell her she was wrong? My law prevents in-fighting and killing humans, but it says nothing about sport fighting. She wasn't breaking my rules, unlike *you.*"

My father sighed as if he found all of this unspeakably tedious, and the Peacemaker scrubbed a hand over his face. "I knew it would end like this," he muttered angrily. "I'm the Dragon of Detroit. I talk to the DFZ every day. I *knew* you were alive, but I understood your concerns and I was *trying* to respect your wishes to remain anonymous. I didn't think you'd try to fight a god alone! Why didn't you ask me for help?"

"Because I didn't need your help," Yong said haughtily, placing one arm on my mother's shoulder and one on mine. "My family was more than sufficient, and unlike you, *they* don't require me to sign away my fangs first."

That was unfair. I didn't know the Peacemaker well, but the one time I'd gone to him, he'd been so nice he was practically bending over. I absolutely believed he would have helped us without cost. I also believed that my father would have rather died choking on his own tail than ask the aid of the dragon he considered a disgrace to the very meaning of the word.

"Don't be too hard on him," the DFZ pleaded with the Peacemaker. "They did it for my sake. If I'd confronted the Gameskeeper directly, there'd have been no avoiding a long and bloody war that would have consumed the entire Underground. Yong and his daughter prevented that. Surely that merits some leniency?"

"Leniency isn't his problem," said the muscular, black-haired dragon with bright-green eyes and a huge sword who'd followed the Peacemaker in. "He's *too* lenient. That's why stuff like this happens."

"Thank you, Justin," the Peacemaker said in a sharp voice, glowering at my father, who looked utterly unrepentant. When it was clear that Yong wasn't even going to give a non-apology for his actions, the Dragon of Detroit's mouth pulled into a hard line.

"We have rules for a reason," he said. "It doesn't matter if you acted at the DFZ's request or not. You knew that killing anyone in my territory was forbidden. You knew I do not allow private military forces into my city. You knew *all* of this, and you still broke my edict. You have knowingly and deliberately ignored every single limit I've put down, and there must be consequences."

He lifted his head, raising his voice so that all the dragons hovering above could hear him. "Yong of Korea, you and all your mortals are henceforth banished from my lands! Anyone found in violation of this will be captured and brought to the consulate to await further punishment. You have thirty minutes to remove yourself from my territory, after which you will be escorted forcibly over the border and most likely into the river."

The big dragon with the sword smirked eagerly at that last part, but Yong merely nodded as if this were entirely expected and waved for his people to start packing up. When my mother and her men rushed to obey, Yong turned to me, and I swallowed.

Here it came. He was going to order me to go home with him. Hell, the Peacemaker had already done it for him. There was no way I could claim I wasn't part of Yong's household after everything that had just happened. I was as good as back in Korea already. But just as the full impact of all of this was hitting me, my father put his hand on my shoulder and asked, "Will you be back for New Year's?"

It was so unexpected, I didn't actually understand what he'd said for a good thirty seconds. "What?"

"Will you come home for New Year's?" he asked again, looking the closest to nervous I'd ever seen him. "You haven't been back to Seoul for a while, and it would give me great pleasure to spend time with you in a nonlethal situation."

"I'd like that too," I replied slowly. "But...aren't you going to order me home?"

Yong shook his head. "The Peacemaker banished myself and my mortals, but you are my daughter, not my mortal. I don't control you any more than she does." He nodded at the DFZ, who nodded back rapidly. "Also, the Peacemaker holds this territory as a dragon. He doesn't have the power to banish humans."

I hadn't considered it from that perspective. I was so used to thinking of myself as a dragon's liability, it hadn't even occurred to me that I could simply *not listen* to the Dragon of Detroit. I glanced nervously at the Peacemaker anyway, just in case, but he was already stomping away, ranting to his tall guard about ungrateful, stubborn dragons too proud to understand the messes they left behind. It was a plight I had great sympathy for. I just couldn't believe it no longer applied to *me*.

"I can stay?" I whispered.

"I'm counting on it," the DFZ said. "Priestess or no, Dr. Kowalski will *kill* me if I let you leave before she's finished your training. And I don't understand the new organizational system you've set up for my treasury at all." Her face grew panicked. "I won't be able to find anything if you leave! You don't even have to serve me. I'll cancel your debt. I'll give you a job! You can be a city employee. I'll even throw in a pension, just don't go! I don't care that you chose your family over me. You still fought for my city and my people, even the ones in Rentfree! Yong has tons of mortals he can rely on, I don't. I *need* you, Opal. Please stay."

The way she begged made me feel warm and needed in a way I couldn't describe. "Well, when you put it like that, how can I refuse?" I said with a grin. Then I grew serious. "But I have some conditions."

Another god would have been insulted by that, but this was the DFZ. Just like her city, she was always ready to bargain. "Name 'em."

"The Gameskeeper didn't come out of nowhere," I said, waving my hand at the wreckage around us. "The fact that he was able to build such a huge empire here proves there's a serious problem with inequality in the Underground. I know you're the ultimate city of the free market, but that doesn't mean you have to leave your most vulnerable to struggle on their own. You always say that people make the city, but cities also determine the lives of those who live in them. By letting your poorest citizens be vulnerable, you make yourself vulnerable as well. You nearly lost all of Rentfree tonight! You thanked Dad and I for saving it, but we shouldn't have had to. This *all* could have been prevented if you'd just taken care of the people down here instead of leaving them to be prey to things like the Gameskeeper."

"I know that," the DFZ said in a defeated voice. "But I keep telling you, I can't change what I am."

"I'm not asking you to change your nature," I said stubbornly. "I'm asking you to *adapt*. The Underground has been a pit of suffering and poverty since Algonquin's rule. It's long overdue for a change, and change is absolutely in line with everything you stand for! We can even start right here." I pointed down at the slagged arena floor. "You're always telling me you want to be a better city. Well, what if, instead of running a tourism hub based on shocking visitors with how terrible the Underground is, we turned Rentfree into somewhere people want to visit for its own merits? It won't even be that hard. The infrastructure to bring people down here is already in place, *and* you've got a huge vault full of world-quality art just waiting for somewhere to show it off."

"Hold up," the god said. "Are you suggesting I open an art museum in *Rentfree*?" When I nodded, her face grew appalled. "Shouldn't that sort of thing be up on the Skyways?"

"Why should the Skyways get everything? They're already full of nice stuff. This place is struggling, *and* we just destroyed its only major employer. If you leave Rentfree like this, it won't matter that we took out the Gameskeeper. Something else will just move in to take his place. But if that something is *you*—which it should be since this is *your* city—we can actually change this neighborhood for the better."

"Do the people down here even want art, though?" the city asked. "I mean, it's a big shift."

"Everyone wants beauty," I said confidently. "It is a big change, but people down here adapt, and all great cities have museums! Now's your chance to add your name to that list and plug a critical weakness at the same time. I'm already organizing your treasury. All you have to do is let me put all that work on display down here, and we're done. With the stuff you've already collected, we can open a world-class museum that anyone can come down here and visit for free."

Her glowing eyes flew wide. "*Free?!*"

"Yes, free," I said, crossing my arms over my chest. "They're called 'public works' for a reason. If you really want to be a better city, you have to invest in your people, and the people down here are poor. You're the richest city in the world. Surely you can afford to give your people one place where they don't have to pay."

The DFZ looked like she was about to have a mental breakdown at the idea of anyone getting anything for free, and I sighed. "If it makes it easier for you, think of this museum as my price for staying. I've always wanted to curate a collection, and yours deserves to be seen by everyone. Give me somewhere where I can show off your treasures to the entire world, not just the rich portion, and you won't be able to get me to leave."

That was phrasing the DFZ understood much better. "Deal," she said, grabbing my hand and shaking it so hard my fingers ached. "Ugh, I'm so glad that's over. I'll come by after practice tomorrow and we can hash out the details. Right now I've got to focus on securing this place. There's so many people trying to loot that even my ability to divide myself can't keep up!"

I nodded. "I'll be there."

The DFZ grinned and vanished, taking her door with her. I was wondering what I'd just gotten myself into when I realized my father was still standing beside me.

"Is that all it takes to win your devotion?" he asked grumpily. "A museum?"

"I always did love showing off my treasures," I replied with a shrug. "And you heard what I told the Gameskeeper. The DFZ is my city. I don't have to be her priestess to want it to be better, and what kind of city doesn't have a museum?"

"Seoul has several," Yong reminded me, his face growing plaintive. "You *are* coming home for New Year's, right?"

I smiled. "Sure, Dad."

"And your mother's birthday," he added. "She wants to see you too. Also Autumn Eve. You can't miss Autumn Eve."

"Don't push it."

My father backed off at once. A sign of his new respect because dragons didn't abandon fights they thought they could win. Not that he wouldn't try again, but it was a big change for us, and I appreciated it.

"I'll visit when I can," I promised, stepping in to wrap my arms around him. "And I'll call when I can't."

"Please do," he whispered, squeezing me back.

That was one of the only non-ironic pleases I'd ever heard from my dad. It was a sign of how much I'd changed, too, that it didn't even make me blink.

I would have hugged him longer, but the Peacemaker's deadline was fast approaching. I barely got time to greet my mother and thank her formally for bringing in the cavalry before Yong and his household piled back into the helicopters and flew away, escorted out of the city by the largest formation of dragons the DFZ had seen since the Second Mana Crash.

"So what happens now?" Nik asked as the Peacekeeper's forces dispersed. "Do you just go back to living in an apartment floating in nothingness?"

"Actually," I said with a sly smile, "I was hoping I could move in with you. Fewer bad memories. That and I'm not entirely sure I *can* get back to my apartment now that I've lost my awesome door-opening powers."

"I think I could make some room for you," Nik said, wrapping his arm around my waist. "But I'll have to find a new job. Cleaning's going to be impossible now that everyone knows my face again, and despite what the DFZ seems to think, I'm not qualified to work at this museum thing you're building."

"You could take some time off," I offered. "We haven't discussed salary yet, but despite being forced into doing something for the public good, the DFZ's still a beacon of capitalism, so I'm sure I'm getting paid." I grinned at him. "I could support you for a change. You could be my kept man."

Nik made a face. "No thanks. I see now why you were so insulted when I offered. Being 'kept' sounds so…useless."

"We'll find you something good to do, then," I promised. "The DFZ has so much stuff, I couldn't sort it all if I had a hundred lifetimes. You can help me go through the piles. That way you could still Clean but we wouldn't have to go to auctions or even out in public unless you wanted to."

"That's your thing, though," he said nervously. "Are you sure you'd want me around?"

"God, yes! I can't tell you how badly I missed you when I was working there alone. And not just your company, either. My expertise is in antiques, art, and historical items, but there was so much other stuff I had no clue about. Just a few weeks ago I had to sort a garage full of classic cars on my own!"

Nik looked horrified. "You didn't junk them, did you?"

I shook my head. "I ended up putting them back in storage, but this is why I need you! One person can't process an entire city's worth of treasure on her own, so what do you say? Want to partner up with me one more time?"

Nik grinned and grabbed my hand, lifting it to his lips until I could feel his smile against my skin.

"Wouldn't miss it for the world."

Thank you for reading!

Thank you for reading all the way to the end of the DFZ trilogy! If you enjoyed *Night Shift Dragons* and the two books before it, I hope you'll consider leaving a review. Reviews, good and bad, are vital to every author's career, and I would be very grateful if you'd consider writing one for me.

This is the end of Opal's series, but I'm definitely not done with the world of the DFZ! If you want to be the first to know I release something new, including more books in the DFZ universe, sign up for my New Release Mailing List! List members are always the first to hear about everything I do, *and* they get exclusive bonus content like the list-only Heartstriker short story, *Mother of the Year.* The list is free, and I promise never to spam you, so come join us! Or, if social media is more your thing, you can follow me on Twitter @Rachel_Aaron or like my Facebook page at facebook.com/RachelAaronAuthor for writing updates, blog posts, and appearances.

Do you need something new to read *right now?* You can see all my books, including **5** completed series, at www.rachelaaron.net

Again, thank you so *so* much for going with me on this journey. You are the reason I get to write every day. Thank you for reading from the bottom of my heart, and I hope you'll stay with me for many more books!

Yours always and sincerely,
Rachel Aaron

Enjoyed the DFZ series?
Need a new book *right now*?!

Try one of Rachel's other completed series!
www.rachelaaron.net

Need more dragons in your life? Try the book that started it all!

As the smallest dragon in the Heartstriker clan, Julius survives by a simple code: stay quiet, don't cause trouble, and keep out of the way of bigger dragons. But this meek behavior doesn't cut it in a family of ambitious predators, and his mother, Bethesda the Heartstriker, has finally reached the end of her patience.

Now, sealed in human form and banished to the DFZ--a vertical metropolis built on the ruins of Old Detroit--Julius has one month to prove to his mother that he can be a ruthless dragon or lose his true shape forever. But in a city of modern

mages and vengeful spirits where dragons are seen as monsters to be exterminated, he's going to need some serious help to survive this test.

He just hopes humans are more trustworthy than dragons.

"Super fun, fast paced, urban fantasy full of heart, and plenty of magic, charm and humor to spare, this self published gem was one of my favorite discoveries this year!' - **The Midnight Garden**

"A deliriously smart and funny beginning to a new urban fantasy series about dragons in the ruins of Detroit...inventive, uproariously clever, and completely un-put-down-able!' - **SF Signal**

The Legend of Eli Monpress

Eli Monpress is talented. He's charming. And he's the greatest thief in the world.

He's also a wizard, and with the help of his partners in crime--a swordsman with the world's most powerful magic sword (but no magical ability of his own) and a demonseed who can step through shadows and punch through walls-- he's getting ready to pull off the heist of his career. To start, though, he'll just steal something small. Something no one will miss. Something like... a king.

"I cannot be less than 110% in love with this book. I loved it. I love it still. Already I sort of want to read it again. Considering my fairly epic Godzilla-sized To Read list, that's just about the highest compliment I can give a book" - **CSI: Librarian**

"Fast and fun, The Spirit Thief *introduces a fascinating new world and a complex magical system based on cooperation with the spirits who reside in all living objects. Aaron's characters are fully fleshed and possess complex personalities, motivations, and backstories that are only gradually revealed. Fans of Scott Lynch's* Lies of Locke Lamora *(2006) will be thrilled with Eli Monpress. Highly recommended for all fantasy readers."* - **Booklist, Starred Review**

The Paradox Trilogy
(Written as Rachel Bach)

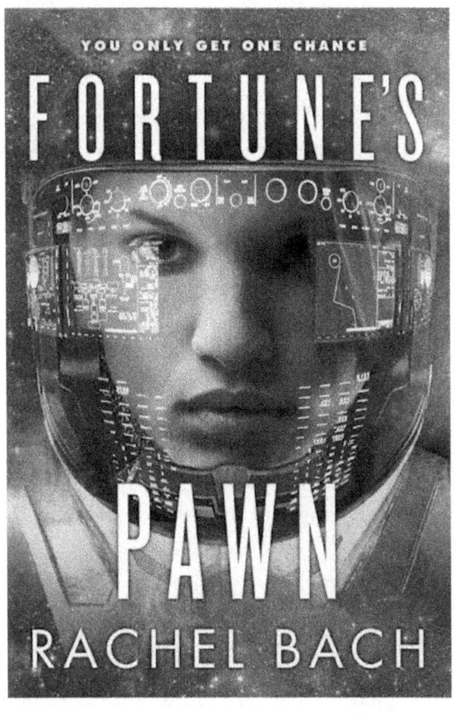

Devi Morris isn't your average mercenary. She has plans. Big ones. And a ton of ambition. It's a combination that's going to get her killed one day - but not just yet.

That is, until she just gets a job on a tiny trade ship with a nasty reputation for surprises. The Glorious Fool isn't misnamed: it likes to get into trouble, so much so that one year of security work under its captain is equal to five years everywhere else. With odds like that, Devi knows she's found the perfect way to get the jump on the next part of her Plan. But the Fool doesn't give up its secrets without a fight, and one year on this ship might be more than even Devi can handle.

"Firefly-esque in its concept of a rogue-ish spaceship family... The narrative never quite goes where you expect it to, in a good way... Devi is a badass with a heart." - **Locus Magazine**

"If you liked Star Wars, *if you like our books, and if you are waiting for* Guardians of the Galaxy *to hit the theaters, this is your book."* - **Ilona Andrews**

"I JUST LOVED IT! Perfect light sci-fi. If you like space stuff that isn't that complicated but highly entertaining, I give two thumbs up!" - **Felicia Day**

Forever Fantasy Online

In the real world, twenty-one-year-old library sciences student Tina Anderson is invisible and under-appreciated, but in the VR-game Forever Fantasy Online she's Roxxy--the respected leader and main tank of a top-tier raiding guild. In the real world, her brother James Anderson is a college drop-out struggling under debt, but in FFO he's famous--an explorer who's gotten every achievement, done every quest, and collected all the rarest items.

Both Tina and James need the game more than they'd like to admit, but their favorite escape turns into a trap when FFO becomes a living world. Wounds are no longer virtual, stupid monsters become cunning, NPCs start acting like actual people, and death might be forever.

In the real world, everyone said being good at video games was a waste of time. Now, stranded and separated across thousands of miles of new, deadly terrain, Tina and James's skill at FFO is the only thing keeping them alive. It's going to take every bit of their expertise--and hoarded loot--to find each other and get back home, but as the stakes get higher and the damage adds up, being the best in the game may no longer be enough.

"Rachel Aaron and Travis Bach have written an amazing story and a realistic LitRPG."
- The Fantasy Inn

"Excellent characters, an engaging story, and geek humor. What more can one ask for?"
- TS Chan

The first in a new gamer/fantasy collaboration from Rachel Aaron and Travis Bach!

2,000 to 10,000: Writing Better, Writing Faster, and Writing More of What You Love *(nonfiction)*

"Have you ever wanted to double your daily word counts? Do you sometimes feel like you're crawling through your story? Do you want to write more every day without increasing the time you spend writing or sacrificing quality? It's not impossible; it's not even that hard. This is the book explaining how, with a few simple changes, I boosted my daily writing from 2000 words to over 10k a day, and how you can too."

Expanding on Rachel's viral blog post about how she doubled her daily word counts, this book offers practical writing advice for anyone who's ever longed to increase their daily writing output. In addition to updated information for the popular 2k to 10k writing efficiency process, 5 step plotting method, and easy editing tips, the book includes all new chapters on creating characters who write their own stories, plot structure, and learning to love your daily writing. Full of easy to follow, practical advice from a professional author who doesn't eat if she doesn't produce good books on a regular basis, 2k to 10k focuses not just on writing faster, but writing better, and having more fun while you do it!

"I loved this book! So helpful!" - **Courtney Milan, NYT Bestselling Author**

"This. Is. Amazing. You are telling my story RIGHT NOW. Book is due in 2 weeks, and I'm behind--woefully, painfully behind--because I've been stuck...writing in circles and unenthused. Yet here--here is a FANTASTIC solution. I am printing this post out, and I'm setting out to make my triangle. Thank you, thank you, THANK YOU!" - **Bestselling YA Author Susan Dennard**

About the Author

Rachel Aaron is the author of sixteen novels and the bestselling nonfiction writing book, *2k to 10k: Writing Faster, Writing Better, and Writing More of What You Love,* which has helped thousands of authors double their daily word counts. When she's not holed up in her writing cave, Rachel lives a nerdy, bookish life in Broomfield, CO, with her perpetual-motion son, long-suffering husband, and grumpy old lady dog. To learn more about Rachel, read samples of all her books, or to find a complete list of her interviews and podcasts, please visit rachelaaron.net!

As always, this book would not have been nearly as good without my amazing beta readers. Thank you so, so much to Jodie Martin, Judith Smith, Christina Vlinder, Eva Bunge, Lindsay Simms, Hisham El-Far, and the ever-amazing Laligin. Y'all are the BEST!

www.ingramcontent.com/pod-product-compliance
Lightning Source LLC
Chambersburg PA
CBHW070819190726
48292CB00006B/2050